Diamonds In The Rough

John I Leggett

* * * * *

Diamonds In The Rough
Copyright © 2017 by John I Leggett

www.johnleggettbooks.com

ISBN-13: 978-0-692-80886-3

A DeWitt Studio Publication

Printed in the U.S.A.

10 9 8 7 6

Acknowledgements

My thanks to the members of the Casco Bay Writers' Project, also known as Brogan's Brigade. (John, Steve, Mary, Anne, Susan, James, Dr. John, Linda, Dan and Beda.) Through their insight and encouragement, the task of putting a novel together became my fictional reality. Each one is a *Diamond in the Rough!*

An additional thanks to my beta readers who pawed through the manuscript—especially during the holiday season—and provided feedback and tactful comments. Steve Bloom, Beda Knight, Wm. Clark Ketcham, Jason Aguiar, my sister Marion Leggett, and my wife, Kathleen.

A thank you to attorneys William Speers, Esq. (my boyhood writing partner) and Dan Knight for legal clarifications.

CONTENTS

LEAVING

THE BOAT

◆ rude awakening

The early morning serenity of the boatyard was shattered by the voice of Ernie Hanson. "You in there?" the dockmaster hollered. "You gotta be. I can smell ya from up here."

Mario Costello recognized Hanson's voice and propped himself onto one elbow before looking down the length of the cabin. Hanson was topside, lying on his belly, with his head in an inverted position in the companionway. As he peered below to see if Mario was on board, his face appeared to be in a teak-framed portrait. Costello, being rousted from a deep sleep, lacked the alertness to focus on the skewed features. He could only imagine the two or three day's growth of whiskers—the dockmaster's signature look.

"Yeah, I'm in here," Mario answered, his voice filled with sleep. "What . . . what the hell do you want . . . what time is it anyway?"

"Time to pay the slip fee you told me you were going to pay last week, and the week before that. I've got guys callin' me for this space. Guys who'll pay a lot more than you pay—or should I say what you're *supposed* to pay."

IT HAD BEEN SEVERAL hours since Mario had guided his thirty-five foot sloop named *Miss Demeanor* into the Melbourne boatyard. The inlet was cloaked in fog, and with her running lights extinguished, the singular mast light, high above the water line, was the only visible proof that a boat was entering. Costello dropped the mainsail and rolled in the genoa allowing her momentum to glide her between boats resting on moorings.

Miss Demeanor's invisibility made the glow from the mast light appear mystical, stealth-like, as she cut through the pre-dawn mist. Costello's familiarity with the waters eliminated the need for the lonely wail of the fog horn that warned others. His eyes searched for the small light that identified his slip space. Upon its recognition, he made the short jump to the dock and looped his bow line in a figure eight around a cleat. The diesel engines of nearby boats grumbled the start of the fishermen's day and were accompanied by cries of gulls, flying as escorts, as they guided boats out of the channel.

After Costello set fenders and secured a spring line, he made a cursory attempt at organizing the cockpit. He had made the sail from Andros Island in two days. The last leg from Miami to Melbourne had been tiring, and although the morning sounds of the Indian River were soothing, they were not necessary to assist in his needed rest. With *Miss Demeanor* safe in her home port, he went below, stripped off his clothing, and crawled into the comfort of the V-berth.

During the next few hours, the sun's reflection washed the hull with a pattern of glittering diamonds. Mario's sound sleep was the reason for his lack of awareness to the yelling that came from the dockmaster. It was the amplification of the voice that now rousted him and gave cause for a response.

"I'll have your money in a couple of days," Mario told him. He swung his legs off the berth and sat up. He was a man that women considered ruggedly handsome. His lanky frame was tanned from days on deck, and at twenty-eight, his muscles were developed and well-toned from years of sailing. Still groggy with sleep, he was annoyed that he'd been caught off guard by Hanson. He was usually successful in avoiding him when he owed money.

"Coupla days my ass!" Hanson yelled back. "I'm losin' my shirt with you takin' up this space. I get my money today or you can anchor this tub out there in the big blue sea. And if I don't get my money today, I'll come by later to see if you've got anything worth taking and help myself. I'm sure I can get a pretty penny for this nice plow anchor you've got sittin' here on the bow—and I'll keep takin' stuff until you pay up. You hear what I'm sayin'?"

When Mario failed to respond, Hanson continued, "Where you been lately anyway? I been lookin' for you all week."

"Sailin' the coast," Mario told him, being as vague as possible. There was no need for Hanson to know he had just sailed in from a run to Cuba. However, the dockmaster's threat about poking around the boat warranted a response. "I wouldn't advise you taking my anchor," Mario told him, "or anything else for that matter. I guess if you did I'd have to pay your shanty up there a return visit, if you get my drift." The comment was made in reference to Hanson's name for the dilapidated building he used as an office. The assumption was he believed the word "shanty" had a more nautical ring to it. A small apartment on the second floor served as the dockmaster's living quarters.

Mario stood in his briefs as he moved to the middle of the cabin in search of the shorts he'd tossed aside before retiring. Finding them, he pulled them on as he approached the hatchway. Hanson's face became clearer. At the closer distance, his inverted features appeared misplaced and absurdly pronounced. His forehead was a chin, his teeth were distorted, and the bristly hairs in his nostrils were tightly packed.

Without bothering to right himself, he continued shouting in Mario's face. "You wanna visit me in the shanty? You just be my guest," he replied. "You're in Florida, now boy," he reminded Mario. "This is a stand-your-ground state. I got a nine millimeter in the office just waitin' to say hello to you if you care to come sneakin' around. "You immigrants think you can come down here and freeload off of us but you ain't gonna do that to *me* my friend."

Although Mario had lived in Florida for several years, he was originally from Massachusetts, and in Hanson's mind, anyone who lived—or had lived—anywhere north of Jacksonville was an immigrant

That said, Hanson maneuvered himself into an upright position and lowered himself into the cockpit. He was a heavy man and as he stepped from the boat to the dock his weight caused *Miss Demeanor* to rock. An empty Jack Daniel's bottle slid across the cabin floor and came to rest on Mario's bare foot.

"By the way, you may want to learn how to put your fenders on," Hanson yelled from the dock. "One of 'em isn't even hittin' anything out here. You're gonna get a nice wear-spot on the starboard side if ya don't fix it."

Mario knew a decent sailor would've made the adjustment rather than criticize the placement, but the dockmaster left it unattended, chuckling to himself as he walked away.

◆ balsam, fish, and lemon

Mario ate breakfast on board and it was well into the afternoon when he went to the office. He eyed the fender that Hanson had referred to. There was, indeed, some danger of wearing paint off the hull if it went unattended. He made an adjustment, not only for his concern for *Miss Demeanor*, but to avoid a friendly boat owner coming along and making the correction in his absence.

Having contraband on board, he had good reason to keep Hanson—or anyone else—away from *Miss Demeanor* for the next two days. Once his Cuba business was concluded, he planned to depart from the Indialantic waters for the last time. He had an afternoon meeting with Carmine—a man he'd been reluctant to have as a partner—but before leaving, he thought it best to patch things up with the dockmaster.

The boatyard had been Mario's home for several years, and other than occasionally being late with the rent, he had avoided conflicts with the guy. Hanson's threat of removing items from the boat and selling them or holding them for ransom was not to be taken lightly.

He was well-known for his tyrannical oversight of the boatyard. On one occasion he put a yacht owner's puppy in a bucket and hoisted it to the top of the mast. The incident was triggered when Hanson discovered the transient couple's yacht was two feet over the allocated slip space, and in his opinion, the husband had lied about the length. The overnight fee was two dollars per foot and Hanson wanted the additional four bucks. The owners, an extremely reserved couple from North Carolina, were horrified when they returned from town to find their dog forty feet in the air and in fear for his life. His whimpering led the man and woman to look up and see the puppy's head and two paws draped over the rim of the bucket.

By their account, he had a panicked look on his face—to which Hanson scoffed—telling the guy he was a jackass to think that animals even had expressions.

The man and his wife were further repulsed when they lowered the dog and found their teak bucket, complete with brass designs that matched the hardware on their boat, had been filled by the dog's need to relieve himself. The incident delayed their departure as the dog, a white Shih-Tzu covered in his own excrement, had to be hosed off and fluff dried. A heated argument ensued regarding the money before Hanson returned to his shanty in a huff. Prior to setting sail the husband hung the soiled bucket on the tiller of Hanson's skiff, and being a conscientious man, he rolled up a check for the additional four dollars and stuck it into the contents.

It was a famous boatyard story, and although Mario didn't own a dog, he realized there could be repercussions if he was on Hanson's bad side. If his meeting with Carmine went as planned, his promise to pay Hanson in a couple of days was well warranted. Once he took care of the fee, he planned to relax for a day or two before setting sail to the Bahamas. He was weary from the risk of running black market goods for Carmine, and if his wallet got thin, he felt he could make a reasonable living running charters for tourists around the islands.

MARIO ENTERED HANSON'S OFFICE to the fragrance of balsam fir. It was the day before New Year's Eve and Connie, the office secretary, was attempting to maintain the fragrance of Christmas. It was also her attempt to disguise the smell of fish emanating from Hanson's bait pail that sat in the corner and repulsed all boatyard tenants. To Connie, the odor was an accepted occupational hazard—a hazard she tried to disguise with lemon-scented mermaids. The mermaids were air fresheners Hanson bought for his truck and came in a package of two. The mermaid kept him company—swinging to and fro from his rearview mirror, smiling at him as he drove around town. Connie often commandeered the second mermaid from the package and hung it over the bait pail. The one currently occupying the hook had lost most of its effectiveness. The holiday season was an excuse to burn the balsam incense which served as a replacement. For two weeks or more, the combined scents of balsam, fading lemon, and fish gave birth to an aroma of unknown origin and served to keep customers' visits quite short. An additional infusion of holiday cheer included a string of blinking lights Connie had tacked up to frame the office window and a ceramic tree on the filing cabinet. Christmas cards were pinned to the bulletin board and peeked through the variety of scrawled post-it notes and bills Hanson had pinned over them. When Mario entered, the smells, the lights, the cards—all of it—served as reminders he was in the midst of the holiday season. Having grown up in New England, he found it difficult to absorb the idea of Christmas in seventy-degree weather.

The bell over the door announced Mario's entrance. Connie was engrossed in a Jackie Collins novel and his arrival caused her to nervously tuck the paperback under a stack of *People* magazines. He was one of the tenants she often fantasized about and she relaxed a bit when she saw who it was. The fact she was hiding one covert reading activity under another didn't seem to register.

Connie wasn't particularly attractive, nor was she very good at running the office. In fact, anyone who dealt with the boatyard on a regular basis knew it was borderline dysfunctional. Her trait of being disorganized was cause for Hanson to give her the axe but he knew she needed the job, and being the womanizer he was, he kept her on and used the threat of her inabilities as leverage for her to make time for afternoon quickies. When days were slow and Hanson needed a respite from doing what little he did, he locked the door, closed the blinds, and they screwed on the old couch to the smell of the lemony bait pail and the hum of the ceiling fan. During the holiday season, they had the additional ambiance of the balsam fir and blinking lights.

The afternoon flings on the sofa were common knowledge among most of the full-time boat owners in the yard. Mario avoided looking at the couch, imagining Hanson lying on top of Connie with his pants and boxer shorts pulled down around his ankles. Connie staring at the ceiling, chewing her gum and counting the rotations of the fan blades while she waits for Hanson to complete his act of sweaty sex. None of the images were anything Mario wanted to think about.

Today she sat in her swivel chair and worked a piece of pink gum that occasionally showed itself. She was wearing shorts that were tightened by the size of her thighs. She studied Mario. His black hair was tousled the way she liked it. From his shoulders his body narrowed into his thin waist and the contours of his chest were pronounced under his shirt.

She thought about what he was going to do to her . . . taking her in his strong arms and carrying her back to his boat to ravage her for the entire afternoon. She became light-headed as her mind played the crescendo from *Victory at Sea* and rose to its peak as if a volcano was about to erupt and then, just as she was swooning with ecstasy, the brass section transitioned into the finale of *The 1812 Overture*. She could feel Mario holding her in his powerful arms and taking her again and again under the explosive firing of cannons. She then, in total exhaustion, collapsed onto his chest as the smoke from the cannons drifts downward like a soft cloud and blankets the two of them in warmth.

"Is he here?" Mario asked. His question gave an abrupt ending to her fantasy and returned her to the reality of the office.

She swiveled in her chair to face him, allowing him to see the wording on her T-shirt. The message, somewhat distorted by being stretched across her oversized breasts, read "Blink If You Want Me."

Mario stood, waiting for an answer, trying desperately not to blink.

"N-no . . . he's out."

"Is he in the yard?"

"Couldn't tell ya," she said, and her jaw started a slow renewal of the gum chewing.

"What about Lester . . . is he out in the yard?" The question was asked in reference to the handyman who was semi-employed. No one—not even Connie—seemed to know what Lester did or had any idea of his schedule.

"I think he's next door at the church," she said. "Reverend Prichard asked him to fix the time clock for the Christmas carols."

"Why, what's wrong with the clock?"

"He said the choir is supposed to sing a carol every hour on the hour from noon until five o'clock but yesterday they were coming on at a quarter past. He asked Lester if he could get them synchronized again. He thinks the program on the computer is screwed up or something."

"Why bother now? Christmas was a week ago."

Mario's comment seemed to strike a nerve and Connie suddenly assumed an official tone in defense of the minister. "Because Reverend Prichard likes to play the carols until the Feast of the Epiphany, that's why! It's a tradition."

Mario studied her for several seconds wondering how a woman who spent afternoons screwing on Hanson's couch could become so indignant regarding the Christians' day of overeating, although he was sure she enjoyed the event. Seeing he'd hit a sore spot, he took a different tack. "I didn't know Lester knew anything about computers."

"He doesn't," she said, her tone returning to normal. "He's just trying to be polite so he said he'd take a look."

Mario suddenly realized he had no interest in what Lester was doing. Even if he was in the yard, it was Hanson he needed to talk to and he returned to questions relevant to the dockmaster. "Well, do you think Hanson *might* be in the yard or not?"

"You can look if you want to," she said, patting both sides of her hair which had a self-inflicted red tint. "But, he probably left outta here already . . . said he was goin' over to West End Marina for some diesel parts or somethin'. If his truck's gone then I guess he's not here. I can take your slip payment though if that's what you're here for." Her jaw continued to work the gum.

"I told him I'd have his money in two days. I just don't want him messin' with my boat. Make sure he knows that. You know how he gets."

"Well, I can tell him but he sure was havin' a hissy fit when he left the office. You ain't the only reason but you're sure high on the list." She then continued with a tone of 'I know something you don't know' warning. "I wouldn't leave your boat unattended if I was you," and then slipped her hand under the magazines to retrieve her romance novel . . . caressing the abs of the guy on the cover as she did so.

"Just tell him I said I guarantee him the money in two days." Mario started to leave but feeling he needed even more reassurance, turned and added, "Tell him I'll throw in a few bucks extra for the wait . . . above and beyond the late fee." Mario didn't want to give Hanson *anything* extra but it would be money well spent to keep him from snooping around the boat. As he turned to leave the second time, Connie sighed. Her eyes followed his backside until the door swung closed and his ass was no longer visible.

3

unlikely partners

Mario walked the three blocks to the Sea Dog. It was a small tavern with an outdoor area. Carmine was already seated when he arrived and had taken one of the few tables that offered the protective shade of an umbrella. It made sense that his partner chose such a table. He was a heavy-set man with a propensity for perspiring. For some reason, he always dressed in a suit—a white suit—but a suit nonetheless.

The two men had become acquainted shortly after Mario's move to Florida. His plan to make a living chartering *Miss Demeanor* fell short of his financial expectations and a chance meeting in a bar one night evolved into a profitable relationship. Carmine dabbled in everything from black market merchandise stolen from warehouses to international piracy. His reputation for being a bit of a scoundrel was the reminder Mario needed to keep up his guard.

"They say a good man is hard to find," Carmine said when they met. "But, a good man with a boat . . . now that's even harder. Sure, plenty of guys with boats sailin' around out there, but a good one? Now that's the guy I'm lookin' for—and it's cash in your pocket if you know what I mean."

Since that first meeting, Mario had been involved in several small operations with Carmine. His boat allowed him to deliver stolen antiques to buyers on million-dollar yachts or avoid interstate highways by sailing a few high-powered weapons to other ports. The small jobs had been Carmine's tests to involve Mario in something bigger and his recent offer to sail to Andros Island and pick up a few diamonds seemed to involve a small amount of risk considering the financial return he'd been promised.

When he arrived at the Sea Dog, a waitress was already at the table taking Carmine's order for a gin and tonic. Mario overheard as he approached and told her to add a glass with two fingers of bourbon over some ice. He sat across from his partner and without any greeting or small talk Carmine got right to the point of the meeting.

"You make out okay?" Carmine asked him. Despite the shade of the umbrella, beads of sweat poured from Carmine's forehead and his shirt acted like a blotter as it soaked up perspiration from his chest. Mario studied the variety of patterns.

"Kinda reminds me of the old Rorschach test," he said pointing to the blots.

Carmine looked down at his shirt, but not getting the connection, ignored the comment and made a second attempt for information regarding Mario's recent trip.

"C'mon, c'mon, tell me . . . how'd you make out?"

"No problems . . . had to motor-sail a bit into the Bahamas but nice winds on the return. I actually got back a few hours earlier than I expected."

"Well, I was a bit concerned you wouldn't make it back today at all. Cut it a little close didn't you?"

"I'm here, right? How about you, everything still on schedule with your guy . . . what's his name?"

"Cohen," Carmine reminded him. "He's flying in tomorrow around noon. Said he wants to meet no later than four. Once he's got the popcorn, he can give it to his popper and we'll be on our way."

Carmine's use of code words and making things more complicated than necessary always annoyed Mario—in this case, sitting in his white suit most likely pretending he was Sydney Greenstreet selling the Maltese Falcon. Mario ignored the use of the word *popcorn* as some sort of code for diamonds that added drama and assumed the *popper* was Cohen's diamond cutter.

Carmine leaned in and his voice took on an air of excitement. "So, tell me . . . how many are there? What do they look like?"

"Looks like there's plenty, but what the hell do I know? They're uncut. They all just look like chunks of beach glass to me."

"Just don't get any ideas about holding any back. You checked them out, right? I mean you weighed them and all like I told you?"

"Yeah, yeah, I weighed them, just like you said." Mario then fell silent while the waitress set their drinks on the table. He was more concerned about the buyer than the process of weighing the diamonds. "So you say this guy Cohen is all right. He's not going to try to screw us around?"

Carmine leaned in and put his arm on the table. "Hey . . . it's *Marshall* Cohen," he whispered, as if adding the guy's first name to the equation made a difference in his integrity. He then continued with the remainder of the buyer's résumé. "He's one of the biggest diamond merchants in New York. He's not a guy who's gonna stiff us. We give him the stones and he gives us a million bucks. You take your half and sail off into the sunset for a month or two."

"He may be a big shot in New York, but I've never heard of him. And now you're tellin' me there's some cutter involved in the deal, not to mention the thugs he sent to meet me at Andros."

Carmine tilted his head and raised an eyebrow and waited for Mario to continue.

"All I'm sayin' is, a lot of people means a lot of possible leaks. It seems like you've got a few too many fingers in the pie, not to mention this Cohen guy is getting five or six million on his end. I still don't see why we don't fence them ourselves."

"Jeezus, Mario, we had this conversation before you left. For one thing, he's paid all the bills so far. For another, uncuts are too hard for guys like you and me to fence. Like you said, they're in the rough and this other guy—who you say has his finger in the pie—is one of the best diamond cutters in the business. He and Cohen go way back."

Carmine studied Mario's face hoping the explanation was convincing. He realized Cohen was a connection worth having and it was in their best interest that the transaction didn't go south. He withdrew a white handkerchief from his back pocket and dabbed at the beads of sweat on his forehead. "Why the hell should we get greedy when we can get them to do the heavy lifting?"

This time Mario nodded in agreement which satisfied his partner. "Besides," he added. "If this goes well, we could shoot for a repeat performance. This guy's got connections we can't match and he's got the money necessary for payoffs. There're a lot of miles between Africa and Florida, my friend, and a lot of heads are paid to look the other way . . . more than you realize. Here, let me show you."

He pulled a pen from his shirt pocket and drew an irregular shape on a napkin, explaining the unrecognizable rendering was a map of Africa. "Before you even got the stones they were here . . . Tanzania," as he made the comment he drew a large X on the eastern coast of the blotch. "Then they traveled west to Mauritania," a second X was placed on the opposite side of his drawing. "From there, the captain of a freighter took 'em to Cuba." With that statement he drew a line to the left and attached an oval on the line's end which was presumably Cuba. "The stones changed hands three or four times just to get 'em there."

Carmine dropped the pen on the table and leaned back in his chair. "And where were you all the time that was goin' on my friend? Coolin' your heels in the tropical breezes of Andros Island, that's where." His finger tapped the napkin indicating the spot where Mario had anchored and waited. "You think the Cuban who brought you the merchandise picked 'em up at the local grocery store? It's a long trail from there to here." This time he put his finger on the first X and then emphatically tapped the middle of the table. "And you didn't even have to go into Cuban waters, my friend. I covered your ass all the way up the line."

"Yeah, I know all that. I didn't come here for a geography lesson."

"Like I said, once we get our money, we're out. We can get our end of business done tomorrow, but bein' New Year's Eve, Cohen wants to get it done early—said he's got plans for the night. His daughter's got a house down here somewhere—Vero Beach I think. Said he's spending the evening with her and his grandkids. He wants to fly outta here Sunday morning and get back to the Big Apple. You can take your cut and then hit the nearest bar."

"Not this time. With this money I don't plan on sticking around Melbourne."

"Don't kid yourself. I know you too well. You'll go through this money like shit through a duck and be callin' me next month for another gig."

"So you say," Mario told him. "In any case, the boat's a bit too hot for a meeting right now."

"Whaddaya mean the boat's a bit hot?"

"Nothin' to do with us and nothin' a little cash won't fix. I assume this guy Cohen is staying at a local hotel right?"

"Actually he's got a condo down here—place called the Ocean View Club. It's right near here on A1A. He wants to meet there."

Carmine sipped his drink. Mario swirled the bourbon around the ice, took a long swallow, and returned the glass to the table. "I gotta run," he told Carmine. "Call me with the time and address and I'll meet you there. Better yet, pick me up at the boatyard." He then leaned in and lowered his voice. "Don't fuck this up. I wanna get this deal done as early in the day as possible and get outta here—the sooner after this guy Cohen lands the better. With good winds I'll be half way to Miami when I ring in the New Year."

After meeting with Carmine, Mario walked to the Dew Drop Inn. It was a more suitable place to drink the afternoon away. He was in no mood to sit at the Sea Dog and watch Carmine sweat away a few pounds while he sipped over-priced gin and tonics.

The Dew Drop was an easy walk from the boatyard and a bar he frequented often. It employed a female bartender who was not only pleasing to the eye but occasionally poured one on the house. He spent many afternoons nursing shots while he eyed her shapely derriere leaning into the cooler to fetch beers for customers.

♦ **three sheets to the mast**

Hanson picked up his diesel parts from the West End Marina and decided to fulfill the urge to wile away the afternoon over a few Yuenglings. The stool he occupied was in a bar several blocks south of Mario. Had they by some happenstance chosen the same bar, they may have made amiable talk and settled the matter of the slip fee. If so, the upheaval that followed later that evening would've been avoided.

Hanson sat and drank while he tried to ignore the bartender's rants regarding the abhorrent use of steroids among baseball players. Had the man serving the Yuenglings taken the time to notice the dockmaster's look of disinterest, he might've guessed the patron was probably not a big fan of baseball.

Hanson had other concerns. He sat and stared at the reflection of his unshaven face in the mirror behind the bar. He was a round-faced seaman in his fifties whose greasy hair was sparse and hidden by a captain's hat. His mug was held in a hand that displayed fingernails and knuckles impacted with grease. Like his fingers, the hat was covered with erratic smudges of oil and diesel fuel. The old cap was such a fixture on his head that on the rare occasion he didn't wear it, people who knew him had to focus on his grizzled face before recognizing him. As the afternoon wore on, he hoisted one beer after another and stewed about the money Mario owed him.

A few patrons came and went, irritating him as they joked with the bartender. Each beer emphasized the annoying glow of the blinking sign that spelled out *Season's Greetings* and by midnight Hanson decided he'd had his fill and slid off his bar stool. It is uncertain whether he remembered eating the several hardboiled eggs or wolfing down a basket of fish 'n chips during the supper hour, but his actions for the remainder of the night were severely hampered by the consumption of far too many Yuenglings. He found the drive to the boatyard was challenged by the steering wheel's refusal to keep his truck in a straight line, and although a citation for driving under the influence would have been a devastating inconvenience, it would have been preferable to what actually took place.

In the hours that had passed since his confrontation with Mario, his infuriation with not being paid his money had grown exponentially. When he arrived at the boatyard, he decided to make good on his threat and pay a visit to *Miss Demeanor* to get his pound of flesh. He walked the dock to the boat, and in a drunken stupor, bellowed out to Mario. "Get your ass out of the boat," he slurred, and "come out here and fight like a man." He continued the bellowing and woke other boat owners. Others, yet to retire for the evening, sat on their decks with their nightly cocktails.

In the midst of Hanson's bellowing, the church clock next door struck the hour of one and a choir of heavenly voices resounded from the steeple speakers. The ill-timed music proved that Lester's attempt to fix Reverend Prichard's choir-singing carols had gone awry. Although he had managed to have the choir sing on the hour, he had mistakenly programmed the hymns to be sung in the a.m. rather than p.m. The choir overpowered Hanson's yelling as they enthusiastically harked to all that the Heralded Angels were singing praises to the new born King. The carol blared forth and woke any remaining residents within several miles of the church. Boat owners stood on the dock but none were actually rejoicing in anticipation of the Feast of the Epiphany. Calls from residents flooded into the Melbourne Police Department complaining about the untimeliness of the choir's rejoicing. The desk sergeant assured callers every attempt was being made to locate Reverend Prichard.

Mario, of course, did not hear the bellowing of Hanson or the singing of the choir because he was sitting at the Dew Drop Inn nursing shots of bourbon.

As the choir ended and chimes subsided, Hanson noticed the padlock on *Miss Demeanor's* hatch, and realizing Mario was not on board, decided to get his bolt cutters from the supply shed. He was determined to get below and see what treasures he could procure in lieu of his slip fee. The bolt cutter idea was immediately tabled when, during his search of the shed, he spied his chainsaw. The saw would not only allow entrance, but cutting into the hatchway would teach Mario a lesson.

He returned to the boat, chainsaw in hand. In his drunken stupor, boarding the sloop was a tactical problem he hadn't properly thought out and his entrance into the cockpit was nothing short of a circus act. The task of balancing himself with one foot on the boat while the other clung to the dock as he wielded his saw would've been difficult for a sober man. It took several attempts and a slight tearing in the crotch of his pants before he made the successful transition onto the boat. The onlookers, a combination of those awakened from the bellowing and those disturbed by Reverend Prichard's boisterous choir, had expressions that ranged from awe to disbelief.

Once on board it took numerous pulls of the cord and adjustments to the choke to get the chainsaw running. Hanson discovered the motion of the boat, combined with the vibrations from the saw, made his attempt to cut through the hatch more difficult than anticipated. The first touch of the saw brought on a violent kick-back and threw him onto the ship's wheel. Pain shot through his back and he fell, dropping the saw. He watched in horror as the unattended chainsaw, which had the mechanical dysfunction of not shutting off immediately, continued to bounce and growl. He watched in panic as it danced between his legs, tore into his pant leg, and continued downward cutting his shoe and a portion of his baby toe before it stopped running. Due to the amount of anesthesia provided by the Yuenglings, the severed shoe and cut toe were temporarily unfelt and unnoticed.

The spectators who'd been aroused from their boats continued watching from the dock and stared in disbelief. Some displayed looks of fear while others laughed and cheered him on. Now, further infuriated, Hanson stood and regained his balance. He retrieved the chainsaw and pulled on the cord. His second attempt to get it running took far more pulls than had been required the first time. It started, sputtered, and stopped several times before he accidently got the choke in the right position and achieved the desired buzzing.

Happy with his progress, he was about to make his second attempt on the hatch when he was struck with a drunken epiphany. He stood and stared at the mast for several seconds and then, pleased with his new idea, he maneuvered himself—with the saw running—onto the cabin. Once he'd made the climb, he set the churning blade onto the mast with the intent of cutting it down. It was the grinding sound that reminded him the mast was metal, not wood, and a spraying of sparks alarmed him and illuminated the harbor. This act of vandalism was accompanied by gasps of disbelief from the onlookers.

Not to be denied, he set the saw to work again and the grinding sounds and continued fireworks were heard and seen throughout the boatyard. The chainsaw bucked and growled for several minutes before he sheered through the mast. Fortunately for Hanson, it was held in check by the standing rigging which probably saved him from being crushed to death. It wavered—teetering—until it came to rest with additional support from the boom. Its irregular position was silhouetted as the boat bobbed gently up and down under a starlit sky. It was that bobbing motion, combined with looking up at the teetering mast that recalled the hardboiled eggs and fish 'n chips. Hanson retched and spewed several sprays of his dinner over a good portion of the boat. The action was accompanied by groans of disapproval from the crowd.

The dockmaster wiped bits of vomit from his mouth with his bare wrist and examined his work. He seemed satisfied. He shut down the chainsaw and again provided entertainment as he stepped back onto the dock. His exit from the cockpit coincided with a wake from a passing power boat which caused the sloop to pitch. As he reached for the railing to stabilize himself, the chainsaw fell between the boat and the dock with a quiet kurplunk. Hanson cursed as his eyes followed the saw into the dark water. He gazed at the crowd and suddenly seemed to be embarrassed. His voice became calm as he worked to regain his dignity. "Iss okay," he slurred. "I'll get that fucker in the morning." In a final glance at the sloop, he noticed her cockpit was spotted with blood, and although he had no idea who had done such a thing, it pleased him to know someone else obviously had it in for Mario.

Having successfully maneuvered himself off the boat, it was time for bed. He walked the length of the dock to his shanty—oblivious to the dripping vomit covering his shirt and without any idea of how he had acquired a limp. His movements during the mast-cutting had caused the toe to separate a bit more and it dangled from the hole in his shoe. Witnesses stepped aside and watched as his trail of dotted blood was nothing short of Hansel and Gretel's bread crumbs. An observation that was confirmed the following day by the local forensic team.

5

I t wasn't until Hanson entered his shanty that he felt the shooting pain from his foot. He turned on the light and stared in horror. His left shoe displayed a jagged tear and a good piece of the sole had been notched out by the chainsaw. Initially, he studied it with a certain amount of curiosity, wondering how anything like that could've happened.

Upon closer inspection, he saw his little toe hanging in an unnatural position and he studied the trail of blood from the office door to where he stood. The sight of the blood brought on dizziness. As rugged a man as Hanson appeared, he had never been able to tolerate the sight of blood, especially his own. The trail led directly to his shoe. The dangling toe that continued to ooze forced Hanson to collapse into a chair on the front side of his desk. The realization of what he'd done was accompanied by a sharper pain. He picked up the phone and punched in Connie's number. "I'm in some trouble over here," he slurred out.

Her voice was filled with sleep when she answered. "Ernie?"

"Yeah."

"What do you mean you're in trouble? What's wrong?"

"Never mind what's wrong . . . just get your ass over here to the office," he demanded.

"What time is it?" she asked and then looked at her clock on the night stand. "Jeezus, Ernie, it's after one o'clock!"

"It may be after one o'clock now but if you want to be working here in the morning, you'll get your ass over here," he repeated. "I'm bleedin' to death."

IT WAS A GOOD twenty minutes before Connie pulled into the boatyard and entered the office. She was still dressed in her pajama bottoms and was wearing slippers but had exchanged her top for a blouse. She was breathing hard when she entered, and without the restraint of a bra, her oversized breasts that Hanson fondled at his daily whims rose and fell beneath the blouse. He sat slumped in the chair, unconscious—a combination of Yuenglings and blood sightings. A few petrified remnants of the hardboiled eggs along with bits of fish 'n chips still clung to his shirt. Connie's entrance, combined with her gasp at the sight of the scene woke him.

"My God, what happened?"

Hanson ignored the question. "I need some bandages," he growled.

Connie looked at his foot. The oozing had subsided somewhat but the dangling toe was still visible as it stuck out through the hole in the shoe. She stepped forward and knelt to get a closer look. She had doctored many injuries for her tribe of nieces and nephews and prided herself on being level-headed during emergencies. Here she saw an opportunity to show her boss a different side of herself. She wanted him to know she wasn't just a boatyard plaything to be abused on slow afternoons.

"You're going to need more than a bandage for this, Ernie. I'll have to get you over to the emergency room. I don't know if your toe is even salvageable." As she spoke the words, she attempted to push the toe back into place. Having already seen its share of unnecessary movement, it was clinging to the foot as if it was a loose tooth hanging by that last thread of skin—the tooth that needed that final push causing the crunching sound that sets it free. Her pushing inadvertently finished the severing and the toe fell into her hand. She gasped again, feeling it was her doing that would cause Hanson to spend the remainder of his life one toe short. She cringed as she watched it roll from the palm of her hand and drop to the floor. She glanced up with an expression of fear and dismay. Hanson had been watching Connie's attempt at doctoring and the sight of the toe coming off in her hand brought on a second round of queasiness. His head rolled back and he closed his eyes, trying to erase the thought of what just happened.

Connie's eyes searched the office looking for anything that resembled a bandage. Seeing only the box of Kleenex on the desk, she remembered her emergency package of Kotex pads she kept in the filing cabinet. She procured one from the box and tore off the wrapper.

"What the hell are you going to do with that?"

"It's a make-shift bandage! If you bothered to have a decent first-aid kit in the office I wouldn't have to invent shit around here every time you break a fingernail." As she spoke, she covered the mangled area that was now one toe short. With the pad covering the hole in the shoe, she searched for something to hold it in place and reached for the plastic hula dancer on Hanson's desk. The hula girl wore rubber bands around her neck that replaced the lei that came with her at the time of purchase. She grabbed the fattest band from the dancer's neck, initiating the hula dance. The doll swayed back and forth, smiling at Hanson. Connie wrapped the rubber band around the front part of the shoe.

Seeing the look on the hula girl's face as she continued smiling and swinging her hips back and forth infuriated Hanson. "That rubber band isn't gonna hold shit," he yelled. "Get that roll of duct tape over there."

Connie followed the direction his finger was pointing, and after retrieving the roll of tape, wrapped the entire end of his shoe. His little toe remained on the floor and continued to stare at him.

"That should hold until I can get you to the emergency room," she told him.

Hanson stared back at the toe. "Bring that with us," he barked.

"I'm not touching that thing again."

"They can sew it back on," he argued. "Go outside to the ice machine and get some ice and something to put it in. Don't argue with me."

Being it was Connie's nature to avoid conflicts with Hanson, she complied. A few minutes later, the two drove out of the boatyard. Connie was behind the wheel and Hanson sat staring out the windshield. The baggie containing ice cubes and his little toe sat between them on the front seat. Hanson was glad they'd brought it along but refused to look at it.

6

♦

it's all in the details

Connie left the boatyard to drive Hanson to the emergency room about the same time Mario left the Dew Drop Inn. If walking under the influence was a crime, Mario was a candidate for conviction the moment he stepped out the door. He'd made the walk from the inn to his boat many times but this particular night had been one of too many bourbons and his cadence slowed as he navigated the sidewalk.

Thoughts of *Miss Demeanor* and his argument with Hanson about the overdue slip fee returned. It would be a good feeling to exchange the diamonds for a briefcase full of cash and end his money problems. As Carmine had said, it was time to sail off into the sunset. His immediate plan was to return to *Miss Demeanor* and get a good night's rest, but for some reason he felt troubled—even a bit paranoid—thinking about the dockmaster's threat to visit his boat and take what was owed him.

If Hanson went on board, there was no likelihood of him finding the diamonds. Over the years Mario had used the secret compartment to conceal money and small amounts of drugs—even one or two handguns. On several occasions, it went undetected during routine checks by the Coast Guard. Hanson certainly wouldn't find the compartment. Mario recalled the incident with the dog in the bucket and wondered if Hanson might do something crazy to the boat. The guy was loony—certainly not above setting it adrift, or blowing it up, or setting it on fire. It would give him reason to rent the slip to someone else for a higher fee. The inebriated thoughts of those possibilities caused Mario to quicken his pace.

THE WALK SEEMED LONGER than he remembered and he was still tired from the lingering effects of his sail from Andros. The winds had been cooperative from the island to

Miami and he had fair winds for the second leg from Miami to Melbourne. Nonetheless, the strenuous work of manning the helm single-handedly had taken its toll. Carmine insisted on no other crew members—a condition to which Mario readily agreed. The offer from Carmine to tag along was also quickly rejected. He was not only a landlubber but Mario knew he would've talked his ear off and been useless on the boat.

He stared up at the black sky he often sailed under. It was dotted by the same stars he sometimes used for navigation and he took comfort in their presence as they glittered and surrounded a small slice of the moon. Mario liked sailing alone, and as tiring as it was, the sail to Andros had been appealing. It wasn't until his meeting at the Sea Dog that morning when Carmine revealed the payoffs to mine guards, couriers, and the captain of a freighter that the omission of complications was brought to light. The initial plan had been made to appear as a simple pick-up of merchandise. Carmine always had a way of simplifying things but if what he said was true, the money was too good to pass up.

"It'll be like a vacation," Carmine told him. "You won't even have to set foot on shore. A courier out of Cayo Ramano will meet you at Andros Island. No Coast Guard, no nothin'." It seemed like a sweet deal—except for going near Cuban territory—a quick round-trip to pick up a package with a big payoff.

"It's too close to Cuban waters," Mario had argued. "It's bad shit to get caught screwin' around down there."

"And you don't think half a mil is worth the risk? What am I saying? I'm embarrassed to even use the word risk. There aren't any risks. Like I said, you're not actually going into Cuban waters."

"And you're sure about the money?"

"Positive. This guy Cohen runs one of the biggest jewelry houses in New York. He's got contacts coming out of his ass."

"If he's got so many contacts, why does he need us? I'd think there'd be plenty of hot diamonds in the city."

"Yeah, there're plenty in New York all right, but every one of 'em's got a serial number tattooed on the underside. The diamonds you're picking up are coming straight from the mines. They're untraceable."

"And all I have to do is pick them up in Andros and sail them back here?"

"Yes. This guy who's meeting you doesn't even know what he's delivering. He's just paid to give you a package."

"Are you saying he doesn't know what's in the package?"

"Right. What's in the package doesn't mean shit to these guys. They work for cash. Could be coconut oil for all they care. Any palms that needed to be greased along the way were lubricated well in advance. You get back here . . . I take the diamonds to Cohen to get the money and meet you for the split."

"You mean *we'll* take the diamonds to Cohen and get the money. You think I'm trusting you to be walking around with a million bucks?"

"Fine," Carmine relented. "You want to tag along . . . be my guest. I just can't believe you think I'd stiff you."

"I think you'd stiff your own mother if it showed a profit."

Carmine ignored the comment. "With this guy's contacts, we can make a profitable habit out of these runs."

"No thanks. This is my last deal runnin' shit for you. This money will be enough to spend my days sailing the Caribbean with a drink in one hand and an island girl in the other."

He continued his walk toward *Miss Demeanor* knowing, once on board, the night air and her gentle rocking would provide the tranquility he needed.

anchors and guns

A few days after the deal had been agreed to, Mario received a call from Carmine telling him the diamonds would be in the hands of the courier in four days.

"The name of the guy you're to meet is Lopez," Carmine told him. From what you said, *Miss Demeanor* is ready to sail and getting there in four days wouldn't be a problem. Anyway, this guy Lopez will be expecting you at the rendezvous so I suggest you leave today."

The call gave Mario sufficient time to sail to Andros Island. He completed the first leg from Melbourne to Miami in less than twenty-four hours. In Miami he picked up a few supplies and took a mooring for the night. He had requisitioned a thousand dollars from Carmine who balked at the amount until Mario reminded him that the nature of the trip necessitated that everything go smoothly. "If I have to go into a port somewhere for one reason or another, this is not a time to scrimp or get help from strangers. *Miss Demeanor*'s as ship-shape as she's ever been but a lot can happen when you're at sea."

From Miami Mario made the thirty-two hour sail to Andros. With fair winds during the day, and motoring at night *Miss Demeanor* made the voyage effortlessly. He lashed the wheel to follow the charted coordinates and stole bits of sleep under a starlit sky. Her running lights guided her toward the island and he arrived the evening before the scheduled rendezvous.

He anchored near the West Side Park as instructed and dozed again while he waited to meet Lopez. In the morning he woke to the warmth of the sun accompanied by the scream of gulls that hovered and dove along the shoreline. He brewed coffee and sat topside while he waited. Not knowing what to expect, he retrieved his .38 from the cabin and placed it under one of the seat cushions in the cockpit.

It was late morning when a boat became visible on the horizon and grew to full size in minutes. It was a high performance Formula 382 FASTech. Mario recognized it to be the type frequently used by drug-runners in Miami—a *Go fast* they called it. Its speed made it an ideal transport for contraband and Mario made the assumption that Lopez used the FASTech for a variety of reasons. The distance from Cuba's port of Cayo Romano to Andros was certainly an easy haul and the inlet near the West Side Park was an ideal exchange point. It was safe from currents and isolated from authorities.

When the FASTech neared *Miss Demeanor* the helmsman powered down and the boat's momentum drifted her toward Mario's starboard side. The guttural sounds of the engines indicated a resistance to the slower speed. Two men stood on the long sweeping bow. One was nearer the cockpit and wore a very visible shoulder holster. Mario guessed the gun it cradled to be a .45 or a nine millimeter. It dangled menacingly in its inverted position with no additional restraints holding it to his body. The second man stood on the bow and held an AK-47. His right hand was on the trigger and the weight of the gun rested in the other. The barrel was aimed at the water. The clip was crescent-shaped and knowing it held at least thirty rounds, Mario realized his .38 was certainly outmatched in any play of firepower.

As an experienced sailor, Mario was taken more by the man's balance than his weapon. His legs acted as shock absorbers and moved in rhythm to the boat's reaction to the waves. It was an ability to be admired. Rather than display any signs of concerns for his footing, the gunman stood as if he was on a beach somewhere, scanning the water for a swimmer or a passing boat. The automatic was an unnecessary part of his look that seemed to display an air of "I'm a casual guy but don't fuck with me."

Both men were dressed in khakis and sported mirrored sunglasses. The one with the automatic wore a gray T-shirt that read *Property of the New York Yankees.* The guy with the shoulder holster wore a white T-shirt with no claims of being the property of anyone. The driver, who Mario assumed was Lopez, was shirtless. His chest and both arms displayed numerous tattoos. All three men looked to be natives of Cuba. The cruiser circled the sloop and Mario noticed the driver eye-balling *Miss Demeanor*'s name on the stern. He circled a second time and then cut the motor entirely. The light slapping of the waves on the boats and along the shoreline were the only audible sounds and seemed to bring an air of calmness to the impending transaction. The FASTech drifted alongside *Miss Demeanor* and everyone remained silent until the helmsman yelled to Mario. "You the man?"

"Looks like it," Mario returned. "Unless you want to check to see if someone's swimming under the boat." The comment was made in an attempt to let everyone know he wasn't intimidated, but as the words left his mouth, he realized he may have planted a seed of distrust. The crewman with the automatic shot a look at the driver whose eyes remained fixed on Mario. He gave a nod and the guy lashed both boats together with the efficiency of a surgeon rendering a suture. He used a knot Mario didn't recognize and executed the maneuver in a way that made it obvious he performed it often.

The helmsman stepped over the windshield and onto the bow. He took a wide-spread stance between the two gunmen. He smiled, exposing a gold front tooth. "I'm Lopez."

"Yeah, I kinda figured that," Mario said.

"You got somethin' to give me?" Lopez yelled to Mario.

Mario pulled the Kennedy half-dollar from his pocket that Carmine had given him for the ritual. Supposedly it proved he was the rightful recipient of the package. Whether it was Carmine's idea or this Lopez guy's, Mario wasn't sure. If he had to guess, any needless cloak and dagger nonsense had come from Carmine. Mario pictured him back in his air conditioned office—sitting in his white suit—pleased with himself as he sent his Humphrey Bogart to get the goods. Mario flipped the coin to Lopez who snatched it in mid flight.

Lopez gave a sharp whistle and nodded to the same crew member who'd secured the boats, signaling him to board *Miss Demeanor.*

He stepped into the cockpit. "I gotta check below," he told Mario, and without waiting for a response walked past him. He reappeared moments later and nodded to the driver, indicating Mario was alone and nothing seemed out of the ordinary.

Lopez gave a second nod to the crewman who had boarded *Miss Demeanor*. He withdrew a package that was tucked into his belt and placed it in Mario's hand.

"You know what's in there man?" Lopez yelled over.

"I know what's supposed to be in here."

"Well, I don't know myself. I'm jes the mailman. So now . . . you got your mail, I need to get my ten G's."

"Whaddaya talkin' about, ten G's?" Mario questioned, feeling the heat beginning to rise up the back of his neck. The gunman wearing the shoulder holster shifted his weight and the guy with the automatic stared at Mario and raised the gun slightly. Any thought Mario had of reaching for the .38 dissolved.

"Yeah," Lopez continued. "I'm supposed to get ten G's for delivering the package. And that's my discount rate. You're supposed to have my money. You see, I've traveled all the way out here on this big blue sea with your package—my two friends and me took great care to get it to you—so . . . where is my ten G's?" As he spoke he made a sweeping gesture indicating the long voyage he'd made across the vast ocean.

"Well, the asshole that told you I was going to have ten Gs is probably the same asshole who told me he already paid you your money."

Lopez laughed. "Hey, I'm jes messin' with you man. Those big shots that hire guys like you and me always spoil my fun by tellin' you they already paid me. I'm jes waitin' for the day when some guy like you believes me and actually gives me the money." There were several seconds of silence while Mario fumbled with the packaging. It was a short piece of PVC pipe. One end was sealed and the other was covered with a screw-on cap. He unscrewed the lid and tilted it causing a cloth pouch to slide into his hand. He pulled the drawstring on the pouch and looked at the stones. He could only assume they were the real thing. He'd never seen uncut diamonds. With Lopez looking on, he pretended to know what he was doing. He continued to stare at the stones and Lopez spoke again. "So, we good man?"

"I have to weigh them."

Lopez shrugged and Mario went below. He spilled the stones onto a small scale and stared at the digital display. The weight was exactly eight ounces as agreed. He returned the stones to the pouch and went topside. Lopez's man had returned to the FASTech. Mario looked at Lopez and nodded. "We're good," he told him.

When the Cuban realized Mario was satisfied with the exchange, he smiled a giant smile, revealing the glittering tooth a second time. Without further conversation, the gunman who had lashed the boats together received a nod from Lopez signaling him to cast off. This was done with a single pull on the line and Lopez fired up the motors. Their deep rumble broke the sound of the slapping waves and the two boats drifted a few feet apart. Lopez gave a quick push on the throttle. As he gunned it, the FASTech growled in response and moved back, allowing more separation from *Miss Demeanor*. He pushed the throttle again, this time with a force that lifted the bow and drove the stern deep into the water. Mario listened to the snarl and watched until it was a speck in the distance. *Miss Demeanor* rocked in the wake of its departure and before going below, Mario made a quick survey of the shoreline. It remained deserted, as it had been all morning. With the exchange completed, he went below and poured himself a double shot.

For the first time since he'd sailed out of Melbourne, he felt at ease. The forecast showed favorable winds for his return trip and with the diamonds safely on board, he envisioned a pleasurable sail home. Sitting below he studied the craftsmanship he so often admired when he spent time in the cabin. The teak was accentuated with a generous amount of brass hardware and the galley was positioned for efficient use of space and convenience. The head contained a full-sized shower which, with her water tanks filled to capacity, lasted for weeks. A panel displayed an array of toggles and lights that controlled his navigational equipment, depth sounders, and the interior cabin lights for nights in the harbor or neighboring ports. Best of all, she was bought and paid for—mostly with money made by charters before sailing to Florida from Cape Cod. Further enhancements had been supplemented with profits from running contraband for Carmine or captaining the boat for select clientele—clients who wanted a weekend with a mistress to go undetected by a wife. It was easy money and Mario had a reputation for being discreet.

He opened the pouch a second time and poured the stones onto a plate. He believed Carmine's assessment of their worth, but their appearance proved to be a disappointment. They were thick and white and chunky. It was hard to believe they would eventually glitter with the clarity their future owners expected. On the other hand, as Carmine stated, they were untraceable. He considered what he might do with his share and whether or not he would keep *Miss Demeanor* or use his new purchasing power to buy a bigger boat. He had owned several, but *Miss Demeanor* had been his home for years and had served him well.

Although he expected the return sail would be easy, it was a long run, even with the favorable winds and the use of his engine. He had lost a good part of the day and he decided to remain on anchor and set sail for Miami the following morning.

He made Miami in a little over thirty hours and stayed an additional night before returning to Melbourne. The second leg was easier than the sail from Andros and he tied up to his slip just before dawn. The greeting he received from Hanson a few hours later waking him to pay his slip fee had been an unnecessary annoyance.

Mario's recollection of the trip and how well *Miss Demeanor* handled herself at sea faded, however, when he reached the boatyard. His cadence quickened as he walked the short distance from the highway. He was ready for a sound sleep and felt good knowing the transaction the next day was going to end all his problems.

♦ pyre of revenge

When Mario reached the boatyard, he noticed the door to the shanty was ajar allowing a small amount of light to spill out onto the porch. Hanson's pickup was evidence he was in for the evening, but the light from the office seemed a bit suspicious. If Mario had left the Dew Drop Inn a few minutes earlier or walked just a bit faster, he would've seen Connie and Hanson leaving for the hospital. What he did see was the uncharacteristic silhouette of *Miss Demeanor*. Her mast was noticeably askew as she sat in what little light the moon offered. The paranoia he felt earlier intensified as he stood and watched it teetering in rhythm with the waves. Its peculiar lean was obviously a sign of something gone wrong and he wondered if his earlier fear of Hanson ransacking his boat was now justified. As he neared her, it became obvious that the mast had been tampered with.

His closer inspection revealed the damage Hanson had done to the hatch and the severed mast. The unrecognizable stench of the spewed hard-boiled eggs permeated the air. In the darkness, however, the spots of blood and chunks of fish 'n chips went unseen. He stood, perplexed, wondering what could've possibly happened in his absence. He ran his hand over the gouge in the hatch. He felt the base of the severed mast and discovered the jagged edge that had somehow been cut through. He studied the scene as he searched the night air for answers as to what possible mishap had befallen his boat.

"Hanson did it," came a voice from behind him. "I saw the whole thing. He was drunker than hell and yelling that you owed him money. Said he was justified and . . . you know, he just kept ranting. First, he was down here on the dock yelling. He woke everyone up and then he left and came back a few minutes later with a chainsaw. He tried to break into your cabin." As the man spoke, he pointed to the hatch, indicating the damage. "When that didn't work he cut off the mast—sparks were flyin' everywhere. Damn lucky it didn't fall on him and kill him. Everybody's pretty much back on their boats now, but there was a bunch of us out here. We all saw it. You'll have plenty of witnesses if you take him to court. I'll sure testify. I've never liked that guy."

"A bunch of you! What do you mean a bunch of you?"

"Hell, he woke up everybody in the harbor."

"If you were all out here, why the hell didn't somebody stop him?"

"What could we do? The guy was a raving lunatic, drunk out of his mind, and waving a chainsaw around."

"Did anyone call the cops?" As Mario asked the question, he realized having the cops around probably wasn't the best idea.

"We talked about it. I guess we figured when you got back you'd decide what to do. We can testify for you but we didn't want to get him pissed off at us. He kept waving the chainsaw around like a crazy man. Hell, at one point he cut his leg or something." This time the man pointed to the blood trail on the dock.

Mario surveyed the dotted pathway and saw it led to the shanty. He started to step back onto the dock to go and settle things but then remembered Hanson's comment earlier that day regarding a gun. He pictured Hanson sitting at his desk . . . waiting for him to come in so he could blast him. Unlike his encounter with the AK-47, tonight his .38 would be enough fire power to retaliate. He turned back to the damaged hatch and dialed the combination on the padlock. He was no better at getting it right on his first attempt than Hanson had been at starting the chainsaw. When he finally succeeded, he removed the lock and threw it onto the cushion with a force of anger that sent it bouncing overboard to accompany Hanson's saw. In the cabin, he opened the secret compartment and procured his .38. As he retrieved it, he failed to notice the pouch containing the uncut stones as it fell into the seat cushions.

He secured the compartment, and with gun in hand, followed the blood trail from the dock to the shanty. The onlookers had reconvened and stepped aside as he pushed his way past them. He had sobered considerably since his return from the bar but remained drunk enough to neglect the formulation of a plan that might display any signs of reason.

Connie had neglected to turn off the desk lamp when the two left for the hospital which gave credence to the glimmer of light coming out of the office. Whether or not Hanson was sitting at his desk with his gun didn't matter. Mario planned to kick the door of the shanty open and shoot the son-of-a-bitch where he sat—or where he stood—it really didn't matter. The dockmaster had destroyed the one thing he owned over a lousy slip fee.

The door of the shanty was open most of the way but Mario felt the need to kick it in anyway. It was a one-room office and a quick look around revealed no one was there. Stairs led to Hanson's living quarters on the second floor but now Mario wondered if his kicking of the door had awakened and alerted the dockmaster who would be sitting up there with his gun aimed and ready. While he contemplated his next move, a voice from the porch hollered in. "He's not in there."

Mario turned, gun in hand, to see a second witness to the fiasco. He recognized the man as one of the boat owners in the yard but didn't know his name . . . Carson or something he thought.

"Whaddaya mean he's not here. His truck's right there," he countered using the .38 to point to Hanson's pickup. "He doesn't go anywhere without his truck."

"He left in a car with some woman. I think it was Connie, the woman who works in the office. She helped him into the car and they drove off. She was driving. I think he was hurt—think he cut himself in the leg or something with the chain saw. She may have been taking him to the ER if he was cut bad enough." The man's eyes remained focused on the gun and his voice was shaking as he recreated the incident.

Mario suddenly felt embarrassed and tucked the revolver into the front of his belt. *Miss Demeanor*'s silhouette had gained more of a lean and he feared the worst if he left her in her current state. "I gotta tend to my boat," he told the man. "You're Carson right?"

"Well, you're close. It's Canton. Alan Canton."

"You think you could get another guy or two and give me a hand? I can't leave my mast like that. If I don't get it down I'm afraid the boat's gonna keep heeling over."

Canton enlisted the help of two other spectators and the three men steadied the mast while Mario freed it. Even in the late hour with a belly full of bourbon, he showed the efficiency of a veteran seaman. In minutes he had removed the boom and mainsail. He then freed the stays that had prevented the mast from falling. Once the stays were removed, he pulled the pins on the roller furling which left the mast free of any attachment to the boat. Mario knew the mast was too heavy and awkward for three men to keep it upright and their yells of concern were no surprise. "Push it to starboard," he yelled, "and then get the hell out of the way."

The mast fell like a giant oak and the kickback at its base nearly sent one of the men overboard. The mast, that stood well over fifty feet, fell with a resounding crash as it landed on three boats that were adjacent to Mario's. The two closest were fashionable yachts and acted as a fulcrum. The mast rocked on their cabins, hammering the third boat—Hanson's skiff. The expensive cruisers were unoccupied during their destruction, although whether anyone was on board or not had been little concern to Mario. The three men looked on in horror as they witnessed the second catastrophe of the night. The crushed yachts sat rocking beneath the weight of Mario's mast. As they bobbed up and down, the mast see-sawed and continued to pound the skiff. A few life jackets and chunks of debris floated in the harbor as water found its way between cracks and seeped into the cockpit.

"Don't worry about those boats," Mario yelled reassuringly. "Hanson will make good on them." In an effort to get the three men off *Miss Demeanor*, he continued with a tone of dismissive nonchalance. "Thanks for the help with the mast."

The men gave each other questioning looks as they filed past Mario and stepped onto the dock. With no capability for sailing, he fired up the diesel. He wanted to get as far away from the boatyard as possible but since his return from Andros, he had not replenished his fuel. The distance he could put between himself and the boatyard was limited. He studied Hanson's skiff. Its severed halves were spared from sinking by the lines securing them to the dock leaving the bow and stern separate entities dangling in the water.

Mario stared at the outboard that sat on Hanson's sinking skiff. His thought was to motor to Miller's Cove, and with limited fuel, he knew the outboard would help. It was an easy removal and transfer to *Miss Demeanor* and it was obvious that Hanson wouldn't be using it in the near future. He knew it might make the difference of making it to the cove. Once there, he could drop anchor. The inlet was well-hidden and would provide safety until he resolved his mast problem. He transferred the outboard and cast off the lines on Hanson's skiff. He stood smiling as parts of her floated away while heavier remnants found their way to the bottom of the river.

Before departing, he made a final visit to the shanty. With the help of a few newspapers and a kerosene lamp, he started a fire on Hanson's desk. He then walked the dock and returned to *Miss Demeanor*, never bothering to turn and see the spectacle of flames that roared into the dark sky behind him. Sparks shot high into the air and were accompanied by loud pops and crackles from the fire. He watched the intensity of the scene in the mirror of the river and smiled.

Almost completely sober now, he pushed his way through the stunned spectators who were still on the dock and strolled to his boat. He adjusted a few items in the cockpit, threw the boom into the cabin, and leisurely motored out of the harbor. As he navigated through several moored boats and looked up at the stars, Lester's ineptness with computers triggered the two o'clock chimes in conjunction with the Mormon Tabernacle Choir's rousing rendition of *Joy To The World*. The carol rang out to the accompaniment of church bells and chimes. He stood at the helm . . . diesel purring . . . and watched as flames licked their way up the shanty. They were sights and sounds to behold. He motored through the reflection of the flames in the water that lay in front of him appearing to onlookers as a demon from hell. The fire roared, the chorus reached its crescendo, and the church bells rang out their joyousness to the world as he left the pyre in his wake.

The burning building beckoned police and firefighters which added the low wail of distant sirens. The boat owners, who had been the audience for the evening's three-act play, stood together with their mouths hanging open. To them the fire was mad revenge—the third act of insanity.

Mario watched the dock people . . . their group profile sandwiched between the blazing shanty and the scuttled boats. Residents in hell, he thought. He glanced in the direction of the yachts in time to witness their final descent. "What a great story all those people will have to tell their grandchildren," he said to the stars.

◆ **this little piggy**

Connie pulled her car into the semi-circle that fronted the emergency entrance to the Melbourne Hospital and killed the engine. Hanson's head was tilted back, his face a light shade of green. After leaving the boatyard, he avoided looking at the baggie that sat on the front seat, separating him from his secretary. The ice cubes hid the toe but he knew it was in there somewhere. His foot throbbed with pain, and with his head back, he closed his eyes to shut out the events of the evening. The thought of his bloody foot brought back his queasiness.

"I think I'm gonna be sick."

"Don't you dare puke in my car," Connie yelled back. Her demand for his restraint caused him to look for a container. Eyeing the baggie, he picked it up and fumbled with the zip-lock, hoping anything exiting his stomach would hit the target.

"You can't use that," Connie yelled. "You think any doctor is going to go fishing around in your vomit to find a missing toe? Open the door and get out if you're gonna throw up."

Hanson opened the door and stretched his head out. The pre-dawn air was chilly and seemed to steady him. He retched, fearing the worst. Connie pictured an array of vomit on her car that matched the drippings on his shirt, but Hanson had nothing left in his stomach. Strands of saliva emerged and drooled out and remained connected to his lower lip. A few strands hung off his chin like tiny icicles until Hanson erased them with his sleeve.

Connie got around to his side of the car and helped him out, wrapping one of his arms behind her head while she held his wrist. With her other arm around his waist, the two hobbled into the emergency room. Hanson held the baggie and clutched it to his chest as if guarding a treasure. The two limped into the reception area where a uniformed cop was sitting. He had been called earlier in the evening to investigate an unrelated gunshot wound and was waiting to question the victim who was still in surgery. When Connie and Hanson entered he approached them to assist.

Seeing the uniform, Hanson began blubbering about his toe and handed the baggie to the officer. "See that the doctor gets this," he told the cop. "It's my toe. Tell him I want him to sew it back on."

Several hours later a young doctor entered the waiting room and informed Connie that, although she had made a valiant attempt to get the toe to the hospital, it just wasn't possible to suture it on. "Unless a body part such as that is procured during a surgical procedure with proper follow-up, it's rare that a toe or a finger can be stitched back on," he told her. "I know people sometimes get that idea from the movies, but that's what doctors refer to as *Hollywood* surgery."

Connie remained by Hanson's side in the recovery room until he awoke in late morning. She considered going home to get dressed and then check in at the office but during her time in the waiting room, a police detective arrived. He was part of the team who answered the call to investigate the carnage at the boatyard. After questioning witnesses at the dock he tracked Hanson to the hospital. He located Connie and explained the destruction of the boats and the burning of the shanty. He went on to say that reports from all witnesses led the police to believe their person of interest was a man named Mario Costello. The department had initiated a BOLO and he told her they expected an arrest within twenty-four hours.

WHEN HANSON AWOKE, HIS immediate concern was to make sure he had five toes on each foot. He had a vague recollection of the conversation with the cop and remembered giving him the baggie. He began questioning Connie. "Did that cop get my toe to the doctor? He did right? I mean, you saw to it didn't you?" He seemed confident the foot had been resurrected until Connie's face betrayed the outcome. "Are you tellin' me he screwed up? Because I'm tellin' you if I don't have five toes on that foot I want that bastard's badge number."

Connie said nothing of the surgeon's inability to suture the toe back on nor did she mention the fact that Mario had destroyed some boats and burned down the office. She felt that any wrath Hanson would bestow following those tidbits of information should be directed toward the doctor and the officer in charge of the investigation, both of whom had promised to check in on Hanson later in the day.

The doctor arrived first. Hanson was sitting upright, pawing at a tray of hospital food. The doctor wasted no time in revealing the details of the surgery and the impossibility of saving the toe.

Hanson stared at the Dixie cup on his tray. "Where is it?"

"Usually in cases such as this, it's put in with the medical waste and destroyed."

"Thrown out with the garbage, you mean," Hanson yelled. "You're tellin' me you just took my toe and threw it in the trash bin."

"I'm sorry, Mr. Hanson, but yes, although I wouldn't exactly refer to the medical waste disposal as the trash bin."

Hanson displayed an uncharacteristic look of despair, as if he'd just lost his best friend or was a child whose teddy bear had been taken away. It was a much different reaction than Connie expected. For the first time since she'd known Hanson she felt sorry for him. It was much different than his reaction an hour later when he was visited by the police. As if receiving the news that spending the remaining days of his life with only nine toes wasn't enough, Hanson received a recap of Mario's performance at the boatyard and his rage intensified.

IT HAD BEEN AN exhausting night for everyone. While Hanson was in surgery, Mario motored to within a few miles of his destination. His intention to get to Miller's Cove was compromised when the diesel engine ran dry. He then discovered that switching to Hanson's outboard was not possible. After considerable work getting it from Hanson's skiff and onto *Miss Demeanor*, he found the shaft was too short. The propeller was a foot shy of reaching the water. This discovery took place shortly after three a.m. He had used up a good amount of adrenalin during the burning of the shanty and the destruction of the yachts. With his energy replaced by exhaustion, Mario anchored *Miss Demeanor* where she sat and went below to sleep.

It was well past noon when he awoke. He brewed a pot of coffee and took a cup topside to survey his surroundings. He was anchored as far from the boatyard as his engine allowed, but was still three or four miles shy of Miller's Cove. In the light of day, he took comfort knowing he was in an area that was well protected. The Route 192 causeway was twenty yards off his port bow with Douglas Park being a short distance to starboard. The park punctuated a row of expensive houses along the riverfront. The causeway continued into Indialantic, past the park and became 5th Street. He knew the area well. A wide variety of shops and eateries dotted the main street all the way to Longboard House. It was only a few miles beyond Longboard where he was to meet with Carmine and Cohen.

An empty bench in the park offered a vantage point that looked out over the water and he realized *Miss Demeanor* would be as visible to anyone sitting on it as the bench was to him.

He sipped his coffee and through the denseness of a throbbing head recalled the events of the prior evening. Surely, there would be repercussions from all that happened. Hindsight told him that burning Hanson's shanty, although justified, had probably not been a good idea. Mario figured Hanson would tell the cops they had argued over the slip fee which was probably the reason Mario burned his office to the ground. He certainly wouldn't mention that he started the war by cutting down the mast.

Even if Mario got his day in court, he had no time to deal with the matter or any of Hanson's nonsense. He needed to get the transaction with the diamonds done and get as far away from Melbourne as possible. He stared at the stump of the mast. The thought of ever sailing *Miss Demeanor* without extensive repairs was out of the question. The lack of a mast was only the beginning. In Hanson's stupor, he made a mess of the deck with his chainsaw and his bleeding. Mario himself had contributed to the disorder when he threw things out of the cabin. Cushions, life jackets, and an array of miscellaneous items were strewn everywhere. Without a thorough check of the boat there was no way of knowing what equipment had inadvertently fallen overboard.

The gouged hatch lay on top of the cabin. Noticing the outboard, he recalled sinking Hanson's skiff and stealing the motor that now dangled off the stern . . . impotent in its attempt to reach the water. Dock lines that were usually neatly coiled into circular patterns appeared as mounds of spaghetti. Sheets, and halyards were entangled in the roller furling with no apparent beginning or end. The furling itself hung over the bow and Mario felt fortunate not to have lost it entirely during the night.

The thoughts and possibilities that flooded his mind became muddled as he recalled the falling mast's destruction of the two yachts. Restitution for those would leave him penniless, although the owners should've had insurance. A good lawyer could argue the falling mast was a direct action of Hanson sawing it off. Even if he was caught, with half a million in cash, he'd buy Hanson off. The shanty wasn't worth shit anyway. His thoughts blurred together. The meeting with Carmine and the buyer was still possible.

As he studied the disarray, he planned his new course of action. Once the stones were exchanged for cash he would take a bus to Miami and buy another boat. From there he could sail to parts unknown—all of it done before Hanson caught up with him. He finished his coffee and prepared to go ashore to get something to eat. After repositioning the hatch he searched the cockpit for the padlock, not realizing it had bounced overboard the previous night.

The thought of leaving the boat unlocked unnerved him but it was early afternoon and he knew his time away would be less than an hour. Not knowing the diamonds had fallen out of the compartment and between the seat cushions, he assumed they were safely hidden. He decided to get fuel for the engine, finish the short distance to Miller's Cove, and meet Carmine with the diamonds. In the cove, *Miss Demeanor* would remain undetected for days—perhaps weeks—certainly enough time for him to get out of Melbourne.

He pulled a gas can from beneath a seat compartment and tossed it into the dinghy. As he rowed to shore, his forward lean reminded him he still had the .38 tucked into his belt. Although he had no need for the gun on shore, he was tired, hung over, and too short on time to return to the boat. His focus was to get something to eat, call Carmine, and get an update on their meeting.

In minutes he was ashore and secured the dinghy in a protected area of bushes along the pedestrian walkway of the causeway. With no wind and only a slight current, the tender would be safe while he took care of business. If memory served him correctly, there was a tavern on Riverside where he could grab a burger. A CITGO sign loomed about half a block away and Mario left the gas can in the dinghy thinking food first, then diesel fuel. As he walked to the tavern, he called Carmine.

"Where the hell are you?" his partner barked. "And what the hell happened last night?"

"What'd you hear happened?"

"I didn't have to hear shit. You're all over the fuckin' news. I'm sitting in my car outside the boatyard. There're cops crawlin' all over the place. They got the crime unit here, the hotshot photographers, three or four news crews, and anybody else involved in law and order in this county. So I ask again, where the hell are you and what happened?"

Mario ignored the questions a second time. "We still on for the meeting with your guy?"

"Yeah, if we can get there before five o'clock, which means you don't get picked up before then. Can you stay out of the public eye?"

Mario looked at his watch. "Listen, it's three-twenty now. Pick me up in front of Squid Lips at four thirty." Squid Lips was a restaurant far enough away from *Miss Demeanor* and Mario knew that Carmine wouldn't make any connection as to where he'd left the boat. If anything unexpected went down, the fewer people who knew the location of the diamonds the better. "I'll bring the package and we can drive over together for the meeting. Under the circumstances, I'll need my share of the money today."

life becomes rosie

Mario entered the Sand Flea Tavern on North Riverside. A smaller sign that followed, in which Mario didn't see much humor, suggested patrons, "Come in and get a bite." Once inside, he perched himself on a stool. His head was still pounding from the prior night's rounds of bourbon. A string of Christmas bulbs framed the bottles behind the bar, and a small artificial tree, topped with a bikini-clad angel, blinked its lights on and off.

He ordered a burger and a Coke but as the bartender pulled the spigot to fill his glass, Mario had second thoughts and instructed him to throw in a shot of rum.

The bartender noticed Mario's condition. "Hair of the dog?" he asked.

Mario gave a slight nod but said nothing.

"From the looks of ya, you started to bring in the New Year a bit early," the bartender added.

Mario said nothing again, but the comment reminded him it was New Year's Eve even though the tavern showed no signs of preparation for the evening.

"Doesn't look like you're putting on any kind of a party in here tonight."

"No. Fact is we're closin' early. This is more a neighborhood bar for the locals. Figure most of our clientele will be home in bed by midnight. If you want any action, I recommend you hit some of the bars along A1A or drive up to Satellite Beach."

"Think I'll pass," Mario told him and started in on his rum and Coke. A man and a woman sat to his left. The man, proving the bartender's point, looked to be in his late fifties and had the comfortable posture of an afternoon regular. He blocked all but the arm of the woman and Mario watched as her hand toyed with the slice of lime on the rim of her margarita glass. He peered into the mirror behind the bar but her reflection was hidden by the assorted bottles of liquor. Had he been feeling better, he would've made a stronger effort to see her.

His only interest was to finish his burger, get the fuel, and motor to Miller's Cove. After a quick shower on board, he would get to Squid Lips and rendezvous with Carmine. After getting his share of the money, he'd have Carmine drive him to the bus depot. In Miami he'd buy a boat and leave Hanson, the cops, and anyone else looking for him in his wake.

Two college-aged guys entered. In the mirror, Mario noticed the admiring glances they gave the woman. The first to enter went directly to a booth. The second ordered a pitcher from the bartender and then joined his friend. Mario recalled his singular year at the Naval Academy and knew the pitcher indicated they were there to make an afternoon of it—perhaps the preamble to whatever New Year's Eve plans they had in mind.

He needed a refill and motioned to the bartender. A pimply-faced kid emerged from the kitchen with the burger. He wore a half-apron, covered with a variety of stains. The cord was looped behind his back and brought around to the front where it was tied off. A dish rag hung over the cord and rested on his hip. As the kid set the plate on the bar, the regular pushed his glass away, picked up all but two singles in front of him, and stood to leave. He hollered a *Happy New Year* to the bartender as he made his exit.

The kid reached under the bar to retrieve a bottle of ketchup and set it next to Mario's plate along with salt and pepper shakers. As he did so, he addressed the woman. Her name was Rosita and when he spoke to her, he pronounced her name with a rolling 'R' and an over enunciated 't.'

"Can I get you anything while I'm out here, R-r-rosita?" For some reason, the way he said it gave Mario an instant dislike for the kid.

"I'm fine," the woman responded without looking up. Her response held an air of annoyance.

With the regular having left the empty stool between them, Mario was able to get a better look at the woman. She was reading a book and he studied her profile. She looked to be in her early twenties and had a face of rough elegance—the likes of which were captivating. Mario realized why she had received the appreciative looks from the college guys when they first entered. Her magnetism held Mario's gaze. She seemed to have a nonchalance that was threatening. She was dark-skinned—probably made darker by the sun—and her hair was coal-black.

Mario made a poor attempt at conversation. "Is that your man?" he asked her, nodding toward the kid who was returning to the kitchen.

"Tommy?" she questioned with a soft laugh. "Not hardly. He just helps out around the place. He thinks if he rolls the R and says my entire first name it sounds sexy—thinks he can get in my pants."

"Your *entire* first name?"

"Yeah, you know, the whole R-r-rosita thing," she repeated as she imitated Tommy's pronunciation.

Mario said nothing.

"I go by Rosie," she said extending her hand. He stared at it and noticed the beginning of an intricate design that crept out from beneath the cuff of her sleeve and spilled onto her wrist. Instinctively, he took her hand in his. It was soft—gentle to touch—and a surge of electricity shot up his arm and continued to his chest. She studied him for a moment before breaking the longer-than-necessary clasp. "How 'bout you? Usually introductions go two ways."

"Mario," he responded, withdrawing his hand. He returned to his burger and the conversation seemed to end. It was an end that he didn't actually want and as he squirted a blotch of ketchup onto his plate he attempted to rekindle the small talk. "So . . . what you said earlier—about Tommy—that's not going to happen?"

"What do you mean, what I said earlier?"

"You know, when he talked to you just now . . . you said he was rolling the r in R-r-rosita because he was trying to sound sexy. You said he was hoping to get in your pants. That's not going to happen?" The tone of his question was filled with an air of intentional humor.

"No," she laughed again. "That's not going to happen."

"Good, good," Mario said, more to the French fry he was dipping in the ketchup than to Rosita. The comment was followed by an awkward silence.

"Sorry," Mario added. "I didn't mean to offend you. I . . . just think it's good," he added.

"What do you think is good? What are you talking about?"

"I just think it's good to know it takes more than a rolling r to get into a woman's pants these days."

She surprised Mario with a laugh that filled the tavern, and as it subsided, she reached for one of his fries. He responded by pushing his plate toward her and she slid over and occupied the empty stool between them.

"Come here often?" he asked her.

She laughed again at the cliché. "Most days," she said. "After I get off work." Mario said nothing and she continued. "I work down the street at Dunkin' Donuts." As she made the statement she gestured to her outfit. He had been so intrigued with her beauty he hadn't noticed the uniform. It was a pants suit made of a lightweight brown fabric and showed very little of her figure but Mario continued to be enchanted by her smile.

"I work the seven to three shift."

"The uniform thing. It's very stylin' on you. Gives you that whole *doughnut girl* kind of look." His voice maintained the same tenor of humor as his earlier comment. "I'm sure you'll be the belle of any New Year's Eve ball you attend tonight."

"The only ball I'll be seeing is the one on TV—if I can even stay awake 'til then."

"No party?"

"Not tonight. My idea of a Happy New Year is curling up with a good book . . . which won't be this one I might add." As she made the comment she lifted the book she was reading to reveal the cover. Mario stared at a textbook by Maslow titled, *A Theory of Human Motivation*. "Psych . . . third year night school," she said almost apologetically.

He gave a sympathetic laugh and then returned his focus to the design on her wrist. "Do they make you wear the long sleeves to cover your tat?" As he asked the question, he pointed to the ink.

"Not really. I just get tired of comments from some of the creeps that come in for coffee." As she answered, she pushed up her sleeve to reveal the end of a snake. The serpent's multiple colored diamonds wound their way around her arm and continued to her elbow. What followed from there was left to the imagination.

"Interesting choice."

"I've had a thing for snakes since I was a kid," she explained. "Actually got the tat idea from my father."

"It's nice work. Does it have a happy ending?"

She pulled the top of her uniform off her shoulder and revealed the head of a viper with a split tongue and fiery red eyes. Mario pictured it spiraling its way up her arm before it peeked over her shoulder. The eyes glared at Mario and the tongue seemed almost animated. Rosita made an action that tightened a shoulder muscle and the tongue moved a bit, making her laugh at Mario's surprised expression. He wanted to see her naked in bed with the diamond-back winding itself around her arm and slithering up and over her shoulder—trace it with his finger starting at the tail and continuing all the way to its piercing eyes. Did she have other tats he wondered? A question that would only be answered by a thorough examination of her entire body. He would have to explore and scrutinize every inch in the quest for other art work—a time-consuming examination that would require his utmost scrutiny.

"Like I said, it's nice work," he told her. "Very nice." The comment was followed by silence. Mario motioned to the last two fries on the plate and they each took one.

"So what does a woman with a snake crawling up her arm do when she's not bagging jelly donuts?"

"School mostly. Once I get my degree I hope I can make a real living. Which is why I'm reading this." She pointed to the text a second time and then closed it. The conversation continued and focused on the complications of balancing schoolwork with her job. Mario sipped his drink, content to listen. He watched the excitement dance in her eyes as she talked and he felt a bit self-conscious realizing his clothes were disheveled and he needed a shave.

The talk eventually turned to the local area. Mario kept his comments short, revealing little of himself . . . telling her he lived on his boat, enjoyed the area, and lied about his plans to settle in Melbourne Beach. He had learned long ago to tell new acquaintances as little as possible about himself while extracting as much information from them as reasonable. He certainly wanted to know more about this woman named Rosita, even though the chance he would see her again wasn't likely. With the fries gone, Mario pushed the plate toward the bartender.

"Unfortunately, I've gotta run," he told her. "Be happy to buy you another margarita though . . . if not right now, maybe later today."

"Thanks, but I've got a few errands to run before the stores close." She then eyed him up and down, seemingly for the first time. "Speaking of running, I don't know where you're off to, but if you're going to any kind of a New Year's Eve party, I hope you stop and iron your shirt," she laughed. "If you don't mind my saying so, a shower and shave probably wouldn't hurt either." She rubbed her index finger across his chin as she made the comment. "I'll bet you clean up pretty good. You got running water on that boat of yours?"

Mario couldn't remember the last time he'd been embarrassed, but he used the opportunity of Rosita's comments as an opening for a brief explanation of his appearance. "I guess last night was a rougher night than usual. You might say I'm not in the best shape right now."

"I think I just did say that. The way you talk sounds as if you have a lot of rough nights."

He was about to continue when the bartender took his plate and replaced it with his bill. "Can I get you anything else, friend? Another round?" he pointed to the near empty glass.

"I'm good," Mario told him and reached for his wallet. Only then did he realize he had left it on the boat. His face colored and he felt the heat rise up his neck. He stared at Rosita.

His expression was all she needed to see. "Let me guess," she said with no hesitation. "You've lost your wallet. Or worse yet, someone stole it." She continued to stare at him and her look was matched by the bartender's.

"You're not going to believe this," Mario started as he switched his attention to the barman.

"And you're not going to believe how many times guys come in here, have a drink, and give me the same line of bullshit you're going to give me," the bartender interrupted.

The last thing Mario needed was any type of confrontation. He ignored the bartender's comment and turned back toward Rosita. "I do have a wallet. I mean, I have money. I musta left it on my boat."

"Right, right. I forgot you have a boat. I'll bet it's a big yacht too." Rosita's tone held an obvious note of skepticism. "Whaddaya say Mike . . . you think this guy owns a big yacht with a wallet on board?"

Mario returned his attention to the bartender. "Look, I'll leave my watch," he told him. "My boat's not far from here. I'll go back and grab my wallet and be back here in fifteen minutes." As he made his plea he slipped his watch off his wrist.

Rosita removed a twenty from her purse and slid it to the bartender. "I got it," she told Mario and then gave him a stare. "Consider it a New Year's Eve present. If you really want to pay me back, you know where I work . . . I'm on the seven to three shift every day but Sunday. That's when I go to church to pray for the homeless. You know, guys with no money," she added with a touch of sarcasm.

"You can count on it," Mario assured her. He tried to discern whether she was a good-hearted woman or perhaps fronting him the money as a signal that she wanted to see him again. "Listen, if you want to wait, I'll get it and come back here right now."

"Can't," she told him. "Just bring it around when you get it."

"Then *you* take the watch."

"Hey, I'm not a pawn broker. Just bring me the twenty bucks if you want to make good."

"I insist," he argued and dropped the watch into the open purse hanging on her chair.

It had been a long time since Mario had felt sheepish about anything he'd done but as he left the tavern he was embarrassed. He hoped to see Rosita again and put things right. His immediate thought, however, was to get cleaned up and get to Squid Lips. He had lingered longer than planned at the Sand Flea and motoring to Miller's Cove would have to wait. Being late afternoon, *Miss Demeanor* would hopefully be viewed as just another boat anchored along the riverfront. He could move her later or simply take his money and run.

Unfortunately, when he stepped outside the tavern, things changed quickly and his plan to meet with Carmine was immediately curtailed. The police BOLO put out the prior evening started what the local cops considered a serious manhunt. Mario's picture had been all over the news and a dutiful citizen who spotted him entering the tavern made a call to the police hotline.

While he sat and ate his burger and chatted with Rosita, a barrage of uniformed cops waited patiently outside the Sand Flea. Once he stepped out the door, two squad cars drove onto the sidewalk. Mario was immediately arrested and taken to the local precinct.

Carmine sat across town at the Squid Lips restaurant, thumping the steering wheel, waiting for his partner to arrive.

11

The interrogation room was windowless and stuffy. Mario sat alone, cuffed to a metal ring in the middle of a small table. The uniforms that brought him into the station bypassed the detention bench where a teen-aged kid was parked alongside a hooker who sat filing her nails. Both were cuffed to the bench which presented an interesting problem for the hooker as she navigated the cuffs to work on her manicure. Mario was paraded through a maze of desks in the squad room, and per the desk sergeant's instructions, was secured in Room B.

The incident on the street had been ugly. Following the first police car cutting off his path on the sidewalk, a second pulled up, nearly running him over. Four officers jumped from the cars, pinned him to the concrete, and cuffed him. During the tussle, his shirt rose just high enough to expose the handle of his .38 and brought a shout of "gun" from the cop who spotted it. The shout triggered an unnecessary amount of roughness. Mario's face was pushed into the sidewalk by one officer while another put a knee into his back. The remaining pair worked the cuffs. People congregated—Rosita among them—and her final vision of the man with no wallet was seeing him thrown into the back seat of a police car.

Now, in Room B, he sat with a scrape over one eye and a head that continued to throb. Whether the pounding was the sustained effect of his hangover or from the recent skirmish on the sidewalk was hard to distinguish.

Instinctively, he checked his watch before realizing it was in Rosita's handbag. He calculated it was near four o'clock—perhaps later—meaning he'd missed his rendezvous with Carmine. He pictured him sitting in his car outside Squid Lips, impatient and worried. By now he had most likely taken a handful of his tranquilizers . . . his "calm me down" pills as he called them . . . and gobbled them up like M&Ms.

Mario studied the interrogation room. Unlike the movies, there was no mirror disguising a one-way glass. He assumed he was being observed by the ceiling cameras mounted in two of the corners. Two chairs were on the opposite side of the table and another camera sat on a tripod behind them. Mario had seen it all before . . . more than once. His past history of barroom fights and hot-tempered disputes provided for many a night's stay at one precinct or another. He knew the routine. Say nothing, admit to nothing. With his wallet on *Miss Demeanor*, today's arrest didn't give the police much information to go on. Evidently Hanson went crying to the cops and gave them his name and description. How much they had pieced together after that was anyone's guess.

His anger was fueled by the missed opportunity of being so close to getting his money and disappearing out of town . . . which he blamed on Hanson. His thoughts turned to Rosita and he wondered if she had seen the incident outside the bar and would he see her again? He certainly wanted to.

It was a good fifty minutes before a plain-clothed detective entered the room. He carried the familiar manila folder. Mario knew it held whatever information they were able to gather during his wait. The cop dropped it on the table. "I'm Detective Benner," he informed Mario, and then used his thumb to point over his shoulder at the camera on the tripod. "You mind if I tape this?"

"Tape what?"

"Well, I guess I'm referring to the conversation we're about to have." He sat down as he spoke and then turned and pushed a button on the camera. Mario watched the red light come on and continue to flash. The detective was about to begin but Mario spoke first. "I don't have anything to say, other than I want my phone call."

"Well, that's unfortunate. I sorta thought the definition of a conversation was the exchange of sentences between two or more people. You not saying anything kind of puts a damper on that."

"The only conversation I'm planning to have is with my attorney. What am I here for anyway?"

Benner ignored the question. "Wow, an attorney. And who would that be? Maybe I could call him for you. I'll tell you what. While we're deciding on your phone call, I'll just review a few things here. You don't have to say anything, I'll just babble on about things you already know." Benner opened the folder and leafed through a few papers. He took a deep breath before exhaling and beginning his speech. "Mario, Mario, Mario," he chided without looking up. "Some interesting information in your file to say the least." He paused but got no visible reaction. He continued as if he was reading a grocery list. "Let's see . . . says here you're on probation in the state of Maryland. Oh, and when we called them a few minutes ago, it seems they didn't know quite where you were. I guess you didn't have their permission to leave."

"I had a note from my mother," Mario responded.

The detective stared at him for a moment and after the pause returned his gaze to the folder and continued. "Oh, and look here . . . we've got aggravated assault, another aggravated assault, drunk and disorderly . . . and oh, here's that phrase aggravated assault again. Hmmm, that third assault must be a misprint. We already had that a couple of times. Tell me Mr. Costello, what *is* it that gets you so aggravated all the time? Why, it also states in your file that you almost—key word here being almost—you *almost* completed two years at Annapolis before getting tossed out for hitting an officer. I guess he must've aggravated you too. Was that it Costello? Did he aggravate you too?"

Before continuing, the detective reached back and turned off the recorder. He then leaned forward as if he was going to tell Mario a secret. When he spoke, the first tone of impatience crept into his voice. "Listen asshole, right now we've got you for arson, destruction of property, leaving the scene, theft, and probably a few other charges we haven't invented yet. And that's just for last night. But you know what, Mr. Costello? All this stuff here, this aggravation you suffer and drunkenness you engage in, and buildings you burn to the ground . . . it's all bullshit to us. We don't even care that you left Maryland in the dust and skipped out on your probation officer—with or without a note from your mother. You know what we care about? We care about where you got the fuckin' gun you were carrying." Several seconds passed before he continued. "Ya see, Costello, that gun puts your balls in a vice right now and I'm the guy who's gonna crank the handle so hard your teeth are gonna fall out."

A pall fell over the room. Benner waited for a response while Mario wondered what the game was. Although the gun was a clear violation of his probation, it was the least of the crimes the detective had reeled off.

"So, you wanna tell me where you got the gun?"

"I think your mother sold it to me. Big fat lady with a mustache. That's her isn't it?"

This time it was the detective who sat in silence. He leaned back in his chair as he closed the folder. He then picked it up with one hand and tapped the edge of it on the table. He stood and withdrew a cell phone from the side pocket of his sport coat. "Go ahead and make your call my friend," he told Mario as he slid it across the table. "But whoever you're callin' . . . they aren't gonna get you outta this mess."

"What about a little privacy?" As Mario asked the question he nodded toward the ceiling camera.

"Like I said, make your call. I'll be back in a minute for the phone so make it a quick one."

When Benner left, Mario leaned forward to accommodate the cuffs and hit the keys for Carmine's number. Carmine had relocated himself from his car seat to a bar stool inside Squid Lips. He was on his second vodka and tonic when his phone buzzed and when he got the call from a number he failed to recognize, he hesitated before answering. "Yeah?"

"It's me."

"Where the fuck are you? I've been at Squid Lips for over an hour. I was just about to call . . ."

"Don't say another word," Mario interrupted. "I'm at the police station and the assholes are probably monitoring the call. They're certainly doing to check on your number to see who it belongs to. When they catch up to you just tell 'em I called you to get me a lawyer—which is exactly what you're gonna do."

"The police station! What the hell are you doing at the police station? You were supposed to be invisible. I told you the cops were scouring the city looking for you. The boatyard's still a three-ring circus down there."

"Obviously Hanson went cryin' to the cops so let's just say I'm not here for afternoon tea. I need a lawyer down here fast. Something's going on that's not kosher."

"Yeah, okay. What about the uh . . . you know . . ."

"Did you hear what I just said? Get a lawyer down here . . . now! I've gotta feelin' these guys are sniffing around for somethin' big time and I don't need any of their bullshit tyin' me up." Mario snapped the phone shut and gave the ceiling camera the finger.

Hearing the disconnect, Carmine closed his phone and downed what was left of his drink. He'd postponed calling Cohen with the hope that Mario would still show. Even a late appearance may have made their meeting possible and temper the Cohen's anger. Now it was time to make a serious decision. He switched from the gin and tonic to a vodka martini. "Just pass the vermouth over the top of the glass," he told the bar maid. "I don't need any of that shit spilling into it. And throw in an extra olive."

As she set the drink in front of him he reached into the pocket of his white suit coat and pulled out his bottle of pills. He repeated the earlier process in his car and tossed several into his mouth and washed them down with the martini. He ordered another, flipped open his phone, and dialed Cohen's number.

12

Jennine Barbosa was a portrait of perfection. She was an elderly woman but her hair, manner of dress, and the way she carried herself were all statements of her assuredness. When she entered the police station, the air of confidence in her stride overshadowed her lack of height or frailty in stature. Her appearance never failed to turn heads and draw attention, characteristics she had adapted from her many years in courtrooms as she successfully defended the guilty.

Several hours had passed since Mario called Carmine with a demand for a lawyer. During that time, Jennine had flown to Melbourne from Savannah. While in the air, she spoke to the district attorney and reviewed the faxed material she'd requested regarding her new client. It was sparse, but Jennine knew knowledge was power and before she met with any client, she absorbed all the information available.

She was acquainted with Jefferds, the DA handling the case. It had been more than three years since they had gone head-to-head in a courtroom. Jennine had been successful in her client's defense but during her in-flight phone call, he gloated over Mario's arrest. "Why he's as guilty as a cream-faced, whisker-lickin' cat who's tryin' to hide the fact that he drank the milk, and I've got all the evidence I need to put him away," he told her.

Knowing most prosecutors exaggerated their claims, Jennine was skeptical regarding what he had and what he could actually prove. At the police station, she had a brief discussion with the desk sergeant regarding Mario's personal belongings before he called a uniformed officer to assist.

"Escort Ms. Barbosa here down to Room B for me."

Her eyes remained fixed on the sergeant and she spoke with a sharp voice she often used to establish her authority. "How long has my client been here?" she asked the cop.

"A few hours I guess, why?"

"Because I'll assume he needs a bathroom break."

He hesitated and seemed like he was about to object until Jennine repeated the statement. "I said my client needs a bathroom break." Her voice remained calm but the sergeant studied the threat that came from her eyes. "Tell me, sergeant, if you had been sitting in a bar drinking for a few hours and then thrown into a squad car and then thrown into an interrogation room, do you think you might need a bathroom break . . . or should I just mention to the judge that you denied him that privilege?"

The sergeant turned his gaze to the uniformed cop who was waiting to escort her to Room B and gave him a nod. "Go ahead Eddie, give the guy a trip to the little boys' room. We certainly wouldn't want him to pee his pants."

During the walk down the corridor there was no conversation between Jennine and her escort. The suit she wore was a crisp gray silk fabric and made quiet swishes as she moved. The only other sound was the sharp click of her heels on the linoleum.

Inside Room B, the officer uncuffed Mario and led him out. When they returned he was again cuffed to the table and Jennine sat across from him. During his absence, she had placed a legal pad on the table, along with an eyeglass case and an expensive pen. Mario studied her. He hadn't heard the demand regarding the bathroom break but wondered if it had been her doing. As the cop made his exit she spoke with the same sharp tone she used with the desk sergeant. "If I find out that someone accidently forgets to turn that off while I'm in here," she said, pointing to the ceiling camera, "I'll be dragging *your* ass into a courtroom." The officer paused as if to say something but then turned and left.

Mario took note of Jennine's age and delicate frame, but after hearing her address the cop any doubts he had regarding her ability to represent him dissipated. Her hardness was far removed from the grandmother-like woman she reminded him of—the grandmother he remembered as a kid, who returned from the hairdresser, meticulous in her appearance. Jennine removed her glasses from their case and somehow managed to put them on without disturbing one hair on her head.

"How'd you know I needed the bathroom?" Mario asked her.

"Clients usually do by the time their attorney arrives. You feel better now? Some cops'll let you sit here all day waiting for you to wet your pants. I've been in stations where the squad room has a pool for guys like you. They take bets on what time your kidney's going to burst."

With her elbows on the table, she put her hands to her chin in an inverted V and rested her head between them. "Small talks over," she said. "Cohen wants his stones."

"What stones?"

"Listen," she started again. "I don't look a day over sixty right now. Do you know why I don't look a day over sixty?" Her tone was flavored with just a hint of the south. Enough to let Mario know her abbreviated drawl was something she'd acquired over time, but not quite southern enough for him to believe she was a native.

"No. I can't say . . . why?" Mario told her.

"Because when I got the call from Cohen to come down here to get your ass out of a jam, I was in Savannah in the middle of my sixtieth birthday party. There I was, having a grand time with some of my oldest, dearest—and most influential I might add—friends. So now that I'm here, . . . do not jerk me around."

"What did Carmine tell you?"

"Carmine didn't tell me anything. He isn't even in the picture any more. Once you called him, he called Cohen to relay the information on you screwin' up the deal. Who do you think called me? Carmine doesn't have any connections in this city. At least not the kind you're going to need. So he's out and you're the hot potato everybody's throwing around. That means I'm your only way out of here. I don't know much about you, but I know you couldn't afford my billable hours long enough for me to look at your rap sheet. So I suggest if Mr. Cohen tells you he wants his stones, you play ball like a good team member and give them to him. You obviously didn't have them on you when they picked you up or they'd be with your personal belongings at the desk. So . . . are they still on that boat of yours, and if so, where's it parked?"

"They're not on the boat," Mario lied. "And as far as any teamwork goes, you can tell coach Cohen that they're safe. When I walk outta here, he gets his stones. Simple as that."

"Okay, then I'll give you the good news first. The shack you burned down last night and the damage you did with whatever poor judgment you used at the boatyard aren't things the cops really care about. If the DA wants to make an issue of what seems to be some kind of a war between you and this Hanson guy, he can have you put away for a year or two. The bottom line is, all that is small potatoes to these guys."

"Then why am I here? What's going on?"

"The stuff I just mentioned is what *was* going on. They were hot to get you off the streets after Hanson filled them in on your little stunt at the boatyard. After they picked you up, however, all that stuff became old news."

"Whaddaya mean, old news?"

"Seems the gun they took from you during your arrest is believed to be the one used three months ago in a convenience store robbery. But it wasn't just a robbery. An off-duty cop happened to walk into the store to buy a paper or something and when the guy saw the uniform he panicked and shot him. Since then, these guys have been looking for their friendly neighborhood cop killer. That gun you're carrying around makes you the lucky winner."

"That's bullshit. I didn't even own that gun three months ago."

"Whether you did or didn't is none of my business. My business is to prove you didn't, and if we can't prove it outright, I need to establish a reasonable doubt. If I can't do that, you can kiss life as you know it good-bye."

"How do they know so soon that it's even the same gun?"

"They don't yet. The ballistic check they ran earlier was inconclusive. They expect to have official confirmation one way or another in an hour or so and if it does check out, you'll be lucky to get out of here alive today. Which is why I want you to take your shirt off while I'm here. I want to get a few snapshots."

Jennine removed a small camera from her briefcase and walked around the table. She pulled Mario's T-shirt up until it encircled his neck and then snapped several photos of his back, and his chest, along with several face shots. "I want you alive for your arraignment," she told him as she pulled the shirt down.

"I didn't have anything to do with killing a cop!"

"Fact is, nobody cares. One of their own was killed and they want the shooter. If you didn't own the gun three months ago and you want to help yourself, tell them who did." Mario stared at the cuffs and said nothing. "Listen," she continued. "This honor among thieves crap isn't going to help get you out of the death penalty. If you know anything about this gun, we can most likely cut a deal."

"Or I can take my chances with ballistics."

"I wouldn't recommend putting your eggs in that basket. However, all that aside, I still need you to tell me where the stones are."

"You mean *Cohen* needs me to tell you where the stones are."

"Anything you tell me falls under attorney/client privilege."

Mario gave a short laugh. "I guess that's a privilege you don't actually need is it? And who is your client, me or Cohen?"

Before Jennine could answer, Benner returned and slapped a report on the table. "Hot off the press," he said to Jennine. "Ballistics confirmed the gun taken from Mr. Costello here is the same weapon that killed our boy." He turned his gaze to Mario. "You should've had that conversation I wanted to have earlier. It's nice your lawyer is here though. She can witness me reading you your rights. We're booking you for murder. You're about to find out that gunning down a cop is going to add up to a bit more than your aggravated assault charges. And isn't it lucky for us that Florida's got the death penalty?"

"C'mon, you read my sheet. You know as well as I do that robbing grocery stores and shooting cops isn't my style. I had nothing to do with that bullshit."

"That's it," Jennine interrupted. "He's got nothing more to say. I want to meet with the DA before we go any further."

"Yeah, well that's not going to happen on New Year's Eve. He's not to be found right now. You were lucky to get him on the phone earlier. So, unless you're flyin' back to Savannah tonight, you can tell your pilot he can shut down the jets 'cause this guy's not goin' anywhere for a while."

There was a long pause before Jennine spoke. "I need a few more minutes with my client."

"You've got five minutes and then we're processing him."

Jennine, still sitting across from Mario, waited for Benner to close the door before speaking. "I know this is a hell of a place to spend New Year's Eve," Jennine said. "But I'm afraid you're stuck with it. There's not a judge in the world that's going to be reachable tonight and these guys don't have any motivation or sympathy for your situation. You're here for whatever New Year's Eve party they've got planned. The best thing I can do for you right now is let you use my phone while you've got some privacy." Her tone then changed to one of disgust, more for the stupidity of Benner than Mario. She slid her phone across the table. "If you need to cancel a hot date for tonight, now's your chance."

"Don't need it," he said, sliding it back. "But what about your influence?" Mario asked the question as if hoping to hear that she had some other bit of strategy to get him out—at least temporarily.

"Me? I've got a jet parked at the Melbourne Airport. I'm flying back to Georgia to blow out my birthday candles before they burn the house down. After some cake and ice cream I'm going to ring in the New Year. I can't pull any strings for you tonight . . . tomorrow either, for that matter. They've not only got you for shooting a cop, but you're sittin' in football country. All your friendly judges will be parked in front of their TVs tomorrow watching a bowl game. The SEC waits for no man. I'll see you again in two days at your arraignment." She leaned forward and put her hand on Mario's forearm. Her voice lowered. "Even when I get you into the courtroom, you're pretty well screwed. Your prior record is enough to keep you in here until trial. There's not a judge in the state who's going to set bail if a cop's death is involved . . . and the shooter has a sailboat on the open sea." She removed her hand from his arm and leaned back in the chair. "So unless I can cut some sort of a deal, you may as well get comfortable in your new home."

"What kind of a deal? You don't expect me to admit to shooting a cop."

"They're going after you because they've got the gun. The DA needs a shooter. I don't think he believes it was you. The guy's a bit of a sleazebag and there's no love between him and me but he's not going to send you up for this if I can prove you didn't do it. Information on the gun is the only card you've got left to play. You telling him where you got it might be your only ticket out of here."

"Might be?"

"They've got several charges right now for your nonsense in the boatyard. If we can get the shooting cleared up, a reasonable judge might rule in your favor, although you should expect to get some time. You did burn a guy's house down, and there was some other business about you sinking a few boats. What the hell were you thinking anyway?"

Mario didn't answer. Jennine continued. "I'll dig a little deeper before your arraignment and see what I can find out. Meanwhile, your memory should show some improvement regarding the whereabouts of Cohen's merchandise." She packed her briefcase as she talked. "I could disappear from this case as quickly as I walked in here." With that, she patted Mario's hand and rose to leave. "Keep your chin up," she told him when she reached the door. "It's never over 'til it's over and the law behind closed doors can be tricky to figure out."

The door opened and Benner entered. "It's gonna be a busy night for us so he's going to booking. If you want to continue your conversation you'll have to wait 'til we're through with him."

"We're all done here," she said. "Oh, and detective," she added, waving her camera. "Other than that scrape on his forehead, my client looks fine right now. So if there's so much as a Band-Aid needed for Mr. Costello because he happens to fall down a set of stairs . . . or if he suddenly gets a nose bleed during the night . . . or falls off his bicycle and skins a knee . . . I'll hold *you* personally responsible."

The detective's expression indicated her threat wasn't taken lightly. He disliked all lawyers but Jennine had gotten under his skin. "Don't know where you parked your car," he hollered after her, "but it's starting to rain and it's coming down pretty hard out there." His comment was an attempt to get in a last word of retaliation and he appeared to relish the thought of her getting caught in a downpour.

Jennine turned and gave him a cold stare and her southern accent suddenly became much thicker. "I don't park my car," she replied. "My *driver* parks my car." She turned and her heels clicked once again on the cold floor. The sound echoed off the walls and Benner stared at her back as she made her exit.

Following her departure Mario was escorted out of Room B and delivered to a uniformed officer with instructions to book him. As he was led away Benner yelled across the squad room. His voice was intentionally loud to catch the attention of everyone in the area. "Hey Costello," he shouted, "Happy fuckin' New Year!"

13

December 31, 2011

5:00 p.m.

Cohen paced the floor of his condo. He became irate when Carmine failed to show with the diamonds. He had explicitly told him that any exchange for the stones was to be no later than four o'clock. After waiting until well past the hour, he made several unsuccessful attempts to reach him by phone. The time frame for the scheduled exchange left little room for error. He had planned his trip from New York to Florida to coincide with the ringing in of the New Year with his daughter and granddaughters in Vero Beach. It was the perfect cover to fly in, get the diamonds, and get back to New York. His daughter had made reservations for a six o'clock dinner at Maison Martinique, a plush restaurant on Ocean Boulevard. Carmine being a no-show, combined with the thirty to forty minute drive for an evening with the family, ruled out any possible exchange that night. He now faced the irritation and red tape of rescheduling his morning flight, and that was with the optimism that he could locate Carmine to get the stones.

Carmine called Cohen a little past five. The message regarding Mario's arrest was slurred into the phone. Discovering the courier was in police custody only served to intensify Cohen's rage.

"What the hell are you blubbering about?" Cohen shouted, trying to decipher the garble. "Are you drunk?"

"Don't worry," Carmine said. "Iss got nothin' to do with the diamonds. He needs a good lawyer though and I don't have any concessions for legal people. You should probably do something because I think he's the only one who knows where the diamonds are."

"You sound like you've been drinking. Where the hell are you?"

"I'm over here at Skid Lips," Carmine slurred again. "I was suppos to meet him here at three-thirty and then drive to your place."

"What do you mean he's been arrested? Where are they holding him?"

"He said he wassat the peece station." Carmine's answer was followed by a drunken burp.

"You know what Carmine? First I was pissed because you were late. Then you didn't even make an appearance. Following that, you didn't call me and you didn't answer your phone when I tried to reach you. Now, you call me—shitfaced I might add—to tell me this guy you hired . . . who you said was quite reliable . . . was arrested and is sitting in the police station. I've got too much money tied up in this deal to put up with this crap."

Carmine's glazed eyes tried to focus on the barmaid while Cohen continued. "Now you're telling me he's the only one who knows where the stones are and you want me to get him a lawyer to get his ass out of jail. What was he arrested for anyway?"

"I think he burned down a guy's house or sompin' like that. Iss his landlord or sompin. . . juss a misunderstanding."

"What the hell are you talking about? I mean, who is this guy?" Carmine was again silent as he searched for an answer. Cohen continued. "Well, understand this. You and I are done. If I have to get this asshole out of jail, I'll deal with *him* from here on out. Any money I spend in the process will come out of your share. In my world of finance, that means your share minus my aggravation leaves you with nothing!" Cohen punctuated his sentence with the slamming of the phone. Before leaving for his daughter's he called Jennine Barbosa.

Jennine was a long-time associate of Cohen and a woman he counted on when legal advice was needed. She was in the midst of her own birthday party which was to continue into a New Year's Eve celebration. Cohen emphasized the immediacy of the situation and her jet touched down in Melbourne a little past seven-thirty.

It was during her return flight to Savannah that she called him with her initial report.

"He's not about to say where he's got the diamonds," she told him.

"Did you remind him anything he said was confidential?"

"Yes, but he's not buying that line either. Figures he's got you in a corner and wants to play *Let's make a deal*. He knows the diamonds are his get-out-of-jail-free card." She filled Cohen in on the gun, stating she could probably get Mario to give the cops the information they wanted. "I don't really believe this guy shot the cop and if Jefferds wants to go anywhere politically, he can't afford to leave any doubt that he put away the real shooter—the press will be all over this. I know he'll cut a deal to find out where your boy got the gun."

Cohen was in agreement. He needed Jennine to get Mario out or cut the best deal she could get. In addition to the money he'd already laid out, the possibility that his involvement with the diamonds might connect him to Mario and sharing a jail cell with the guy was not out of the question.

"Do whatever you have to," Cohen instructed. "And I'm putting the emphasis on *whatever you have to*."

10:00 p.m.

Cohen sat in the living room of his daughter's house. His fury regarding the earlier faux pas with Carmine had been softened by the innocence of his three granddaughters. After returning from the restaurant, the family dipped cherries, miniature marshmallows, and orange slices into the chocolate fondue his daughter had prepared.

While waiting for the ball in Times Square to welcome in the New Year, the girls were cuddled together on the couch. Two listened as Cohen read *The Princess and the Pea* while the youngest slept in his oversized lap.

Carmine, still at Squid Lips, remained on his bar stool. Having failed to get anything to eat, the martinis were a catalyst for his pills and began dictating his every action. He discovered his tongue wasn't working correctly and stopped trying to talk to people. Fortunately, he had no need for communication with the woman serving him drinks who, since his arrival, had evolved into a dark fuzzy creature with a very large mouth full of extremely oversized white teeth. After all, it was New Year's Eve, and not being aware of his pill popping, the waitress continued to replace his empty martini glass as he signaled for refills. Since his arrival, the once audible conversations of nearby patrons had become a myriad of indescribable utterances mingled with boisterous laughter. Periodically, the room spun in one direction and then reversed itself. Carmine held on to his stool during those spinnings and noticed the faces of people sitting near him looked like an arrangement of floating Picassos.

Jennine stood among friends in the living room of her home in Savannah. Some had lingered from her birthday celebration which had continued uninterrupted while she flew to Melbourne and back. Many at the party hadn't noticed her absence. It was a lavish estate, consuming many acres, and people congregated around the pool or walked through the gardens and numerous paths that wound through the grounds. New arrivals, not as familiar to Jennine as the birthday crowd, arrived to help ring in the New Year. Servers employed by the catering service scurried to and fro with trays of hors d'oeuvres and fresh drinks for those who didn't care to walk the few feet to the bar. In the great room, a pianist played a mix of soft jazz and old favorites. Her guests sipped cocktails and prepared to ring in 2012. Unlike Cohen, the last thing on her mind was Mario Costello. She had little interest in a crazed sailor who apparently doubled as an arsonist. Cohen, on the other hand, wanted his diamonds.

Her call before she landed seemed to satisfy him for the moment, but there was no question as to her loyalty. Cohen held the purse strings, and once the stones were secured Mario's chance of a viable defense lessened. With midnight only two hours away, Jennine slipped into her study and pulled the heavy double doors together. She set her drink on the desk and picked up the phone to make her annual call to her son in Boston.

Mario was now quite sober. He had been booked and put into one of five cells. It was much smaller than the two across from him . . . one of which was presumably the drunk tank. Every precinct had one—the area where harmless idiots sat in waiting while they sobered up. The cell on his left was empty and the cell to his right held a snoring inmate he had yet to meet. Despite the attorney's attempt to intimidate Benner regarding any rough treatment, his handling had been anything but gentle and he massaged the soreness on various parts of his body.

The neighboring inmate turned out to be his only company until the first two inebriants for the tank were brought in . . . one singing, the other holding on to the cop for support while he continued to question why he was there. The clamoring woke the occupant to Mario's right. He was a young kid who wasted no time in proudly confessing to Mario that he'd been arrested for breaking and entering. "I woulda got away with it too," he told him. "But my driver saw a cop car and went chicken-shit. He burned rubber and left me in the house. When the cops caught him he spilled everything, he even gave 'em directions to where I was . . . and then he gets to go home 'cause he's a minor and I'm stuck here all night."

"Impressive," Mario told him and then moved to the other side of the cell.

The first two drunks for the tank proved to be the beginning of a long parade. Others were escorted in and the cage began to fill. By eleven-thirty there wasn't much room left. Most were early rowdies arrested at house parties that had gotten out of hand. The overflow, which included a trio of transvestites, was put into the cell adjacent to the tank. When the costumed ladies arrived, cat calls and whistles bellowed from the occupants of the tank and the trannies responded by assuming womanly postures and teasingly sashaying past the drunks.

As Mario watched, he realized if he wasn't in such a predicament it would've been great entertainment for the evening. The once solemn area was close to reaching a feverish peak. Laughter and shouting filled the corridor and several renditions of Auld Lang Syne were sung in a variety of keys. One or two of the drunks managed to get their noisemakers past their body search and were blowing paper horns that unraveled as they honked and splayed out like paper swords. The noisemakers targeted the cheeks and noses of fellow drunks who made unsuccessful attempts at grabbing them away.

Mario recalled Benner saying it was going to be a busy night. It now seemed an understatement with the non-stop parade of drunk and disorderlies. As midnight drew closer, Mario thought of Rosita and how nice it would be to be with her. Maybe if things had gone differently . . . .

Was she really going to stay in and read, he wondered? Oddly enough, the thought of her possibly being out with someone at a party initiated a pang of jealousy. He promised himself he would see her again.

11:30 p.m.

Cohen's attempt to convince his granddaughters that the Princess could actually feel the pea under a pile of mattresses was a losing debate. The girls had the same doubt anytime the story was read. The discussion was tabled when a fresh batch of cherries and orange slices arrived from the kitchen and the chocolate fondue was reactivated.

Carmine was reluctant to leave his barstool to make another journey to the men's room. The combination of booze and pills had put him over the edge. During an earlier trip, he tried to save steps by cutting across the dance floor. After being bumped around in a pinball fashion by the couples who actually belonged there, he teetered and fell to one knee. In the process, he grabbed for the stabilizing force of a woman's shoulder and tore the sleeve of her dress. He then stood and tried to smooth it back in place, apologizing over and over for his clumsiness.

After returning from the men's room, he focused on his barstool which he found quite difficult to mount.

Jennine mingled with her guests. One of the servers was responsible to cue the pianist at the stroke of midnight. A five-minute warning was given for those in the pool area to allow them time to congregate with those in the house.

Mario sat and observed the drunks. He was somewhat amused when a cop entered and bellowed to everyone that they should shut the hell up if they wanted to get through the night in one piece. In the few seconds of quiet that followed, Mario heard one of the drunks whispering. It sounded like a phone conversation—perhaps with a wife or girlfriend. The drunk was explaining that he had car trouble and may not be able to get home. Fellow inmates snickered in the background as they eavesdropped and enjoyed their comrade's predicament.

It wasn't the conversation Mario was interested in as much as wondering how a prisoner got through the squad room and into a jail cell with a phone. Obviously, in the confusion of the night, the steady parade of characters had opened the door for a lapse in security.

Mario recalled his attorney's earlier use of her phone, saying, "If you have to call and cancel a hot date . . . ." Although he had no use for a phone when she made the offer, he now felt a compulsion to make a call . . . a call to Rosita.

"Who you talkin' to?" Mario whispered across the narrow space separating the cells. His question was waved off by the drunk in his attempt to continue his deception.

"I need to use your phone. I have to make a call too," Mario continued.

The drunk then covered the phone and addressed Mario directly. "If you shut up, I'll let you use it when I get off. You think what I'm doin' here is easy? My fiancée's bullshit!" He continued his explanation to his future wife who was obviously unconvinced regarding the sincerity of his tale. After hanging up, Mario pushed him again for the phone. "Just one quick call," he told him and held his arm out through the bars.

"One call," the drunk responded, "and then I want it back."

"Whaddaya gonna do if he keeps it," a member of the cage asked. "Ya gonna call a cop? You ain't even supposed to have a phone in here." A chorus of slurred statements and laughs followed.

"I'll give it back," Mario assured him. "I just need to make one call."

"Yeah, he's gotta call his stock broker," a voice yelled from the darkness. That comment was followed by a comment from one of the transvestites. "I'll give you my number, honey. You can call me anytime." The tranny's offer was followed by more hooting and hollering as, by now, they had become an accepted part of the jailhouse entourage.

Reluctantly, the drunk slid the phone across the floor. Mario stretched to reach it and pulled it into his cell. With his lack of technical knowhow, it took several minutes for an explanation on how to get the number of Dunkin' Donuts from a woman named Siri. When he called, a clerk answered. He sounded young, perhaps a teenager conned into working on New Year's Eve.

"I was calling to see if Rosie's working tonight," Mario lied. "Actually, I was hoping she wasn't as I think she deserves New Year's Eve off."

"Who is this?"

"Oh, I'm sorry," Mario continued. "This is her uncle. I'm calling from Miami . . . just wanted to wish her a Happy New Year." A strange quiet fell over the jail cells as the inmates seemed to lavish in the deception that was taking place. It was as if they were Mario's silent cheerleaders.

The clerk at Dunkin' Donuts hesitated. Mario recalled the psych program Rosita had mentioned at the bar. "Thought I'd see how school was going, and you know, see if she needed any money for books or anything. I don't have her home number. Maybe you could help me out. If not, I guess I'll have to wait until I get up to Melbourne in a couple of months."

"We're not really supposed to give out that information ya know?"

"Yeah, sure, I understand. Listen, I'll just wait until I see her. It's just that it's been sort of a tradition that I call her on

New Year's Eve." Another few seconds of silence followed Mario's comment.

"Hold on a second," the clerk told him. "I'll see if I can find her work card."

ROSIE ANSWERED THE PHONE with a sleepy hello. As predicted earlier in the day, she had curled up with a book for a New Year's Eve read. Somewhere in chapter three, she dozed off and the pages telling of Atticus Finch fell to the floor. Mario's call woke her to the vision of the muted television. A celebrity was interviewing people while others in the background milled around Times Square. They appeared drunk and were most likely hooting and hollering so she left the TV muted.

"I called to wish you a Happy New Year," Mario whispered into the phone.

"Who is this?" She was still not awake and tried to put a face to the voice.

"I kind of need a favor."

"Who *is* this?" she asked again.

"It's Mario. You know, the guy who owes you twenty bucks."

"Jeezus, what are you doing calling me . . . and how did you get this number?"

"I guess I should've told you I work for the CIA," Mario laughed, not wanting to reveal his source.

Rosita continued to stare at the muted crowd on the television. The camera switched to a close up of the ball reminding her why the TV was on at all. "Let me guess. You want to meet me at midnight so I can buy you a New Year's Eve dinner." Her voice seemed to be tempered somewhat from her initial reaction.

"Hey, I already apologized for the wallet thing, didn't I? Although that's not a bad idea," he responded.

"Well, I hope you're not calling for bail money. Are you still in jail?"

The question caught Mario by surprise. "Oh, so you know."

"Of course I know. I was outside the Sand Flea when they took you away. What'd you do anyway?"

"Just a minor mix-up, but yeah, unfortunately, I'm still in jail. A real Happy New Year if you know what I mean. Listen, I'm not sure what the weekend holds for me and I was wondering if you might do me a favor."

"I thought I already did you a favor."

"Yeah, I know and I appreciate that . . . but I really need some help with something and I don't actually know anyone around here." There was a momentary silence before Rosita spoke. "You don't know me either," she told him.

"I know enough."

Another pause followed. "It's illegal isn't it—what you want me to do I mean."

"No, trust me. I wouldn't put anything like that on you. I just need you to check on my boat for me." This time a long silence followed and Mario began to feel hopeful. "Listen, I wasn't kidding when I told you I left my wallet on board. Do me this favor and you can even get the money I owe you. I'm not sure exactly how much is in it, but there's at least five hundred." Mario knew there was at least that much remaining from the money he'd extracted from Carmine before leaving for Andros.

"And that's all I have to do. Just check on the boat?"

"Yeah, and keep an eye on it for me . . . just for a couple of days—'til I get out of here. You know, just check it from shore once a day . . . make sure no one's messing with it. It's not far from Dunkin' Donuts."

"Where exactly is it?"

Mario was about to say Douglas Park when he realized he had far too large an audience. He moved to the farthest corner of his cell and cupped his hand over the phone. "You know where Douglas Park is?" When Rosita paused, he continued. "That little park right off Riverside and Main Street."

"The one at the end of the causeway?"

"Yeah. You can actually see the boat from the park."

"And you want me to just go over there and make sure it's all right?"

"Well, I'd need you to make one trip to the boat first. I left it unlocked. I need you to go to a hardware store and get a padlock and then row out to the boat and lock the hatch for me. I just want to make sure it's secure."

"How am I supposed to get out there?"

"My dinghy's tied up in the bushes at the end of the causeway. *Little Miss* is written on the stern plate. It's probably the only dinghy there. Just row out and lock her up and while you're out there, you can get your twenty bucks out of my wallet. When you get back to shore, just leave the dinghy in the same spot."

"And that's it?"

"That's it. Or if you wouldn't mind, just go to the park occasionally and make sure she's still there."

"How long are you in for?"

"I'm not sure. Tomorrow's Sunday and I can't get an arraignment on Monday 'cause of the holiday."

"I'll consider it," she told him.

"I need you to do more than consider it. This is important to me. The boat's all I've got." Rosita said nothing. "Listen, there's at least five hundred dollars in my wallet. If you do this, you can have it all."

"And there's nothing illegal about it?" she confirmed.

"No, nothing."

"If I get in any trouble doing this, I'm not keeping quiet about anything. I don't know what you've gotten yourself into, but I'm not going to be sitting next to you in your cell."

"Okay . . . thanks . . . listen, I gotta go. You have a Happy New Year."

"Yeah, you too . . . at least mine will start off better than the one you're having."

If he didn't know better, Mario thought he detected a slight bit of sympathy in her response.

"If you do me this favor, it'll be a good start."

"Good night," she said, and the tone of her voice convinced him *Miss Demeanor* would be secured.

11:59 p.m.

Cohen sat in his shirt that was now covered in chocolate as a reminder of his granddaughters' tutoring in the art of fondue dipping. They counted down the final ten seconds of 2011 together. As they counted, his thoughts rewound the day's events—the mix-ups, and the conversation with Jennine. He felt confident she would cover all the bases which, in essence, meant she would cover his ass.

Jennine and her guests toasted in the New Year as they touched Waterford glasses together that were filled with expensive champagne. The pianist played Auld Lang Syne on cue and as guests rang in the New Year, they showed their mutual affection for one another by demonstrative air kisses on each other's cheeks.

Rosita thought about Mario and wondered whether she should get more involved with her dark stranger. Just before the countdown on her TV reached zero, she turned it off and went to bed.

Mario continued to watch the drunks in the cage as they played dress-up. By midnight, the occupants of the tank had convinced the transvestites to give up their brassieres, wigs, high heels, and anything else that would assist in a comedy routine. The trannies, happy to be accepted into the brotherhood of drunks—which seemed to have an unspoken allegiance—reached into the adjacent cell and fastened the bras over the shirts of their new neighbors. The third bra was twirled around lariat style by a guy trying to walk the length of the cell in high heels. The impromptu antics and fashion show that followed took the hooting and hollering to a new level of intensity.

The officer who had bellowed earlier about the noise entered the cell area again, took one look at the chaos, gave a wave of defeat, and left without a word. The prisoner's rendition of Auld Lang Syne was in mixed voice and Mario believed they were probably having as much fun there as they would've had at any party.

Carmine was politely asked to ring in the New Year at a different location and found himself staggering down the block in search of a new habitat. Within minutes, he found himself in his second bar of the evening. His immediate need upon entering was to make another trip to the men's room. Being it was almost twelve o'clock, he made several unsuccessful attempts at distributing kisses to women along the way. At the stroke of midnight the singing of Auld Lang Syne filtered in through the bathroom door. He made a desperate attempt to locate the row of urinals before realizing he was in the ladies' room.

14

The jailhouse party continued into the early hours of Sunday morning. Fatigue and the earlier infusion of alcohol caused the drunks to drift off amidst a chorus of snores and farts. The stench was worsened as they exhaled stale beer and a variety of liquors. Added to this was the smell of vomit that had missed the toilet, not for lack of aim, but because one of the inmates had passed out while sitting on it.

It wasn't until the shift change at seven the next morning that anyone was released. Loved ones arrived to claim the bodies. Those who had reported their friends or spouses missing had been contacted by the clerk who was glad to do the paperwork and send them on their way. Unlike the usual protocol, the New Year's Eve drunks were released on one hundred dollars bail until their court appearance the following week.

Shouts came from the outer office as wives argued about the fine or for having to wait for someone else to bring the money from home. One by one, the arrestees were released. Mario sat in his orange jumpsuit and watched the exodus. Some were awake; others had to be rousted and woke wondering why they were wearing a brassiere over their shirt. Those few were embarrassed, not only by their appearance, but what they may have said or done during their on-stage performances the night before. By eight o'clock the tank was emptied except for the three transvestites still waiting to be rescued. A friend of one of them arrived and was persuaded to post bail for the other two. They paraded past Mario in their mini-skirts, smoothing out any wrinkles.

The tallest was still irritated by their treatment, incensed that her mother's necklace had been confiscated. None were allowed to rescue their wigs that were scattered about the drunk tank, but the cop retrieved their high heels, presumably to eliminate a law suit for making them go barefoot. They paraded out, struggling to make themselves presentable. The bitching continued regarding the appearance of one another's makeup and the wretched condition they were forced to suffer during their overnight stay.

Shortly after their exit, a custodian entered. The name "Barry" was embroidered over his shirt pocket. He used the handle of the mop that was stuck in his bucket as a steering lever and maneuvered the pail into the drunk tank. He studied the mess but showed little surprise at the task before him. He turned around to look at Mario. "You must be the cop killer," he said. His voice was calm and his matter-of-fact tone made it a statement rather than a question.

"So they tell me."

The brief exchange brought new life to the kid in the next cell who was the only remaining occupant. The discovery that Mario was a cop killer seemed to inject a heightened admiration for his neighbor in orange. As much as he wanted more details, he was reluctant to engage in conversation with a killer and moved himself out of Mario's reach.

The custodian went right to work. There were no beds in the tank and his nonchalance of wiping down the benches, cleaning the toilet, and mopping the floor seemed routine. During the cleanup, the cop who had made the earlier trips to get men being released entered carrying Styrofoam containers and a bottle of spring water. He gave one container to the kid, along with the water, and then passed the second breakfast through to Mario with no inclusion of anything to drink. The cop crinkled his nose and gave a couple of exaggerated sniffs at the odor—a blend of the disinfectant the custodian was using and the variety of aromas from the night before. "Bon appetite," he said.

"How about a cup of coffee to go with this?" the kid asked.

"Yeah, I'll get you a winning lottery ticket too."

Mario knew not to ask. Not to ask for coffee . . . or water. He knew to not ask for anything and to eat what they gave him and keep his mouth shut. The kid opened the lid. It contained a breakfast burrito along with a few potato puffs. "How about some ketchup for these potato things in here?" he yelled after the cop.

"This ain't the Holiday Inn. You can eat 'em the way they are or don't eat 'em at all. Your choice."

Mario tossed his container on the bed and the kid asked if he could have it. Mario slipped it through the bars. "Did you really do what he said earlier? Did you kill a cop?"

"So they tell me, but don't believe everything you hear."

"How'd you do it, man? You gutted him, right? Yeah, I'll bet you gutted him."

"I'll tell you what. If I have time to make myself a shiv while I'm in here, I'll show you."

The kid moved to the opposite side of the cell for the second time and remained there until his release just before noon. Mario was left as the lone remaining prisoner and didn't see the kid again until his arraignment.

THE NEXT MORNING, MARIO was taken from the cell and returned to Room B.

"If you're going to question me again, I want my lawyer."

"Your lawyer is why you're here," the cop told him, and after cuffing him to the table, he left the room.

The kid who entered next looked to be fourteen or fifteen, sixteen at best Mario thought. He extended his hand and then noticed Mario was cuffed to the table and withdrew it. "Shane Morrow," he said. "I work with Jennine."

Mario said nothing.

"She sent me down here to get some information about the case."

"What kind of information? And where the hell is she?"

"She's home but she'll be here on Tuesday to handle your arraignment. She's just a bit busy today."

"Busy? I'm her client. How busy can she be?"

"Look, I just do what she tells me okay? She needs some information and she's not going to fly down here on New Year's Day to check on a few facts."

"How many cop killers have *you* defended?"

Morrow was taken back, as if the fact that Mario was charged for the murder of a cop was information that had been left out of his briefing.

"Actually, I'm in mergers and acquisitions."

This news was disheartening to Mario and he shifted uneasily in his chair. "So you're tellin' me that Jennine, who works for this hotshot guy named Cohen, sent a green lawyer who knows nothing about criminal law down here to see me?"

"Cohen's dead," he said.

"Whaddaya mean, Cohen's dead?"

"I think the term *dead* is self-explanatory." Morrow's tone then became irritatingly defensive. "And for me being green . . . taking a deposition and getting some needed information to keep your ass out of prison is so trivial, Harvard doesn't even bother to cover it." His annoyance was reason enough to mention Harvard. "And I've been given enough information from Jennine to keep things afloat for now."

"What happened to Cohen?"

"Let's just say the procurement of the stones you have didn't sit quite right with other associates that normally make those acquisitions. Cohen was involved in a terrible accident."

"Then why is he still covering my ass?"

"He's not. It's just . . . well, let's say some of his silent partners still maintain an interest in the merchandise you hold."

"Sounds like Cohen had too many associates and silent partners to think he could remain healthy in all this."

"Which brings me to my most important question . . . where's the boat?"

"If that's what you flew down here for you wasted a lot of fuel. The boat is safe, the diamonds are on the boat, and when I get out of here, your new associates can give me my cut in exchange for the merchandise."

The banter continued for several more minutes until Morrow realized there was no deal to be made. He had used Jennine's jet to fly down from Savannah. He called her on the return flight to fill her in on the lack of progress. She in turn called Cohen.

"Did Morrow tell Costello I was dead?"

"Yes. He told me he didn't flinch when he mentioned it . . . so much for putting a scare into him. He's not giving up the diamonds until he's out and walking around. How do you want me to proceed?"

"Can you get him off?"

"Like I said, he has to give up the gun. It's the only leverage I've got and he's keeping his mouth shut."

"Put some pressure on. Remind him how uncomfortable prison can be when people on the outside who don't want him in there can pay people on the inside to make his life a living hell."

◆ trial and errors

Horace Fairchild, a judge in his mid-sixties, stood in a pair of plaid Bermuda shorts and supported himself with his putter. His wide girth exaggerated the plaid but they were his lucky shorts and being overweight was a condition that never prevented him from wearing them. He eyed the golf ball at his feet and studied the distance to the cup and calculated how it would be affected by the nape of the office carpet.

He took his weight off the putter and placed it behind the ball as he prepared for a light tap. The pistol holstered on his hip rubbed against his forearm and he slid it back an inch or two on his belt. The gun was a working piece of memorabilia from the war and he was fond of dismantling it once a week for cleaning and then reassembling it. He wore it under his judge's robe—a habit he adopted decades earlier—after being nearly shot by a lunatic who charged through the metal detector and got off a couple of rounds aimed at the female defendant before the security guards corralled him. It turned out the woman was the man's wife who was charged with prostitution. The husband wanted her to know he wasn't too pleased about it. As the guards escorted the man out in cuffs, Fairchild yelled to the officers to "make sure he got no conjugal visits" to which those in the gallery who caught the irony got a good chuckle.

Fairchild continued to eye the putt. Marcus Callahan, a lifelong friend, sat in a soft leather chair and watched the procedure. "Just hit the damn thing," he said. "You're not going to make the shot anyway."

"And you pay the green fees today if I do?"

"Absolutely." Callahan said. He tossed down the last swallow of scotch from the glass he was holding.

"Just think," Fairchild said, "when I retire next month, I can take you for green fees every day. Loser does pay, right?" Callahan set down his glass and responded with a grunt.

Horace then studied the ball with a renewed purpose. The stroke that followed was smooth and steady and the ball travelled across the rug and made the familiar sound he heard so often as it entered the artificial cup. He was pleased with himself, more for making the shot than winning the bet, although taking his old friend for a few dollars made him smile. He and Marcus had a ten o'clock tee time and planned to get in a round of eighteen before the afternoon heat.

Having won the bet, he set his putter aside and donned his judge's robe. "This shouldn't take long," he told Callahan. "Two arraignments. One of them is that guy they grabbed for shooting the cop a coupla weeks back." He then tapped his gun. "See . . . you should get yourself one of these."

"Jeezus, Horace, it was twenty years ago when that guy got a gun into your courtroom."

"Yeah, and if he hadn't been such a lousy shot I may not be standing here today. Look at this cop case . . . the guy's off duty and gets whacked by some asshole." He tapped the gun again. "I'm never in court without it."

"And other times?"

"Hey . . . it'll be in my golf bag, don't you worry."

When he entered the courtroom and walked to his bench, none of the seated participants had any idea his robe was nothing more than a black façade covering a white cotton golf shirt, a loud pair of shorts, and a loaded sidearm. The first issue on the docket was the arraignment of the kid who'd been arrested for breaking and entering. Justice was swift. The New Year provided for a long weekend and the public defender that'd been coerced into duty entered a plea of guilty. Bail was set, the gavel tapped and Judge Fairchild was of a mind that he was halfway to the golf course.

The clerk was about to read the charges against Mario when an interruptive clambering from the rear of the courtroom announced the entrance of Ernie Hanson. His foot was still heavily bandaged and he was making use of a lightweight aluminum cane that struck most of the benches he passed in getting as close to a front row seat as allowable. Connie trailed behind him carrying a folder stuffed with papers which contained the evidence Hanson needed to prosecute his case.

He intended to take Mario for every cent he had in restitution for the total loss of his skiff, damages for the two yachts, and full payment for the shanty which Mario had burned to the ground. Somewhere in Connie's menagerie of folders were numerous photographs of the ashes. He also held Mario responsible for the loss of his little toe and was planning to ask millions for pain and suffering. To Hanson's dismay, when the proceedings got underway, his concerns did not coincide with those of Judge Fairchild. The charges read were limited to the "officer shooting" to which Jennine entered Mario's plea of not guilty—her request for bail was denied—and a date was set for a preliminary hearing. Judge Fairchild glanced at his watch and saw he and Marcus could easily make their ten o'clock tee time. He banged his gavel to end the morning's business and stood to leave.

Hanson panicked. He jumped to his feet, wincing from the weight applied to his four-toed foot. "What about me?" he yelled to the judge.

Fairchild, now standing, returned a surprised look. "What about you?" he questioned. "Who exactly are you?"

"Ernest Hanson, Your Honor." Hanson limped forward a bit as he answered and then leaned on his cane, seemingly for a bit of sympathy. "He wrecked my boats," Hanson said, pointing to Mario. "And then he burned my house down. Who's gonna pay for all that?"

"If that's true Mr. Hanson, I'm sure you'll get your day in court. Unfortunately, this is not the day."

"But I was told this was going to be taken care of today."

Fairchild looked at Jefferds. "Do you know anything about these other charges?"

"Yes, Your Honor. We've did make several attempts to contact Mr. Hanson regarding the additional charges but he's been unreachable. Without being able to contact him, we proceeded with the charge regarding the shooting of the police officer. We actually tried to contact Mr. Hanson again this morning but, as I said, we were unable to reach him.

"Maybe that's because my phone was in my office when he burned it down!" Hanson yelled, pointing to Mario.

Fairchild thought about the first tee and showed signs of impatience. "Where is your attorney, Mr. Hanson?"

"I'm gonna represent myself, Your Honor. I'm not wasting any money on an attorney."

The judge sighed and reseated himself. "Are you certain you want to proceed without an attorney, Mr. Hanson?"

"Yes, Your Honor."

Judge Fairchild then addressed Jefferds. "What's your plan of resolution for Mr. Hanson here?"

"An arson charge has been filed but there seems to be some conflicting testimony regarding damages to several of the boats in the harbor. If Mr. Hanson is in agreement, I was going to suggest we bring in an outside arbitrator to determine a settlement."

Fairchild gave another long sigh before addressing the DA. "With so many things pending here, I suggest you sit down with Ms. Barbosa and get the matter straightened out before you leave today." He then turned to Hanson. "You can rest assured that Mr. Costello will be appropriately punished if found guilty on the charge of arson. If you want to agree to an arbitrator settling the issue of restitution regarding your boats, we may all be able to get on with our lives a bit sooner. And I strongly suggest that you retain an attorney to represent you in the matter."

Hanson started to protest but was stopped by the raised hand of the judge. "I'm now going to tap my gavel one more time and when I do, this court stands adjourned. Anyone still thinking he or she has further business may very well be found in contempt."

It was the formality of the courtroom and the demeanor of Judge Fairchild that brought Mario to his senses. He could see that Hanson was in for a good screwing if he was appearing in court without the foresight of retaining a lawyer. He began to feel like a character in a play. A role he'd played too often. Things that had gone wrong in his life flashed through his mind—the desertion by his father, his expulsion from the high school sailing club, and his dismissal from Annapolis. He envisioned another ill wind filling his sail and decided it was time to take advantage of Jennine's expertise. He recalled her comment during their initial meeting that he had only one card to play. When the bailiff came forward to return him to his cell, he leaned over and grabbed her arm. "I get it," he said. "Tell the DA I'll give up the gun."

♦ **nothing but the truth**

Two days after Mario's arraignment he and Jennine sat in a small room with Jefferds and a younger DA wannabe. As Jennine had told him, the DA wanted to know where the gun came from. Although Jefferds wouldn't admit it, he didn't actually believe Mario was the guy responsible for killing a cop. His history of arrests for being drunk and disorderly were well documented, but robbing grocery stores had never been part of his MO.

"I got the gun from The Trunk." Mario began.

"What trunk?" Jefferds shot back.

"It's not a *what* trunk, it's a *who* trunk. It's the name the guy goes by who sold me the gun. You know, he sells out of the trunk of his car."

"I need his real name," Jefferds said.

"The Trunk's the only name I was given. I'm pretty sure I lost his business card."

Jennine stiffened at Mario's sarcasm and gave him a piercing stare. Jefferds became irritated. "If you think that information is getting you a ticket out of here, think again. Ms. Barbosa here told us you could explain the gun. So unless we can put the weapon in somebody else's possession during the time of the shooting, you can plan on an all expense paid vacation courtesy of the state of Florida. Do you know the real name of this Trunk guy or not?"

Mario exchanged looks with Jennine. "Try Norman."

"Norman? That's the name you're picking?"

"No, that's the name of the bartender at The Bitter End on Fifth Street. He can not only tell you who the guy is, he can set you up for Saturday."

"What's so special about Saturday?"

"The Trunk's kind of a one-night-a-week guy for business. You want a gun, you tell Norman. Then Norman gets a location from The Trunk—usually behind a shopping mall or a supermarket—but always between two and three a.m. You rendezvous with The Trunk, pick out the piece you want, and you both go on your merry way. I'm sure Norman gets a cut."

Jennine then jumped in and told Jefferds to turn off the camera. "If this Trunk guy knows it was Mario that turned him in, he's not going to do my client the favor of getting him off the murder charge. If you plan on grabbing him, you're going to have to do it with a sting operation and keep Mario's identity out of it. You have to set up the bartender."

"We don't have to do squat. As far as I'm concerned, I'm lookin' at the shooter."

"You know as well as I do that I've got enough reasonable doubt here to sway any jury you put in front of me—and if he walks you're not going to look too good standing there holding your ass after the spanking you'll get from the mayor's office."

Jefferds stood to leave. "I'll follow up on this. If any of it pans out, we can talk."

IT WAS THREE MORE days before Mario heard from Jennine. "You're off the hook for the shooting," she told him. The detectives picked up the bartender. Once he was threatened with aiding and abetting in a cop killing, he turned green and told them everything they wanted to know. The Trunk was picked up behind Publix Market on A1A Saturday morning."

"And?"

"And he told them he bought the gun a couple of days after the shooting and sold it to a guy a few days later. They showed him some pictures and he picked you out as the guy he sold it to. There's no way they could continue holding you on the murder charge, although they've certainly got you for possession, in addition to your antics in the boatyard."

"Did they get the shooter?"

"The Trunk gave up the name the next day. He only knew his street name, but made an ID from a mug book—seems he was somewhat of a regular customer. The guy's a two-bit street hustler. Anyway, he'll spend the rest of his days sitting on death row."

"What about The Trunk . . . and Norman?"

"Chances are they'll walk in exchange for their testimony."

"And me?"

"I got Jefferds down to eighteen months," she told Mario.

"What are you saying, eighteen months? So everybody gets a free ride but me? What about a pass for giving up The Trunk? They didn't have squat until I gave them the missing piece of the puzzle."

"Yeah, well, unfortunately you rubbed Jefferds the wrong way. He wanted to send you up for three to five for the possession charge and the destruction of the boats. And let's not forget your little escapade that involved playing with matches. You should thank me for the reduction to the eighteen months—I figure fifteen if you behave yourself. The negotiations were tricky. His reduction to eighteen months was only because Cohen stepped up to the plate and settled with the insurance companies for the damages to the two yachts. He also agreed to buy a trailer for your friend Hanson to use as a live-in office. Although you need to know it's all coming out of your share of the deal."

Mario sat with a mystified look. "Whaddaya mean Cohen settled with the insurance companies? That kid you sent down here told me Cohen was dead."

"Yeah, well he's alive again. Let's just say Cohen ran a bluff and you called him on it. Think of it as you winning round one, but don't get too cocky with a minor victory. Things in Cohen's world can change overnight. You might be a tough nut to crack and think you won a battle here but if you screw with Cohen, you're liable to meet some of those associates that supposedly killed him. Those guys do exist and Cohen has a long arm when he wants to reach out and touch someone. In addition to the eighteen months, I also got the judge to agree to Bower Correctional. It's a country club compared to where he could've sent you. For a tough guy like you it should be a walk in the park." Her voice held a touch of sarcasm or perhaps bitterness. Mario was getting off with a light sentence, but Cohen hadn't been pleased with her failure to get the location of the diamonds. "On top of everything else, I had to deal with the Hanson fiasco," she continued. "He certainly didn't like the deal that was offered. He wanted millions for pain and suffering for the loss of his toe but seeing as how the jerk cut it off himself, the arbitrator didn't have much sympathy."

Mario knew Jennine was right, but he was still holding the diamonds and Cohen was the man with a million dollars. Carmine had become invisible during the whole ordeal so the million was his for the taking—his salary for doing the time. *Miss Demeanor* was his hole card and he wasn't about to show it.

"So, that's it? I get to go away and cool my heels for fifteen months?"

"No, there's one more rub and Hanson's not signing off on the arbitration papers until he gets his just desserts. He wants your boat," she lied. "That's why *we* need to get to it first."

Mario's exclusion from meetings with the arbitrator left him to believe Jennine was acting on his behalf. He was forced to accept anything she relayed to him as the truth.

Jennine's information regarding *Miss Demeanor* being on the negotiating table meant Mario would have to give up its location. Under Cohen's instructions, she offered the boat to the arbitrator arguing that, even without a mast, it more than compensated for the loss of Hanson's skiff. She and Cohen felt it was the only way they would get Mario to give up the boat's location without a fifteen month wait. Jennine liked the idea. It was a much better plan than sending out a search party to find it.

"Hanson was adamant," she said. "He won't sign any release unless your boat's part of the deal. Don't forget, you destroyed his and he didn't get any monetary compensation for it. Although he was the one who cut your mast, you were the one responsible for it falling on the boats so the arbitrator saw it as dual negligence. However, you're going away, and like I said, he felt even your damaged boat was fair compensation for Hanson's skiff. Obviously, we have to get to the boat before he takes possession."

Jennine told Mario that Hanson laughed during arbitration. "He said you wouldn't be needing a boat where you were going anyway."

Mario became incensed by the additional demand Hanson had added. *Miss Demeanor* was not only his prize possession, it was his only possession. Giving up the location of the boat to anyone other than Rosita wasn't an option.

He considered the deal and in Jennine's explanation regarding the forfeiture of *Miss Demeanor* he saw an opportunity to stop any future search for the boat entirely. His idea would also allow Rosita to keep an eye on it with very little interference. If Cohen could run a bluff about being dead, he decided he could just as easily kill *Miss Demeanor.*

"There is no boat," he said. "I mean, there is a boat, but it's sitting under thirty feet of water at the bottom of the river." Brilliant, he thought. The idea not only halted any search for *Miss Demeanor*, but Hanson would be shit out of luck.

Mario continued. "Hanson must've somehow cut a hole in the hull while he was waving his chainsaw around the night he cut down my mast. She started taking on water a few miles off shore and I had to abandon ship."

"Where exactly did this abandonment take place?"

"How the hell should I know? It was dark, I was drunk. I was lucky to even make it to shore."

"Are you telling me that Cohen's diamonds are also thirty feet under water?"

"No. I took them ashore with me. They're safe. And until I get my money, they're *my* diamonds, not Cohen's."

Jennine tried to read whether he was telling the truth. The story was far-fetched but plausible. She then reflected on the agreement she'd made with the arbitrator.

"Does Hanson know any of this?"

"No."

"Fine," she said. "You sign off on the boat agreement and everybody walks away happy, or at least until Hanson discovers the boat he inherited is thirty feet under water."

"And once he signs off, it's a done deal?"

"Yes. I'll see the agreement states he gets full title to the boat. I'm not obligated to tell him it sank."

Mario smiled. He was sorry he couldn't be present when the bastard got the news that *Miss Demeanor* was a sunken, mastless, water-filled mess. That thought, coupled with Jennine's promise of getting him out in fifteen months made things somewhat palatable. When Mario agreed, however, Jennine pushed him again on the location of the stones, reminding him that his time inside could be easy or hard depending on Cohen's agreement to provide certain amenities.

"I guess if anything does happen to me, Cohen will never see the stones. I'm also guessing if I gave them to you, my life would pretty much be over."

Jennine knew the diamonds, when cut, would yield millions. Cohen had no choice other than agree to wait out the fifteen months.

TWO WEEKS LATER MARIO stood before a judge and entered a plea of guilty to the charges of vandalism and destruction of property. The terms of the agreement written by the arbitrator were read and entered into the record. Hanson was again present. Throughout the hearing both men sat grinning ear to ear. Hanson, overjoyed at the prospect of getting Mario's boat, and Mario because he knew Hanson had yet to be informed that *Miss Demeanor* was sitting somewhere at the bottom of the Indian River.

FINDING THE BOAT

◆   the big brass pole

Two days following the incarceration of Mario Costello, Andy Dugan's minivan, filled with T-shirts, shorts, and several toolboxes crossed the Route 192 causeway into Indialantic, Florida. Other than the loss of a filling in Georgia while eating a piece of pecan pie, the three day drive from the town of Boothbay Harbor, Maine had been uneventful.

Andy was a recent graduate from the Maine Maritime Academy, and following years of studying boat design and engineering, he wanted to stretch his sea legs a bit before delving into a professional career. His aunt's declining health prevented her from making her annual trip south, and knowing her beach house in Florida needed attention, she offered Andy a rent-free stay in exchange for some light repairs. They were mostly cosmetic—the replacement of a worn step . . . the painting of window trim . . . the fixing of a broken shutter, and the like. With Andy anxious to celebrate his recent graduation, her offer was timely. He certainly preferred putting his carpentry skills to use on a house in Florida to working eight-hour days in the bone-chilling cold of another Maine winter.

He had never seen his aunt's house, nor had he ever been to Florida, but in recent weeks he fantasized about the three months ahead. While residents back home were splitting firewood and chopping ice from their windshields before shoveling their way out of a driveway, he would be meeting new friends and getting some beach time. He would forego the *chowdah* and *lobstah* to which he was accustomed and trade such delicacies for coolers of beer, the study of bikini-clad women, and the hope of doing some sailing.

Sailboats had always been his passion. At the age of three, he ran up and down the decks of a one hundred fifty foot, gaff-rigged schooner. It was the last of Maine's four-masted windjammers. The schooner was owned by *Ocean Tour Boats* and captained by Andy's father. Three times each day, she was boarded by tourists and sailed out of Boothbay Harbor. The midmorning sail included coffee with croissants from a local pastry shop, while afternoon patrons were treated to fine wines accompanied by crackers topped with a variety of cheeses. The sunset cruise added the romantic flair of champagne and couples of all ages held hands while they enjoyed views of Maine's rugged coastline.

The ship was manned by a crew of eight, along with Andy, who had been potty trained in the ship's head rather than a traditional bathroom. He also ate most of his meals in the galley—unlike other kids his age who ate in kitchens. At the age of four, he was put to work on board the schooner.

At the conclusion of his father's welcoming speech, Andy was handed a belaying pin, and dressed in his long-sleeved blue and white striped shirt and bell-bottomed pants, gave his rehearsed talk. "This looks like a rolling pin," he began. "But it's a blayin' pin." The unintended mispronunciation of the word gained immediate favor with patrons. "There're lots of holes here so you can move it fore and aft." As he made the statement, he gestured to the holes near him on the starboard side of the schooner and explained fore and aft by pointing to the bow and stern. Holding up a piece of rope, he continued. "On a ship, a rope is called a line and if a line is attached to a sail, it's called a sheet. After the pin is where you want it," he continued, as he placed the pin in a hole, "you wrap the sheet around the pin to trim your sails." He began making the motion but then turned back toward the crowd and added, "trimming the sail means adjusting it so it catches the wind the right way." The comment was nonchalant rather than condescending.

He then wrapped the sheet in a figure eight around the pin's top and bottom and locked it in place using a cleat hitch. His tone was friendly and informational, and being an adorable four-year-old, he was a great hit with the tourists.

"And what else is a belaying pin sometimes used for Andy?" his father asked on cue.

The question was Andy's signal to steal the hearts of the crowd. "Well," he said, as he smiled at the onlookers, "my mom keeps one in the kitchen and if my father comes home late, she hits him over the head with it."

This answer to his father's question always elicited a chorus of laughs from the crowd. It concluded Andy's role in the short tour of the ship and he gave a gracious bow and the laughs were followed by a round of applause.

When the schooner sat in port, Andy's other job was to ensure the large brass bell near the ship's wheel was kept highly polished. His father, a robust man who was one of Boothbay's most lovable characters, made a special effort to compliment his son on the bell's appearance. "That bell is so bright that on cloudy days, it's my little piece of sunshine," he told Andy. And then always added, "other than you that is."

As his childhood continued, Andy lived sailboats. At home, his bedroom was referred to as his stateroom. And he never went up or down stairs . . . he went topside or below. It was his passion for sailboats that led him to the Maine Maritime Academy and his experience in the craft of sail far surpassed the knowledge of his peers. During his years of study, he worked during his summer vacations as one of the official crew members on his father's schooner. After graduating, he spent a final summer sailing the Maine coast, and when fall arrived, he helped the family prepare for the long winter. Two weeks after a gala New Year's Eve party with friends, he packed the van and made the drive to Florida.

On the day he crossed the 192 causeway into Indialantic, it was his love of sailing that drew his attention to a sailboat that sat anchored near Douglas Park. With his knowledge of sailboats, he recognized it immediately to be a Beneteau— a thirty-four or thirty-five footer. It was a French company, but also built boats in South Carolina. They were known for their high performance, luxurious comfort, and ease of sailing.

For some reason, however, this Beneteau had no mast and her deck displayed a haphazard array of seat cushions, life jackets, tangled lines, and other equipment that had been strewn about. He pulled off the highway, parked, and climbed out of his van to study her. Had she been sitting in dry dock sporting a *For Sale* sign, he would've climbed on board for a closer look. Not that he was in the market . . . sailboats just seemed to draw him like a magnet. Whenever an opportunity presented itself to investigate the sleek contours and interior designs of a craft, he accepted the invitation. Andy watched as it bobbed in the water, beckoning someone to put her shipshape. . . clean her up . . . sail her away to ports unknown.

To commuters it most likely blended into the seascape while tourists who passed on their way to the beach may not have noticed her at all. Andy wondered why she'd been left—sitting unattended—cluttered with debris that detracted from her elegance. She was obviously a boat that was meant to fly . . . meant to suck the wind into her sails and cut through the ocean, heeling to one side, with the spray of saltwater washing over her bow and covering her freeboard while she held that delicate balance between safety and peril—speed versus caution. Without a mast, she appeared half-naked and Andy pondered the fate of this monument to neglect that beckoned a captain. To a sailor—any sailor—a sighting of a craft in such disarray was somewhat of a mystery . . . and Andy Dugan was a sailor.

Following the boat's inspection, he climbed back into his van and studied his aunt's written directions. As noted, the causeway emptied onto Fifth Avenue into Indialantic. At the end of the street, he was to turn right at Longboard House, continue to Ocean Avenue, and take a left. It was then a few short blocks to the final right turn where he was directed to continue on A1A for what appeared to be five or six miles to his aunt's beach house.

Over the past few days, however, Andy had learned his aunt's estimates of distance were somewhat lacking in accuracy. After making the final turn, he noticed his aunt had also neglected to mention the bikini bar that was part of a restaurant called *Sand On The Beach*. It was adjacent to a small pub, called the 911 Club and Andy, wanting to get more specifics on his aunt's directions, figured the pub would be a good place to get a cold beer and celebrate his arrival.

It was just after four o'clock when he entered. The bartender was killing time wiping bar glasses while wait staff hustled around the dining room. Stainless steel carts filled with stacks of dishes were being wheeled in and busboys were setting up the buffet line and arranging tables. The smell of food waiting to be brought in from the kitchen to fill the waiting containers permeated the area. A long bar ran across the back wall. It was well stocked and inverted wine glasses hung from an overhead rack.

The décor reflected the restoration of the original building—an old fire station—and the walls maintained the flavor of exposed red brick. An antique bell from a fire truck was mounted behind the bar and was surrounded by plaques and framed pictures of firemen. Other remnants of firefighting apparatus were in various locations on walls or hanging as mobiles.

Andy continued to survey the furnishings as he walked to the bar. Old fire hoses were mounted in glass cases near tables along the wall. At the end of the bar an antique fire alarm sported a dangling hammer. A brass plate above it read "Break Glass for Bouncer" with a second plate below it reading "Anyone breaking glass will be bounced." His eyes stopped when he spied the big brass pole. It ran down from the second floor that once housed the firemen's quarters. It was firmly anchored about six feet from the corner of the bar leaving enough room for patrons to squeeze through.

The bartender took note of Andy's admiration for the pole. "The place used to be an old firehouse," he said. "When it went up for sale a couple of years ago two guys from New York flew down here and grabbed it up. They left as much of the old fire gear as they could, renamed her the 911 Club. Now they've got a gold mine goin'. They just sit up there in New York and rake in the money."

Andy gave an appreciative nod as he sat on a stool at the short end of the right-angled bar and ordered a draft. The busboys continued to clatter dishes as they set tables in preparation for what he later learned Floridians called the "Early Bird Special."

The bartender noticed Andy's interest. "Snowbirds will be drifting in soon," he said. Andy gave a quizzical look.

"You know, the old folks who spend a few months evading the northern cold. They get in and out early for dinner so they can get to bed by eight. They'll be comin' in for the buffet. It's a pretty good spread if you're hungry."

Andy continued to watch as linen tablecloths were set in place followed by plates, silverware wrapped in napkins, and too much glassware for his taste. It was a bit fancier than the type of restaurant he would've chosen for a meal, and his draft was overpriced. He made a mental note that it might be a place to bring a date but it wasn't a bar for sitting and drinking.

The bartender was friendly, and with no other customers, he continued to make conversation.

"Just drive down from up north?"

"What gave it away?"

"Early January . . . no tan . . . not so hard to figure. Where you from?"

"Maine."

"Wow, that's a helluva drive. How long did it take you to get down here?"

"A few days," Andy said, without adding any details.

"You looking for work? I mean, I'm guessing you're not retired yet, unless you made some fortune in the computer game and sold your soul to Silicon Valley."

"No, I'm good . . . work I mean . . . just here for a few months." He refrained from continuing with more information but the bartender pursued.

"Oh yeah? What've you got lined up?"

"A bit of carpentry work on a relative's house," Andy said, still trying to remain as vague as possible. "Haven't actually seen it yet, other than some pictures . . . the house is supposed to be on A1A somewhere near here. The number's seven thousand and something." Andy pulled out the slip of paper from his shirt pocket with the address and tossed it onto the bar.

The bartender glanced at it. "Yeah, yeah. House numbers in the seven thousands are probably about eight or nine miles. Just keep goin' down A1A. You'll see a place on the right with a big sign for the New England Eatery—I think that's around five-thousand or so. The house you want shouldn't be too far after that. Odd numbers are on the left so it looks like you'll be livin' on the beach side." He seemed to be finished with the directions when hit with an obvious afterthought. "Hey, you follow college football?"

"Some, why?"

"If you're goin' down that far, you're gonna go right by Doug Flutie's place. You know who Flutie is, right?"

"Isn't he the guy who threw a pass that beat somebody in a bowl game or something?"

"Not just any pass, baby. A forty-eight yard 'Hail Mary' with six seconds left on the clock to beat Miami. Anyway, he's got a house down there. It's not too far so you'll go right by it."

Although Andy had some recollection of the event, he wasn't as enthusiastic as the bartender over the thirty-some year old victory.

"Incidentally, when you get started on your carpentry work or whatever, there's a guy who comes in here all the time who's pretty well connected. He can probably get you a deal on any kind of building supplies. You know . . . lumber or whatever."

Andy nodded in appreciation of the offer as he continued to look around. "Is it always this deserted in here?"

"Hell no. It'll get pretty wild in here tonight . . . you know, after the snowbirds go to bed and the real people come out. We've got a band that comes in and sets up around eight-thirty. They draw a big crowd."

With news of a band, Andy returned his attention to the brass pole. "So, should I assume when the music starts this pole here is put to better use by some dancers?"

"Yeah, I wish," the bartender laughed and Andy ordered another draft.

18

Mario sat in the exercise yard next to a con named Silo. Silo was serving twenty to life for manslaughter. His father, a Nebraskan farmer, gave him the nickname when he was thirteen. At that time he stood two heads taller than his classmates. He now stood six feet six inches and weighed in at somewhere between two-hundred eighty and three-hundred pounds—with very little body fat.

He and Mario worked side by side in the laundry room. Silo yanked piles of shirts out of the huge dryers and heaped them onto a stainless steel table. Mario folded them and stacked them according to small, medium, and large. Several shirts from each load routinely fell to the floor and were ignored by Silo. Not needing any enemies of a man that size, Mario retrieved the dropped shirts and added them to the appropriate piles. As they worked, he tried to make small talk but the conversation was one-sided—Mario talked and Silo either said nothing or made grunting sounds. After two days of piling and folding, the giant finally spoke. What surprised Mario was hearing the words come out as a complete sentence.

"Stay in my vision," Silo said. And then, in case Mario wasn't clear on the instruction, he repeated an expanded version for clarification. "When we're in the yard with the other cons I mean, stay in my vision."

Mario wondered if the order was some kind of a threat, and reluctantly, he pressed his fellow inmate on the issue. "Stay in your vision? What does that mean exactly, stay in your vision?"

"I'll make sure nobody kills you . . . so stay in my vision."

Considering Silo's size and reputation, the information was comforting to Mario but also raised another question. "Why are you making sure nobody kills me? Not that I'm complaining," he added.

"Because a Mr. Cohen is paying me to keep you alive. You know a Mr. Cohen?"

"Yeah, I know a Mr. Cohen." Mario felt relieved, discovering he had been assigned protection for the next fifteen months. Although Bower County Correctional had a security level of "medium," there were enough bad elements on the inside to make it dangerous. Yard fights between inmates were common. Crude weapons were available for those willing to trade for cigarettes or other items from the commissary. Two or three stabbings a month were not unheard of, although they were seldom fatal. Mario was certainly a target. He was not only a newcomer, but more or less an anomaly among the general population. His two tattoos were military in nature which gave him very little standing with inmates who were inked with tats of swastikas and barbed wire necklaces. He had no obvious standing with the Hispanics or the Blacks . . . the religious fanatics prayed too much . . . and hanging with the gay population didn't seem to be a viable option. For those reasons, he couldn't rule out the possibility of harm, or perhaps death, which were ever-present during disputes in the exercise yard.

He was certain no one on the inside knew anything about the diamonds and Silo wasn't the type to question *why* he'd been hired to protect Mario as long as he was paid on time. Receiving word that he was assigned a bodyguard meant Mario's message to Jennine regarding his safety got through. Cohen obviously realized that hiring Silo as a precautionary measure was a minor investment in comparison to the financial yield he would reap from the diamonds.

When the two men became joined at the hip, Silo eventually opened up to Mario, telling him he'd been incarcerated after being led astray by evil men. He didn't actually use the word incarcerated when he told his story because he was hard pressed to use words having more than two syllables. He told Mario the story about moving to Florida to find a new life. He figured with his size and strength he could become a lifeguard like the ones he'd seen on the Baywatch reruns, but it didn't quite pan out the way he expected. He soon ran short on money. It was then he fell in with the wrong crowd. They recruited him to act as a lookout during the robbing of a factory. During the holdup, he was forced to hit the night watchman. The punch sent the guard out a third floor window which, as Silo very seriously pointed out, was closed at the time.

The three-story fall through the plate glass window was fatal but Silo's court appointed attorney bargained for a plea of manslaughter in lieu of murder. It was also agreed during the plea bargaining that because his mental capacity seemed to be a bit lacking, the court would allow him to serve his time at Bower County rather than one of the facilities that housed the more violent cons.

As he relayed the story to Mario, he seemed filled with sadness and remorse regarding the killing of the watchman. Mario viewed his protector as an "optimistic lifer." He was midway through the sixth year of his sentence but still believed his inept public defender would find a major oversight in someone's testimony and declare a mistrial. The fact that his plea bargain had eliminated any trial in the first place never seemed to register. Mario thought it best to keep his mouth shut. As the days progressed, he found having the giant by his side was advantageous. As ordered, he remained within Silo's vision. Other than a minor yard skirmish, things had been relatively peaceful.

The incident occurred the second week into Mario's stay. He was lifting weights in the yard when one of the muscle heads, who had no actual intent to lift, told Mario to, "get the hell off the weight bench." It was common practice for one con to test another and find out how far he could be pushed. Mario was in Silo's line of vision, so had no interest in succumbing to the demand. There was little doubt his new found bodyguard would intervene and teach the guy a lesson. His complacency, however, was misguided. Mario continued to lift and when the bar was cradled between reps, the muscle head snatched it from its resting place and set it on Mario's chest. The inmate then straddled Mario and pushed down on the bar, pinning him to the bench while a second inmate bloodied his face. A few additional blows to the body area followed before the guards stepped in and broke up the mêlée. The members of the fracas were separated, and evidently, the guards didn't feel the incident warranted any further disciplinary action. All parties were ordered to return to their respective corners, and Mario returned to sit with Silo.

He wiped a bit of blood from his nose and felt a small lump beginning to grow on his forehead. "What the hell were you thinking?" he asked Silo. "Didn't you see those guys beating the shit out of me?"

"Yes, I seen them."

"Then why didn't you do something?"

"I'm paid to keep you alive. It doesn't count if you're just getting the crap kicked out of you. You're still alive aren't you?"

"Barely."

"I try not to hit people anymore. I don't want to kill anyone else. But if they were killing you I would've stopped them. As long as you're alive I still get paid."

In the days that followed the beating, Mario stayed close to Silo in the laundry room, during chow time in the dining hall, and while in the yard with inmates. Everyone interpreted their camaraderie as a deterrent to avoid any future conflicts. Fortunately for Mario, none of the cons were aware that Silo was only a preventive measure against death. Beatings were still allowable.

♦ i know a guy

W hile Andy and the bartender discussed the possibility of pole dancers, flashing blue lights appeared in the rearview mirror of a jeep, several miles down the highway. For the driver, the possibility of being pulled over was an occupational hazard. He maneuvered the vehicle out of the flow of traffic and brought it to rest on the shoulder. His license and registration were in his outstretched hand before the trooper got to his jeep and he handed him the items without any exchange of words.

The cop gave them a quick once over. "Any idea why I pulled you over today?"

"Yes, sir. I'm guessing I was a bit over the limit."

"Just a bit. I clocked you at eighty-seven."

"I'm sorry. I'm trying to get this to the hospital and every minute counts." He patted a case sitting on the passenger seat. The hand was dark—tanned from many hours of surfing—and was a direct contrast to the white container it rested on. Stenciled red lettering clearly identified the contents as HUMAN ORGAN & TISSUE FOR TRANSPLANT. The stenciled words surrounded a staff entwined by a singular snake depicting the Rod of Asclepius.

The cop eyed the container and then pointed to it. "What hospital?"

"Eastside Pediatrics. It's . . ."

"Yeah, I know where it is," the cop said, cutting him off. He studied the driver's attire—loud-colored baggies and a T-shirt that asked "What would Vlad the Impaler Do?" A Boston Reds Sox cap failed to cover the dreadlocks that spilled from beneath it and fell to his shoulders. "You on staff at Eastside?" the cop's question held a tone of skepticism.

"No, sir. I work for a messenger service out of Jacksonville." As he spoke, he fished his employee ID badge that hung around his neck and was tucked inside his shirt. He held it up to confirm his employment. The photo on the ID was perhaps a year old, but the name *Oliver Henshaw* matched the name on the driver's license.

While the cop studied the ID, Oliver spoke with a tone of urgency. "Look, this kidney's for a nine-year-old girl. They told me it was a rush. I'm sorry about the speed. Whaddaya say? Can you cut me some slack? I've only got a couple more miles to go here."

"Yeah, I know where it is. Maybe I should give you an escort. How'd that be?"

Oliver knew the cop was fishing—perhaps trying to legitimize the juxtaposition of his appearance and the importance of his delivery. It wasn't the first time he'd been pulled over while on a run. His lack of being well groomed in addition to his questionable attire was always suspect. "Sure, if you've got the time I'd appreciate that," he said.

The cop pondered Oliver's response. He appeared to be on the level and there were possible repercussions if he delayed the delivery. "If you think you can keep the speed down for the next few miles it'll probably be faster than me callin' in to get the okay. Just keep in mind that delivering a transplant doesn't give you a license to break the law."

"Yeah, sure. Sorry about the speed. It's just . . . you know, it's for a little kid."

The trooper returned Oliver's license and registration and rested both hands on the door of the jeep. "I'll run some interference behind you until you get back into the flow of traffic so keep me in your rear view mirror."

Both vehicles pulled back onto the highway and Oliver watched as instructed. Less than a mile later the police car made a U-turn through the median and the blue lights flashed again as the cop found another mark. Oliver pressed down on the accelerator, flew past the entrance to Eastside Pediatrics, and then slowed to the speed limit. He continued over the 192 causeway, and once into Indialantic, followed the same path Andy Dugan had taken and pulled into the 911 Club. Before getting out of his jeep he opened the Human Organ and Tissue container and removed a paper bag containing a quarter of a pound of grass. He walked around to the back and entered through the kitchen door.

Soon after his entrance, the conversation between Andy and the bartender was interrupted by the muffled sounds of an argument coming from the kitchen. The double doors separating the two areas swung open and the yelling became amplified. Two men busted into the dining area at a full sprint. The first was Oliver Henshaw. His sun-bleached dreadlocks fluttered behind him as he sprinted in the direction of Andy's bar stool. The second man was a yard or two behind him and was dressed in a waiter's uniform. He was holding his ass with one hand, bellowing something about the stove, and waving a soup ladle in the other.

Andy watched as they neared the end of the bar. Oliver could see his path was heading him into a table, and to slow himself, he reached out with his left hand and grabbed the big brass pole. His momentum propelled him around it in a one hundred-eighty degree turn. As he spun, he lifted his legs to his chest and the waiter, having closed the gap, caught Oliver's kneecap square in the jaw. He reeled backward and fell to the floor.

"You fucker!" he yelled.

Andy could see the waiter's front teeth were red with blood.

"What the hell did you do that for?" He put his hand to his mouth. "Jeezus, I think my front teeth are loose."

"Sorry man, but you shouldn't have started the shoving match in the kitchen. For all I knew you were gonna start swinging at me. What'd you chase me in here for anyway? I sure didn't intend for you to catch my knee with your face. I was just tryin' to stop myself from running into the table."

"You didn't have to push me onto the top of the stove either. I think I burned half my ass off."

"Hey, I was just tryin' to get the dope back and get you off me. I didn't drive all the way over here with that shit just to find out you don't have all the cash."

The bartender suddenly became nervous as their shouts regarding a dope deal gone bad escalated in volume. He slapped his hand on the bar. "Ollie, Ollie . . . keep it down, man."

Andy sat and continued to sip his draft, somewhat amused at the show.

Oliver extended a hand and helped the waiter to his feet. He continued holding his hand over his mouth and inspecting it for signs of blood. "Look what you did," he said, pointing to his top teeth. They're loose."

Oliver looked around. Other than Andy and the busboys picking up the few toppled chairs, the bar was still deserted. Most of the waiters who worked there did business with Henshaw and they didn't seem to have much sympathy for their co-worker who was short on cash. Stiffing Ollie was an act that could jeopardize future deals for all of them.

Henshaw, on the other hand, seemed to show remorse over his role in the skirmish. "I'm sorry, man. I didn't know if you were gonna take a swing at me in the kitchen with that thing or not." Ollie pointed to the ladle as he spoke. "But if you want to buy shit from me, you need to have the cash up front. I'm not running a credit agency here."

"What about my teeth? Who's gonna pay to have my teeth tightened?"

"Don't worry, I know a guy."

"What?"

"I said, I know a guy. A guy who fixes teeth and stuff—if it's anything serious."

"Does he tighten teeth?" The question was so comical Andy almost laughed out loud. The comment, however, reminded him of his encounter with the pecan pie and he stuck his tongue into the hole the lost filling had left. He interrupted Ollie's attempt to console the waiter and injected himself into the conversation. "This guy you know . . . does he do fillings?"

Ollie studied Andy momentarily. "Yeah, sure he does fillings."

"Is he any good?"

Ollie lifted his eyebrows and looked at the bartender as if needing a second endorsement.

"Hey . . . Ollie here is the guy I mentioned earlier—the guy with connections. If he says the dentist is okay, you can take it to the bank. He only knows good people."

"Okay then," Andy said and held out a hand. "Andy Dugan."

Ollie took the hand and shook it. "Ollie," he said.

The waiter turned to go to the kitchen and Ollie grabbed his arm. "Don't touch the dope," he warned. "I'll take out enough to cover the money you do have but don't pull this shit again or you can find another dealer."

The waiter made his exit, still covering his mouth with one hand and rubbing his ass with the other. Ollie took a seat at the bar and Andy pushed him for the name of the dentist. As their conversation progressed, tales turned to the sea and they found they had much in common. A friendly competition rose as Andy told stories of perils during sailing in the offing and Ollie countered with the dangers of surfing in shark-infested waters. Although Ollie had never been personally attacked, he was quick to point out the ever-present dangers and mentioned guys who had been less fortunate.

Andy liked this new friend; a guy who took life in stride, was mellow to the core, and seemed to live for the moment. Even when he stood his ground with the waiter, he had remained low-keyed and rational. They chatted into the evening over beers and food from the buffet until the band arrived. The place filled up quickly and the loudness of the music made conversation difficult. They agreed to get together again and called it a night.

The bartender had been right in stating Ollie was well connected. When he had used the phrase "I know a guy," in reference to the dentist, it was the first time Andy heard him say the words, but in the weeks that followed, it was a phrase he heard often. Ollie *always* knew a guy. If you needed anything done, something repaired, or an object located, Ollie knew a guy who could do it, or a guy who could repair it, or a guy who could find it. It was as simple as that. He always knew a guy.

home sweet home

It was dark when Andy arrived at his aunt's cottage. His later than expected arrival curtailed any initial inspection of the house in which he was to spend the next few months. The adjacent homes appeared dark inside and Andy assumed they were either empty or occupied by snowbirds who had retired for the night. After concluding an already long day drinking with his new best friend Ollie, he wanted sleep. His only thought was to get inside and find a bed. Investigating his new surroundings could wait until morning.

He grabbed a small backpack from the minivan and fumbled his way inside. In the darkness he felt around the obvious places near the door and found a light switch. The house was small—one-story—and his initial survey of the interior was cursory. From the front room, he could see into a small kitchen. A quick look around revealed a bedroom and half bath off one side of the living room and he found the opposite side had a larger bedroom with a full bath. Another room, presumably a third bedroom, had been converted into a reading area. He retraced his steps and turned off the lights before returning to the master bedroom. There, he stripped off his clothes and crawled into bed. It had been a long drive . . . a long day . . . and he slept soundly.

WHEN ANDY WOKE, HE was disoriented. The bedroom was black—cave-like in fact. He focused on where he was and how he got there, finally recalling the previous night at the 911 Club. Things began to register. Florida . . . he was in Florida . . . his aunt's house. Small pin-pricks of light were scattered on the floor and the sound of heavy wind swirled around outside.

His eyes continued to adjust and silhouettes began to appear. He recognized the outline of an antique lamp on the nightstand. The base of it was glass and had been filled with seashells. He clicked it on and realized his entry the night before failed to reveal what the morning explained. Hurricane shutters shielded every window from potential storms but denied the interior of any daylight. Once he learned the reason for the darkness, he found a crank and opened the shutters allowing him to stand in a sundrenched bedroom. He discovered the wind he heard earlier turned out to be the crashing of ocean waves.

The room had sliding doors to a small patio, and to his surprise, he saw the beach was no more than a stone's throw away. He threw on a pair of shorts, slid the glass doors open, and spent the next several minutes exploring his surroundings. The patio was covered—a lanai of sorts—and the slate floor was cool beneath his feet. A stone walkway grouted with tiny seashells ran from the patio to a small yard filled with a variety of sea grasses. A few more steps put him on the beach. He stood and took it all in . . . inhaling the air that filtered itself through the salt. None of what he saw had been visible in the dark of night and Andy was astounded by the stretch of sand and the expanse of the ocean. It was different from the coast he loved . . . absent of the rocky cliffs. The gulls of Maine were replaced by terns and sandpipers. Pelicans swooped overhead and dove for their breakfast. Andy liked this place called Florida. He liked the warmth, the scents, and the sounds. It would be a good winter.

On his return to the house, he studied the exterior. It was small in comparison to those on either side but had the traditional stucco finish that seemed to be popular. The color was similar to the beach sand. The neighboring houses displayed the same type of metal shutters that protected his aunt's windows. They were closed indicating the houses were unoccupied. The thought of having the additional privacy was appealing.

He investigated the house's interior a second time, but unlike the previous night he used a bit more scrutiny. It was modest but comfortable. In the light of day, the bedspreads showed their pastel colors . . . window curtains were drawn closed but had tie-backs to allow for more light during the day.

A small end table covered with a white doily had a lamp with the same pastels in its shade as the bedspread. It was surrounded by framed photos taken years before. One seemed more paramount than the others, and depicted two teenagers posing in front of an ice cream parlor. Each held a cone and they had assumed facial expressions that embodied the fact that the ice cream was dripping down their fingers. A closer look revealed it was his aunt and his mother. Other photos were strategically placed on available spaces or hung on walls. Like his aunt's home in Connecticut, no space was ignored when it came to her passion for knickknacks. The second bedroom was similar in its decor, but housed two single beds.

The third bedroom had been converted to a sitting room and was furnished with an antique desk, several bookshelves, and an oversized recliner. The shelves contained a multitude of jigsaw puzzles, a few beach-reads along with novels by Agatha Christie, Nora Roberts, and John D. MacDonald. A small table sat beneath the window and supported a sewing machine. Andy found the adjacent cabinet contained a variety of bobbins, spools of thread, old Sucrets tins—one filled with needles, a second containing straight pins—and a drawer filled with bits and pieces of fabric.

He spent the remainder of the morning pawing through drawers and cupboards and made a mental inventory of what was in the house. Closets were stuffed with sheets and pillow cases, towels and washcloths, doilies, a first aid kit, shampoos, soaps, toilet paper . . . anything and everything needed for survival. Many of the items were kept fresh by lavender sachets. It seemed the only missing ingredient for his immediate need was caffeine. The discovery of the Tupperware container with a few tea bags reminded him that his aunt never drank coffee. He brewed a cup of tea and made a short list of groceries to carry him through the first few days.

His investigation of the house, followed by a trip to the market, took most of the morning. The afternoon was dictated by Ollie's assurance the night before that his dentist friend would fit him in for the filling.

"I'll call and let him know you're coming in after lunch," Ollie told him. "He's cool . . . he'll take good care of you." Ollie explained that Jimmy was hard to reach by phone and insisted on making the call for him. "Just get yourself over there any time after lunch. I'll call his cell and clear a path for an appointment."

Andy left through the side door of the house which took him through the garage—another area he found commanded neatness. One wall held an array of hanging tools for outdoor work along with a garden hose and a gas-powered trimmer. The opposite side had a built-in work bench. Shelves over the bench displayed flower pots in a variety of sizes along with small bags of leftover mulch and compost. A lawn mower sat next to a hanging bicycle, and other than a faded oil spot on the floor, it was as orderly and regimented as a military complex.

Andy climbed into his minivan and retrieved the information for the dentist that was stuffed in the cup holder. He studied the name and address Ollie had scrawled on the bar napkin. The dentist's location meant a return trip over the causeway which would include a second opportunity to check out the boat he'd seen. As he studied the napkin in the light of day he became a bit concerned when he read the name Ollie had written down. It hadn't seemed as objectionable the night before when they'd been drinking and Ollie assured him the dentist could certainly replace a lost filling.

The thought of reconsidering his fate was, perhaps, triggered by the cold shower taken earlier. He had forgotten his aunt's reminder to throw on the breaker for the hot water tank. With his appointment still looming, the cold shower was the first of two sobering events that afternoon. As he drove to Melbourne, he continued to question whether or not he should allow his tooth to be filled by a dentist known as "Jimmy the Gasser."

◆   **painless**

Jimmy the Gasser's office was located in Historic Downtown Melbourne. It was on the second floor of an old building that also housed a small thrift shop. Jimmy and the store owner were the only two occupants of the building. The hallway was dimly lit, possibly to hide the cracks in the plaster, along with the stairs and stair rail—all in desperate need of a coat of paint. Mismatched pictures of lighthouses, seascapes, and tropical birds covered the walls, but unlike the beach house, they were askew and displayed no attempt to achieve any aesthetic sense of spacial coordination.

When Andy entered the waiting room, a girl who looked to be seven or eight was sitting alone thumbing through a *Vanity Fair* magazine. Elton John was coming through a singular speaker that was hanging from wires protruding from the ceiling. A second pair of exposed wires, presumably for the other speaker, dangled a few feet away and were attached to nothing. The receptionist greeted him. She was the bubbly, friendly type. Andy explained that he was there to get a filling replaced. His friend Ollie, who was a mutual friend of his and the dentist, was supposed to have called that morning to let the dentist know he was coming in.

"Never called me," she said. "But knowing Ollie, that's no surprise. Do you really need a filling or are you just here for a checkup?" The word *checkup* seemed to be emphasized as she asked the question.

"Yeah, I really need a filling. He can do that, right? I mean, he's a real dentist, right?"

"Of course he's a real dentist. And yes, he can do a filling for you. I'm sure he'll squeeze you in if you want to have a seat. Do you have cash? Did Ollie tell you Jimmy doesn't take checks or plastic?"

Before Andy could answer, a door at the end of a long hallway opened and a nurse escorted a woman toward the reception area. Despite being a bit wobbly, she seemed to be wearing a big smile.

"You wanna just sit for a few minutes, Annie?" the nurse asked her.

"No, I think I'm okay. C'mon, hon," she said, motioning to the eight-year-old. She pulled two twenties out of her purse and handed them to the receptionist. As they were leaving, she muttered something to the girl about having to stop at the drug store on the way to school to get her prescription filled.

The door at the end of the hallway, still open, was then filled with the silhouette of a man who made his way toward Andy. "Can I help you?"

Although a white medical jacket seemed to be the only telltale sign of attire identifying him, Andy assumed it was the dentist. He was wearing jeans and sneakers and the medical jacket was worn over a Hawaiian shirt. He was in his mid fifties, tall, and much too thin. His facial features were sharp, pointed.

"Jimmy the Gasser?" Andy questioned.

The receptionist and the nurse gave a quiet laugh.

"It's just *Jimmy* here in the office," he said. But from your question, I can guess Ollie sent you over. You here for a checkup?" Again, the word *checkup* seemed to be emphasized.

"Didn't he call you? He told me he would call and let you know I was coming."

"Ollie's not real big on phone calls."

"I need a filling replaced. Ollie told me you could take care of it. I lost it to a piece of pecan pie on the drive down here from Maine."

"Really! Yeah, I guess driving can be dangerous that way." Jimmy, who had a passion for his own wit, followed the comment with a laugh. A ratta-tat-tat sounding laugh—much like the sound of the imaginary machine guns kids make when they're playing soldiers.

"Well, come on down, let's have a look."

Since entering the office, Andy had become somewhat reluctant about having any work done. He considered the fact that Ollie hadn't made any advance call and realized it might be a way out of what could be a dental catastrophe. "If Ollie didn't call to set this up, why don't I make an appointment and come back another time?"

"Hey, it's your lucky day. I think the guy who was scheduled called and cancelled. I can take you right now." He looked at the receptionist, as if for confirmation.

"Yeah, that's right. I got a cancellation a while ago," she said, and then flipped through a register on her desk—presumably the appointment book. From what Andy could see, most of the pages had large empty spaces for available appointments. Before he could say any more, Jimmy the Gasser took his arm and escorted him down the hallway. As they walked, he was followed by the nurse who had assisted the wobbly woman.

In the inner office, Andy seated himself in the chair and scanned the walls for a diploma—any diploma—that might have the name of a reputable dental school. The nurse went for a bib and when she went up on her tiptoes to retrieve it from the cabinet, Andy noticed the shortness of her skirt. She then turned—as if choreographed—smiled a pretty smile, and leaned forward to secure the bib around his neck. Her uniform top was low cut, and as she hovered over him, he found himself staring at a healthy amount of exposed cleavage.

When she backed away, Jimmy the Gasser was looking at Andy and grinning. "How was it?" he asked.

Andy's face reddened at being caught looking. "How was what?"

"The pecan pie, man, how was it?" The nurse's laugh seemed to be synchronized with the sound of Jimmy the Gasser's machine gun. Andy reddened a little more but let it pass.

When the laughing subsided, Jimmy became all business. "Okay, let's see what we've got here." Jimmy pushed back on Andy's chair, making him perfectly horizontal and blinded by light.

"Top left side," Andy told him, and the probing that followed seemed professional enough.

"Yeah, yeah, here it is . . . or I guess I should say here it isn't," another burst from the machine gun filled the room. "Ah, not so bad," he said. "Jolene, mix me up a small batch of cement will ya?" He returned his attention to Andy. "I'll have you outta here in no time." The comment was accompanied by the rolling of a large canister toward the chair.

With the blinding light in his eyes, Andy could only make out what looked to be a large scuba tank on wheels. He couldn't actually read the writing on the tank but he did catch a glimpse of an obviously large red warning label.

"No novocaine?" Andy asked.

"Hell, if I used novocaine I wouldn't have any patients." The habitual laugh followed.

THINGS ANDY REMEMBERED AS he drove home were the nurse securing the plastic mask onto his face and Jimmy laughing while telling him not to worry about Jolene doing anything to him while he was under because if she did, she was real good at it. After that comment, he felt the pleasant sensations of the gas taking over his body and he played with the colors that danced around in his head. He had a vague recollection of seeing Jimmy and the nurse passing the mask back and forth while machine gun bursts were fired over his head. A short time later, he found himself sitting bolt upright in the chair. All three of them were acting like fools. Jolene was sitting in the corner of the room holding her stomach to slow the laughing and Jimmy was turning his drill on and off to the beat of the song coming from the radio.

Andy remembered why he was there and was conscious enough to check the tooth. He rubbed his tongue over the original hole and was pleased to find it filled. It seemed smooth enough and the thought of his tooth being repaired offered some relief. He climbed out of the chair and recalled Jolene escorting him down the long hallway much the same way she escorted the wobbly woman.

He remembered Jimmy shouting from his office door. "Don't go chewing on that side for a couple of hours . . . and don't do anything I wouldn't do," which was followed by a final ratta-tat-tat.

At some point, the nurse helped Andy procure a few bills from his wallet. His fingers felt numb when he handed them to the receptionist. He had no recollection of getting to his car, but concluded that the drive home was probably quite pleasant. Later that day he found an appointment card in his shirt pocket offering a complementary *checkup*.

♦ guess who's coming to prison

A few days after the incident on the weight bench, Mario was unexpectedly called to Warden Weatherhead's office. It was not a good sign. Reasons for being called to see the warden ranged from being transferred to another facility—one that would not include Silo—or the elimination of time off for good behavior because of the yard fight. Mario mentally prepared his defense as he was escorted to the office.

As it turned out, neither was the case. He had been summoned for a reason he was unprepared for. When he entered, Weatherhead sat behind a large desk and was thumbing through a manila folder. It was reminiscent of Detective Benner looking through the folder at the time of his arrest. Mario was told to sit and Weatherhead continued with his thumbing and neglected to look at him when he spoke. "Do you think you belong in here, Costello?"

"I guess it doesn't matter much what I think, Warden. The DA thinks I belong in here so it seems the issue's been settled."

"Hmmm," the warden had yet to look at Mario, and his perusal through the file continued. "I've had an interesting request." Mario said nothing and Weatherhead repeated his statement. "I've had an interesting request." This time he raised his eyes with a look that reminded Mario that he was to respond appropriately when the warden was kind enough to address him.

"Really . . . what kind of request?"

"I've got a letter here from a professor . . ." he lifted the letter a few inches from the folder and held it in both hands. He glanced at the bottom of the page to remind himself of the sender's name. "Goodwin. You ever hear of a professor by the name of Goodwin?"

"No, sir."

"He's from a university up near Melbourne. That's your neck of the woods if I recall."

"Yes, sir. It was until I changed my address to your house."

Weatherhead returned a cold stare. "He's requesting that we allow one of his students to follow an inmate through the incarceration process starting with his entry on day one to his release. You know, the big finale when he gets out of here."

"Sounds like a fun project. Who's the lucky guinea pig?"

"It could be you, Costello, if you play your cards right. It seems you were identified by name." The warden paused. Mario said nothing. "Which is why I asked if you know this Goodwin guy."

"Like I said, never heard of him."

"How about a woman by the name of Márquez. Does that name ring any bells?" The tone of the question was suspicious causing Mario to straighten himself in the chair, unsettled by what might be coming.

"Márquez?" Mario searched himself but had no recollection of the name. "No. Don't believe I have any Márquez in my Rolodex."

"Well, you can understand why I'm a bit curious as to how your name got onto a letter from two people you don't know."

"Like I said, I don't know them and I'm really not interested in being part of any study." He shifted his weight again hoping the movement would initiate his dismissal from the warden's office.

"The student says she knows you."

"She?"

"Yeah, she. Evidently she was present at the time of your arrest, which gives her a leg up on the project. I assume she convinced her professor that witnessing your extraction from society has given her the advantage of starting from square one." The warden studied Mario, searching for a telltale sign that might suggest there was more to this request than even the professor knew. "So . . . you say you don't know the woman in this photograph here?" As he asked the question he spun the folder around and tapped his finger on the photo. "This Rosita Márquez?"

Mario stared at the picture. The girl seemed younger than he recalled from the Sand Flea Tavern but it was certainly Rosita. The same Rosita he hoped to see more of when he got out—the same Rosita who was hopefully keeping an eye on *Miss Demeanor.*

He maintained his composure, hoping the heat crawling up his back wasn't turning his neck red and giving anything away. He tried to sound unnerved with his response as he shook his head. "No, don't recall her. She *may* have been on the street and saw the cops pick me up . . . I was a little busy at the time."

Weatherhead leaned forward and put both elbows on the desk. "Ya see, the thing is, Costello . . . I've been looking over your file and you seem to be one of the few guys in here that has an IQ that reaches way up there into double numbers. I can see some advantages for us if some college kid comes in here and leaves with a good report. You know, you could put us in a good light with the public. Some positive PR would go a long way with the locals." His tone then became a bit condescending regarding Mario's role in the project. "Why you can talk about how nice our facility is and how well you're being treated by the guards, and when you're all done here, you can tell her how wonderful it feels to be rehabilitated."

It appeared the warden was in favor of the project, but Mario felt if he seemed too anxious, Weatherhead might become suspicious. "Like I said Warden, I'm not really interested." He looked Weatherhead in the eye hoping he'd played the right card.

"That's too bad. The whole idea could've helped you, too, Costello."

"Helped me? How?"

"I get requests like this off and on and I don't usually cuddle up to this kinda thing, but . . ."

"But?"

"Like I said, this could be good for both of us. Let's say if you were to go along with the idea, a favorable report from the university could knock two or three months off your sentence. Combined with the three month reduction for good behavior, you'd be outta here in a year—not to mention the fact that this student's rather easy on the eyes wouldn't you say?"

Mario was silent as he stared at the floor and pretended to ponder the offer. It would certainly be an advantage to have contact with Rosita, but a quick answer might be interpreted the wrong way. "What would I have to do exactly?"

"Apparently just a few interviews. She'll probably come in once a week for a while. I think if we agree to this charade we can pretty much set the terms." Mario said nothing. "So what do you say then? You want to give this thing a go?"

"You said a two or three month reduction on my sentence?"

"Providing the results are positive and you make us look good."

"You give me a guarantee of three months . . . in writing ... with a copy to my attorney and you've got a deal."

Weatherhead hesitated, closed the folder, and tapped the edge of it on his desk. "Okay, Costello. I'll give you the three months. But rest assured, we better come outta this lookin' like we're the Florida Hilton, you got that?"

Mario nodded. "I can do that."

"Then I'll push the paperwork through and work out some kind of a schedule." Weatherhead then instructed the guard to return Mario to his cell.

IT WAS TWO WEEKS before he was brought to the visitor's room. Rosita sat waiting. Unlike the prisons that housed the more hardened criminals, Bower County's visitors' room was filled with tables that allowed inmates to sit and talk without the interruption of a glass partition or use of a telephone. It was congenial, but with no touching. A singular guard oversaw the room, and ceiling cameras were mounted at each end. Despite the "no touching" rule, when wives and girlfriends first arrived, they often leaned over and kissed inmates. Some guards let it go—others gave them a sharp warning.

When Mario neared his table, he alerted Rosita to the cameras by pointing to one of them with his eyes as he sat down. He leaned in as if it was part of his sitting motion, and without moving his lips, whispered. "Don't forget to introduce yourself."

When Rosita did so, she extended her hand but before Mario could take it, the warning came from the guard. "No touching!" he said.

She pulled her hand back and opened her briefcase. She took out a legal pad along with a form that displayed the university's letterhead. She gave Mario a brief explanation of the project and how each psych student was expected to have a final thesis. She was the only student allowed to participate in a study using an inmate making the thesis part of her visit true. She explained the timetable to Mario, telling him the warden had agreed to Saturday meetings during visiting hours.

Mario kept an eye on the guard. If he was bothering to listen, all that was evident was the confirmation that the young woman was there for a college study. In any event, Rosita's appearance lent itself to the guard's visual attention rather than any interest in what was being said.

"I obviously have your name," she continued after the preliminaries. "But I have to fill out this form before we get started. Is that okay?"

Mario nodded, admiring her business-like attitude. Even *he* was beginning to doubt there was anything covert involved.

"Address? When you're not staying here that is."

"I live on my boat," he said.

"That sounds exciting. Where do you keep it?"

His answer was slow in coming. Mario hadn't seen a woman in over two months and Rosita was prettier than he remembered. She was dressed in chino pants and a flowered blouse. The tattooed serpent's head peeked out from her shoulder. Her perfume drifted across the table, and strangely enough, returned him to their first meeting at the Sand Flea Tavern. He focused on her smile, as well as her eyes, that danced while she waited for his answer.

"Well, I used to keep her in the Melbourne Boatyard," he told her. "Although as I told my attorney, she's at the bottom of the river now . . . had a bit of a problem before I was arrested." He gave a forced laugh.

Rosita continued with questions and comments that were strategic and well thought out. As they spoke in code, Mario gained an admiration for her intelligence. During their allowable time, she got the message across that *Miss Demeanor* was where he'd left her. "Your boat's probably fine," she told him. "I'll bet you can salvage it when you get out of here. Was it worth a lot of money?"

He pondered the injection of money into the conversation. Other than the few hundred dollars from his wallet, they never had an opportunity to discuss compensation for her keeping an eye on *Miss Demeanor*. Mario wondered if she was viewing the cash as a down payment. He grew uneasy, but realized he had to be careful not to upset their arrangement. She was fishing for a deal.

"I think the rent for my slip fee was a few hundred a month. Something like that."

"That sounds like a reasonable price for someone to pay . . . for living accommodations, I mean. I guess it's having the peace of mind knowing everything is secure. You do want that peace of mind, right? Perhaps it's better your boat sank. I can't imagine they're paying you any kind of a wage in here, are they? I mean, if you did need to come up with a few hundred a month for someone to keep an eye on it you'd be in a real predicament."

"I have some money set aside," Mario said. "It's just not accessible right now but I'll have access to it when I get out of here."

Rosita rested her chin in both hands and continued to toy with Mario. "Hmmm, that does seem to be a problem." And then she perked up with what seemed to be an AHA moment. "Hey, if you did need some money, maybe a friend on the outside could get the money you set aside and put it in your account here in the commissary. I could check with your financial advisor if you want to give me a name."

If Rosita had been a man, Mario would've risked additional time to reach across the table and administer a strangle hold. The thought of her extorting money to keep an eye on *Miss Demeanor* wasn't in his game plan. Not knowing if she was serious and his enchantment with her beauty were the only things that stopped him.

"It wouldn't be possible," he told her. "No one really knows much about my situation and I really can't access my money until I get released."

"And that will be?"

"If your report goes well, and I expect it will, I can get out of here in about ten months."

"My, that seems like such a long time to be cooped up." This time as she spoke, she pulled down on the bottom of her blouse and revealed a bit of cleavage. "Do you think you can make it that long?" The question was teasing and a smile played on her lips. "Of course," she continued, "if you have to wait until you get out of here to access your money I would expect a certain amount of interest will accrue."

"I'm sure you're right," Mario said. His body heat rose from his anger and his fist became visibly clenched. "Unfortunately, I'm not sure what the current rate of interest might be. Maybe you could tell me what you think."

"I guess if you were figuring say . . . four hundred a month, the ten months would make it four thousand. With interest . . ." Rosita paused and jotted the number five-thousand on her pad, circled it, and spun it around for Mario to read.

He glared at the figure and then exhaled. "You understand then, that would be paid *after* I get out . . . and the boat is as I left it."

"Let's say, the *day* you get out, shall we?"

Mario gave an affirmative nod toward the figure on the pad. He realized the importance of securing a suitable overseer of *Miss Demeanor,* and once he exchanged the diamonds with Cohen, he could certainly afford five grand.

When the interview ended, Mario returned to his cell knowing *Miss Demeanor* was still anchored where he'd left her. Rosita had been checking her every day and now would continue to do so with the understanding there was five-thousand dollars at the end of her tunnel.

Rosita wondered if his willingness to pay for *Miss Demeanor's* protection was a sign of the boat's value or if he had other reasons—reasons he seemed reluctant to discuss. It appeared his only goal was to keep the boat sequestered. Rosita had ten months to find out why.

23

Two weeks into his stay, Andy sat with a letter from his aunt tucked in his back pocket. His morning routine had evolved into taking a cup of coffee to the beach and pondering the day ahead. It was often followed by a ride from Ollie to Sebastian Inlet. Since the two met at the 911 Club, they had become close. Ollie was a guy who needed nothing more than a surfboard and a joint to be happy. Andy enjoyed the company of the born-and-raised Floridian and often sat on the beach reading while Ollie sat bobbing on his board waiting for the perfect wave. Today, however, he needed a bit of alone time to think and had declined the invitation.

In Maine, he usually spent time observing the ocean from the cockpit of a sailboat. But since arriving in Florida, his view from the beach offered a different perspective. He sipped his coffee and watched large boats in the distance. Most were making long journeys to specific destinations while smaller boats were day sailing in whatever direction the wind took them. In addition to boat watching, his morning entertainment was often provided by the antics of sandpipers. They chased the waves into the sea and then stood pecking at food until the ocean came crashing back to force their retreat. The only missing ingredient in his stay was, quite obviously, a sailboat. "I'm sloopless," he told Ollie on more than one occasion. "I need to get me a boat."

But it was not a day to worry about getting a sailboat. It was a day to ponder the recent letter from his aunt. He retrieved it from his pocket and read it a second time. It was certainly a letter having the potential for ruining his planned winter vacation. He scanned it again to confirm the message. It was the first letter she had sent since his arrival. It started with her reiterating the comments she made on the phone. She was relieved that he got there safely and hoped he was enjoying the warm weather. It continued with the usual chat about Connecticut getting its share of snow. It was the second half of the letter that caused the dismay. Other than her tactful reminder of his agreement to do some minor repairs around the house, she wrote her recollection that the roof needed new shingles.

A check for five-hundred dollars was enclosed along with a Post-it note asking him to "please keep all receipts as I'll need them for my taxes," and "if you need more than this, let me know."

Since arriving, his tool boxes had been unloaded and moved into the garage but had yet to be opened. His initial survey of the house provided him with a mental list of what needed to be done and the length of time needed for each job. Knowing they were one or two day tasks, he planned to take care of them when convenient, leaving time for a leisurely three months in the sun. Shingling a roof under a baking Florida sun was not part of his game plan. Additionally, he feared the enclosed check would not cover the cost of materials and he knew his aunt's fixed income left her strapped for cash. Asking her for more seemed a bit skewed since he was given the cottage rent free.

He would need help and while his new best friend Ollie was always cordial and willing to give advice, it was far from being a friendship that allowed for having him carry bundles of shingles up a ladder in lieu of surfing. After all, Ollie made no secret of the fact that he made an easy living selling pot. Andy had been made aware of his friend's lifestyle since the scene he witnessed at the 911 Club the day he arrived. When the surf wasn't quite to his liking, the two spent time at Ollie's apartment or at Harry Berry's—a bar that catered to the arts and entertainment crowd.

The owner claimed to be a distant relative of the vaudeville performer, Harry Berry, whose band consisted of seven female musicians known as *The Sunkist Vanities* and their dog *Fanny*. Patrons were greeted in the entryway by a life-sized 1942 poster of the vaudevillians advertising the act as "One hour and twenty minutes of fast, clean, entertainment."

The bar was more or less Ollie's place of business and at night he got phone calls from customers that were filtered through the bartender. It wasn't the type of place that fit Ollie's personality, but most of the clientele were artists, musicians, or actors who were discreet and had the ability to pay for their dope up front. They were certainly a classier clientele than those who visited his apartment.

Ollie's bungalow had a different atmosphere. The coffee table in the living room was usually embellished with a good-sized bong, an open baggie with a few buds, and a variety of other drug-related paraphernalia. When people dropped by, Ollie seemed to be unnerved by the presence of any of it and most guests seemed to be comfortable filling the bong and firing it up without invitation. The smoking was usually followed by a trip to his bedroom where an exchange of money was made for various amounts of pot. He also had several organ transplant containers, similar to the one used the day he drove to the 911 Club. The containers lined one wall of his room and were arranged by size. Different sizes were used in conjunction with what organ someone needed transplanted. The corresponding containers designated the weight, dope strength, and price. Sales in the bedroom were semi-discreet but it was difficult for Andy to miss the transactions. When clients reappeared in the living room, they were usually making feeble attempts to conceal their purchase. Most wore T-shirts and shorts, and being stoned, often had difficulty finding a pocket.

ANDY SET THE LETTER down and pictured Ollie sitting among other surfers waiting for the wave that would allow his body to become "one with the board" as he put it. He thought about the statement the bartender at the 911 Club had made saying if he ever needed anything, Ollie was the person with connections. After reading the letter a final time and deliberating his options, he called Ollie at his apartment and caught him before his afternoon siesta.

"Shingle the roof!" he yelled into the phone. "She wants me to shingle the freakin' roof!"

"Did she give you a budget?" Ollie's question was filled with his usual calm. His "Zenness" he called it.

"She sent a check for five-hundred but that's certainly not going to cover it. She said to let her know if I need more but she doesn't have that kind of money."

"Okay then," Ollie said. "Not to worry . . . I know a guy."

◆ ## pedros plumming

A few days after the phone call to Ollie, Andy was fixing his morning cup of coffee and heard a thunderous noise in the driveway. His first thought was the Wednesday trash collection had been changed for some reason. When he checked the window, a large flatbed truck was backing into the yard. The cab was painted a dull orange which initially camouflaged the numerous areas of rust. Smoke billowed from the exhaust pipe that dangled and made occasional scrapes on the blacktop. Hand-painted lettering on the door of the cab covered faded letters that had been painted over—presumably the name of the previous owner.

The new lettering read *Pedros Plumming*. The misspelled words were linked together with an oversized letter P with *edros and lumming* following after it. The letters were a dark gray, varied in size and displayed obvious brush strokes. As Andy studied the sign, he thought of his mother and smiled. She taught ninth grade English at Boothbay High School and he had been weaned on *Warriner's English Grammar and Composition*. Despite the omission of an apostrophe and the letter "b" in plumbing, he knew how pleased she would be if she was there to see the sign's author had at least known enough to double the consonant before adding the "ing."

After maneuvering the vehicle to a near miss into the fence, the driver switched off the ignition and emerged from the cab. Andy had already made his exit from the house and was prepared to give directions to a guy who was perhaps lost.

The driver was a heavy-set man and beamed a knowing smile when he saw Andy approaching. A singular gold tooth sat adjacent to a large empty space on one side of his mouth while the teeth on the other side searched for different directions—indicating he would've benefitted from braces during his childhood. Andy immediately thought of "Jimmy the Gasser."

"You get shingles?" the driver asked, holding up a piece of paper. His eyes darted back and forth from the paper and the house as he searched for matching numbers.

Andy's glance moved from the gold tooth to the flatbed. The truck was loaded with stacks of shingles, roofing nails, strips of flashing, and other materials—all the items that were on the list Andy had given Ollie. As Ollie's patented phrase of, *I know a guy* rang in his ears he stood staring at the Pedros Plumming sign. Obviously, this was *the guy*. A guy who was either a plumber making a few bucks on the side or a guy who sold shingles and was using a friend's truck. He was certainly a fitting encore to "Jimmy the Gasser." Andy realized his second experience with a guy Ollie knew was about to begin. He stared at Pedro and then rubbed his tongue against his new filling. Jimmy had come through and the new filling seemed to be holding.

Ollie had given Andy a very low price for the materials and forewarned him of an eventual delivery. He now realized he should have expected nothing less than Pedro and his plumbing truck. Andy decided it was probably best not to think about where the materials came from or their method of delivery.

"Yeah, roofing materials go here," Andy told Pedro.

"You got cash, yes?"

As per Ollie's instructions, Andy had cash. "I've got cash," he said.

"Where you want I put these?" The question was followed by another friendly smile.

"Can you put half here and half on the other side of the house?" Andy combined hand gestures with the question as Pedro's English seemed limited. Whether it was the verbal instructions or the gestures, Andy wasn't sure, but the hearty grin remained. "Okay, okay, some here, some there," he said.

Andy continued to gesture as he talked, and motioning to his shorts, explaining he would change into other clothes and help him unload the truck.

"No okay," Pedro said. "I put some here and some there. You go inside." This time it was Pedro who was gesturing and letting Andy know he understood and could handle the unloading. "I put some here and some there, and then *you* put on roof, si?" Pedro's laugh that followed indicated he realized Andy had a lot more work to do when he left.

"Okay, si," Andy said.

From inside the house, he watched Pedro open the other door of the cab. Two children got out. A girl, perhaps twelve, and a boy—two or three years younger—most likely her brother. Empty pallets were placed on the ground where Andy had indicated and the three worked to fill them. Pedro set bundle after bundle of shingles close to the edge of the truck and the kids each took an end as if they were carrying a stretcher. Methodically, they piled the bundles on the pallets with precision. Andy noticed the girl was particularly picky if a bundle was askew. When they reached the halfway point, Pedro fired up the truck, disturbing nearby neighbors a second time, and moved it to where the remainder of the bundles was to be placed.

When Andy saw they were about finished, he went outside carrying three cans of Pepsi.

"I thought you could use these," he said.

Pedro eyed the sodas and beamed another smile. He then put his arm around the girl's shoulder and began introductions. "These are my helpers," he said with a voice bursting with pride. "This is my daughter Louisa. She's actually the supervisor, and this is my son Manny."

Andy handed each a can. The children's faces and arms gleamed with sweat as they reached for them. Their looks of appreciation were evidence that a Pepsi was an unexpected treat. Pedro took the remaining can as he pulled a handkerchief from a back pocket and wiped his forehead. "We thank you for these," he said, lifting his can. "What do you two say to the gentleman?" Andy was given two more thank-yous and then Pedro scurried them back to the truck.

"Ollie said two-hundred, right?" Andy fanned out ten twenty-dollar bills.

"Si, two hundred. You need more stuff, you call Ollie. He knows me."

Pedro climbed into the truck and fired up the engine. This time Andy noticed curtains moving in the house across the street. The gears ground into reverse and the truck from Pedros Plumming backed out of the driveway. The kids in the cab waved through the crack in the windshield, and in the same manner the truck had arrived, it rumbled down the highway leaving a cloud of black smoke.

♦

25

Shortly after Pedro's delivery, Ollie arrived—indicating he'd been kept apprised of the entire schedule. He sat at the kitchen table and rolled a joint while Andy made coffee and fried up some eggs. While Andy cooked, Ollie worked on a drawing of a map of A1A which emphasized the location of Andy's house. When finished he stuffed it into his pocket. They shared the eggs and Ollie fired up the joint to go with their second cup of coffee. Andy gave a detailed account of Pedro and the delivery of the shingles.

"I'm a bit surprised Mike used Pedro for the delivery," Ollie said.

"Mike?"

"Yeah. He's one of the guys I do business with but I didn't realize Pedro was still in the area." He took another sip of coffee followed by a toke on the joint. This time, when he spoke, his voice was cracked as he attempted to hold in the smoke. "So, now we need to get those shingles on."

Andy was taken aback by the offer of Ollie to actually help shingle the roof. "I was going to wait until a cooler day," Andy said. "It's supposed to be really hot all week."

"Don't worry about it. This isn't a job you have to do, man. We'll fix a couple of cups of coffee for the road and I'll take you over and introduce you to Mike. Mike runs the labor pool in town. Don't worry, he's cool."

Before leaving, Ollie tore open a wrapper on a bundle of shingles and threw one in his jeep. "We need to make a stop at the liquor store on the way. There's one next door to Publix Market."

At the liquor store, Andy was instructed to get a bottle of tequila and to make sure it was Cuervo Gold. Equipped with the shingle and the bottle of Cuervo, Ollie drove out toward North Palm Avenue to a less populated area of Melbourne. He pulled in behind a grocery store and shut off the engine. A small man sat out back at a picnic table under the protection of an umbrella. He was tapping his hand on the table to the beat of the music flowing from the back door of the store. Ollie waved and held up the brown bag that shielded the bottle of tequila. The man waved back and then approached.

"Lookin' for Mike," Ollie told him. "Is he around?"

"He's in the store. You want him out here or you want to go inside? I can get him."

"Yeah. Ask him to come out would ya?"

The man left, and within minutes a tall man appeared from the store. He was thin, and as he walked to the jeep Andy noticed he wore a face that exhibited a life of hard times. His worn features were dark and sharp. Ollie handed him the tequila. The man pulled it half way out of the bag, and seeing the label, gave Ollie an approving grin. He twisted the top off and took a long swallow.

Ollie put his hand on Andy's shoulder. "This is my amigo, Andy," he told Mike. Andy and Mike recognized each other with nods.

"His house," Ollie continued. "His . . . ah . . . his casa . . . new roof." He then reached behind Andy's seat and pulled out the shingle, as he made a hammering motion.

"Crew," Ollie said. "Tomorrow . . . Mañana . . . Andy's casa."

The tall man took another pull from the bottle. "Si, tomorrow."

"Small roof," Ollie said, using his hands to make what looked like a small box . . . as if the man had any idea what he meant. He again pointed to the shingle. "Cinco amigos."

"Si . . . cinco amigos. Tomorrow." The man stood grinning. Ollie retrieved the map he'd made and handed it to Mike who studied it at length.

Ollie pointed to the house number on the paper. "House numero, okay?"

"Si . . . okay. Tomorrow," and then he made the same hammering motion. "Cinco amigos tomorrow," he added.

Ollie turned to Andy. "Let me have a twenty."

Andy fished out a twenty and Ollie showed it to Tequila Mike. He then held his hand open and touched each finger and his thumb with the bill as he counted. "Unos, dos, tres, cuatro, cinco. Cinco amigos . . . este . . . una dayo," he said, using his own rough brand of Spanish to let Mike know it was a one day affair. He held the twenty up again presumably indicating each man was worth a twenty.

"Si, si, okay, okay." Mike now seemed to be the one irritated at the idea that Ollie was being condescending regarding the task.

They drove out of the alley and Andy remained quiet for the first fifty yards before saying anything. "Am I to understand you just hired five guys to shingle my aunt's roof?"

"Yeah, twenty bucks each. Don't worry, Mike's cool. Plus, after materials and paying these guys, you still got two-hundred left of your aunt's money right? And now I've introduced you to Tequila Mike. He may not speak much English, but he rules a work force that's second to none. If you ever need him for anything, he knows you now and you know where to find him. Just make sure you bring the tequila. He doesn't meet if there's no bottle. He'll also want a twenty for himself when the job's done. Just give it to the foreman."

"How do I know who the foreman is?"

"He's the guy who'll have his hand out for the money when they finish the job. Just tell him the extra twenty is for Mike. He'll be expecting it anyway."

"So now I spend tomorrow on a hot roof supervising guys who don't speak any English?"

"That's where you're wrong, my friend."

"What do you mean?"

"You're not going to be on any roof tomorrow. I'm sick of hearing you moon over not having a sailboat so tomorrow we're goin' out to sea."

"You tellin' me you finally found a guy with a boat?"

"No man, no boat. It's time you learned how to surf!"

IN THE WEEKS THAT followed, Andy and Ollie spent most days together. The crew sent by Tequila Mike completed the roof in just less than two days and Andy gave each worker an extra ten dollars. They had done an outstanding job and it gave Andy confidence in other guys Ollie knew—each having a name which fit their identity or their individual skill. Guys like Rembrandt, who painted houses and was called in to take care of the exterior trim. He scraped, sanded, primed and painted with the patience of Job for the cost of what Andy had expected to pay for paint. Ollie introduced him to "Bobby the Clipper" who came once a week with two other guys and the three of them took care of mowing the lawn, edging the walkway, and trimming the shrubs.

Most of the guys Ollie knew were hired through Tequila Mike, who always took his bottle of Cuervo and a twenty dollar cut. They spoke very little English, never had real names, and were more than likely in need of a green card. Through it all, Andy asked no questions. The work done was always top-notch and inexpensive. He often returned from the beach at the end of a day and broke out a six-pack to share a cold beer with whoever was working on the house. Communication was kept to a minimum, but the men were always grateful and pleasant to be around.

Three months flew by quickly, but when it was time for Andy to pack his belongings and return to Maine his aunt's house was, as promised, in pristine condition. He took several photographs of the exterior along with a few pictures of work that had been done in the master bathroom.

The tiler's resumé was brief. "The guy does great work . . . he's like a cosmetologist of tiling," Ollie told him.

Of course being on his knees during much of his tile laying profession, and his chubbiness forcing his pants to slip down, he was known among local contractors as "Joey Ass Crack." But like all the guys Ollie knew, Joey Ass Crack did good work. When the job was completed, it was more than Andy had hoped for. His own skills were limited to carpentry and he admired the facelift Joey had given the shower.

During his entire stay, his only forfeiture of enjoyment had been the lack of sailing. Despite the fact that Ollie always knew a guy, his contacts with sailors and boats seemed to be limited. Andy's complaints of being boatless during the three months received little sympathy and Ollie had only managed to get him one day of sailing. It had been a twenty-four footer in need of much repair.

The night before departing for Maine, Andy and Ollie sat in Harry Berry's reminiscing about their time together. Andy recalled experiences with guys Ollie knew and they shared laughs over Andy's awkwardness on a surfboard. It was a mutual hope that Andy would return the following winter to allow them to pick up where they were leaving off.

"When your aunt sees all the work you did on the house and how great it looks, how can she deny you, man?" Ollie's tone was encouraging.

"Yeah, well, I don't want to lie to her so I'll have to explain very carefully as to how the work was done and who did it, if you know what I mean. Besides, if her health is better she may opt to come down here herself."

With a long day to follow, Andy called it a night. The two shook hands and embraced. Ollie pulled a joint from somewhere and slipped it into Andy's hand. "A special doobie," he said. "Fire it up when you're drivin' through one of those redneck states you're goin' through."

The following morning, before leaving the peninsula, Andy made a brief stop at Douglas Park for one last look at the abandoned boat. It had remained where he first saw it for the entire time he'd been there. Algae had formed on the waterline and seemed to be creeping up the anchor rode. He had checked it often during his stay and now felt a certain kinship to the sloop. His continuous thoughts of her phantom owner and mysterious past had remained with him since that first sighting. He snapped several photos before driving away, and during his trip back and the months to follow, he often thought of her.

If he did return for a second winter, he was not about to allow for a repeat performance of reading on the beach or falling off a surf board. Another winter meant the procurement of a boat. He intended to spend his days sailing. And if by chance . . . some very strange chance . . . nothing changed in this slow-moving place called Florida, he knew exactly where to find one.

26

Rosita stood in the dim light of morning and surveyed her reflection. It was a challenge to dress in a manner conservative enough to appease prison officials, yet seductive enough to have Mario notice her. It was the third month into her weekly visitations to Bower County Correctional and she wanted to look nice. Saturday mornings had become routine for the two of them and she enjoyed their time together.

The drive from Melbourne Beach to the prison was just under an hour. Before leaving the peninsula she pulled into Dunkin' Donuts for coffee. Donnie was working the drive-thru and told her the coffee was on the house. He was one of several teenaged co-workers who fantasized about her. His inquiry as to where she was headed went unanswered. As she drove to Bower, she sipped her coffee and glanced at her briefcase, the contents of which would allow her to actually touch Mario when she arrived.

From the first visit, the pair played their roles to perfection. Guards were aware of the warden-sanctioned study. Her growing familiarity with prison officials, combined with her charm and beauty, bought her an acquired trust. She and Mario found their game involving covert activities quite humorous.

During visits, she injected code phrases into their conversations. Statements such as, "the movers haven't shown up yet," or "my company still hasn't come." The statements let Mario know that *Miss Demeanor* was still anchored where he'd left her or no one had paid her a visit. The comments took place during the first ten or fifteen minutes of each visit. As Rosita dispensed information regarding the boat's status, the embedded language was mentally transposed. Although anything overheard by nearby inmates or the duty guard went unnoticed, Mario always seemed to show signs of relief knowing *Miss Demeanor* was safe.

Once the information was passed along, the remainder of the time was used for Mario's responses to questionnaires or performing problem-solving tasks for her psychological profiling. The instruments compiled data for Rosita's thesis, and with each new procedure she discovered Mario's intelligence level and problem solving abilities went far deeper than the façade he put forth. He continued to demonstrate an ease of accomplishment as she assigned him increasingly difficult challenges. She no longer viewed him as the man she met on a bar stool in the Sand Flea Tavern—the man she witnessed being thrown to the sidewalk by police before they cuffed him and dragged him off to jail. As they worked together each week, a progressive understanding of their personalities, thoughts, and feelings emerged with all of it spilling onto the table.

Whether it was the development of their relationship as psychologist and patient, counselor and client, or barstool companions at the Sand Flea Tavern was unknown, but any business arrangement between the two regarding being paid to keep a watchful eye on *Miss Demeanor* had fallen by the wayside. Whatever the reason, their time together fused them into a trusting relationship and it was something they both needed.

Rosita's plan for the day's visit was to begin administering one of the subtests of the WASI—an instrument for measuring intelligence. The test would require Mario to arrange red and white cubes on the table top and recreate illustrated patterns. In this case, it meant the prohibited crossing of the blue line—the line that ran down the center of the table to ensure nothing was ever passed between a visitor and an inmate. Wives, girlfriends, mothers, daughters, siblings—it made no difference; touching was prohibited at the table and it was a regulation that had no flexibility.

Mario lived for Saturdays and with each meeting he became more anxious for his release. He was no longer content to sit across from her as a convicted felon. He viewed the blue line with contempt. He wanted to touch her . . . hold her . . . to shower her with kisses . . . to be the reason for her contagious smile. He wanted to sail away with her to unchartered islands where they could run naked on a beach and make love under the stars.

It was the blue line regulation prohibiting any tactile show of affection in the prison's restricted environment that brought them together—as if prison officials were playing the role of concerned parents attempting to keep love-struck teenagers apart—all of it making their inability for physical touching a catalyst for their emerging feelings.

For all intents and purposes, the blue line was to be observed the same way a goal line was seen on a football field. The imaginary plane extended upward, and if broken in a football game, the result is a touchdown. In the visitors' room, however, to break the plane meant expulsion. The explanation was clearly outlined in the **M**anual **O**f **R**egulations for **V**isitors or, as Rosita referred to it, the book of **MORV**. Regulation number 2.a on page four clearly stated that visitors passing *anything* over the line risked losing all rights of visitation. The book was given to guests prior to their first visit along with a form to be signed and returned stating they had read and understood the two-hundred and eighty-four pages. The book of MORV referred to the center line as the *yellow line,* but following its first printing, the yellow line was deemed loud and offensive and the Board of Prison Officials agreed to have it repainted. The new color was "Ocean Blue" a reflection of Warden Weatherhead's wife's selection from the color chart at Home Depot.

In Mario's case, Rosita was allowed to cross the blue line within the warden's established parameters when she passed test materials. She was to spread the items on the table, push herself back, and announce she was "crossing testing materials." The guard then glanced over to make a visual inspection, and with the authority of a Vegas pit boss, nod his approval. Only then was she to slide items across the blue line to within Mario's reach.

Rosita enjoyed such crossings. It was her one opportunity to touch Mario—a brief touch—but a touching just the same. During their very first passing, she slid her hands over the line as she pushed materials toward him. When his hands reached for them, she extended her little fingers and touched his wrists. It was a touch she let linger before she slid her fingers down the length of each of his hands . . . reluctant to let go of the moment. It was a move she had since perfected and Mario noticed the lingering. Her slow withdrawal became a moment of risk for each of them—a moment of defiance as they chanced a reprimand from the guard. Their eyes always locked, confirming the message of their mutual affection. It was Mario's only physical contact with Rosita during his incarceration and they were touches he cherished.

WHEN ROSITA ENTERED THE visitors' area that morning, her greeting was cordial, but professional. Her handbag was checked at the point of entry, but as agreed, her briefcase was allowed through. Pens were not permitted, and one of her two pencils was confiscated with a reminder that she would be checked in the exit area to ensure the other left with her. Her appearance was modest as suggested in the book of MORV. Apparently, conservative dress eliminated inmates getting overly excited by the site of women in skimpily clad attire. Since her first visit, she also wore tops with sleeves that covered her tattoo.

Rosita never missed a week, and as the two sat, separated by the blue line, they always used their entire allotment of time. As their trust in each other grew, Mario talked about his childhood, his questionable past, and his unforeseen future. He told Rosita about growing up in Cotuit, Massachusetts. How his father, a lobsterman, lost an arm while hauling up traps and how the incident left him wallowing in self-pity. His father turned to the local tavern for comfort, and although he had always been a womanizer, the trait became more profound after the accident, perhaps to assure himself that a man with only one arm could still score with the ladies. Between his hours on the boat and his time at the bar, there was little left for a home life. His father's bitterness reached its peak when Mario was twelve. He became belligerent, took up with a local whore, and was physically abusive to Mario's mother.

Rumors of the torrid affair filled the small town of Cotuit, and on a warm summer night his father and the whore stepped onto the lobster boat and motored off into the sunset. The desertion scarred Mario and made future adversaries of such men—men who drank too much and took advantage of women—men like Hanson. During his self-revealing talks with Rosita, he realized how many of his actions imitated the drinking and barroom fights of his father. The act of being a womanizer, however, was a trait he had never adopted. After his father left, Mario became very protective of his mother and as he got older he felt obligated to protect any woman being disrespected. He realized it was that commitment, often combined with drinking, that led to his hot-headed behavior. The same behavior listed as *aggravated assaults* on his record.

As he talked about himself, Rosita became intrigued by the man on the opposite side of the blue line. She began to understand him and see another side of the man who owned nothing more than a boat—a boat for which he had paid money to keep secret—and she wanted to know why.

♦ **dog days of summer**

During the return drive to Maine, Andy made a brief stop in Connecticut to apprise his aunt of her requested renovations on the cottage. His descriptions were accompanied by photographs, and as he disliked the idea of lying to her, he chose his words carefully. He included a vague acknowledgement of his occasional solicitation of advice from local contractors. He even pointed out that, not having done much tiling himself, he hired a professional to do the work needed in the master bath. He was careful in the telling and avoided mentioning the name "Joey Ass Crack." He stayed to share a cup of tea and homemade lemon cookies and their discussion led to his aunt's deliberation on what to do with the beach house.

She always had a tendency to think out loud, as if to get others input. "I just don't have the desire to travel anymore," she told him. "I don't want to sell it just yet and if I keep it, I'll have to have someone go down there and look after it again next year . . . you know . . . do a few other things that need doing. It's not good to just let it sit unattended. And of course I don't feel right continuing to ask you, Andy. You've got your own life to live with your friends up in Maine."

The comment was made with his aunt's flavor of total honesty. There were no hints of deception or prompting of an acceptance by Andy to fulfill any obligation to an old woman in despair. In fear she might possibly forget making the statement, he jumped on the opportunity to have another winter on the beach.

"It won't interfere with my plans at all," he told her. "I'm actually enjoying some flex time before I dive into a full time career. I figure once I get started with whatever I plan to do with my degree, I'll be tied down for quite a while. I probably won't have time to travel or do anything."

Accepting her offer, however, did alter his plans. A return to Florida the following winter certainly eliminated employment at home that required a long-term commitment. His desire to design and build boats for a prestigious company would have to be put on hold for an additional year. His aunt, knowing her beach house would be in the best of hands, was delighted that he was willing to take on another winter.

His April return to Maine proved timely. Work in the Boothbay boatyard was plentiful. Moorings overseen by the harbor master had to be inspected and secured after the long winter, dry docked boats were unwrapped and hoisted from their cradles, slips were prepared for both local owners and transients, and a myriad of tasks that went with the season needed to be performed. Andy, having grown up working on the Boothbay schooner captained by his father, had worked for the harbor master during his summer vacations while at Maine Maritime. He was well liked and had many friends in the area which made procuring employment an easy task. He not only knew his way around the yard, but was experienced with the heavy equipment and the day-to-day operations.

Work days in spring involved long hours. Boats were lifted into the water and towed to moorings. The store in the boatyard was flooded with owners needing everything from chocks and cleats to life vests and flare guns. Many were experienced sailors who could fend for themselves while others were unsure if starboard meant the front or the back of the boat. In short, preparing for the boating season involved two months of fast-paced action in both the yard and the marina's store before Andy was ushered into June.

Eventually, the full-time clients had their boats secured to their moorings and work settled into a routine. Owners often hired Andy to tune their rigging and do a general refurbishing of the brass or teak. Others, who purchased an old boat or had left a boat unattended for a season, hired him to do extensive repairs. Andy was in his element, and while completing those jobs he often thought of the refurbishing needed on the boat that sat anchored on the Indian River.

In July, old friends dropped by towing day sailers, and former classmates from the Academy often sailed into the harbor on larger boats. Offers to go sailing were in abundance and invitations were readily accepted. It was a summer that combined working, sailing, and partying. He often thought of Ollie and how he would've enjoyed this carefree life. He considered that it may have been Ollie's influence that put his professional career on hold while he took some time for himself.

On the other hand, it may have been attributed to the arrival of his boyhood friend Frankie. Andy and Frankie had not only grown up together, they had raced J-Boats through high school. After graduation, their paths changed when Frankie's father insisted he carry on the family tradition of attending Harvard. He was from a family that had more money than he could ever spend, and after fulfilling his father's prerequisite for life, he sailed *Carpe Diem,* his father's forty-foot Hinckley, into Boothbay Harbor and announced he was there for the summer.

For Frankie, however, the boat was more of a living accommodation than a form of recreation. Once the Hinckley was put on a mooring, she remained there unless coaxed by others—usually Andy—to take her out. On those occasions, Frankie could usually be found below deck with a gin and tonic in one hand while his other groped a bikini-clad female. He slurred clichéd lawyer jokes while the drink spilled into the bikini top and then apologetically swooped down to lick the gin from the cleavage. The summer was Frankie's last hurrah before taking his highly-paid anointed position at his father's law firm. Any women he was with on Carpe Diem were, more than likely, vying for the position of becoming Mrs. Frankie.

Shortly after Frankie arrived, Andy met Evelyn. She was with a small group who came on board for a rare day of putting out to sea. Like Andy, she had a passion for sailing and the two became one for the remainder of the summer. They had a knack for teaming up and getting Frankie inebriated enough to drop the Hinckley off her mooring and actually sail her. Being a well known party boat, *Carpe Diem* never had a shortage of crew members, although many paid the price for mixing too much alcohol with sailing.

At summer's end, owners had their boats pulled for the winter and Andy reversed the process used in April. He worked into November and finished up just prior to the Thanksgiving holiday, which he spent with Evelyn and her family. Before returning to Florida, he cut and stacked firewood and made preparations for the long winter his parents were about to face. He looked forward to seeing Ollie again and sharing new adventures that seemed to follow his friend and guys he knew.

After ringing in 2013, he said his good-bye to Evelyn and climbed into the same minivan that had made the trip a year earlier. He took three days to make the trip, and during the drive he not only thought of Ollie, but of the sloop that sat anchored on the Indian River. He wondered what might have happened to her . . . if it was possible she was still there . . . sitting unattended . . . waiting for a captain to sail her. It was not to be a second year of standing on a beach while he looked through binoculars and watched others sailing.

Ollie's burner phone was unreachable, and knowing he systematically replaced it, Andy concluded he had tossed it for a new one. In a last ditch effort Andy called Harry Berry's to check and see if, by chance, the bartender knew Ollie's whereabouts. If Ollie could confirm the Indian River sloop was still there, he planned to track down the owner and perhaps trade a bit of work in exchange for some sailing time. The phone conversation with the bartender was brief. He remembered Andy and gave him a warm greeting but had no news regarding Ollie. "Not here, Andy," he said. "He came in a few times after the night you left and I haven't seen him since. I don't know what happened to him. He probably took up residence on a barstool somewhere else. His type likes to move around if you know what I mean."

Andy reflected on the last night he and Ollie spent at Harry Berry's. They shared beers while they relived their three months and stole glances at Kentucky beating Kansas in the final game of March Madness. Now the lack of any contact caused Andy concern regarding the whereabouts of his friend.

Other than thoughts of the boat and his missing friend, the drive was uneventful. This year there was no loss of a filling—although when he drove through Georgia and saw the billboards advertising *The Finest Pecan Pie*, his tongue instinctively rubbed across his filling. He thought about "Jimmy the Gasser" and smiled.

sweet vanilla

While Andy rang in the New Year in Boothbay Harbor, Mario stared at the ceiling of his cell. His skin was damp from the heavy air that always seemed to hang within the concrete walls. As he lay naked on his bunk, his first thought was of the thirty days remaining on his sentence. A thought that was interrupted as he and the other cons had their stillness shattered by sirens in nearby cities and towns sounding their welcome to 2013.

It was his second consecutive year to be locked in a cell for the event. Unlike the previous year, there was no entertainment by comical drunks or transvestites. Nights in Bower Correctional were quiet. The only sounds heard after lights out were the snores of inmates in concert with the clang of heavy gated doors and muffled conversations from the guard station. Occasionally a quiet tune drifted from a radio until it was silenced or confiscated.

By day most cells displayed pictures of wives, or girlfriends, or family members. At night they became unrecognizable blotches on the cell walls. Mario had no pictures, knowing a photo of Rosita would be seen as inappropriate, possibly suspicious. She was recognized as a college student and he was her research project, and as agreed, his sentence had been reduced by three months for his cooperation in her psychological study.

Mario continued to remain under the watchful eye of Silo. Recently, however, Silo had formed a friendship with a Ravi Shankar wannabe and had learned to meditate. The meditation seemed to offer some relief for his continued depression over killing the night watchman. He often meditated during yard breaks, and when he sat in his cross-legged posture, his enormous size injected a bit of comic relief to the act. His strength, of course, dissuaded any comments from fellow cons.

After learning the technique, he passed the practice on to Mario who also found it to be a form of relaxation. When the signal was given for "lights out," he often used the technique to help him drift off. Unlike Silo, he began with thoughts of Rosita. Her visit a few days earlier had been good. After the usual round of coded information regarding *Miss Demeanor*, she administered a small amount of testing before a bit of casual conversation. Their talk eventually turned to his usual standby—his other means of escape—which was sailing. New Year's Eve was no different. It was the discussion that week about his childhood and his first boat.

"I guess you could say it all started with *Sweet Vanilla*," he told her.

"Sweet Vanilla?"

"Yeah. She was my first boat, and how sweet she was," he reminisced. It was the thought of the visit that caused his mind to drift and return him to his childhood. He felt the tiller of *Sweet Vanilla* in his hand and the wind fingering his hair as he began to meditate about the first day he sailed her. It was a hot day in August . . . skimming across Cotuit Bay . . . the mainsail holding that perfect arc as she heeled over and the rhythmic spray of salt water washed his face and bare chest. He licked the droplets from his lips and tasted the freedom. He knew immediately the boat had been worth the four weeks of back-breaking labor he and his two friends had endured to get her.

"BEIN' AS YOUNG AS you are, I can't legally pay you boys a salary," Mr. Turner told them. "But if you want to put in some hours every day for a month or so, I've got an old sailing dinghy out back I could let you have. It's a fourteen-footer. She needs a bit of work, but I'm sure you fellas could get 'er shipshape in no time. You could probably have some fun with it once you got her up and sailing."

The three arrived at Turner's brickyard six days each week and piled bricks and concrete blocks onto pallets that sat waiting for the forklift to raise them onto Mr. Turner's flatbed. Cape Cod boomed with construction that summer and work in the brickyard never let up. The days were long and hot and Mario and his friends loaded pallets into the dead heat of afternoons and then biked to the ocean to plunge into the salty water to erase the brick-red dust from their arms and faces.

Two or three times each week they journeyed to the back area of the yard and surveyed the boat that was soon to be their reward. It was perched upside down on sawhorses, high enough to stoop under and get their heads up inside it. Their conversations echoed within the chamber as they inspected their treasure and discussed the renovations they would make and where they would get the necessary materials.

It was a sailing dory that had been there for years and was well beyond the time of shipshape rehab Mr. Turner indicated. The agreement, however, was made sight unseen—not that seeing it would've made any difference. A boat of their own in any condition was worth toiling with bricks for the month of August, and when their weeks of hard labor ended, Mr. Turner was true to his word. On their last day of work, he presented them with a sheet of paper that confirmed their ownership.

"Can't give you a bill of sale," he said. "Like I told you, you're too young for me to hire you on here, but this paper says the boat's yours. It's all fair and square." As an aside, he pointed to a notation at the bottom of the page that stated the boat was to be removed from the property within seven days.

None of the boys realized their deal to provide four weeks of labor for Mr. Turner's boat was also a strategy to get the eyesore off his property. The three stared at the document, pleased to see the Turner Brickyard letterhead at the top. It seemed to make the transaction more official. There they stood, the proud owners of a fourteen-foot sailing vessel. At the very bottom of the document, in small letters, Mr. Turner had hand-written the words "as is," evidently an afterthought on his part.

Along with the letter, he handed Mario a small tobacco tin. "I was over checking out the boat the other day," he said. "I found this tin wedged up between the bow and the seat. I guess since it was in the boat, it belongs to you boys." He rattled it before handing it to Mario. It was an old tin labeled Sweet Vanilla, an old brand of tobacco. Mario and his friends opened it and found an assortment of bills and some loose change that totaled exactly thirty dollars. "It was in the boat so I guess it's yours," Turner repeated.

When Mario got older, he sometimes questioned whether it was a gesture of kindness or guilt. He knew he and his friends had gone over every inch of that dory, and there had never been any tobacco tin wedged between the bow and the seat. At the time, however, the extra thirty dollars wasn't questioned and was reason enough to elevate their opinion of Mr. Turner.

With the help of Mr. Turner, the dinghy was loaded onto his flatbed truck and moved to Freddie's house. Freddie was the youngest of the trio and his father had agreed to let them have the use of one half of the family garage while they got it shipshape. After being unloaded, they spent what little was left of the summer making repairs. The work continued into fall and winter. Fingers became numb as they lovingly transposed the old dory into a vessel they were proud to claim as their own. The first supplies were purchased from the thirty dollars in the tin that they kept hidden in the garage rafters. The money was always referred to as Sweet Vanilla, and when they realized there was no name on the boat's stern plate, the decision to name her after the brand of tobacco was unanimous. The three of them spent every spare minute scraping, sanding, patching and painting and by the end of spring they had repaired the hull, refinished the seats, and brought the few pieces of teak trim to a finish any boat builder would've admired.

IN THE TOWN OF Cotuit, most of the local fishermen congregated in Bonnie's Café just prior to sunrise. It was their time for coffee and a sharing of complaints about life as they knew it. The topics usually started with the current screwing they were getting from local politicians and then turned to town gossip. During the lengthy refurbishing of the dory, it was occasionally one of the items on their agenda. Some felt Mr. Turner had taken advantage of the boys; others suggested he regretted the deal once he saw the dory being returned to life. Other talk revolved around the question of where the boys procured the tiller and the rudder—two items needing to be replaced due to the storm damage that initially put her in dry dock. The fishermen knew the replacement rudder the boys needed was a bit pricy and the one the boys managed to acquire was oversized for the fourteen-footer.

"It sure weren't somethin' the boys got from Sears Roebuck," said one.

"It's none of our nevermind," returned Brad Endmont. "They're good boys. Prob'bly didn't do nothin' any of us didn't do at their age." The comment stemmed from the consensus that the rudder was one that may have been taken off a wreck in McGill's boatyard. McGill was an old windbag who operated a salvage yard some twenty miles up the coast near Osterville.

The Osterville fishermen were friendly rivals of the lobstermen in Cotuit, and if parts were being borrowed from salvaged boats sitting in McGill's yard, the Cotuit fishermen found it to be a bit humorous. Especially when they considered McGill's incessant bragging about his tight security comprised of numerous cameras and the latest in technological hardware. It seemed on the night of an alleged break-in, the perpetrators used a good old-fashioned can of spray paint to render the high-tech cameras useless.

Rumors and suspicions aside, Mario and his friends were well-liked around town and the restoration was an act of blood, sweat, and tears. Where they obtained needed parts didn't seem to be much of an issue to the locals. "If any items go missin' from McGill's boatyard and mysteriously show up somewhere else, it's none of our affair," said one.

On the day of the launch, many of the fishermen, perhaps recalling their own misspent youths, helped Mario and his friends get the dory to the wharf. In their closer inspection of the repairs, the locals marveled at the use of inventive problem solving in areas of rigging that had been improvised due to the absence of money. When *Sweet Vanilla* was slipped into the water, cheers from those present could be heard for quite a distance. They continued to an elevated pitch when she remained afloat.

All eyes then fell to the mainsail. It sat on her deck in a folded heap waiting to be hoisted. It was in need of repairs when the boys took ownership—another problem that needed solving. Mario was the most industrious of the trio, and with the tobacco tin empty, he made a deal with a local sail maker. It meant more labor—this time in the sail shop—but he learned the basics of sail-repair and rendered the stitches and patches needed to get the sail in shape. The first official hoisting was a beautiful sight with the scars and patches seemingly going unnoticed.

Early that summer, *Sweet Vanilla* was in constant use, being boarded and sailed by a crew of one, two, or all three of the owners on a daily basis. Each of them was skillful enough to sail her single-handedly, but Mario's proficiency at the helm was a natural talent. The idea of harnessing the wind to propel himself over the ocean took him to places he'd never been. He loved the silence as he skimmed across the water, and although sailing with friends was thrilling, it was when he sailed alone that he found a certain peace. Whenever he had time to sail, he was on the water. When he didn't have time, he made time.

In July, Freddie's father was transferred to Illinois, and Kevin, the third member of the trio, fell in love with Dolores Parker, the best looking eighth-grader in the school. Kevin was then relegated to the beach to spend time with Dolores and her friends.

"You use the boat," he told Mario. "I'm going to the beach. You should think about coming along. She's got some good-lookin' friends."

"I'll pass," Mario told him.

"Okay, suit yourself. I guess it was always your boat anyway . . . I mean, you always did the most work . . . had the passion ya know? I'll let you know if I want to use her. I'm thinkin' I might take Dolores for a sail sometime."

Kevin did take Dolores out for a sail . . . once. She screamed most of the time, yelling "It's too tipsy," and, "We're going to fall in the water!"

It was her fear of heeling over that ended Kevin's sailing career. For the remainder of the summer Mario sailed alone and continued sailing into the crisp winds of fall when the scent of burning leaves drifted from shore and filled the air.

It was the smell of autumn combined with the wind combing his hair that put Mario into a deep sleep that night. He never heard the snoring of nearby cons, the muffled conversations of the guards, or the slamming of the heavy metal doors.

⚓ ⚓

TAKING THE

BOAT

29

◆   **Un So**

When Andy Dugan made the drive from Maine to Melbourne the second time, he envisioned the three months ahead in a different light than his previous year. Although he drove the same minivan filled with the same T-shirts and shorts along with his two boxes of tools, this year would be a winter of sailing.

During his nine months in Maine, the boat sitting anchored on the Indian River was constantly in his thoughts. Initially, he intended to find the owner and propose a swap—the use of the boat in exchange for needed repairs. If the owner was willing to trade its use for some of Andy's elbow grease, it could be a sweet deal.

He also realized seeing the boat where he'd left her wasn't a realistic possibility. But once over the causeway, as unbelievable as it was, she was there . . . bobbing . . . beckoning . . . as if awaiting his return. Surprisingly, however, his anticipated feeling of excitement turned to anger. Her apparent lack of use, combined with the obvious neglect that had continued in his absence, had stripped her of any remaining dignity she may have had.

He parked his van and walked to a bench that faced the water—the same bench Rosita occupied during her lunch hour each day. In fact, had he driven onto the peninsula an hour earlier, the two would have run into each other.

He studied the increased growth of algae that seemed to glue the Beneteau to the river. From the waterline it crept up the anchor rode and was only a few days from contaminating the bow sprit. The disarray of cushions, life jackets, and tangled lines on deck, coupled with the outboard still dangling off the stern rail, made it obvious no one had been on board since he'd left. The thought that no one had bothered to care for her remained a mystery, it was a disgrace to sailors everywhere.

It was time to forego any protocols or ethical means of identification. The boat had obviously been abandoned and the idea of seeking out her owner vanished. According to the Law of the Sea—if there was such a law—he could claim her. She was salvage . . . plain and simple. He was uncertain regarding the required legal distance from shore for such a claim, but it somehow seemed irrelevant. "I found her adrift at sea," he would tell people. Who would be the wiser? There was no longer any reason to find the rightful owner. No need to spend hours of intense labor for someone else in exchange for the joy of sailing her. It was obvious the Beneteau was an orphan, and like any orphan, she needed to be adopted . . . cared for . . . treated with the respect she was due.

He was certainly no thief, but this wasn't actually stealing and he felt good about his decision. He softened the idea by telling himself he would simply borrow her. It was the right thing to do. He would take her somewhere and work on her in hiding. Ollie would help of course—Ollie would love a plan of high seas piracy. The two of them would get stoned and procure the boat in the wee hours of some morning. Ollie would know a guy and he and Ollie and the guy he knew—possibly multiple guys—would move the boat, fix it up, and Andy would sail it for three months. Before returning to Maine, he'd anchor her right where he'd found her. The rightful owner would be pleased to find her in pristine condition.

WITH A NEW URGENCY to find his friend, he drove to The Harry Berry Room. Although his phone call to the bar had yielded no information regarding Ollie, he needed a more face-to-face response from the bartender. When he arrived, Bobby recognized him and was cordial. "Haven't seen him in eight, maybe ten weeks," he said. "I know he's around . . . I mean, he's not in jail or anything. There've been a few guys in here who've seen him. You know—a few of his old customers. But like I told you on the phone, guys like Ollie tend to move around a lot. You might wanna check some of the other bars in the area."

The bartender's suggestion was certainly viable, but a search he would have to postpone until he was settled in at his aunt's cottage. His first idea was to drive to Sebastian Inlet the next morning. If Ollie was still in the area, he would be surfing that part of the peninsula. If not, other surfers might know his whereabouts.

When he arrived at the inlet, he found Ollie's jeep parked in the overlook. He made the short walk to the beach, and shielding his eyes with one hand he scanned the row of bobbing surfers that sat waiting to catch a wave. They reminded him of the crow shoot in the booth at the carnival. Today they sat on their surf boards, cawing at one another while they waited. It didn't take long to spot the familiar profile of his friend. Andy watched as Ollie lay on his belly and initiated his paddling motion before snapping to his feet and taking his familiar posture. He rode a fairly good-sized wave until it flattened. The ride ended near the shoreline where he made a graceful turn and paddled back to rejoin the other crows.

"Looking for somebody special?" The question came from a kid who looked to be nine or ten. He was covered in sand and carried a boogie board under his arm.

"I was, but I found him." Andy said. "It's the guy just getting up on his board." Andy didn't bother to point. Ollie was up again and the only upright surfer.

"Oh, you mean Un So."

"Un So?" Andy questioned.

"Yeah man, that's Un So. He's one of the best out there."

"Are you sure we're lookin' at the same guy? 'Cause the guy I'm lookin' at is Ollie . . . " Andy had to search his memory to recall Ollie's last name. "Henshaw, Ollie Henshaw."

"I think you got the wrong guy. That guy on the board is Un So."

Andy let the comment go and watched Ollie catch several more waves before he called it quits and waded out of the water. He spotted Andy immediately and his face brightened. "It's about time you got down here," he said, as if it was a reprimand. "How you been, man?"

Andy studied his friend. He was more sun-darkened than he remembered. His dreadlocks were a bit longer, and his teeth seemed whiter. Ollie dropped his board and the two embraced. He had the smell of the sea on his wetsuit and Andy's T-shirt acted as a blotter.

"You don't look any the worse for wear," Andy told him. What've you been up to? I called Harry Berry's tryin' to track you down."

"Yeah, I don't hang my hat there anymore," he said. "I've moved my office to . . ."

Before he could finish his statement, the kid with the boogie board ran up and interrupted. "This guy said your name is Ollie. Is that right? I thought your name was Un So."

Ollie dismissed the kid with a laugh and a ruffling of his hair. He picked up his board and he and Andy walked to their vehicles.

"Un So?" Andy asked.

"It's what I go by these days."

"Whaddaya mean, what you go by?"

"I've gotten into this whole new thing lately—lunariumism they call it. It has to do with phases of the moon and stuff." As he loaded his surfboard onto his jeep he pointed to a new sticker pasted across the dashboard of his jeep that read, "Without inner peace, outer peace is impossible".

"Un So?"

"Yeah. Un So is my lunarium name."

"So I'm supposed to call you Un So."

"Well, everybody else does."

"When did this all come about?"

"I guess since I met Ding-Lee. She got me into it."

"Ding-Lee?"

"Yeah, well that's her lunarium name. She got me into the whole lunarium thing. We're seein' each other now. It's pretty regular."

"So you're tellin' me that now you read your horoscope in the paper every day."

"It's more than that, man. For example, did you know there's a certain time between moon phases when decisions people make just don't have any meaning. You know . . . no consequences one way or another."

"Let me guess. Ding-Lee is short for Ding-a-ling." Andy's comment wasn't received with the humor intended.

"Don't mock it man, I'm serious about this shit."

In the parking lot they made plans to get together later in the day at Ollie's new office—a bar called Captain Ahab's. Andy wondered whether Ollie's dealing was now dominated by customers having strange lunarium-derived names but he said nothing.

CAPTAIN AHAB'S TURNED OUT to be a hookah bar and Andy got an instant education regarding the finer points of communal smoking. Like most hookah bars, Captain Ahab's had circumvented the tobacco laws by offering a variety of herbal shisha. Clientele either pulled out their pouch containing their personal favorite or purchased one of the blends available at the bar. Bowls that sat on tables and usually held peanuts contained a wide variety of disposable mouthpieces.

Had the hookahs been filled with grass or hashish, Andy felt it was an appropriate place for Ollie to frequent, but he soon realized he wasn't meeting Ollie, he was meeting Un So. No alcohol was served at Ahab's, which meant the lunariums weren't bellying up to the bar for drinks. Andy's anticipatory mug of cold draft was put on hold. He found Ollie at a table nursing an ice tea between draws from the tip of the hookah in his mouth. The place was noisy and they spent the first few minutes yelling comments back and forth in an attempt to catch each other up on the past few months.

"So, this is where you're hanging your hat these days," Andy hollered. "I guess it's a good thing I found you at the inlet because I don't think I would've thought to look for you in this place." He dismissed any idea of discussing the sailboat or acts of piracy until they were in a quieter environment. While they talked, a belly dancer occupied the dance floor and turned her attention to one table after another as she gyrated around the room.

Ollie took a toke from the hookah and exhaled a molasses smelling smoke. "You should try some of this. Or there's other stuff here if you don't like this one." He pointed to a display rack behind the bar that offered a wide variety of herbal tobaccos. Tins advertising Coco Buzz, Apple Bottoms, Green Ice, and Kali Drizzle lined the shelves normally reserved for bottles of liquor. "That Green Ice there is kinda spearminty.

The Kali Drizzle is kinda like . . ." he stopped to search for the right words. "Grape bubblegum," he said. "This is actually a good place to do business. Most of these people put a lot more than shisha in hookahs once they get home if you get my drift."

"So, nobody smokes any illegal stuff in here?"

"No, man. This place is strictly legit. It's just a good place to find customers who partake at home."

"And this is part of your new lunarium life style?"

"Well, a lot of people who believe in the lunarium phenomenon hang here."

"And this is where you met Ding-Lee?"

"No way, man. Even this non-tobacco type stuff is off her chart. She's a veggie. You know, a purist when it comes to what she puts into her body."

"That must raise quite a bit of havoc with your diet of fast food."

"We make it work. Some of what she throws together for meals is actually pretty good."

It was obvious to Andy that Ding-Lee had not only taken over Ollie's heart, but apparently everything else. When it came to women, he was a giant tuna swimming around just waiting for a big hook. The new name and the scene at the hookah bar made Andy realize he was resigned to live through Ding-Lee's current spell of intoxication until the big tuna hooked himself on a different barb.

♦ crème de la crêpe

Andy waited several days before approaching Ollie with his idea regarding his planned appropriation of the boat. The lunarium approach to living was still forefront in Ollie's mind and Andy wasn't sure what his friend's response would be. Despite this new belief, the window of opportunity for addressing Ollie when he was straight was limited to the time period between him getting out of bed and having his first joint of the day—usually with his morning coffee. The situation was further complicated with the addition of his new romance.

He drove to Ollie's and found his bungalow empty. The landlady informed him that he had gone to Crème De Le Crêpe for breakfast. It was one of the routines Ollie had not changed. It was a restaurant on New Haven Avenue not far from Jimmy the Gasser's office and it was Ollie's favorite morning spot. A local couple owned the place—a French woman named Jacqueline who made the best crêpes Ollie had ever eaten and her husband, Cecil, who oversaw the business and kept things running smoothly. Jacqueline was friendly and hollered to regulars from the kitchen. She trusted no one else to do the cooking. Ollie referred to her as an "Artist in Crêpistry."

When Cecil wasn't in the office working on the books, he greeted customers and oversaw the dining area. Going to Jacqueline's for crêpes was one of the few things that got Ollie "off island" as he called it when a drive forced him to leave the penninsula.

When Andy arrived, his friend was at his usual table hunched over a cup of coffee. The restaurant was bustling with the morning crowd. The familiar sound of china hitting china echoed around the dining area as cups went to and from saucers and melded into quiet conversations at tables. The smell of fresh-brewed coffee was immediate. Andy pulled out a chair opposite Ollie and seated himself.

There had been no plan to meet at the restaurant, but Ollie spoke as if he had been waiting for Andy's arrival. "I already ordered. You want something to eat? It's all good here, man." "Yeah, I know. I've sampled it often." Andy studied Ollie's eyes. They were glazed over and he realized the window of opportunity had already closed. On second thought, the idea of high-seas piracy might be better received if Ollie was stoned.

Andy was never as frequent a visitor to the restaurant as Ollie, but was a familiar face. Cecil approached the table, menu in hand, and greeted him, mentioning it was good to see him back in the area. Andy returned the greeting and responded briefly to Cecil's inquiries—filling him in on how things had gone while he was in Maine and how he was glad to be back a second year. "Just coffee," he told him.

Ollie eyed his friend who, like himself, was not in the habit of journeying off island.

"Must be something pretty important to bring you here if you didn't come for breakfast. What's up, man?"

Andy saw the question as an opportunity to get right to the boat. "Do you remember when I came here last year?"

"I guess so. We've probably come here three or four times. Why?"

"No, I didn't mean here to the restaurant, I meant to Melbourne Beach."

"Yeah, I remember. We met during that whole thing at the 911 Club. That waiter was tryin' to stiff me for some dope."

Cecil arrived with Ollie's crêpes and set them down along with Andy's coffee. Two were filled with fresh strawberries, the third oozed out a rich chocolate. They waited for Cecil to leave before Andy continued. "Remember me tellin' you about a sailboat that was anchored on the peninsula side of the causeway?"

"Remember? Of course I remember. I mean, I don't remember the boat so much as you talkin' about it the whole time you were here. Kept sayin' what a waste it was to just sit there with nobody sailin' it."

"See, that's exactly what I'm talkin' about. You're like everybody else who lives down here. You go about your daily activities without seeing any of the shit around you. You must've passed that boat a hundred times since I left."

Ollie ate a piece of his crêpe before responding. "By you telling me I passed it a hundred times I'm guessing you're saying it's still there?"

"It's not only still there, it hasn't moved since I left."

"What makes you so sure?"

"Remember last year when we saw it and it didn't have a mast? I mean, it is a sailboat. Anyway, it's not only still sitting there—and still without a mast—but the hull is all covered with algae, not to mention the same crap we saw strewn all over the deck hasn't been moved or been cleaned up."

Ollie forked another piece of crêpe into his mouth. "Not that unusual down here. It's not like Maine where people have to get their boat out of the water for the winter. Besides, it's on the river, right? I mean, it's not even sitting in salt water."

Andy took a sip of coffee. He knew he had to be careful broaching what he had in mind. "Listen, that boat is a thirty-five foot Beneteau. People just don't leave those sitting around. I'm thinking of checking it out a little more closely this year, if you get my drift."

"Good. Maybe if you get a boat I won't have to listen to your whining for three months. What are they askin' for it?"

"I'm not actually looking to *buy* it, man. It's just sitting there. Like it's there for the taking if you know what I mean."

"Well, somebody owns it." Ollie continued eating, content to let Andy take point on the conversation.

"Okay, here's the thing. You haven't noticed it because you don't care much about sailing. Although I have to say, as you frequent this place a couple of times a week, I'm not sure how you could miss it."

"Probably because it's on the 192 causeway."

"Yeah, it's anchored off Douglas Park."

"Well, that explains it. I usually shoot down Eau Gallie to North Riverside. Anyway, if you're tellin' me you're gonna try to find the owner and want my advice, I can follow you from here. I'm headin' over to the inlet as soon as I finish eating. I can take a look at it with you if you want me to, although I don't know much about sailboats. Now, if you want my advice on what kind of surfboard to buy then I'm your man."

Ollie's eyes continued to display a stoned glaze as he made the comment confirming Andy's guess that he'd hit the bong before driving over. It also explained his order of the strawberry and chocolate crêpes. It was one of Jacqueline's specialties and sometimes shared by couples for a dessert rather than a breakfast meal.

Andy continued as if Ollie's suggestion was a good idea. "Great. You can follow me back. We can pull into the park and check it out together. You can see the disrepair yourself. I'll need your help on this anyway." Andy hoped appealing to Ollie's Good Samaritan side might sway him when he heard his plan.

"Ah, I see your strategy now . . . the disrepair brings the price down, right?"

"Forget the price, man. I'll tell you what it means. The disrepair means no one cares about the damn thing and we can officially claim it as salvage."

"Well, I'm not sure you can conclude that no one cares about it. Maybe the owner lives in Europe or something and just uses it when he's in town." As Ollie spoke he wiped his plate with a finger and then licked it to get the last remnants of the chocolate filling.

"C'mon, man. Be serious. The algae alone is a surefire clue. The anchor rode is covered so thick it's hanging off it like sphagnum moss. The crud goes up five or six inches above the water line on the hull, and there's never been a mast on it. You don't sail a sailboat without a mast. I'm tellin' ya it's ours for the taking."

The excitement in Andy's voice continued to grow and caused Ollie to look around to see if other patrons were paying attention to their conversation. He raised an open hand to curb his friend's enthusiasm. "Okay, man, I concede. You found a boat on the river that nobody seems to care about. But like I said, *somebody* owns it."

"Yeah, well I've been thinking about a few possibilities as to why it's been sitting there so long."

"Like what?"

"I figure the worst case scenario is the owner anchored the sucker and then died. If that's the case, his body might still be on board." Andy then hesitated, and thinking he might need more of a hook to get Ollie involved added, "Murdered maybe."

"Aha!" Ollie rebuked. "But if somebody did murder the owner, why didn't the murderer take the boat . . . I mean, he could've just put some weights on the body and dumped it overboard." Andy recognized the tone of residual giddiness, probably from earlier tokes on the bong. Ollie's idea brought on a few snickers as he talked until the visual of the dead body inside the boat brought him to the point of slapping himself on the knee.

This time it was Andy who had to calm Ollie and the attention he brought to the table. "Just get serious for a minute. Suppose I throw out the idea the boat was involved in a drug deal? Guys are always stealing boats down here and then using them to transport drugs, right? When they don't need them anymore they just leave 'em. Maybe something went wrong and the boat is full of cash or . . ." The idea of a boatload of marijuana had brought a look of interest and Andy saw an unanticipated opportunity. "What if a dope deal that went wrong never got finished and there's a ton of marijuana on board . . . that's just sittin' there for the taking?"

Ollie sat back and put both hands in his lap as he looked around in thought. Andy knew he'd hit on a weak spot.

"Prob'bly be moldy by now," Ollie commented, which started him laughing again. "However, if those two scenarios you're puttin' out there are some sort of multiple choice test, then I pick 'A' and go with the murder idea."

"Really? So you give my story some credibility?"

"No, I just think if any of what you're suggesting is true, it would be more exciting to find a dead body on board than a pile of moldy grass."

The discussion as to which scenario was more plausible was interrupted when Cecil placed their bills on the table with an appreciative thank you. Andy pushed his toward Ollie. "For being so closed-minded about this whole thing, you can pay for my coffee."

"And I suppose I also take care of the tip."

"Hey, you ate the crêpes man, not me. I just had coffee."

They made their exit, and realizing it might be his only opportunity to get Ollie on board with his plan, Andy continued his rationale into the parking lot. "Like I've been saying, if the boat's been abandoned, it's salvage and we can take it."

"Now that's another thing. You keep using the word we. How did the *we* get into the plan. I'm a surfer, man. I like to keep the shoreline in sight if ya know what I mean. I'm not interested in taking a boat way out in the ocean. Too scary for me."

"I look at it as a right," Andy argued. "You know, the pirates' law of the sea . . . at the very least it's the law of salvage. The boat is adrift and we should take it."

"There's that *we* again. And I thought you said it was anchored."

"A minor technicality," Andy countered.

"Even if you're right, it's the *we* and the *our* words that concern me." Ollie had the keys to the jeep in his hand and pointed them at his friend. "Listen man, just because you want to do a little sailing doesn't mean you can come down here to Florida and pick out a boat and take it. What are ya planning on doing when your three months are up? You gonna hoist anchor and sail it back to Maine?"

"I'm not sure yet. I have considered just borrowing it while I'm down here and then we can put it back when I leave. I've got to work out a few details. That's where I'll need your help."

"What kind of details?"

"The first thing we'll have to do is move it to a location where we can work on it."

"*We* word again."

"Well, I figured you'd know a guy—a guy who might have access to a boatyard. We need to get it somewhere we can check it out without a lot of peering eyes. If we can hoist it out of the river and get it onto a cradle, we could check out the underbelly and see how seaworthy she is."

"Well, we know one thing you're gonna need, and that's a mast," Ollie responded. "A big hummer mast to say the least. And they don't come cheap."

31

the plan

A ndy led the way from Crème De Le Crêpe to Douglas Park. The minivan wove in and out of traffic on New Haven Avenue and onto the causeway. Ollie followed behind in his jeep laden with two surf boards. In the rearview mirror, Andy watched his friend's vehicle weaving for a different reason than traffic. He could see Ollie in his rear view mirror wrestling with a matchbook in an attempt to light a joint.

As he traversed the causeway, Andy knew there was more to investigate before he made his claim by right of salvage. Whether or not he had convinced Ollie to assist him was still questionable. The thought of a drug deal that had gone wrong—although it was only the implanted fabrication suggested at breakfast—might be the enticement needed. Even a small-sized shipment would be payment enough to compensate "guys he knew" if others were needed in the operation. Neither Andy nor Ollie had any hard-core criminal element in their makeup, but each had enough larceny in their bones to rescue a neglected boat with a stash of marijuana. After all, in the boat's current condition it would be an act of kindness. If they pulled it off, the possibility of Andy sailing it to Maine was a decision to be dealt with later.

During the drive from the restaurant to Douglas Park, smoke continued to waft from the driver-side window of Ollie's jeep. The park was small but offered a few parking spaces for visitors, and they pulled into adjacent spots. Andy was first to get out of his vehicle.

Ollie's arm was hanging out the window as he extended the last bit of the joint to Andy. When it was waved off, Ollie flicked it away and leaned into the back seat. He pawed through several layers of wetsuits, swim fins, and other items. "Always prepared," he announced and withdrew his Bushnell binoculars.

The two walked to an area that allowed for an unobstructed view of the boat. The embankment was occupied by two men and a woman. The men were fishing while the woman sat on the singular bench. She held a book in one hand while her other rocked a baby carriage by its handle. A pit bull slept at the base of a tree with its leash unattached to anything solid. He lifted his head surveying the newcomers and then returned to napping. Conversations between the three were in Spanish and either they couldn't read English, or hadn't seen the "no dogs allowed" signs that were posted throughout the area.

The body language accompanying the men's talk suggested they were discussing the failures of their fishing exploits. One was casting a net from the embankment. With each cast it became entangled when the weighted ends caught on one another. The catch of the day seemed to be clumps of algae and an occasional Styrofoam cup. The other fisherman held a pole and stared into the black water of the Indian River, perhaps thinking a good stare might entice nearby fish to take his bait. Their banter was ignored by the woman who sat reading while she rocked the carriage.

Encountering three other people was reason enough for Andy and Ollie to seek a better vantage point. The two walked up the sidewalk adjacent to the causeway and sat in one of the breaks in the foliage. The boat was actually closer to shore than Andy realized. The morning sun warmed them, and for a few minutes they studied the boat in silence—Andy contemplating its history—Ollie staring through his binoculars while waiting for what was next.

"Yeah, I remember this tub now. Looks pretty bad. You sure you want that thing?"

"I won't be sure until I get on board for a closer look. I'll need to make a list of what we're going to need and what kind of money I'm lookin' at. I'm hoping most of the fixing up involves spit and polish along with a good dose of elbow grease. Can you get a boat so we can get out there some night this week?"

Ollie had yet to relinquish the binoculars. Ignoring the question, he relayed information he was getting from the binoculars' closer look. "It's got registry numbers on the hull, maybe you could contact the Coast Guard and get the name of the owner. By the looks of it, you could probably get it pretty cheap. It would sure eliminate a lot of covert bullshit if you just bought it outright."

"The whole point of the operation is to keep a low profile. The last thing I want is to have the Coast Guard snooping around," Andy countered. "I mean, look at it. It's ripe for the pickin'. So, what do you think?"

Ollie's head had swiveled and he had refocused the binoculars on a young woman coming off the causeway on a bike. "Why I think that is one fine looking cyclist."

Andy pulled the binoculars away. "Keep your mind on the boat. We're on a mission here. I asked you what you thought."

"What do I think? Hmmm, first and foremost, I think we shoulda got a couple of coffees to go."

Andy's question had been asked more out of politeness than to get an actual appraisal. Despite Ollie's time spent on the water, his knowledge of boats was limited. He continued to peer through the glasses and spoke out loud as if he was dictating notes for Ollie to jot down for future use. "She's not sitting low in the water so we can assume there's not much weight inside."

Ollie shaded his eyes from the morning sun and made an attempt to be helpful. "No dinghy," he said. "I guess that means your dead body theory would eliminate a suicide."

"Not necessarily. I mean, it's true that if it was a murder, the killer would take the dinghy ashore. However, if it was a suicide, the dinghy could've pulled loose and drifted off. If anything, it gives credence to one of my theories."

They continued to sit in silence, not realizing the ridiculousness of what they were suggesting. Andy then continued with more verbal notes. "There's an outboard hangin' off the stern, but I can't tell the horsepower. A boat that length should have its own diesel engine so I'm not sure why she's got an outboard hanging off the ass end."

"But what about the dinghy, man? I mean, if the killer rowed ashore, he certainly didn't carry it away on his back . . . or *her* back. Maybe the guy was killed by a jilted lover."

Andy ignored the dinghy question and continued to scan the boat. "Bow sprit looks good . . . topside looks good—despite a lot of miscellaneous crap all over the deck. We'll have to get on board and see what she looks like below."

"That shouldn't be too hard. It's only about twenty yards out. Hell, you could swim to it if you wanted to . . . and there you go with the *we* word again. You need to keep in mind that I don't need a boat. I've got two beautiful surf boards sittin' on my jeep. That works for me."

"Yeah, I realize that, but you can't tell me you're not a little curious. Anyway, we can't swim out there in broad daylight. We'll have to make a night visit. We should check the hull, probably not much bottom paint left on her. Even in the river here, it gets a bit salty. We'll need some equipment. You don't happen to have an underwater light by chance?"

"If I can find it. I haven't done any scuba diving in a coupla years."

"Well, next chance you get, see if you can dig it up. I need to know whether or not this boat is worth taking."

"What about the missing mast?"

"Yeah, it's something to think about. We'll need a crane to step a mast on a boat this size. It'd be nice to have access to a yard with the right equipment. You and I sure as hell can't step it."

"Well, you're the boat expert, my friend, but whatever it needs, I'm sure you'll figure it out."

"So, does that mean you're with me on this? I don't want to have to rely on some unknown conspirator from the yellow pages."

"If I do find a guy, and if I do help you get it somewhere—and those are two big 'ifs,' then I'm done with the project. Once the boat is on shore, I'm out of it . . . and the timing will have to be right."

"Whaddaya mean, the timing will have to be right? The timing will have to be in the dark. Obviously anything we do will be late night or during the wee hours of the morning. What were you thinking?"

"Lunarium, man. I'm talkin' about the lunarium calendar. We have to time it around the whole Void of course thing. You know, when the moon changes. If the timing's bad, it's not good karma."

"That's what I'm sayin' too. We're sure not gonna take her under a full moon. The darker the better."

"It's not the full moon I'm worried about. Lunariums aren't werewolves, man. It's the time *between* the moons that matters. Remember me saying that during the void of course we don't have to worry about certain consequences. It's like a weak spot or something. I'll check with Ding-Lee and see what's what."

Andy put a hand on Ollie's shoulder. "Then please tell Ding-Lee that the sooner the better. With my luck, just when I'm gonna claim her, the dead owner will show up."

32

♦   perigee vs apogee

Andy and Ollie left Douglas Park and went their separate ways. Ollie drove to Sebastian Inlet to surf and Andy returned to his aunt's cottage. Each carried different thoughts regarding the boat and how it came to be left anchored on the Indian River. Other than a brief thought regarding the boat's unchanged appearance from seeing it a year earlier, Ollie hadn't given the sloop much thought—although the possibilities of finding kilos of dope or crates of cash were now given a certain amount of consideration.

Andy spent the rest of the morning sizing up the house. Most of the work was completed the prior winter leaving him with ample time to engage in sailing activities. Any touch-ups were negligible and a few hours each week would be sufficient to get things done. He'd already made the decision to do the lawn work himself and any major repairs could be pawned off on guys Ollie knew.

Once he settled in, he found a tablet and jotted a few notes to back up his tactical thinking on the boat. Moving a sloop that size without drawing attention to the task required a certain amount of planning. There was also the procurement of a mast—an expense that warranted consideration when establishing the boat's worth. He had confirmed his initial estimate on the length of the sloop to thirty-five feet. It was essential to find out if the investment was worth the trouble to move it and put in the time and money needed to make her seaworthy.

HE WAITED ANOTHER TWO days before catching up with Ollie for an update. After getting several messages at Captain Ahab's, Ollie returned his call. "There're two boatyards on the island. The closest one to you is run by a guy named Hanson. The other one is West End Marina which looks to have more equipment as far as getting your boat out of the water or putting up a mast. You said you'd need a crane, right?"

"I need to look at it first before we do any moving," Andy said. He stifled his tone of annoyance knowing Ollie had foregone the step of getting on board for an initial inspection. On the brighter side, Ollie's response regarding the boatyards was a sign indicating he was willing to help. "I don't want to line anything up for major repairs before I know if the boat's worth the trouble."

"Yeah, yeah, I know. I didn't make any commitments with anyone. I've just been checking around to see what's available. I don't know the kind of equipment you need. You're gonna have to make the final decision on where you wanna take it."

"I've got the same two places on my list so I'll give them a call and get some preliminary info and some prices. What about getting out to the boat? You said you might be able to find something to get us out there."

"Yeah, all taken care of. A guy I know said he had an old inflatable dinghy we can use."

"Can you get it for tonight? I want to get rollin' on this."

"I can get the boat for tonight, but it's not a good night for it."

"What's wrong with it?"

"Void of Course, man. The moon's just not right. We need to wait until tomorrow night when the moon changes."

Andy bit his lip when he heard the phrase *void of course* but knew it was a touchy subject and not to be made fun of. "Okay then, tomorrow night," he conceded. "Can you get the dinghy and meet me at the park around midnight?"

"Lunarium wisdom says we'll have to be done *before* midnight or we could have bad karma, man. Make it eleven, and I could use some help getting the dinghy. He said it needs to be inflated. How 'bout I swing by and pick you up around ten and we'll get it and go from there?"

"Yeah, okay. I'll see you around ten."

THE NIGHT IN QUESTION was not the vision of precision planning that Andy had foreseen. Ollie arrived somewhere in the neighborhood of ten o'clock, and during the drive to his good buddy Eric's house, he reminded Andy of the time constraints in which they had to work. "Like I told you on the phone, I'm gonna have to get this caper wrapped up before midnight."

"Yeah, I know. The moon will be in full bloom by then and you've got to get the pumpkin home."

"I keep tellin' ya, it's got nothing to do with the full moon. Followers of the Lunarium calendar are believers in the differences made by the path of the moon, man. Tonight, for example, Ding-Lee said the moon is in perigee, which means it's closest to earth and that's a good sign for us. After midnight, it begins its orbit into apogee and that means negative vibes for us, if you know what I mean."

Ollie's brief dissertation on lunariumism seemed to have some credibility to Andy until Ollie added the words, "Or something like that" at which point Andy's concerns for his friend resurfaced. "So, all these lunarium people you're hanging out with now . . . do they all smoke as much pot as you do?"

"Some do, some don't. Like I told you, Ding-Lee's body is a temple. I guess that's where we part ways. Speakin' of parting ways, Ding-Lee isn't real thrilled with my role in this boat thing. She thinks we'll probably get nailed for killin' the dead guy."

"You told her there's a dead guy on board?"

"Well, I had to give her some excuse. I couldn't tell her we were stealin' it. Like I said, she's not totally on board with this idea, if you'll excuse the expression."

The conversation ended when Ollie pulled the jeep into Eric's driveway. Loud yelling came from inside the house as partiers competed with Iron Butterfly's Metamorphosis vinyl rendition of *In-A-Gadda-Da-Vida*. The open back door led into the kitchen where they found Eric in a haze of marijuana smoke attempting to mix cocktails. The blender was covered with stickers of flowers and peace signs. To Andy, it seemed they had stepped through a time warp. Several of the houseguests were clustered around the counter and were involved in fragmented chatter involving everything from the best beaches to the worst politicians. The clatter of the blender added to the blaring stereo forcing an increase in everyone's volume as they tried to be heard. Eric, who was scanning the entourage, caught Ollie's entrance.

"Hey, my man! How you been, guy?" he yelled over everyone. He then made a waving gesture to the kitchen guests. "This here is one of my oldest friends. Ollie . . . er . . . a . . . what the hell's your last name again?" which was followed by a hearty laugh.

Several joints were being passed around the kitchen and a woman in her forties wearing too much make-up offered Andy a lipstick covered pipe. Andy took a hit out of politeness and passed it on to Ollie who took up the next introduction. "And this is my good friend Andy." And then added, "from Maine," which was followed by a chorus of "Hi Andy from Maine!" from everyone in the kitchen.

The blender was finished mixing and Eric began pouring a blue concoction into waiting glasses. Rather than shake Andy's hand, he filled it with a glass. Continuing to be polite, Andy sipped the drink, containing more alcohol than needed. Eric handed a second glass to Ollie as he leaned in to whisper and yelled over the crowd noise. "There's some blow in the living room if you want to take a quick stroll. Help yourself. It's on the mantel, or at least that's where I saw it last time I looked. Take Andy from Maine too," he added.

Ollie seemed to melt into the crowd. Others entered from doorways that led to various parts of the house or made an exit to the living room to snort a little blow. The flow caused a trading of places with occupants presumably from the living room who swapped space with those in the kitchen. Iron Butterfly was replaced by an old bootleg Dylan album and Andy turned his attention to the back door. He could see into the yard and his eyes searched for some sign of a dinghy. With no luck, he elbowed his way toward the host. Before he could say anything, Eric yelled in his ear. "So, where abouts are you from in Maine?"

"Up near Boothbay," Andy shouted back. Eric's eyes were glazed over and he was tipsy in his effort to reach his glass filled with the blue concoction. "You down here for a visit?" he slurred.

"Three months."

"Hey, that's great. A great time of year too." He took another sip. "You'd be freezin' your ass off up there in Maine now, wouldn't ya?"

"Yeah," Andy yelled over the noise. "Heard they got fourteen inches yesterday." It was the exact kind of small talk Andy wanted to avoid. Ollie had said nothing about a party. They were there to get a dinghy and Andy wanted to get it and get out before Ollie got too messed up on the booze and the coke.

Eric teetered a bit and Andy jumped on the opportunity for a more serious question. "Ollie mentioned you have a dinghy we could borrow . . . an inflatable or something. Is it somewhere handy? I mean, I could load it onto the jeep while I'm waiting for Ollie."

Eric stared into space. One of the guests sporting a golf shirt with an alligator on it handed him a joint. After taking a long toke and exhaling, he somehow remembered Andy's question. "Yeah, yeah. I've got an old dinghy in the shed out back there. But you should come back and get it tomorrow, man. Just stay and party tonight. Hell, you can sleep here if you just got into town."

"I think we're planning on getting it tonight so we can get an early start in the morning. We're gonna get in some early fishing."

"Fishing!" he slurred out. "I thought Ollie said you were stealing a boat. Some sailboat or something."

"Anyway, where is the dinghy?"

"Oh, it's out in the shed. You better get Ollie to help you though if you're getting it tonight. There's all kinds of shit piled up out there. There's a light switch by the door for the yard light and there's a light in the shed if the bulb's still good."

Andy decided to investigate before pulling Ollie away from the party. The yard light was a yellow light Eric had purchased because it advertised scaring mosquitoes away. It threw a small amount of illumination over the back door and was little help in lighting the outdoor path. Once at the shed he found the second bulb wasn't working at all and went to the jeep to retrieve Ollie's underwater light. The door of the shed hung on one hinge and the light's beam fell onto piles of junk and debris that filled the entire interior. Bed springs, old pallets, a wheelbarrow, and other gardening tools sat in the midst of stacks of newspapers and magazines, paint cans, brushes, hoes, rakes, shovels, swimming noodles, oars from a rowboat, life jackets, and miscellaneous other oddities that Eric had accumulated over the years. Andy began throwing things out of the way when he heard Ollie's voice from outside the shed door.

"You find it, man?"

"Everything but."

"Well, if Eric says it's out here, it's out here."

"I'm sure it is. He's got everything else in the world out here."

For the first time, Ollie realized Andy was using his underwater light. "Probably shouldn't be using that thing for this. Too bright. You'll burn the bulb out."

Before Andy could respond, he heard the voices of several party members walking toward the shed with Eric leading the pack. Some were holding up lighters, and with Bob Seger bellowing from the house, the lighters gave a concert appearance to the yard. Most partiers were unaware of why they were out there but had followed the leader in his quest to find whatever it was he was looking for.

"I think the dinghy's over in that far corner if I remember," Eric hollered in to Andy. "You may have to move some of that other shit. It's in a stuff bag, I think." The comment reminded Andy that the dinghy still had to be inflated.

"Don't worry though, man," Eric slurred. "There's a generator in there somewhere and I think it still works. It'll inflate that thing in a matter of minutes."

Andy finally spotted an oil-stained stuff bag via the lettered instructions for inflation and concluded he had found the dinghy. Ollie climbed over several obstacles to assist in pulling it out from under a card table. It was at that precise moment the police car pulled into the yard and parked behind Ollie's jeep.

◆   eels that go bump in the night

The unplanned arrival of the police initiated Ollie's fear that he and Andy would remain trapped in some void of whatever course they were on for the rest of the night.

They had been summoned to Eric's party by neighbors who were not only concerned about the loud music, but had suspicions regarding burglars breaking into the shed. Eric's house was more or less a regular stop for the local police. When the black and white had arrived the two officers gave him the usual warning and told him to "tone it down a notch or they'd have to take more drastic measures."

Andy instinctively turned off the underwater light and he and Ollie took a seat in the shed. Eventually, one of the officers flashed his light inside landing the beam on their faces, along with two other partiers, and instructed them to step out into the yard. The officer asked Eric if he knew Andy and Ollie, and after some hesitation, Eric admitted that they were, in fact, part of the party.

The inquiry as to why everyone was in the yard while an empty house was blaring music was answered by Eric as he explained that someone had suggested a snipe hunt. The cops failed to see any humor in the response but a slightly more sober person stepped up and explained that one of the women had become ill and stepped outside for some air and they all followed her out to make sure she was okay.

Although the cops didn't buy that story either, it was at least an answer they found respectable. Having better things to do with their time, they reiterated their warning, telling everyone to get inside and keep the music down. If they had seen any joints thrown to the ground and stomped on when they first arrived, it seemed to be an issue they were ignoring.

Once the police departed, most of the party returned to the inside of the house. A few of the more adventurous remained outside to assist with the unpiling of junk and retrieval of the dinghy.

Ollie's mention of Ding-Lee's warning was reiterated when the generator failed to start, leaving them with an uninflated dinghy. The suggestion was made by one of the more stoned party-goers that if enough people had the small factory-equipped compressors used in emergencies for their car tires, they could use them to blow up the dinghy. The idea was voted on and the process got underway. The inflation was further delayed when two small holes were found. The fix for the holes was a combination of window caulking and duct tape.

"It'll hold for tonight anyway," Eric assured them. "You're just going out to steal a boat, right?" To which others traded questioning glances. Andy then suggested to Ollie that perhaps he should've put the entire idea in the newspaper that day so all the journalists in town could get an exclusive on what they were doing.

The final piece of the puzzle, to ensure the punctures wouldn't leak, was the use of a substance from a can of compressed gel. Once the bicycle owner gave his sworn testimonial of the product's use in the repair of small leaks, the nozzle from the can was attached to the dinghy and the can of gel was pumped into the inflatable.

By midnight, the entire party had been moved to the yard. Trays of cookies were passed around along with bags of chips followed by plastic containers of different dips. Andy's last vision of the partiers was a yard filled with sleeping bodies. Some on broken chairs they had removed from the shed, an amorous couple snuggled together on a hammock, and a few slept in parked cars. Two or three hard-cores sat at the kitchen table and were debating whether or not Long Island is really an island.

IT WAS SOMETIME BETWEEN two and three o'clock in the morning when Ollie pulled off the causeway and he and Andy unloaded the dinghy. Andy used the singular plastic paddle they were able to find in the shed and the two companions maneuvered their way to the anchored sailboat.

Ollie continued to mutter his concerns regarding the time frame, claiming the lunarium calendar was no longer favorable. Andy was more concerned about his own condition than Ollie's thoughts of the moon.

"I'm not sure why I'm feeling so weird," he told Ollie. "I mean, I took a few tokes at the party but I didn't think the stuff was that strong."

"Blue Kool-aid," Ollie explained.

"Blue Kool-aid?"

"Yeah. If I recall, Eric always doctors it with something. You know, gives it a little extra kick."

"I hope you don't mean acid."

"No, nothin' like that, man. Just a little boost of something. You'll be fine in the morning."

They reached the boat and Andy tied them off. The two fumbled onto the deck and into the cockpit where they found the hatch padlocked. While Andy searched a few of the logical places a boat owner might hide a key, Ollie found a small length of pipe and broke off the hasp.

"What are you doing? That's a teak door. It'll cost me fifty bucks to fix that."

"From what I see this boat needing, fifty bucks is the least of your worries." Ollie then made a sweeping gesture inviting his friend to be first to go below. Andy flicked on the light and descended the companionway to the cabin. The Beneteau had been a showpiece in its day, but the light revealed the toll the year of neglect had taken. He stood in two to three inches of water and continued to wave the light into various crevices and into the V-berth. The air was stuffy and was filled with the smell of the river.

Ollie pushed him a bit forward and stepped into the water himself. "Jeezus, the damn thing's sinking."

"I don't think so," Andy told him. "This water's more likely from rain that got in. If she had a serious leak she would've been under a long time ago."

"I don't see any dead body."

"You sound disappointed."

"I guess I was hoping for something to reward our trouble. So, whaddaya think?"

"About the dead body?"

"No, man. About the boat. Whaddaya think about the boat. Are ya takin' her or not?"

For the first time since they'd left the party, Andy smiled. "I think she's got real potential. I think if her underbelly checks out okay, I've got myself a sailboat."

Ollie's eyes followed the beam of light as Andy continued to pan the inside of the cabin. "Are we seeing the same boat here? Because I think whatever Eric put in your cocktail may have seriously damaged your eyesight."

Andy ignored the crack. "I'm going under to check out the hull. Where's the underwater light?

"Still in the dinghy. But if you're goin' in the river, I don't know why we even bothered with the dinghy. We're only twenty feet from shore. And me . . . why am I here? It's past midnight. We're into lunar apogee, man . . . not good karma."

Andy went topside and retrieved the light and a swim mask from the dinghy. From the water, he could see the boat's name on the stern. "I think this might be a good sign," he whispered up to Ollie. "The boat's name is *Miss Demeanor*."

"You may have to change that to *Grand Theft* after we steal it."

"I'm not stealing it. It's salvage, remember? Besides, I may even put it back someday." With that, Andy disappeared into the blackness and Ollie watched the underwater light sink deeper as if it was the eye of a giant sea serpent.

Although the hull was covered in algae, it appeared sound and Andy felt it was a boat worth the taking. Satisfied with his investigation, he was about to return to the ladder when he turned and found himself wrapped in a giant eel. The eel seemed to glow in the light and he panicked, immediately thinking it was an electric eel with a ferocious bite. In his panic, he instinctively pushed at it, and in doing so, lost his grip on the light and it tumbled to the murky bottom. It sent a beam upward, illuminating the eel that continued to wind itself around Andy's legs and waist.

His lungs burned from the lack of oxygen and with no light to guide him, he fought to get to the surface. The eel be damned, he needed air to survive. His head bumped the hull.

He clawed at the boat's bottom but the algae was slippery and he struggled to find anything solid. He gave a final kick, hoping to propel himself upward and his flailing arms finally broke the surface. His wrist cracked onto a piece of metal which turned out to be the bottom rung of the ladder. He kicked again, not yet feeling a bite, and scrambled to pull himself on board.

Ollie was leaning over the starboard side with the flashlight aimed at the dinghy. Andy dragged himself into the cockpit scraping his shins on the ladder rungs as he did so. Feeling the boat rock, Ollie turned to address him. "I think we've got a problem here."

"Yeah, no shit. I was just attacked by an eel down there. Those things are vicious. I'm lucky the sucker didn't bite me." Andy's tone was one of annoyance with his partner's unawareness of the situation and apparent lack of concern.

"Was it a big bright green one?"

"Yeah, so you saw it. Why the hell didn't you help me or something?"

"It's still here, man. Take a look."

Andy peered into the river. The green eel seemed to be lurking under the dinghy and then Ollie moved the light away from the inflatable to show Andy the long stream of green gel that had leaked out and followed them from shore. "Kinda like Hansel and Gretel wouldn't you say? I think we done sprung a leak with our tire gel. I think it's still comin' out. I suggest we get ourselves back to shore before we lose the inflation in our inflatable." He laughed as he spoke and Andy realized Ollie had no idea of his earlier state of panic.

"Where's my light?"

"I dropped it during the eel attack."

"Dropped it . . . man, you gotta go back in and get it. That light cost me over two-hundred bucks."

It was ten or twelve feet to the light, but Andy spotted the glow among the muck at the bottom and retrieved it before they paddled to shore.

"Did you find out what you wanted down there?"

"Yeah, I did. We're good to go. I'll call and check out the boatyards tomorrow. Can you get us a motor? We can't have the boatyard come and get it. They have to believe it's ours."

"Yours you mean. And once it's at the yard, I'm out of it remember?"

If the shoreline had been another ten feet, they wouldn't have made it. The last of the green eel streamed out behind them as Andy continued to paddle to shore with the dinghy's buoyancy disappearing along the way. When the shore was reachable, Ollie gave the command to "abandon ship."

They folded the collapsed dinghy and stuffed it behind the back seat of the jeep. "I'll get it back to Eric tomorrow," he told Andy. "I'll go in the morning before his brain wakes up and stick it back in the shed. I don't know if I can get the green slime off or not but if he doesn't use it again for a year or so, he probably won't remember any of last night anyway."

"Well it wasn't like we got it in great condition to begin with."

The two sat in silence on the drive to Andy's beach house. He climbed out and spoke for the first time. "Wasn't the best night I ever had."

"Yeah, some real screw ups. But it wasn't our fault, man. Eric's party and a bum inflatable put us past midnight. Put us into apogee."

Andy gave a quiet laugh and then turned toward the house. Ollie's voice called after him. "Apogee, man. I'm tellin' ya . . . defying the moon is bad karma."

On the night of Eric's party, Rosita tossed and turned in her bed. She had no knowledge of perigee or apogee or any other gee, for that matter. The stars and the moon, regardless of their states of being, were no more than a peaceful umbrella under which she usually found protection from her worries in life.

It was thoughts of the impending release of Mario and wondering what their future held, combined with school, and work, and finances . . . everything buzzing around in her head like a swarm of restless bees. Just after one o'clock that morning, she got up and dressed herself. It was not the first night of restlessness that forced her from her bed, and the one remedy in which she found solace was walking. After dressing, she left her flat and walked to the bench in Douglas Park. She had claimed the bench as her own shortly after her relationship with *Miss Demeanor* began. It was there she sat and guarded the anchored sloop that contained so many mysteries. Whether or not the sloop would provide the answers she sought was still to be determined. As she walked, the sky cheated her of a bright moon to light her path, yet rewarded her with a multitude of stars. Under their calming influence, she sat at peace while she observed Mario's other woman bob gently on the river. He would be sailing her again soon. With his three month reduction for participating in her study and his ninety days for good behavior, he was scheduled to be released at the end of January.

As she looked out at *Miss Demeanor,* the absence of moonlight sent her attention to a light beneath the boat—a light that had no reason to be there—a light that wavered and flickered beneath the water before disappearing. It was followed by the sound of splashing water and then suddenly, the silhouette of a figure climbing on board.

A second light illuminated the far side of the boat and displayed a pattern of flickerings. She continued to watch and saw a second figure emerge and the two silhouettes stood on deck. The flashlight beamed across the water and a muffled conversation between the intruders drifted toward shore. Loud whispers . . . hearing what she thought might be the word *wheel* . . . and then the talk became frantic, mentioning an attack of some kind. The figures disappeared for a moment and then reappeared as they paddled a small boat toward the causeway. She continued to watch as they loaded the boat onto a jeep and drove off.

Mario's boat had been undisturbed for a year, and now there was unexpected activity in the middle of the night. She questioned whether her sighting was a random break-in or if the intruders were on board looking for something specific. Or, with only a few weeks until Mario's release, was there some connection. He was always evasive about the boat, leading her to believe there was more to *Miss Demeanor* than he was willing to tell her. The duty of keeping a watchful eye on the sloop now presented a problem. Mario needed to be informed of the intruders, but they had agreed to avoid any suspicion in their relationship by having no contact during the week. Unless the men returned, there wasn't much more she could tell Mario than what she had seen. For the few remaining days before Saturday she increased her surveillance. In addition to the regular checks during her lunch hour, she walked to the park each evening. Her visits revealed no further evidence of the men's return.

On Saturday, she cut the first part of the ritualized pretense short. Mario seemed surprised but also noticed a difference in her body language. She wasted no time in mentioning the intruders. "We might have a problem," she said.

"What kind of a problem?"

"It's the boat. The other night I couldn't sleep so I walked to the park to clear my head. It was late. When I got there someone was on board. It looked like there was a light on inside . . . you know, below deck maybe. I wasn't sure so I waited to see what was going on. Another light was streaming out from underneath the boat. Then a guy got out of the water and climbed on board. The two of them started talking. I couldn't make out much of what they were saying . . . sounded like something about the wheel or something but it didn't make any sense. Maybe he was saying peel, or deal. Then the one guy went back into the water and came up with a light and then it seemed like they were looking for something in the water. They must've tied up their boat on the opposite side because at first I didn't see a dinghy or anything, but then I saw them paddling some kind of raft back to shore, one of those things you blow up you know . . . one of those inflatable rafts. They had a jeep parked right off the causeway like they knew exactly what boat they were targeting."

"What did they look like?"

"Too dark to tell really. Couldn't get a license plate either, but it looked like one had long hair. At first I thought it might be a girl but he was too tall and his motions didn't fit a woman. They must've let the air out of the raft 'cause they collapsed it into the jeep and took off."

Mario mentally reviewed the picture Rosita painted. It didn't sound like intruders that would be connected to Cohen or Hanson . . . possibly some guys who'd had their eye on the boat for a while and had noticed its lack of activity.

"Can you get out there and check it out?"

"How? The dinghy's gone, remember? Drifted off months ago."

"Can you get any kind of a boat?"

"There's an old kayak in the yard that belongs to my landlady. I've never seen her use it. She mentioned once she didn't even know if it still floats."

"I'm too close to getting out of here to have anything happen now. You've got to get out there . . . give people the appearance that someone's using it or something."

"I can give the kayak a try. I mean, I'm pretty sure she'd let me use it."

"This afternoon then. Don't wait. I need to know what's going on."

"Maybe it's time you tell me what *is* going on," she said. "Just what exactly is so important about that boat?"

"It's my home remember? When I get out of here it's where I'm hanging my hat. I don't need anyone messing with it, or worse yet, thinking it's there for the taking. It's been sitting there for a year now."

"Yes, it has been a year, and I guess I thought by now you'd trust me enough not to lie to me."

Mario said nothing for a few moments. "Listen, I can't involve you in whatever I was in before I took up residency in this place. Just do me the favor of checking everything out."

"Do you want me to contact you if I find anything?"

"No, it's too risky at this point. Stick to the plan of no calls. You can fill me in next week."

The agreement to restrain from using the phone made it a long week for Mario. The following Saturday, he was sitting in the visitors' station long before Rosita arrived. If pacing had been allowed, he would've worn a path in the cement floor. Once there, she began with their normal preliminaries. This time, Mario broke her off. "Forget that," he said. "What's going on with the boat?"

"The padlock was broken off. Whoever it was set the hatch back on when they left, but they sure weren't concerned about breaking in. Other than that, I didn't see any visible damage below but that may be because the boat's got a few inches of water inside."

"Probably from some of the heavy rains." Mario said.

"It looks like they went through the compartments. Some of them were open but I don't know if they opened them or not. Like you said, it's been sitting for a while, tossing and turning with the wind. Some of the doors could've jarred themselves loose." She paused. Mario said nothing and then Rosita made a quick change from the subject of *Miss Demeanor*.

"Who's Maggie?"

"Maggie?"

"Yes, Maggie. I found a letter . . . to you . . . from Maggie. Some note about the Commodore dying or something. A lot of the ink was blurred because it got wet." Rosita paused and then continued in a tone of caution. "Went on to say she missed you, hoped to see you at the funeral. Did you go?"

Mario's mind was on the diamonds until Rosita broke the reverie. "Hey, I asked you, did you go."

"What? Did I go where?"

"To the funeral. Did you see your girlfriend Maggie at the funeral?"

"Jeezus, she's not my girlfriend. I knew Maggie when I was in high school," he confessed. "I mean, we didn't go to high school together. I was in high school and she was in college. We raced sailboats together. It was a summer thing. The Commodore was her grandfather. He helped me out a few times so yes, I went to the funeral and no, I didn't sleep with her."

"I didn't ask you if you slept with her."

"Not verbally," Mario said. "It was your eyes that were doing the asking. And what the hell were you doing reading my mail anyway?"

"It wasn't mail. It was just a note. You told me to look around." She decided not to pursue the topic further and returned to the discussion of the intruders. "Well, in case our friends have plans to go back to the boat I left them a present."

"What kind of a present?"

"I went back out the next day and left Penelope in the three inches of water."

"Penelope?"

"My water moccasin. Did you forget about my pet snakes?"

Mario hadn't seen her tattoo in so long he had forgotten about her fascination with snakes. "You left a water moccasin on the boat?"

"Sure. Penelope's better than any burglar alarm, and like all water moccasins, she's *very* territorial."

"And she'll stay there?"

"She'll hang around for a few days anyway . . . until she gets hungry. After I put her below I closed the hatch and leaned an old life jacket against it. That way I can check the jacket from shore every day to see if anyone's gone below. If anyone does go on board, she'll either give them a reason to stay topside or bite 'em in the ass.

In the week that followed, Rosita checked *Miss Demeanor* from shore twice a day. Through binoculars, she saw no movement of the jacket. As far as she could tell, the two figures she had seen on board had not returned. With that information relayed to Mario, and still believing the diamonds had been safe in the concealed compartment for over a year, he felt cautiously reassured.

◆ the commodore

Following Rosita's departure, her inquiry into the note from Maggie and thoughts about the Commodore rekindled Mario's memories of his freshman year in high school. It was the year he discovered the Cotuit High Sailing Club. Membership required high academic standards and motivated Mario to take his studies seriously. With his knowledge of sailing, he was not so interested in the instruction regarding the craft of sail as he was in the fleet of small racing boats for card carrying members. Additionally, the coach was well versed in seamanship. Aside from learning the techniques and strategies of racing, Mario learned about dead reckoning, sailing by the stars, and the use of a sextant. He was taught to read the sea, when and how to reef a sail, proficiency in anchoring, the proper handling of lines, and procedures involving safety and survival skills. The sailing club gave him a family, and in that environment, he felt at home.

His time in the club was short-lived. In his sophomore year, he was summarily dismissed from the team for his involvement in a lunch room fight. The incident was triggered by an off-color comment about his mother's inability to keep his father at home. During the incident, Mario accidentally punched the intervening teacher which left the administration with no choice other than a three-day suspension and his dismissal from the club.

With extra time on his hands, the love of sailing lured him to employment at the Cotuit Yacht Club. It was common knowledge that when employees had time off they were allowed to use the small sailboats the club used for lessons. The Sunfish were smaller than *Sweet Vanilla*, but faster, with more maneuverability. The Club also had a fleet of racers, more sophisticated than those he used at school, but were off limits to anyone other than yacht club team members. Mario spent the afternoons and weekends of early autumn scrubbing pots and sweeping floors in exchange for minimum wage and the privilege of sailing a Sunfish.

The yacht club was ruled by the iron hand of Commodore Barkley—a seventy-two year old retired navy officer, who like every other male member of his family over the course of generations, was the overseer of the Yacht Club's Board of Directors. He usually took his afternoon cocktail on the deck that overlooked the harbor. From his Adirondack chair he sat and admired *Ellie*—his 1999 forty-foot yacht that had been custom built in Maine. He loved the yacht as much as he had once loved his third wife, for whom the boat was named, and who now vied for its ownership in their on-going divorce. Unlike the vintage Herreshoff-styled *Ellie*, wife Ellie was in her late twenties, and on the rare occasions they sailed together, she slathered herself in oil and stretched out completely naked on the bow. Ellie had no knowledge or interest in sailing, but knowing the Commodore's affection for the Herreshoff she informed her attorney that no settlement would be reached that did not include her acquisition of the yacht.

When the offer was put on the table, Barkley was quoted as telling her attorney, "You can tell the little bitch I'll scuttle the damn thing before she ever gets her hands on it!" The fact that she was sitting next to the attorney when the comment was made did not lend itself to tempering the situation.

On days Mario didn't work in the kitchen, he usually took advantage of the club's policy allowing off-duty employees to use the smaller boats. It was during one of those sails that he was noticed by the Commodore. It was a gusty day, and he watched as Mario maneuvered the Sunfish around the bigger sailboats that sat on moorings—gently urging it through each change of the wind. He handled the boat with the experience of a veteran sailor, displaying a natural quickness—left hand on the tiller—right on the sheet. Barkley studied the assuredness in Mario's decisions and admired his ability to factor the wind and the currents to strategize his tack. When he returned and secured the boat to the dock, the Commodore summoned him to his office. When Mario entered, Barkley stood looking out the window. He addressed him without turning to recognize his presence. "It's Costello, right?"

"Yes, sir."

"I'm told you work here at the club . . . in the kitchen."

"Yes, sir."

"I watched you sail in just now, Costello. There're some tricky winds out there today. You're a good helmsman—too good to be in the kitchen fixing salads and whatnot."

The heat rose in Mario's neck and his tone turned defensive. "I had permission to use the boat. We're allowed during our off hours." He let the comment regarding the fixing of salads and whatever the *whatnot* was slide. He had nothing to do with the preparation of food but felt it wasn't his place to correct the Commodore.

"Relax, son. I know the rules. I made most of 'em. Hell, I prob'bly broke most of 'em too at one time or another. I didn't call you in here to question your right to use one of our boats. I called you in here to recruit you." As he made the statement, he turned and faced Mario for the first time. He sported a handlebar mustache, white with age and wax-groomed to a meticulous upward curl. Its whiteness matched his hair which was full and wavy. His eyes were a deep blue or, perhaps, appeared so from the reflection of the water outside. "You do know we've got the fall regatta coming up in a few weeks—the last hurrah before we pull the boats for the winter."

"Yes, sir," Mario said, more relaxed now. "I've watched some of the races. Unfortunately, I'm not eligible to race. It's a 'members only' affair." Mario's new tone reflected an irritated air of the club's elitism. It was ignored—if noticed at all—and Barkley continued.

"Ever do any racing?"

"Raced a little on the school team. Other than that, a few races with friends—usually in Cotuit Bay, sometimes around Dead Neck. I've got a sailing dinghy my friends and I fixed up."

Barkley studied Mario for several seconds before continuing. "How'd you like to trade kitchen work for dock work? You know . . . tend to the small boats, like the Sunfish you had out there today. The boats the members' kids take out. I could fix you up with a job to . . . you know . . . keep 'em shipshape . . . oversee their rigging . . . and so on. When the kids go sailing, you'd be responsible to check them for safety vests, that sort of thing. Maybe you could give some of the little ones lessons." The idea seemed to be a positive afterthought to the offer. "Hell, parents are always buggin' me about a program so their kids can get lessons."

Before Mario could answer, the Commodore continued. "Most of the time the little ones don't even bother securing the boats. They just leave them to drift off and then I've got to get somebody to motor over to the cove and round 'em up. Think you can handle something like that?"

"Sure, I'd like that."

"Well, that's *my* part of the deal."

"Your part of the deal?"

"Yes. Your part, in addition to working the dock, will be to represent the club in this year's regatta."

Mario got a twinge in his stomach. He loved sailing and racing, but his experience in the honors club had been limited to a few races. The Yacht Club regattas were more competitive and the races were taken very seriously by the members.

"When you're not working, I'll want you to familiarize yourself with one of the Lasers. Ever sail one of those? You'll find they're a bit different from the Sunfish . . . they're sleeker, more vulnerable to heeling over. If you're not careful, you'll be drinking the water rather than sailing on it. I'm sure you'll find it a bit different from that sailing dinghy of yours as well." His tone indicated a bit of indignation regarding the dinghy.

"You'll need to learn a few new skills. The Laser's a bit longer than the Sunfish. The club races them in the fourteen foot class." His voice lowered as if he was about to share a secret with Mario. "I want you to get to know the Laser as well as you know your girlfriend's belly." With the statement, he turned and again looked out the window. "And if you don't know what I'm talking about today, you will by the time the regatta rolls around. I want you making love to your boat out there." A sweeping gesture accompanied the statement as he arced his arm over the harbor. He then turned and looked at Mario again. This time he put both hands on his desk and leaned forward putting his body weight on his arms. He continued to stare at Mario but appeared to speak past him rather than to him, as if he was addressing the entire room. "I want you to learn to urge her along . . . play with her . . . tease her into doing what you want . . . caress her like you'd caress the thighs of a good woman . . . make her glide through the waves with the wind singing in her sails all the way across the finish line." For Mario, the silence that followed was awkward.

"As I said, sir, I'd like to race here, but to be eligible . . . ."

The Commodore cut him off with a wave of his hand. "I'll take care of the eligibility nonsense." Although he was a slender man, Mario pictured him having full command on the deck of a ship shouting orders. "You just worry about winning, son. Because when you cross that finish line I want every other boat in the race to be behind you."

"I appreciate the offer but why me? I mean, I'd be glad to race, but the Club always has several entries . . . guys who sail the Lasers all the time."

"You told me you've seen some of the regattas. If that's true then you haven't seen one of our racers cross the finish line first in the last decade. Hell, those guys who race for the club are all pansy-assed sons-of-club members. Most of 'em don't know a halyard from a winch handle. The only reason they get in the race at all is to work on their tan and then go to the big dance afterward. They spend most of the evening with their girlfriends out on the terrace. Those guys are more interested in tryin' to figure out how to unhook the back of a bra, and of course, after the girls spend the first five minutes pretendin' they don't want their tits fondled, they spend the rest of the night screwin' in the back seat of a car. I'm lookin' for somebody who can bring home the gold, son. Why, last year one of those clowns from Osterville went home with the prize." The name Osterville was said with the contempt that indicated they had lost to a third world country.

Mario pondered the idea and the Commodore pushed for an answer. "What do you say? Can you win us the damn cup or not?"

"I'll do my best."

"Okay then. I'll call Marcus down in the kitchen and tell him today's your last day of playin' with fruit salads. Tomorrow you and I will sit down and hammer out your new schedule."

Mario turned to leave.

"Costello?"

"Yes, sir?"

"You said you'd do your best. You understand your best will be first place . . . just something to remember."

Mario left the office and Barkley placed a phone call to Brian Napers, the business manager. "Put the Costello family on the membership list," he instructed. "The family of the kid who works in the kitchen—or used to. I'm moving him out to the docks. We need some help out there with the boats."

Napers explained to Barkley that a work change had to be processed through personnel. He then questioned adding a new membership that hadn't been voted on, hinting neither action came under the jurisdiction of the business manager.

Barkley didn't like to be questioned on club decisions and his continued conversation was shouted into the phone. His words penetrated his office door and echoed halfway down the hallway. A pause followed each of the Commodore's orders and was heard by those within earshot. "Then get personnel on the horn and tell them to get to it . . . yes, that's what I'm saying. . . I'll take care of that as well . . . then call whoever you need to call to get him transferred out of the kitchen. . . I told you . . . on the dock . . . I don't care, just do it!" A longer pause followed before he barked into the phone to conclude the message. "Then put it on my account for now . . . whatever you need to do, just do it!"

The next day the business manager rekindled Barkley's demands during his cocktail hour. Disturbing him on the deck while he enjoyed his Captain Morgan on ice was the manager's second faux pas in as many days. Napers informed the Commodore that as far as a family membership went, Mario had no family per se.

"The kid lives with his mother. She's a secretary at the Cotuit sheet metal plant. Word is his father ran off with some harlot years ago and left them high and dry." Napers offered the information in hopes the membership idea would be dropped.

He used a tone that inferred Mario's mother's employment as a secretary made her more or less a felon.

Barkley absorbed the information while his index finger made circles around the ice cubes in his drink. He then spoke to the business manager with a tone of nonchalance. "Well, there's no rule that says you have to be married to have a membership. Just go ahead and give the membership to the kid and his mother."

Napers shifted his weight from one foot to the other. His eyes darted around the sundeck to avoid Barkley's stare. The Commodore caught the hesitancy and was pleased the situation was causing the manager some frustration. Napers turned to leave and Barkley, enjoying the moment, decided to add more fuel. "What kind of a salary was the Costello kid getting for the kitchen work?"

"He's one of our minimum wage employees, sir."

"Give him a raise then. The kid can probably use the money. Tell him it goes with the new position."

Napers stiffened and took the tone and posture of an English butler. "And how much of a raise would you suggest, sir?"

"I don't know," and then, not wanting to leave the decision to the manager, added, "give him an extra buck an hour." Barkley watched as the reddened neck and stiff backside of the business manager left the sundeck. He smiled and sipped his cocktail.

36

The Costello family's elevated status as members in the Cotuit Yacht Club was never realized by anyone in the community. Not having applied for the membership, Mario's mother was a bit puzzled by the letter stating she had been accepted. Her confusion ended when Mario explained the situation. Newsletters arrived and kept her abreast of club fund raisers and social events. The bill for the annual dues which, in her case, would've amounted to more than her salary, was written off by the Commodore.

Mario learned what he'd been told about the Laser was true. It was faster and sleeker than boats he was used to. He took second place in the fall regatta, losing to a racer from the Camden Yacht Club. Barkley wrote it off explaining Mario hadn't had much time to familiarize himself with the boat. The second-place trophy was a feather in the cap of the older club members. The regatta was the last official race of the season but club racers practiced their skills against each other into the fall. In those rounds, Mario confirmed the merit of Barkley's bragging about his new protégé by never losing a race.

A FEW DAYS INTO the following summer, Mario was prepping the Laser for a morning sail when the Commodore made a rare appearance on the dock. He stood peering through binoculars at one of the other boats owned by the club. "You see that other Laser out there?" he asked Mario.

Mario stopped playing with his sail and acknowledged the second racer.

"Let's you and I have some fun today. Take your boat out there and tell that sailor you've got fifty bucks that says you can get to the first buoy and back before she can."

Mario stared at the Commodore. Over the past eight months he had become used to his eccentricities and wagers with board members.

"She?"

"Looks like a she to me," he said as he continued eyeing the boat through the binoculars. "Unless you're concerned about losing to a female."

"No concern," Mario said.

"Well then, go get her. Don't worry son, I'll cover the bet if you lose."

"I don't plan on losing," he quipped back. "What if she won't race?"

"Oh, she'll race all right. Her parents are members here at the club and she comes here every summer. Racing seems to run in her blood. Sorta like you."

The Commodore's prediction was correct. When Mario neared the second Laser a girl sat holding the tiller. She looked older, perhaps a college student. She was wearing a modest two-piece bathing suit, although the top was covered with a yacht club T-shirt. "Whaddaya say to a little race—out to the buoy and back?" Mario nodded toward the channel marker. When the challenge was tossed across the water she gave a genuine laugh.

"Did that old guy on the dock put you up to this?" As she asked the question, she nodded toward the Commodore.

"I'm not sure I'm supposed to answer that."

She laughed again and with a graceful pull on her tiller, came about and brought her Laser abeam of Mario's. "See ya at the finish," she said, and with an easy continuous glide, she started toward the buoy.

Being caught off guard Mario had no choice other than watch as she increased the distance between their two boats. At the buoy, however, Mario gained an advantage as they came about and he was able to steal some of her wind. The two Lasers sailed side by side briefly before she again took a slight lead and when they entered the area of the wharf, she was first to inch past their agreed finish line. She tossed her head back and her face projected an easy smile. She coaxed the Laser to where Barkley stood and secured it to a dock cleat. The Commodore stood smiling.

Mario joined her and the two stood face to face. Only then did he notice how pretty she was. Her smile seemed to light up the dock and her blonde hair, still tangled from the wind, was cut short, making a perfect frame for her face. Mario took in each feature before remembering he had lost the race. He turned and gave a sheepish glance to the Commodore who broke the awkward moment.

"Meet your new partner," he said.

"New partner?"

"That's right. I'm moving you up to the two-man division and I'm teaming you two up for this year's regatta."

"Two-*person* division," she corrected.

The Commodore beamed another smile. "Yes, I stand corrected. The two-person division," he repeated. He turned to leave but after taking a few steps looked back with a final word to Mario. "And you better get along with her . . . she's my granddaughter." With no further words, he left the dock.

"Maggie," she said holding out her hand. Her smile flashed again. This time Mario noticed her lips. They looked soft, despite the sun and the saltiness of sprays they were subjected to. Her tanned skin accentuated the whiteness of her teeth and her nose and cheeks displayed a faded spray of freckles from younger days.

Mario liked her immediately and took her hand in his. "I had you, you know," he said. "You must've caught a lucky gust of wind just before the finish."

Maggie tossed her head with a move he came to see often as she laughed again. "Why don't we discuss it over lunch? I'll forgive the fifty bucks you owe me as long as you're buyin'."

The Commodore knew they were a matched pair. Like Mario, she had been weaned on boats. During lunch, he discovered she had just completed her first year of college and was in Cotuit for the summer. Her parents had a vacation home there, and as a child she had spent most summers away from her home in Boston. Being the Commodore's granddaughter, she always had the run of the club, and like Mario, grew up using a small sailboat to navigate her way through the many inlets and islands around Cape Cod.

Their friendship was immediate and when the two became a team, they continually won trophies in the two-person races as well as capturing titles in their individual events. On days Mario raced, his mother took advantage of her new status to sit in the members' viewing area to cheer him on. It was there, in the warmth of sunny afternoons, she watched him sail to one first place finish after another. He sailed with a relaxed confidence, handling the tiller and sheets as if they were extensions of his being. By choice, Mario's mother never mingled with members before or after races, nor did she ever see the pretentiousness of the Club's interior.

Race days were always punctuated by an evening social. Mario and Maggie usually attended together and rumors surfaced regarding a romantic interest between them. She laughed when Mario mentioned her grandfather's comment regarding the pansy-assed sons-of-club members going after the girls at the dances.

"I can hear Grampa saying that," she laughed. "They're the same pansy-asses who give you a hard time because you beat them every time you race. Don't let them get to you," she said, and assured him that none of the pansies would ever have a chance of unhooking *her* bra at a Club dance—or anywhere else for that matter. Her statement about the team members was true. They were not only jealous of his superior skills with racing, but shunned him for his lower standing in the community. Many were jealous of his relationship with Maggie, but she never gave Mario any reason to believe it was anything more than platonic. The friendship was filled with sincerity and Mario knew that while being a free spirit, any pledge of fidelity was to her boyfriend back on campus.

Mario was relegated to be viewed as her teammate, or worse yet, a younger brother. His role was never confused with the guy she dated at school. The friendship sometimes made their daily practices feel like a photo shoot for a swimsuit catalogue. Maggie arrived each day wearing what seemed to be a never ending assortment of bathing suits. Her nonchalance was indicative of her unintentional teasing but Mario's opportunities to steal glances and fantasize at her near nakedness were always present. During the laziness of calm days, attempts at actual sailing were futile and they often floated in the stillness of the water while they revealed their thoughts and dreams. Those were days Mario cherished—days the sail luffed gently as it tugged at the line—trying to urge them along—while the two of them ignored it and chatted through an entire afternoon. On those days, Mario studied her every move and often hated the friendship that she felt for him knowing it interfered with his feelings. He always thought of them as his bitter-sweet days of summer.

Maggie and Mario were the team to beat in the two-person competition. Mario also continued his success in the single division. With persuasion and encouragement from the Commodore, he and Maggie were eventually partnered with another team and moved up to the J-24 class. They were bigger boats and the four-person crew, once again, put the Yacht Club in the winners' circle. The Commodore was proud of the racing team he had put together. He loved his granddaughter and took great pride in Mario.

It was an unforgettable summer of racing, and when school began, the Commodore kept Mario on at the club while insisting he maintain a high average in his studies. As a former naval officer, he preached that all endeavors were to be achieved at their highest level. Summers that followed allowed Mario to gain a reputation in racing circles and the Commodore pushed him to set his sights on college.

In spring of his senior year, he was summoned to the office. Barkley sipped his Captain Morgan from a snifter while Mario ran a finger up and down the condensation on his glass of Pepsi. Their history allowed for a casualness few people enjoyed with the old man.

"I wanted to talk to you about a couple of things," he said. "First, I just got word that Maggie won't be racing this summer. She's taking part in some program connected with her studies that allows for a summer internship and she'll be off to Europe."

The news was disturbing to Mario. He stared at the droplets of water running down the Pepsi glass and shifted in his chair.

"I realize it's probably a bit of a disappointment to you, but if that's what she wants to do then she should do it."

Mario found it awkward to show displeasure while trying to act happy over her choice.

"Could be good timing, however," the Commodore continued. "I've been thinking of moving you up to crew in the men's division this year. They've had good results in the past but there's an opening on the team and I think you're the sailor they need to get them to the top. It'll be a nice feather in your bonnet as well. You game for that?"

Mario took a sip of his drink and set it down before answering. The thought of not racing with Maggie still lingered but the men's division involved the best sailors in the club, some who'd raced internationally.

"What about the individual class?"

"I was actually hoping you'd continue with that as well, as long as you can handle both. If push comes to shove, however, I want the men's team to be your priority."

"In that case, I'm in," he said.

"Good. I know you're going to enjoy the shot of adrenalin you'll get racing on the men's team. Anyway, enough about racing. Let's take a different tack. Item two—something else I wanted to discuss today—is your future. I know we've had a couple of talks regarding college, but you seem to be dragging your feet a bit on weighing anchor on applications."

Mario looked at the Commodore with raised eyebrows but let him continue.

"Because you've been hemmin' and hawin' about it I called a couple of my old navy buddies this week . . . in addition to a senator friend of mine." Barkley lifted his glass and swiveled the contents but didn't take a sip. "How'd you like to attend Annapolis?"

This time, Mario knew some kind of a response was expected but the words were slow in coming and seemed to come from somewhere else. "I'm not sure I'm cut out for Annapolis."

"Well, you've got the grades, and you're certainly seaworthy. I can get you in the front door if you want to find out. There'd be an interview of course, some other odds and ends to take care of but nothing you can't handle."

The thought of a military life had never occurred to Mario, although Annapolis was hardly comparable to enlisting. A long and detailed conversation took place between the two before

Mario accepted the Commodore's offer. His summer was then filled with racing and the study of old military manuals the Commodore supplied, indicating their necessity in getting a leg up on the other cadets.

In the fall, Mario packed for the Academy. Before leaving Barkley reminded him that "getting into Annapolis is hard enough. Staying in is often more difficult," and then added, "I heard a quote once that is a good one for you to remember . . . *'If you lose your temper, no one else is going to find it for you.'* You need to think about that. You're a fine sailor, son, but you always seem to carry the weight of a plow anchor on your shoulders." He then wished Mario good luck before adding "Now, go become an admiral," which were the last words Mario ever heard him speak.

TWO MONTHS LATER **A** heart attack took the Commodore's life in as peaceful a passing as could be expected. It was also the last time he saw Maggie. The two stood together at the funeral and endured the loneliness of taps.

His return to the academy was difficult. It was the constant thoughts of the Commodore's determination about life and his competitive spirit that got him through the remainder of his first year. In his second year, Mario's history repeated itself. During a weekend in town, he and a few other cadets were having drinks at the Armada Tavern. One of the locals began maligning a coed from the University of Maryland, and Mario stepped in to put the guy in his rightful place. Within minutes, a skirmish broke out between several midshipmen and a few townies, resulting in police arrests. The inflated damages to the bar totaled over fifteen hundred dollars.

When the city court concluded its findings, the standard reprimand from the administrators at Annapolis was still to follow. Mario and two other midshipmen stood and listened to a degrading lecture from a junior officer. Without flinching, the officer recited articles (b) and (h) verbatim from the academy's code of conduct. He was quick to inform the midshipmen that item (b) clearly stated that:

"Physical abuse of any person, or conduct intended to threaten imminent bodily harm or to endanger the health or safety of any person was cause for disciplinary action" as well as item (h) which he went on to say was:
"Intentionally inciting others to engage immediately in any unlawful activity, which incitement leads directly to such conduct."

The reprimand, along with the attached disciplinary report and restitution to the bar owner, was meant to put a black mark on the records of the midshipmen. It was punishment enough and would've sufficed. But during the rebuke, the junior officer took it upon himself to infer that Mario's actions were idiotic and stated the coed Mario stepped in to rescue was probably nothing more than a cheap college whore anyway. The comment brought Mario's anger to a fevered pitch. To him, the officer was more than likely one of those pansy-assed, sons-of-a-club member types the Commodore detested, and Mario knocked him out cold with a single punch. Had the Commodore been alive, he might've smoothed the incident over with academy officials, but no longer having that endorsement Mario was dismissed.

He returned to Cotuit and for several years he procured seasonal work on charters that sailed tourists around Martha's Vineyard and Nantucket. After five seasons he had put enough money aside for a down payment on a neglected thirty-five foot Beneteau. During her refurbishing he captained her for small charters of his own and took tourists for leisurely sails in the afternoon or romantic sails in the moonlight.

Realizing a warmer climate meant year-round sailing, he sailed *Miss Demeanor* to Florida and attempted similar charters. In Melbourne, he secured a slip at Hanson's boatyard and made his home on the Indian River. Making a living with charters in Florida, however, was more difficult than doing business in Cape Cod. Being one of hundreds of sailors who owned a boat and had the same dream, he found the competition fierce.

Without contacts, and a dwindling bank account, he fell in with Carmine—a man whose tongue was loosened by drink—a man who told him there were ways a guy with a boat could "make some quick money" if he was interested.

It all seemed so long ago. Mario now stared at the ceiling of his cell and recalled Carmine's scheme to sail to Andros. "No risk," he said. "It'll mean big money for both of us . . . all you have to do is sail down there and pick up a few diamonds . . . what could possibly go wrong?"

And now, Cohen had evidently removed him from the picture—banned him from his circle of influence. In the darkness of confinement, Mario became anxious. Anxious about his impending freedom and his own deal with Cohen. As the day of his release grew closer, he began to feel a sense of paranoia. Nothing had gone right in his life and the possibility of getting out of prison, becoming rich, and sailing off into the sunset with a woman he loved just didn't seem to fit.

Questions filled his mind. Did Rosita really care for him or was she playing him? Did Cohen get to her? Did she know about the diamonds? Was her offer to pick him up on the day he got out because of her true feelings or was it a trap? He attempted to answer the questions with logic and reason, realizing a man's brain being locked away can play tricks. He tried to meditate and focus on positive things as Silo had instructed.

Two weeks he thought, trying to calm himself. Two weeks until he would walk out of prison. He pictured Rosita leaning against her car—arms crossed until she saw him—and then she would run to him and throw her arms around his neck and he would finally be able to hold her, touch her, caress her every being. Within those thoughts he convinced himself that his paranoia was unjustified. Two weeks, he thought. Two weeks to a new beginning.

38

♦   trailer trash

Ernie Hanson was a man who carried a grudge. During the twelve months of Mario Costello's incarceration, he had changed very little. The only visible change was his limp. For that mishap, he still blamed Mario. Any thought of his own stupidity during the night of his self-inflicted amputation never registered. He felt Mario's sentence of eighteen months was hardly enough punishment for the man who sunk his skiff, stole his outboard, and burned down his beloved shanty. His anger was compounded when he discovered Mario's boat, which he was given title to by the court appointed arbitrator, was sitting somewhere at the bottom of the Indian River. The consolation that Mario would never sail it again didn't carry the satisfaction he needed. His insistence during arbitration of getting title to the boat was to infuriate his enemy, knowing if he was awarded ownership of *Miss Demeanor,* it would eat away at Mario like a cancer.

As the proprietor of the boatyard, Hanson used the insurance money to have a trailer pulled onto the lot. Similar to the shanty, it served as both office and living space. It was to be a temporary fix until the building of a new structure, but after the hook ups for electric and plumbing were completed, he recognized the trailer provided a better venue for his afternoon sex with Connie. The convenience of having his bedroom just a few feet away from her desk eliminated any remorse over the old couch that had gone up in smoke. Connie, as inefficient as ever, continued her search for employment that didn't require sex on demand. She had recently become friendly with the salesman who provided much of the marine hardware for the yard, and if things got serious with the guy, she was ready to tell Hanson to find another playmate. She had already cut him off from his afternoon romps, thinking it was better to lose her job than losing the prospect of a husband.

The morning Andy called the boatyard, Hanson was out of the office. Connie jotted a few notes on a pad as he made his inquiries.

"I was calling to check on your facilities," Andy said from the other end. "I'm looking for a yard that has a boat hoist. I need to get a sailboat out of the water for some work and I want to get a mast stepped at the same time."

"We have a small hoist here, but if you just need to step the mast, he won't have to take the boat out of the water. What size is it?"

"It's a thirty-five footer, but it's not just a matter of stepping the mast, I'll need to order a new one. There's part of the old one stuck in the sleeve. I need to get that out first."

There was a pause as Connie digested Andy's problem.

"You say that part of the mast is still stuck in the boat?"

"Yeah, it was bent in half during a storm a while back and the weight of it made the boat so lopsided I had to cut the rest of it off," he lied. "I'll have to motor it in to have the work done. That's why I'm calling. I need to know what kind of equipment you have and what kind of a time frame I'd be looking at."

Connie was silent again as she scribbled information on a note pad.

Andy continued. "I need to check out a few other things while I'm having the mast taken care of so I'd like to get her into a cradle or up on jacks."

"Well, Mr. Hanson isn't in the office right now but I can have him call you when he comes in and you can discuss the details with him."

Andy, aware he was going to contact West End Marina with the same questions, was reluctant to give out his number. "I'm gonna be hard to reach. I'd rather call him if you know what time he'll be back."

"Well, you're guaranteed to reach him between twelve and one. He eats lunch here in the office. Closer to one would be better. He gets cranky if his lunch is disturbed. You know, give him time to fill his belly," she laughed.

Andy hung up the phone and called the West End Marina. The owner was in the office and this time Andy got the answers he wanted. West End had all the right equipment and could order and step a new mast.

"I'll have to check around and put some figures together before I can give you a quote on the mast and labor, but the mast price is going to be the same wherever you have the work done. I've also got a few connections so I might be able to find you a used one if you can live with that. You said it was a Beneteau?"

"Yeah, a thirty-five footer."

"You realize you're lookin' at a mast that's gonna run ya a pretty penny. Like I said, I might be able to fix you up with a second-hand mast and save you a few bucks."

Andy knew there was no need for any further conversation with Hanson's boatyard. West End Marina had the equipment he needed and it was obvious from his conversation with the owner that the guy knew his business. It was Andy's failure to make a return call to Hanson that resulted in Connie's scrawled note remaining pinned on the bulletin board with other phone messages. A note that read:

35-footer
needs mast (broken off)
some other stuff

♦   let's make a deal

The owner of the West End Marina returned Andy's call the following day. "I've got good news and bad," he told Andy. "I've located a mast for you, but like I said, it's gonna run ya a pretty penny. It's in a yard about forty miles south of here by boat. You could pay to have it shipped here or—and I hate to say this—you could motor down there and let them do the work. How's your engine?"

"I'm not sure. I may have some water damage. That's one of the things I need to check out."

"So you've got no mast and no engine. What the hell happened to that thing?"

"You might say it's a case of serious neglect."

"Well, anyway, the guy wants sixty-five hundred for the mast. It's not the original and I think his price is a little high, but this guy knows boats and he said it can be retrofitted. Of course, the sixty-five hundred doesn't include labor and you're probably lookin' at close to a hundred bucks an hour. But he's got the equipment and more manpower to do the job than I have. If there's any way you can get your boat to him, I'd say that's the way to go. I can do some more checking but I'm not real optimistic. You're lookin' for a pig in a poke."

"What about that possibility of finding me a better price on a used one?"

"The one he's got *is* a used one. But if money's tight for you right now, you may want to surf the net on your own and see what's out there. If you can get your boat here, I can at least offer you a slip and we can check out your engine. My guys can probably get her motor up and running."

It was a decent offer, further convincing Andy that West End Marina was the boatyard he wanted to do business with. The conversation ended with a lingering decision on the mast.

Sixty-five hundred to repair one piece of the puzzle was certainly not a realistic figure for his plan to refurbish the boat.

Once again, it was Ollie who knew a guy that might be able to help. "Let me check on a few things," he told Andy. "I might have a solution." Considering Ollie had shown opposition to the whole idea of stealing the boat, Andy was surprised at his friend's response.

The next morning Ollie stopped by with the pretense he was returning the inflatable. Andy sat at the kitchen table staring at a long list of needed repairs and an estimated cost for each. The first number was the sixty-five hundred dollars for the mast. The smallest amount was a figure of one hundred dollars he had penciled in for miscellaneous cleaning supplies. After getting the price for the mast, he realized how ridiculous the list of minor items appeared.

They drove to Eric's house and returned the dinghy to the shed before Eric had time to inspect it. Inside, they found him sitting in the living room. He was dressed in a T-shirt and what looked like pajama bottoms. Unlike the house's appearance the night of the party, there was no evidence of drugs or paraphernalia . . . no boisterous banter from their host and no loud music. Andy also noticed a change in Ollie's behavior as if the entire morning—the return of the inflatable and seeing Eric—had all been staged. His assumption was soon confirmed. After declining to join Eric for a screwdriver, they accepted beers and sat in the living room. Eric seated himself on an overstuffed easy chair; Andy and Ollie took seats on opposite ends of the couch that faced him. Ollie started the ball rolling. "Eric here may have a solution to your boat problem."

Eric's eyes focused on Andy. "Ollie says you're good people," he started. "Assuming that's true, I'm going to spill out some information that could get you your boat." Andy said nothing. "I know you're aware that Ollie deals a little dope on the side . . . he's got a nice little business going here."

"Yeah, I'm aware of all that."

"Good. What you're probably not aware of is that Ollie gets his drugs from me. Whether or not he told you that is irrelevant but it's a fact." Again, Andy remained silent. He didn't look at Ollie, but sensed the presence of a different psyche coming from his friend.

"In our business, everybody answers to somebody a bit higher up, so of course my supplier is the next step on the food chain, so to speak. The bottom line is, I've got connections that go to a rung of the ladder that even Ollie hasn't stepped on."

"I'm not sure where you're going with this," Andy said.

"As luck would have it—and it would be your luck I'm talking about—there's a shipment coming in and I need a boat to connect with it and move the shit to Miami. I've got guys with boats that I usually deal with but Ollie here explained your problem to me and I thought maybe we could help each other out."

Andy shot a look toward Ollie.

"Hey, man, I'm just being the middle man here trying to help you out. You kept tellin' me you want this boat and this is a way to get it. You can listen to the plan and then you decide what you want to do."

"I'm not really in the drug dealing business," Andy told Eric in a tone that indicated he was a bit insulted at the idea.

"Okay, then we can end the discussion right here."

"Jeezus, at least hear him out, man. It's a good deal. He's talkin' about a free boat and some cash in your pocket to boot."

Andy figured he'd gone this far and he still had some beer left. "Okay, what's the plan for a free boat and cash in my pocket?"

It was then Eric who shot a look at Ollie, as if wondering if his friend was as anxious to get this boat as he had been told. He returned to Andy. "Whether you buy into this or not, anything I tell you is between the three of us. I'm sure you realize the higher up the ladder you go, the more complicated things get, especially with information."

"Agreed," Andy said nodding.

"Okay then, here's the deal. There's a boat coming in sometime in the next few days. It'll be off shore near West Palm Beach. It'll be carrying a shipment of marijuana that has to get to Miami. We run smaller boats into Miami, not only for the convenience to our marina down there but to eliminate the attention bigger boats draw. Big boats in small ports have a tendency of attracting custom agents which is something we try to avoid. A boat like yours . . . you know . . . a boat needing obvious repairs has a good reason to be going into the marina. It's a perfect cover."

Andy sat and stared at the bottle in his hand and Eric continued. "Okay, you haven't told me to shut up yet, so I'll keep going. The crew will transfer the grass to your boat, which, from what Ollie here tells me, you'll limp in to our marina—which will be a nice touch by the way—and our guys will unload the merchandise and hand you a satchel of cash."

Andy stirred in his chair and was about to speak but it was as if Eric knew it wasn't a deal he was interested in and he raised a flat palm in the air. The signal stopped Andy from voicing any opposition and he continued. "That's not all, my friend. Tell him about the marina, Ollie."

"Yeah, you'll like this. The marina is not just a cover for the operation; it's a fully functioning facility with guys who've been working on boats for years. In addition to the cash we'll get paid, you can give me a list of everything you want fixed on the boat. You know . . . mast . . . engine . . . anything you need to get that sloop in shape, and in a matter of days, you'll sail out of there with a new boat." Ollie knew Andy well enough to know that he wasn't yet convinced. "Don't decide right now, man. Sleep on it." He then addressed Eric. "That works for you, doesn't it?"

"Sure. If Andy here doesn't want in—it's like I said, I've got other guys with boats I can send out there. You called me remember? I'm goin' out of my way to help you out. My other guys don't need their boats repaired at the company's expense."

THE WALK TO OLLIE'S Jeep was made in silence. Once underway, Andy started in on his friend. "What the hell are you thinking? Stealing a boat isn't risky enough? You want to add drug running to the equation?"

"Hey, man, you called me in a jam and I found you a way out. You can take it or walk away. It's the dream boat you've been moonin' over, fixed to your specs I might add, and a few bucks on the side."

"And where do you fit in to all this? If I went along with the insanity, I mean."

"I'll go with you. I mean, I'd expect at least half of the money. I am the dealer here, if you recall."

"At *least* half?"

"Yeah, I mean . . . you're getting the boat out of the deal. Maybe you should get the boat and I should negotiate for all the money."

"What kind of money is this guy talkin' about? I guess I didn't let the conversation get that far."

"I'm not sure. It varies from dealer to dealer. Street value on a pound of good shit right now goes for three to four hundred an ounce. If you figure three hundred, a pound would net a guy around five grand . . . double that to ten thou for a kilo and . . . well, you might get as much as ten per cent if all goes well. And even a guy without a calculator can figure out that ten percent of ten thousand is a thousand bucks a key and that ain't bad. He's probably talkin' twenty to twenty-five keys."

"Yeah, or twenty to twenty-five years if all doesn't go well."

"All I can tell you, my friend, is sleep on it. If you want to go for it, I'm in. It's gonna be more weight than I'm used to, but it is what I do for a living."

hard decisions

Mario sat in his cell. It was Tuesday. With three days of incarceration remaining, he was counting down the hours until his release. A guard arrived to tell him he had a visitor. Not being Saturday and having an agreement with Rosita that no contact would be made at other times, he had no expectations of seeing anyone. He was taken to a small room rather than the regular visitors' area. A young man waited. It was several seconds of studying his face before Mario recognized him as the young lawyer who visited him a year ago after his arrest—the attorney who specialized in mergers and acquisitions. Mario sat down and the attorney got right to the point omitting any pretense of a friendly greeting.

"So, Friday's the big day, Mr. Costello. How's it feel to be getting out of here?"

"I cry every night thinking about how I'll miss this place," Mario responded. "What the hell do you want?"

"Why, it's time to pay the piper, my friend. Or to be more precise, it's time to repay the guy who's kept you safe in here. In short, Cohen wants his merchandise. Your game of pussyfooting around ends Friday and I'm here to tell you how it's going to work."

Mario said nothing and the lawyer continued. "A car will be waiting outside. You'll get in it. You'll instruct the driver to take you wherever the hell it is you need to go to get Mr. Cohen's product. The driver will take you there, and after confirming the goods, he'll give you a briefcase containing the half million you're owed—minus any expenses Mr. Cohen's accrued along the way to keep you safe. Once that's done, you'll get out of town . . . never to be seen again."

Mario remained silent while he studied the attorney's face for several seconds. "What's your name again?"

The attorney's face reddened as he seemed to be thrown off balance by the question. "Morrow . . . Shane Morrow."

"Oh, yeah," Mario returned. "Well, I'll tell you what Mr. Morrow, when I walk out of here on Friday, I'm gonna get in the car of a woman I've been waiting over a year to be alone with. The odds of me getting into a car with a guy who probably has a face that looks like ground hamburger isn't that appealing to me. You can tell Cohen he'll get his *product* as you call it within twenty-four hours. It's gonna take me at least that long to say hello to my woman. And when I do deliver the product, the price was one million, not a half million."

"I'm afraid things have changed since you've been on the inside. First of all, the million was for you and your friend Carmine. Who, by the way, is currently cooling his heels for three to five for illegal transport of whatever it was he was mixed up in. In addition to that, you may have forgotten that Mr. Cohen has been footing the bill for your protection over the past twelve months. I'll also remind you that once you're outside the gates of heaven here, you won't have Silo to protect your ass. If your woman is waiting outside, you need to think very carefully as to which car you get into, otherwise you may not have a girlfriend to be alone with." He paused, but there was no response from Mario "We'll see you on Friday, Mr. Costello. Enjoy your last few hours."

Morrow then stood and pushed the button to signal the guard. Mario's return walk to his cell was filled with thoughts of his release, uncut diamonds, and now included thoughts of Rosita's safety. Even the handing over of the stones gave him no guarantee of getting any money from Cohen, or keeping him alive for that matter. He had much to think about and seventy-two hours to come up with a plan. His advantage was knowing the boat and the diamonds were safe.

AS MARIO SAT ON his bunk thinking about the message delivered by the attorney, Andy Dugan sat at the kitchen table thinking about a boat. He stared at the tablet covered with calculations. The sheet listing the estimated cost of repairs had been put aside and he looked at a new set of numbers. Ollie had said a conservative estimate for an ounce of prime reefer would sell for three-hundred dollars. The figures he'd written down and calculated several times told him a cut of ten per cent would be roughly one thousand dollars a key. Ollie had guessed twenty to twenty-five keys for the shipment. Even after an even split he would not only have the refurbished boat, but a wad of cash. Eric had mentioned, as the boat was stolen, a name change along with any legal papers needed for ownership could be arranged. "I've got guys who can provide you with documents that will pass any Coast Guard inquiry," Eric had said.

Andy made the calculations one final time and got the same results. He knew dealing was profitable, but he had never actually worked out any figures. It suddenly became clear why Ollie did what he did. Even on Ollie's smaller scale, the profit margin was well over what he desired from life.

It was a restless night for Andy. Like his rationale for stealing the boat, he tossed and turned while he mulled over the morality and consequences of transporting a boatload of grass to Miami. After all, it was only a small amount of marijuana and it was going to get to the potheads who wanted it whether he took it there or not. The odds of being suspected and searched by the Coast Guard were minimal and there were plenty of cavities on board to hide a few keys. Even if the Coast Guard checked them at point of entry, it would be a superficial exam. Like Eric said, the boat was obviously going into the marina to have work done.

The clock on the nightstand clicked off the seconds for over an hour before he found the comfort of sleep. In the morning, he sat and stared again at the figures on the tablet. The numbers seemed to leap off the page and he came to the realization that a trip to Miami was the only way he would gain ownership of the boat sitting on the Indian River. The few days of moderate risk would be worth the time. "Someday," he said out loud, "I'll have a story to tell my grandchildren . . . a story of piracy on the high seas. I'll tell them how their grandfather stole a boat and ran drugs for a cartel." With that thought he smiled. He scrolled down the list of numbers in his cell phone and called Ollie.

When Ollie answered, Andy's voice was calm and determined. "I'm in," he told him.

41

After receiving the news from Andy, Ollie set the wheels in motion. He set a second meeting with Eric and picked Andy up on the way. Eric met them at the door. His demeanor was more cordial than their first meeting, as if Andy getting on board with the plan made him an accepted member into the fold. They all shook hands. Eric's other hand held a Bloody Mary complete with a stalk of celery. Andy and Ollie declined his offer to join him, and similar to their first meeting, they substituted cold beers. In the living room, they sat in the same seats as the day before, but the table between the couch and the chair displayed several lines of coke and a stub of a plastic straw.

"Help yourself," Eric told them.

Ollie snorted two lines and handed the straw to Andy who inhaled two shorter lines. The taste of the coke immediately trickled down his throat and he took a swallow of beer as a chaser. Eric got right to the point. "It's good to know you're in on this." He raised his Bloody Mary to toast the union. "To Andy from Maine." The touching of glasses was omitted and the three drank before Eric continued. "Anyway, I'll give you a couple of days notice and you can head out to rendezvous with my guy. I'll call Ollie on his cell. Your boat's all set to go, right?"

"Yeah, sure," Ollie lied.

Since making the decision to be part of the operation, Andy had many questions he needed answered. "Where's he going to be, I mean, where are we supposed to meet the guy with the boat?"

"Once you're on the water, I'll give you the coordinates. I've got ship to shore equipment here along with a hand-held GPS you can take. From what Ollie's told me most of the equipment on board probably isn't operational."

"Where's the stuff coming from?" Andy pushed.

"Hey, you know," Eric made waving gestures in the air. "It comes from here . . . it comes from there . . . doesn't really matter as long as it just keeps coming, right?"

Before Andy could get in another question, Eric cut him off. "So, tell me about this boat you guys are stealing. Is this something we should be worried about being reported?" Ollie viewed it as a matter of interest, but Andy wasn't sure if it was a legitimate concern or a diversion to stop him from asking questions.

"It's been sittin' untouched for over a year," Ollie told him.

"You said it's a thirty-five footer if I recall."

The statement initiated another question from Andy. "How much will we be picking up? I'll need to know the weight."

"I won't really know until everything's set, but they know the size of your boat and it won't be much, especially bein' your first outing. Who knows, you may like the deal and we can use you two for regular runs. You'll be fine."

For Andy, this was to be the only run he was going to make and he still had questions. "Once we pick it up, where in Miami do we take it?"

"You'll get the location of the marina when you transfer the goods to your boat." The statement was made with a tone of finality indicating Eric was tired of all the questions from a newcomer. "I'm beginning to think you're some kind of an undercover cop or something."

The comment split the air. "C'mon, c'mon," Ollie broke in. "He just wants to know where he's goin', man. Back off."

Eric nodded and then gave a slight laugh. "Okay, I didn't mean anything by it. Make your list of what the boat's gonna need to get it back in shape. I'll get the information to the marina so there won't be any delays in getting you out of there and back up here to Melbourne." The combination of coke swirling in his head and Eric's evasiveness brought a feeling of uneasiness to Andy and it was the topic of conversation on the ride home.

"I'd like to have more information than Eric's willing to give us."

Ollie, who had taken an additional snort of coke before leaving, brushed off his friend's concerns. "That's the way it works. They give out little bits of info when you need it. Be thankful they're cautious. Everything's gonna be fine."

After being dropped off at the beach house, Andy called the West End Marina. It had become imperative for him to get a closer look at the boat. "I'd like to get the boat over to your place as soon as possible, but I'm not sure what kind of shape the outboard is in and the engine is halfway under water. I'm sure the battery's dead anyway. Just something else I'll need to replace."

"I've got an old six horsepower outboard here in the yard I could let you borrow to get her over here if that helps. I'll be here until five if you want to swing by and pick it up. You said the boat was near Douglas Park. You'd only have to motor a couple of miles to get it here."

Ollie was unreachable. Andy drove to the marina and discovered the shaft on the outboard that had been offered wasn't long enough to reach the water from the stern. "I've got a small aluminum boat at the dock. You could stick the outboard on that and push your boat in. Shouldn't be much of a problem for that distance. Hell, you're on the river. It's not like you're gonna encounter thirty-foot waves."

With the boat loaded on top of the minivan and the motor stowed, Andy drove to Ollie's house. There was still no sign of Ollie so he parked in the driveway and waited. As assumed, Ollie had been out catching waves and when he pulled in, he walked to the van. He motioned to the inverted boat on the roof. "What's going on?"

Andy nodded toward the outboard in the rear of the van. "We're on for tonight. West End let me borrow the boat and an outboard. I figured we could hang out here until it gets dark and then head over."

"I don't know, man. I should probably call Ding-Lee. We should probably check to see if we're anywhere near a void of course if you know what I mean."

"Screw the void of course shit. I thought you said that was a good thing. Now I'm not so sure you know what all that lunarium stuff means. I've got to get this boat and motor back to the marina. When it gets dark, we're out of here."

Under the pretense that he was planning to call Ding-Lee anyway, Ollie phoned her, and without revealing any details of the evening's plan, inquired as to whether or not the lunarium timetable was in their favor. Luckily, the timing of the change from one moon to the next seemed to be with them.

The plan was simple. They sat and drank a few beers at Ollie's place until well after sunset. On the way to the sloop, they smoked a joint and reviewed the step-by-step details. It was close to ten o'clock when they got to *Miss Demeanor* and parked in a grassy area just off the causeway. It wasn't until the boat was unloaded from the van that Andy realized they had no way of getting back from the marina unless they returned in the borrowed boat.

"Motoring back to the van will just take too much time," Andy said. "Besides, then we'll still have to take everything back to the marina." Neither seemed to realize their discussion under the influence of drugs and alcohol was not making much sense, but they agreed to tie the boat at the shoreline and return to Ollie's apartment to get his jeep.

"The outboard will have to go with us. I'm not leaving it for someone to come along and steal it. We're taking enough of a chance leaving the boat here," Andy told Ollie.

"You've been in the big city too long. This is Florida, man. Nobody's gonna touch it. They hang people down here for boat rustlin'." Andy shot him a look. "That's real comforting to know, seein' as that's the reason we're here in the first place."

"Not sailboats, man. They just hang guys who steal fishing boats."

Another hour passed while Ollie got his jeep and parked it at the marina. It was close to eleven o'clock when they returned to make the second attempt at getting the boat. They motored out, and without bothering to go aboard, Andy grabbed hold of the anchor rode. After the year of sitting, the anchor's fluke was immersed in bottom mud too deep to be easily freed. He withdrew a knife from his sheath and cut the line. *Miss Demeanor* bobbed a bit, as if taking a deep breath and welcoming her freedom.

"You think this outboard is powerful enough to tow this thing?" Ollie asked.

"Don't plan on towin' it," Andy told him. It's much easier to push it along. We used to do that with the schooner I worked on to get it out of the harbor."

Andy instructed Ollie to climb on board *Miss Demeanor* and secure a line from the tender to the sloop's stern as a safety measure.

"In case you start to drift off," Andy told him.

With Ollie in the cockpit, Andy began the short trip to the West End Marina. At first, there was a slight bit of resistance, perhaps showing her reluctance to leave the comfort of her resting place, but then she eased forward a bit. Andy gave a slight turn on the tiller handle and sent a slow surge of power to the outboard. With the motor purring, they nudged *Miss Demeanor* along and made the slow move down the river. Ollie sat at the helm and lit a joint in celebration of being underway. He glanced up at the starlit sky and then down at Andy. "Not exactly like rustlin' cattle, is it?"

"No. I'm not sure if cattle rustlers got stoned."

The river was peaceful which seemed to be in conflict with their deed. The outboard purred quietly and they continued to push *Miss Demeanor* along until she was in the parameter of the marina and safely secured. The aluminum boat and the motor were returned to the main dock as instructed. For the first time since returning to Florida, Andy enjoyed a feeling of relief. He felt comfort in knowing he was finally the owner of the boat he had obsessed over for an entire year.

42

Thursday was a day things seemed to occur at twice the speed of life. It started with Andy's irritation at himself for oversleeping. Wednesday night's involvement in stealing a boat and not getting in until the wee hours of the morning were a contributing factor. His intent was to get to West End Marina early and get a jump start on surveying *Miss Demeanor*. The list of items and repairs he expected were to be in Eric's hands by noon. The idea of motoring a stolen boat from Melbourne to West Palm Beach and then adding the additional crime of loading it with twenty-five keys of marijuana bound for Miami gave him a continued sense of uneasiness.

Ollie seemed to be fine with the whole operation, but as he said, this is who he was—what he did in life—and maybe any consequences that occurred along the way were expected as part of doing business. Andy, on the other hand, intended to design boats, eventually get married and have children, and live a normal, uneventful life like other husbands.

He dressed quickly and got to the marina shortly before noon to find *Miss Demeanor* had already been lifted out of the river and was resting comfortably in a cradle. The cushions from the cockpit had been thrown over the side to the ground along with those from the cabin and the V-berth. All of them showed visible signs of mold.

Andy climbed the ladder to inspect the progress on deck. A worker who looked to be in his fifties was removing the last portion of her mast. "This sucker was a real mess. What the hell happened to this thing, if ya don't mind me askin'?"

"After a storm bent the thing in half, I cut the rest of it off," Andy lied. "I didn't really have much choice in the matter."

The worker shrugged and then tossed the remains of the mast's stub over the side where it fell and bounced off one of the cushions. A stirring came from below deck and Andy gave a questioning look toward the worker.

"Your partner's lady friend is below," he explained. "Been down there most of the mornin' scrubbin' away and gettin' things organized."

"Is he down there with her?"

"No, he left outta here about thirty minutes ago. Said he'd be back by lunch time."

Andy climbed down the companionway. The woman he presumed to be Ding-Lee had her back to him. She was spraying a cleaner on the teak trim and cabinets and wiping them down. The smell of bleach and Windex filled the cabin.

"Ding-Lee?" Andy asked.

She turned, and for the first time Andy faced the woman in Ollie's life who was ruled by movements of the moon. He saw instantly why Ollie had become so infatuated. She was pretty—not beautiful—simply pretty. Her hair fell just short of her shoulders and had a natural messiness to it. It was her body that was exemplary. Every inch was toned from her regimen of daily workouts—as if chiseled by a sculptor from the Renaissance era—and very little of it was hidden. She was wearing cut-off jeans that were short enough to expose the pockets that hung down from inside and a T-shirt that had been cut to less than half its original length. It was difficult for Andy to avoid staring. It was something about the exact proportionality of her body. As they exchanged glances, her face brightened into a welcoming smile.

"Andy?" she asked, extending a hand.

He continued to take her in. Her T-shirt was soaked through from a playful water fight with Ollie earlier in the day, and her breasts lifted it to expose a stomach that was young and tight. He had already surpassed the appropriate amount of time one might expect a polite person to use as he stared at her nipples that were straining to poke through her shirt. She noticed the direction his eyes had taken, yet didn't seem to be concerned by any of it. He composed himself and brought his eyes to focus on hers. "Yes, I'm Andy."

"One of the guys who works here drilled a hole in the bottom of the boat to let the water out," she told him. Her opening words of their conversation sounded as if she'd known him for years. As she made the statement, she lifted a foot that was in several inches of water. "He said he could plug it once it drained and it wouldn't let any more water in. He said he had his doubts if your engine was going to run again though. That's full of water too."

"Yeah, that's one item I'm here to check on. How about the cabin? What've you found so far in the way of damage?"

"Well, I didn't get into the bedroom in there yet," she said, pointing to the V-berth. "And I think this area in here just needs a good cleaning. There's mold and stuff but this cleaner works pretty good."

Using the excuse that he wanted to go through the cabinets to check things out, Andy stayed below. After all, Ding-Lee was his best friend's girl and he felt a certain obligation to get to know her.

"So what do you normally do, when you're not cleaning boats for strangers?"

"Mostly I make jewelry and sell it on the beach or across town in Tomosca Park."

"What kind of jewelry?"

"Mostly stuff I make from sea shells. Sometimes I use sea glass . . . oh, that reminds me, I found a pouch full of some sea glass stuck down in the boat cushions this morning. Ollie said I could have it but I guess I should ask you since it's your boat."

"Well, actually, I acquired the boat from another guy. But sure, knock yourself out if you can make something out of the stuff. It's the least I can do. I appreciate you helping out here." He continued to open drawers and doors in a half-hearted attempt to see how much elbow grease was going to be required to get the cabin to a livable state. "You said you mostly made jewelry. What else do you do?" He expected an answer that might be related to some kind of fortune telling or moon appraisals.

"I cut hair."

"Really? Maybe you should try that skill on Ollie. I think he could use a little trim now and then."

"That's how I met him. I used to go to the park one day a week and cut hair for some of the old guys, you know . . . the homeless guys. And then one day a guy came up to me and asked if I'd cut his hair and he said he'd pay me five bucks. Anyway, he must've said something to his friends because the next week he showed up with four other guys. Well, to make a long story short, the next time I was there a guy told me he'd pay double if I took my top off while I cut his hair."

Andy raised an eyebrow and tried to avoid looking at the nipples still straining to poke through the T-shirt. "A topless haircut?"

"Hey, that's no big deal to me. I used to live in a nudist colony. I mean, I don't see anything wrong with showing off the human body so I said sure, why not, and stripped off my shirt. That started my career as a topless hair stylist, but then too many guys started comin' around—I think maybe just to gawk, you know, so I stopped doin' it all together."

"What about the cops?"

"Well, there was *one* cop who came and stood by the bench while I was there. He said he was just there to protect me so nobody stole my money. Anyway, I just do the jewelry thing now but I'm savin' up to go to beautician school. I could cut your hair though if you want me to, I wouldn't charge you anything and I'd keep my shirt on, of course."

"Yeah . . . of course." Andy contemplated the offer. "I think I'll pass for now."

"Okay, just let me know if you change your mind." There was a long silence before she spoke again. "Did you *want* to see my boobs?"

Andy choked a bit at the question. "I think it might be a bit inappropriate. I mean the whole topless haircutting thing seems a bit provocative to me anyway, don't ya think?"

"Yeah, I guess," she said and they both shared a good laugh over the thought. Another moment of silence passed before she asked him, "What's that pavocative thing you said mean anyway?"

Before Andy could muster a response, a yell from Ollie came from outside the boat and Andy went topside. Ollie was standing next to his jeep and pointing to an outboard that was sitting in the back seat. "Long shaft," he shouted. "Bought it this morning. It's a nine horse." He then held up his phone. "Eric called, we gotta hit the trail . . . today!"

Andy climbed down and gave a quick once over to the outboard. "What'd you pay?"

"Half a pound," Ollie told him, and they both laughed.

The afternoon was a scramble. With the exception of the two life jackets containing the least amount of mold, everything else containing cloth was hauled to the dumpster. The boat was drained dry and plugged to prevent any incoming water while at sea. Crane operators put their chores on hold to lift *Miss Demeanor* back into the water and Ollie made ready. Andy made a quick trip back to the cottage to get a sleeping bag, a cooler, and a plastic air mattress. En route to the marina he stopped and picked up some ice and a minimal supply of nonperishable food. Ollie mentioned he had done the same but Andy knew their ideas of survival gear differed greatly. By the time he returned, *Miss Demeanor* was at the dock with the outboard mounted. She was as ready as she was going to be to run drugs to Miami.

During the hustling and bustling at the West End Marina, Hanson's office was also busy. The salesman from the marine hardware supply dropped by and proposed to Connie. He was being transferred and the move offered a new start for both of them. She accepted the proposal which would not only give her a new lease on life, but end her ties with Ernie Hanson. It was Thursday, and in her haste to tidy up office affairs, she left the next day's billing slips and other end-of-the-week chores for Hanson. She decided she would tell him nothing. At five o'clock on Friday she would take her paycheck and walk out the door without a word. On Monday Hanson could fend for himself.

WHILE CONNIE PLANNED HER elopement, Mario packed his few personal items in the standard box issued to outgoing inmates. He had waited over a year to walk out the doors of Bower Correctional, and in nineteen hours he would make his exit and get into Rosita's car. She had arranged a vacation weekend at a nearby beach resort, and after getting better acquainted, he planned to get the diamonds from *Miss*

Demeanor, meet with Cohen, and get the money needed for him and Rosita to get away and make a fresh start.

After packing his personal items, he went to chow and had his last dinner with Silo. Back in his cell, he selected a magazine from his box and leafed through it until he was interrupted by a guard. "You've got a phone call," the guard told him.

Mario assumed it was the second-string lawyer from mergers and acquisitions with a final reminder regarding his release.

"Not interested," Mario told him.

"You might want to take it. She sounds pretty upset. She said it's an emergency. I checked with the warden and he said you could take it, seein' as how you're gettin' outta here tomorrow."

"She?"

"Yeah . . . and like I said, she sounded pretty upset."

When Mario got to the phone, the message from the other end of the line was piercing.

"It's gone," Rosita sobbed.

"Whaddaya mean, it's gone? What's gone?"

"Your boat . . . it's gone. I finished my shift and walked to the park like I always do. When I got there the boat just wasn't there. I looked up and down the river thinking she might've broken loose and drifted, but it's nowhere. It's all my fault for not watching it better."

"Okay, okay, just stay calm. If it's gone, it's gone. There's nothing we can do today. Pick me up in the morning like we planned. We'll figure it out together. And this is not your fault."

Mario was deep in thought for the remainder of the night, mentally playing out every possible scenario of the missing boat. The same answer continued to surface . . . Hanson had found the boat. He found it and took it to his boatyard. He figured he owned it, and now he had it. Mario's only hope was that Hanson hadn't found the secret compartment and the diamonds, although it was unlikely. He would gladly give up *Miss Demeanor* in exchange for the stones. It would be easy. He would stake out the boatyard and wait for Hanson to leave. It would only take a few minutes to get on board and get the pouch. The problem was time. Cohen had waited a year to make this deal and the wolves were circling. He couldn't put things off any longer. For Mario and Rosita, the timing couldn't have been worse. Of course, for Andy Dugan, the timing was just about right.

MIAMI

◆ **releasing the hounds**

Friday Morning - February 1ˢᵗ
8:00 a.m.

Mario made final preparations for leaving Bower Correctional. His small box of personal items was tucked under his arm as he was walked through the final procedures. His scheduled release for nine o'clock was on time and in just over an hour, he and Rosita would be on the highway. In lieu of the romantic weekend they had planned, they would be searching for *Miss Demeanor.*

Rosita looked in the mirror one final time before leaving her apartment. In an hour she and Mario would finally be together. There would be no interference from a watchful guard, no surveillance cameras, and there would be no separation by the blue line that denied any touching. To be held in his arms was a twelve-month longing she had endured with understanding. She and Mario would find *Miss Demeanor* and then spend the romantic weekend at the luxury beachside hotel she had taken great pains to arrange.

Connie prepared the morning pot of coffee for the last time. At five o'clock, she planned to leave and never return. Tension between her and Hanson had grown exponentially during the past weeks. Her refusal to submit to his sexual desires and his threats to "throw her out on her ass," had peaked. She hummed as she fixed the coffee, knowing in a few days she was getting married.

Hanson had yet to emerge from the back bedroom of the trailer. His snoring was pleasant to Connie's ears because the longer he slept meant less time she had to put up with him. She knew he would sleep until nine-thirty or ten leaving her only seven hours to listen to his incessant rants regarding her stupidity.

Cohen was on the phone confirming his expectations for his hired men. Instructions were reiterated a final time to ensure Rosita would never make it to Bower Correctional. His men would take her place. They would secure Mario's cooperation and get him to hand over the diamonds. Not being a man of severe violence, killing Mario wasn't in the equation. Cohen's instructions were to administer a thorough and proper beating before dumping him into an alley. Anything short of a hospital stay would be insufficient.

Ding-Lee sat on Melbourne Beach and made pieces of jewelry using a technique she had learned in one of her many craft classes. The technique involved wrapping wire around the beach glass she had found in the pouch on *Miss Demeanor*. With no one giving them a second thought when the stones were first discovered, she had no idea she was making her jewelry with rough-cut diamonds. Once the stones were wrapped, she attached them to delicate silver chains. The larger ones were fashioned into necklaces, the medium-sized into earrings, and the very tiny stones, not being of much use to her, were thrown into the ocean. The largest of the pieces she wrapped with a piece of waxed thread and gave to Ollie before he left. The waxed thread would allow him to wear it around his neck while surfing. She told him it would bring him good karma.

◆ no ser cebo de pescado

The first day of February brought on a renewed taste of sailing for Andy. It had been several months since he had been out to sea, and although he had no mast and was propelled through the ocean by a small outboard, it felt good to be on the water again. He and Ollie had motored through the night and were free of the Indian River. The laboring outboard propelled *Miss Demeanor* toward West Palm Beach. The lights along the shoreline guided them throughout the night, and since sunrise the coastline served as a comforting escort. Andy continued to man the tiller while Ollie made coffee and rolled a joint to get the day started.

Shortly past Port St. Lucie, they received the call from Eric on the ship to shore. Andy listed the coordinates for their rendezvous with the ship that was carrying what they estimated to be twenty to twenty-five kilos of marijuana.

Ollie sat cross-legged on the bow absorbing a light spray of salt water. He was dressed in a pair of lightweight cotton pants and a long-sleeved L.L. Bean shirt he had taken from Andy's duffel bag. Andy remained in the cockpit and scanned the horizon for the ship awaiting their arrival. Ollie was first to spot it. It started as a speck but loomed larger with the use of binoculars until it became recognizable with the naked eye.

"Is it the trawler?" Andy asked.

"I could probably tell you if I knew what a trawler looks like."

"See if you can read the name then. It should be on the bow. Eric said it was the *Bonnie-K.*"

Ollie peered through the glasses a second time and after a long pause confirmed it was the ship they were to meet. They neared the vessel and secured *Miss Demeanor* amidship which provided easy access to the deck. A man wearing a shoulder holster holding an inverted automatic weapon helped secure the line. For the first time, Andy realized what he and Ollie were involved in and he wished he hadn't gotten so stoned that morning.

The gunman spoke in a matter-of-fact tone. "You Captain Dugan?"

"Yeah, I'm Dugan," Andy responded, surprised by the title.

"Captain wants to see ya. He's in the pilothouse." He then nodded toward another crew member who also wore a sidearm, but one not as menacing as the automatic. "He'll take you to the bridge."

His escort was a burly man. "Gotta frisk ya, mate," he told Andy, and made a gesture indicating he should raise his arms in the air. Andy complied and the gunman made quick work of patting him down before instructing him to follow. As he was led to the pilothouse he noticed distinct differences in the appearance of the crew. Most looked like what he expected commercial fishermen to look like—weathered skin, rough calloused hands, and dressed in appropriate fishing gear. Others were dressed like the man leading him. They wore sidearms and stood in strategic areas on the deck, hidden from approaching boats. They brandished heavy weapons and their posts gave them the advantage of defending their cargo against intruders or an avenue to disappear below deck to avoid being seen by the Coast Guard or other authorities.

Inside the pilothouse, a crewman surrounded by gauges and switches drank coffee from a Styrofoam cup. The captain was seated at a desk and a third armed crewman stood close by. The captain stood and smiled as he extended a hand to Andy. "Welcome aboard. I'm Captain Lombardi . . . you know . . . like the football guy." The handshake was powerful, yet not the bone crushing type some men use to prove their strength. "I'm guessing you're Captain Dugan." And then added, "Of the good ship *Miss Demeanor*."

Andy accepted the handshake and their eyes locked. It was obvious he was being studied by Lombardi and he felt a bit uneasy. The response to his expression when *Miss Demeanor* was mentioned was further proof that Lombardi could read people.

"Eric and I keep in close contact," he told Andy. "Even when I'm out here on the high seas."

He was a slender man. Andy guessed him to be in his late forties. The long sleeves of his khaki shirt were rolled to the elbows and the dark hair on his arms glistened from the heat of the cabin. "Come . . . let's take a short walk. I like to show off my ship and it will take a few minutes for my men to get your boat loaded before you can get underway."

Andy was led to the main deck. Lombardi filled him in as they walked toward the stern. "She's an eighty-five footer . . . steel hull . . . solid for our needs."

"What do you fish for?" Andy's question was more to make conversation than anything else. It also served as a pretense to let the captain know his lips were sealed regarding anything he observed while on board. He wanted to confirm he viewed the ship as a fishing vessel, not a ship having anything to do with running drugs.

"Not much this time of year. A lot of the fishing ends in January. We're heading south and then west to spend some time in the Gulf."

Andy didn't push the topic of fishing and they continued in silence until they reached the stern where two sharks were hanging on giant hooks. One had been gutted; the other hung in waiting. A crew member appeared as if on cue.

"Ahhh, what good timing for us, Captain Dugan. It seems as if Jimmy here is in the midst of making some chum. Ever used chum for bait, Captain Dugan?"

"I don't really fish myself, but I'm familiar with it. I grew up near fishing villages in Maine. Never really fished for anything that called for chumming the waters. I spend most of my time sailing."

"Well, this container here is already started." He then turned to the crewman. "Jimmy, maybe we should show Captain Dugan how we gut a shark."

The crewman withdrew a knife the size of a Bowie. Its serrated edge gleamed under the sun. Lombardi neared the hanging shark and stroked its underbelly the way a person might pet a dog. His eyes locked again on Andy's and he talked as if giving a lecture at the aquarium. "Sharks . . . ferocious in the water . . . but out of their element . . . defenseless." He continued staring at Andy, "everyone needs to stay in their element, don't you think?" As he asked the question he extended his hand and the crewman placed the handle of the knife in his open palm. "Otherwise," he continued, "we become weakened." At the word weakened, he plunged the dagger into the shark's underbelly, "we become . . . unable to protect ourselves."

He ripped the shark open, stepping back as the guts spilled out and fell to the deck. A stench unequalled by anything Andy had ever smelled permeated the air. The crewman, seemingly oblivious to the odor, grabbed a small shovel and scooped the shark's innards into the container.

Lombardi picked up a cordless drill with a long attachment secured in the chuck and ran his hand down the eighteen inch shank. It ended in a hollow square-shaped blade. "A deadly tool, Captain Andy. Why, I've known careless men who've caught their hand inside the square here and lost some of their fingers—some who now wear a hook for the rest of their days." He held the end toward Andy. "Touch it," he said. "You'll see what I mean when you feel the sharpness." Lombardi's finger remained on the trigger and Andy hesitated.

"It's okay, it's clean," Lombardi encouraged. "Feel the blade."

"It isn't the cleanliness I'm concerned about. It's more the thought of wearing a hook the rest of my days if the trigger is accidently pulled." Andy gave a short laugh attempting to indicate he meant no offense.

"Ahhh, and that is where trust comes in my friend. Like the shark in the sea who trusts us to feed him when we chum the water. But if he's not careful, he winds up sunbathing on my hook with his belly ripped open. But you and I—we're in business together now and we must trust one another." He poked the square toward Andy again. "Go ahead . . . feel it."

Andy reached out and ran his fingers over the razor edges.

"It's called a chum cutter," he told Andy. "Here, try it." He held out the drill and motioned to the container of fish remnants and the guts of the shark. "Give it a good mix."

"I think you'll get a better batch if your man Jimmy here does the mixing."

"But it's a custom. You can't come aboard a fishing trawler and not stir the chum. The stirring brings good luck, not only to you, but to all on board. Go ahead—stick it in there and pull the trigger."

Andy stiffened, knowing he was now a player in the captain's game and his deliverance of a message. Lombardi's hand offering the drill remained outstretched. It was obvious that mixing the chum was not a suggestion. Andy was being schooled in the rules of survival in the world of running drugs. He took the drill and submerged the chum cutter deep into the mix and pulled the trigger. There was an immediate churning of the contents which spewed splatterings everywhere. The inner whirlpool threw specs of blood and bits of intestines and fish heads around the inside of the container. Much of the blood sprayed upward, dotting Andy's face and his clothing. The captain immediately stepped in and signaled him to stop.

"My apologies, Captain Dugan. I didn't realize how much was in there. I didn't expect such a backlash." Lombardi's tone failed to reflect his sentiments. He took the cutter from Andy and handed it to the crewman before placing a friendly hand on Andy's back. "We should go. Jimmy can finish up here. He'll add some dry oatmeal and corn and a bit of clam juice before he finishes his recipe. I shouldn't tell you, but Jimmy has a secret ingredient that he believes his chum gets him more sharks than anyone else. He has the cook grind up bones if the stock needs extra bulk. It's amazing to think that all the fish heads, and guts, and bones—all of it—simply disappear into the bellies of more sharks . . . leaving no trace . . . and then it starts all over again."

Lombardi's message had been effectively delivered, and with no offer of a towel to wipe his face or his clothing, Andy was paraded past the crew wearing the signs of initiation of someone new to their business. On board *Miss Demeanor*, he would wear that same message to Ollie.

Before he stepped off the *Bonnie-K*, Lombardi put a hand on Andy's shoulder. "North of the Keys Marina," he said. "Repeat that."

"North of the Keys Marina," Andy repeated.

"Good. Keep that name in your head but never write it down." He then handed Andy a slip of paper. "These are the coordinates. Chart your course. You're expected. Once you're in the marina secure your boat. While you and your man check in at the harbor master's office, your cargo will be offloaded by my men. The harbor master will make arrangements for you to meet the Librarian who will give you your money."

Lombardi's hand began to tighten on Andy's shoulder. "This is your first time with a shipment," he began in a fatherly tone. "But you must realize how risky our business is. The men on this ship have families to take care of—wives and children—mouths to feed. We must be very cautious who we trust and who we work with." As he spoke, his grip tightened. It felt as though his index finger and thumb were going to meet if he continued to squeeze, and Andy struggled with the pain.

"You seem to be a nice young man, Captain Andy. A man who may or may not help us again. A man who is too nice to stand before me with a . . . a face speckled in blood and clothing covered with the stench of fish guts." He paused and looked out to sea. "We have a saying in our business. No ser cebo de pescado."

"I'm afraid I'd need that in English," Andy told him.

Lombardi's translation was accompanied by a look Andy had not seen that day—a look a person might give as a show of concern over the death of a good friend. He leaned in close to Andy's ear and whispered. "It means . . . don't become chum."

◆ timing is everything

9:00 a.m.

Mario walked through the gates a free man. He stood outside the perimeter walls that had housed him for twelve months and stared at the long roadway that wound its way to civilization. A dark sedan waited. A driver sat behind the wheel, while a second man stood outside the vehicle holding the back door open. A third man was clearly visible in the rear seat. He had flicked open a switchblade and was using it to scrape out whatever was under his fingernails before wiping the blade on his trousers. There was no sign of Rosita.

Cohen sat in his Ocean View condo waiting for his men to return with his diamonds. His afternoon flight to New York was booked. He made final preparations for his departure. He smiled to himself as he pictured a blood-covered Mario lying in an alley with multiple fractures and broken ribs.

Connie put the week's receipts into the bank pouch and left to make her Friday deposit. It was a task she had planned to ignore that week but it was an excuse to get out of the office and she took it. Hanson was still sleeping. Before leaving, she turned the coffee pot off and dumped what was left into the sink figuring he was going to have to make his own coffee from now on and he may as well get used to it. She scribbled a note to let him know she had gone to the bank and pinned it on the bulletin board. She slammed the door as she left, knowing it would wake him.

Hanson woke in anger. The slamming door had shortened his oversleeping. He made his way to the coffee pot and was incensed when he found it empty. He scanned the office and spotted the note Connie had left. When he tore it off the bulletin board, he saw the week-old note beneath it that had been buried among the clutter. As he read it, his body went numb and the blood seemed to drain from his head. He read it a second time trying to digest the meaning of the words:

> *35-footer*
> *needs mast (broken off)*
> *some other stuff*

Rosita was in a frantic state as she watched the tow truck lift her car by the front bumper in preparation to be towed. She had emerged from her apartment to find both front tires were flat. She immediately attempted to contact Mario. In her one attempt at calling the prison, she was informed that it wasn't possible for him to get to the phone, but the guard would deliver the message and let him know she was having car trouble. The message was never delivered.

Ding-Lee prepared her bag of homemade jewelry consisting of items made from sea shells, driftwood, and the rough-cut diamonds. Being Friday, it was one of the three days she spread her wares on a blanket and sold items to people in the park. Her business was well known through her unsparing distribution of business cards. They were printed by a guy Ollie knew and given out around town in abundance. Unknowingly, a card given to the owner of the West End Marina may have put her life in jeopardy.

◆ rovelli and romance

Rovelli and Romance was a combination of names one might associate with a legal firm or a Broadway dance team. Neither was the case. Tommy Rovelli took up boxing in the ninth grade and spent his spare time in the Fayette Street Gym either working the bag or sparring. He wasn't very good at boxing and by the time he was twenty-six his face had been bludgeoned to a permanent puffiness. In addition to his enlarged face, neither eye closed properly and he had difficulty hearing out of his left ear.

George Romance had played right tackle for the East Side High School football team—not because he was a good football player—but because he weighed in at three-hundred plus pounds and opponents had a difficult time getting around him. He was often ridiculed by classmates, but always from a safe distance.

Rovelli and Romance met in high school, and being mutually unpopular, formed a friendship. Between classes, they extorted money from weaker students. Anyone refusing to pay received a beating. Other bullies in school sometimes allowed for one warning before administering a pounding but Rovelli and Romance wasted no time with preliminaries. It was pay on demand or get bloodied. It was rumored that the combined I.Q. of the two didn't equal double digits.

One of their many victims in high school was Marshal Cohen. Years later, when Marshal became a success in the jewelry business, he occasionally looked up his old nemeses and offered them work. They were two guys who could get the job done—whether it was the breaking of bones or a simple beating—they were guys he could count on.

For that reason, Mario's toughness was no match for the two men who greeted him when he left the prison. His refusal to accept their offer of transportation was met with several body blows from Rovelli and finalized with a strike to the jaw before he was thrown into the back seat of the car. Romance had finished scraping under his nails and put the point of the switchblade to Mario's throat. The point punctured the skin and Mario felt a small trickle of blood flow down his neck and pictured it staining his new prison shirt.

"Cohen's a bit tired of fuckin' around, Costello," Romance told him. "We need directions so why don't you just tell us where to go."

"Tell you where to go? I think you know where you two can go."

The comment was met with an elbow from Rovelli that glanced off the side of Mario's head. Romance pushed the knife a bit deeper.

"The boat's gone," he told them. His voice was raspy and Romance eyed Rovelli and gave a look of approval regarding their way of handling the interrogation.

"Yeah, we know. It's at the bottom of the river."

"Don't be such an ass. The boat never sank." Mario's body was forced upward off the seat and the knife remained in his throat.

"If you want to ease off a bit, we might be able to help each other," Mario told them.

Pressure eased a bit on the knife. "Okay asshole, let's help each other. You first."

"No, first you're gonna tell me what's going on with Rosita."

"Your girlfriend's fine."

"You'll have to excuse me if I don't take your word for that. You can tell Cohen that until I talk to her I'm not tellin' you shit."

"You got a number for her?"

"I do."

Rovelli handed Mario his phone. "Call her."

When Rosita answered and heard Mario's voice she began apologizing for not being there when he was released, explaining her flat tires and adding that the garage guy said they'd been slashed.

"Is the car good to go now?"

"Just about, where are you? I can pick you up."

"I've got two escorts right now, but maybe they can take me to a place we can be alone together." Mario hoped Rosita got the message and would go to the hotel where they had planned to spend the weekend. After talking in code for twelve months, it was second nature for both of them to read things into what was actually said. Before she could respond, Rovelli snatched the phone from Mario's hand and ended the conversation.

"Okay asshole, now you know your girlfriend is fine."

"The stones are still in the boat. It was sitting undisturbed until yesterday. Either somebody was waiting for my release, or we've got one hell of a coincidence. At first I thought it was Cohen's doing." He then paused before continuing. "Personally, I don't believe in coincidences. So if it wasn't you two morons who took the boat, I think I know who did. If so, the diamonds are still on board."

"I guess then you just need to tell us who you think took the boat."

"And I guess if I do that, you'll just let me get out of the car and go on my merry way." Neither of the men said anything. "I'm assuming your silence means you don't have a clue what you're supposed to do now so why don't we call Mr. Cohen and see what he has to say."

Mario's comment struck home. He had taken away any leverage they had with Rosita and they knew trying to beat information out of Mario didn't seem to be a viable option. Rovelli dialed Cohen's number and filled him in.

"Put Costello on," Cohen instructed.

"I need twenty-four hours," Mario told him.

"Why should I give you twenty-four hours? In twenty-four hours you're gone and I'm screwed."

"I'm not goin' anywhere without the money I'm owed. Until I get paid I've got no reason to run." Cohen remained silent and Mario continued. "I know we've never met, but don't mistake me as someone who does business like your friend Carmine."

"That guy's no friend of mine."

"I can do without him, as well," Mario told him. This is now a simple business deal between the two of us. Give me twenty-four hours and I'll get the stones. We can still do the exchange at your place if that suits you. Once I've got my money, I'm gone. If you want to continue playing games with these goons you sent to pick me up, we're not going to get anywhere. Otherwise, you can tell them to drop me off where I say. I'll keep this phone and you can call me. I'll have the goods and you'll have the cash."

"Put Tommy on."

"Is Tommy the ugly one or the guy who needs Weight Watchers?"

Rovelli yanked the phone from Mario and Cohen gave him the order to take Mario where he directed and let him out. "Let him keep the phone. Tell the driver to follow on foot. Costello's gonna assume we're following him so tell him not to get careless. You and Romance take the car and get over to the boatyard where he used to keep his boat. I don't know if he had anything goin' with the guy who owns the place, but see what you can squeeze outta him. I want all the bases covered on this."

◆ **calling it quits**

W hen Connie returned, Hanson was out of the office and limping toward her car before she could get the door open. The note torn from the bulletin board was clenched in his hand. He waved it in her face. "What the hell is this?"

Connie stared at the paper being pushed at her as she tried to gain some semblance of what Hanson was yelling about. She chewed a large wad of pink gum and stared at the paper until she recognized the week old notation. "It's a note I wrote that should've been thrown out. The guy didn't follow up. I guess I just forgot to take it off the board."

"What guy?"

"I don't know, some guy who called about getting his boat fixed. He didn't leave a name or anything. I think I told him to call back and talk to you."

Hanson pointed to the note again. "What did he mean he needed a mast?"

"He said his was damaged or something and then he had to cut it off so he needed a new one . . . and a yard with a hoist." Connie had opened her door and climbed out of the car during the exchange and the two stood face to face. "He might've mentioned he was going to try West End Marina and see what kind of equipment they had, I don't remember."

"Did he say what make the boat was?"

"Jeezus, Ernie, I don't know. He said he'd call back is all."

"Did he use the word Beneteau?"

"I told ya, I don't remember all the conversation. Maybe if you were in the office more often you'd get more business. You're the one who's supposed to check the board for messages. It's not my fault he didn't call back."

"You're a stupid bitch, you know that?"

Connie turned and stomped toward the trailer. Hanson hollered after her. "And when you get inside, do something useful and make a pot of coffee."

Hanson followed her in and while she complied with his demand for coffee, he called West End Marina and asked the owner if he had received a call about a boat needing a mast.

"Yeah, I did," the owner told him. "Pulled in here yesterday. We hauled it out of the water and started doing some work on it."

"A thirty-five foot Beneteau?"

"Yeah, that's right."

"Do you remember the name of the boat?"

"Hard to forget. *Miss Demeanor* . . . probably named after a few of the deeds done by the guys that motored her in here. Sounds like you know the boat."

"I own the damn boat! Don't say anything to the guys who brought it in. I'm on my way over."

The owner of West End Marina didn't care much for Hanson and took a small amount of pleasure in delivering bad news. "Come over if you want, Ernie, but it won't do ya no good. That ship has sailed, my friend. Or maybe I should say motored. They never did get a mast on her. They got a phone call and told me to get her back in the water and then they took off outta here bein' pushed by an outboard."

"They? Who's they?"

"Couple of young guys. A little on the crazy side if you ask me. They didn't waste any time getting outta here."

"Did they say where they were going?"

"Said something about Miami."

"Did they say *where* in Miami?"

"Didn't say where, but for the work they want done they're gonna need a yard with some heavy equipment."

Hanson put the phone down and looked at Connie. The coffee was about ready and he told her to fix him a cup. "This is a major fuck up," he yelled. "Actually, *you're* a major fuck-up. Didn't you put two and two together and think that the thirty-five footer with no mast might be mine? The one that asshole Costello ran off with and then said it conveniently sank in the river somewhere?"

Connie had her back to Hanson, and although she spat in the water when she first made the coffee, she leaned over and spit in his cup before filling it and taking it to his desk. "I've got to get to Miami. I need you to get online and Google a list of boatyards down there. Don't bother with the little ones. I'll give you a call when I get there and you can give me the list over the phone. Meanwhile, start calling them. See if anybody's got a sailboat scheduled to come in to have a replacement mast stepped."

Hanson carried his coffee into his living quarters and threw a few items of clothing into a small duffle bag. As an afterthought, he tossed in his Glock. He knew if the boat was being motored to Miami he could easily be there ahead of it. During the drive, he envisioned the entire scene. Two assholes who he presumed had stolen the boat would motor into the marina. He would casually walk out on the dock with two policemen behind him and present them with his documentation of ownership. He'd watch their faces drop while the cops ceremoniously put cuffs on them. The thought, however, seemed somewhat anticlimactic. He played the scene a second time and then realized he'd left the papers of ownership in the office.

He pulled out his cell and called Connie. "I need my papers," he yelled into the phone.

"What papers?"

"The papers proving I own the boat. The ones I got from that arbitrator guy. They're in the filing cabinet. I'm too far along to turn around so I want you to overnight them to me."

"Where am I supposed to send them?"

"I'll get a motel room somewhere and call you." As he thought about a motel, he realized it would be to his benefit to wait until *Miss Demeanor* had any repair work done and paid for before he presented the thieves with his papers of ownership.

"On second thought, I'm gonna wait around down there for a while so get a courier to drive the papers down here and hand them to me personally. I don't want to take any chances with this."

"That's gonna cost a pretty penny, Ernie. Are you sure you don't want me to overnight them?"

"Are you fucking deaf? I told you to get a courier and have him drive them down here!"

"Okay, okay. Where in the filing cabinet?"

"There's a folder way in the back of the top drawer. It's labeled, *asshole's boat.* There's a blue packet of papers in the folder. Send the whole damn packet . . . make copies of everything before you give it to the courier. It's the only proof I've got. What about the list of boatyards . . . where are you on that? I want you callin' those people today."

Connie paused as she thought about the opportunity that presented itself regarding her quitting. She hadn't planned to tell Hanson for fear of his temper, but being out of his reach gave her the courage she needed. "Actually, Ernie, it'll have to be today. I mean, I'll only have today to get the list."

"What's that supposed to mean?"

"I'm quitting, Ernie. I've had it with your bullshit. I'm not going to be here when you get back."

A silence followed before he responded. Connie was pleased she'd shut him up for once, and while she waited for his response, she pulled the pink gum out of her mouth and stretched it out like a spaghetti strand before tipping her head back and preparing it for reentry.

"So, I'm supposed to get on my knees and beg you not to go, is that it? You think the office is going to fall apart because your pea brain isn't there? And who do you think is going to give you a fucking job?"

"I don't really need a job. I'm getting married."

"Well, congratulations to you and to whoever the asshole is who's gonna put up with your bullshit."

"Ya know, Ernie, you might want to be careful what you're sayin' if you want your precious papers to be delivered to Miami. I can always forget to call the messenger service."

"If you wanna quit, you go right ahead. But if this is your last day then you'll follow orders and get those papers to me."

"I guess that request would include a month's severance pay?"

Another silence. "Two weeks . . . and that's a gift."

"I'm afraid I'll need a whole month. You want me to find a messenger or not?"

"You're a shit you know that? A real shit! Consider the month's pay a wedding gift. You'll need it after the guy leaves you high and dry."

Hanson ended the conversation by throwing the phone to the floor of the cab. He returned his thoughts to *Miss Demeanor* and gave a loud laugh as he flicked the tail of the scented mermaid dangling from the rear view mirror. "Whaddaya say, baby," he said to her. "How'd you like to hang your pretty little ass in the cabin of my new sailboat?"

As always, she smiled back.

♦ marielitos

M ario instructed the driver to pull over and let him out two blocks from the hotel where he was to meet Rosita. The immediate area was a busy part of the city and he knew it would be difficult for either Rovelli or Romance to get out and follow. He ducked into a small candy store. The clerk behind the counter gave a greeting and went back to reading her book. There was no hesitation on Mario's part as he walked the length of the store, went through a curtain that led to a back door, and made an exit to an alley. From there, he entered a small mini-mall and continued into another busy street. As he walked, he called Rosita. She had, in fact, picked up on his clue.

"I'm at the hotel. Room 428. What the hell is going on?"

"Just stay where you are. I'm two minutes away."

THE GREETING IN THE hotel room was not as he had imagined during his many nights of incarceration. The embrace from Rosita seemed half-hearted as she struggled to decipher what was happening. She began questioning the events of the morning—wanting to know who the men in the car were when he called earlier—how could he be in some kind of trouble only minutes after his release . . . and was any of it or all of it connected to her slashed tires?

"It's complicated," he said. "I told you before, I don't want to get you involved."

"I'm already involved. I've been involved since day one. I'm the one who's been doing the dirty work here. It's been me standing watch over your boat which, by the way, certainly triggered a reaction when you found out it was missing. I can't believe a boat in that condition is that important. What's on that boat? Is it drugs . . . because if you're mixed up in running drugs, I'm out right now."

"Did you bring me some clothes like I asked?"

"Clothes? Didn't you hear what I just said? I need to know what's going on." This time Mario saw the pleading in her eyes.

"Let me shower. I need to get the stink of prison off me. I'll shower and get dressed and then we'll talk. I'll explain the whole ballgame—or at least the condensed version—I don't know how much time we have."

After showering, Mario emerged from the bathroom wrapped in a towel. He hadn't gained any pounds during the past year, but lifting weights with Silo had redistributed what he did have. His arms and torso were chiseled.

Rosita seemed more relaxed and she moved toward him and put her arms around his waist. "You know, before you tell me things that may cause me to walk out of here, maybe we should have that greeting we've both been looking forward to." As she spoke, her hand slid to the tuck holding the towel around his waist. She gave a slight pull and it fell to the floor.

His hand went to the sash that was holding her sarong in place, "Two can play that game," he told her and with a quick tug, it too fell to the floor. Rosita unbuttoned her blouse and with a move of her shoulders, it floated off and rested on the sarong. Not knowing her morning was going to begin with a trip to the local garage, she had dressed in her bikini for lounging poolside at the hotel after picking up Mario. The bikini top was fastened in the front and Mario unhooked it and let it drop. Her bikini bottom had small shoestring bows on each side, and sliding his hands down from her waist, he pulled on them. The two stood naked.

His hand moved to her wrist and brushed the tail of the serpent he hadn't seen during his time inside. Seeing it for the first time in the Sand Flea Tavern seemed like such a long time ago. He traced the serpent with his finger, studying the rise and fall of her breasts as he did so. Rosita stood staring—studying him as if seeing him for the first time. Mario pushed her onto the bed.

"No foreplay?" she questioned, smiling. The comment seemed to break any tension in the moment and Rosita gave a soft laugh.

"Not today."

"Oh? And what is it you have against foreplay?"

"I've got nothing against it. But I've been thinking about you every day for ten months. Foreplay's over!"

IT WAS LATE AFTERNOON when Mario showered again. This time accompanied by Rosita. They then dressed and went to the hotel restaurant where they ordered lunch and Mario did his best to tell his story. While he talked, Rosita picked at her salad. Sometimes with a fork, other times she fingered pieces of lettuce or cucumber, always attentive to what Mario was telling her.

"It was supposed to be an easy gig," he began. "A quick trip to Cuba to pick up a small package of uncut diamonds and sell them to a fancy New York jeweler—a guy named Cohen. With the money from the deal, I'd have enough to get out of the rut I was in . . . maybe get a bigger boat and do some charters . . . start over. Anyway, I had a gun on board for protection which, if you've done any traveling on the ocean, is understandable. When you saw me get picked up for smashing a guy's boat—which was retribution by the way for cutting off my mast—the cops told me the gun had been used in a murder . . . a cop killing. I mean, it was a gun I bought from a guy in a back alley somewhere. That kinda put burning the shanty on the back burner."

"Burning the shanty?"

"Yeah, I guess in the process of getting even, I kinda burned the guy's house down." Rosita's eyes grew wide at the new information. "Anyway, you were there when I was arrested so you know the rest of the story. That was my welcome into the New Year, remember?"

Rosita looked around the dining room. "You remind me of a guy I grew up with . . . you know . . . always getting accused of stuff he didn't do."

"Somebody from school?"

"No, my father."

"Your father? You've never really said anything about your father—or your mother either for that matter."

"I guess there're a lot of things you don't know about me. It's not so easy talking with guards listening to your every word."

Mario feigned looking around the restaurant. "I don't see any guards in this place. Tell me about your parents."

"My father was a Marielito—you know . . . it's what they called the Cubans who migrated to Miami back in 1980. They left from Muriel Harbor which is how they got their name. Anyway, it was part of an agreement between Castro and Carter, and with people not trusting how long Castro would keep the agreement, Cubans were clammering to get out. My father was only twelve so he didn't talk about it much, but my grandfather said that although Fidel was running the country, a guy named Raul Castio was his right-hand man. Not only his right hand man for decisions, but a ruthless enforcer.

I guess the first crossings were nights filled with fear. People pushed and shoved and fought their way into any available boat—many in such poor condition they were doomed from the start. Everyone wanted a richer life and figured any boat was better than living in poverty. People from Miami arrived to help transport friends and relatives back to Florida. Seventeen hundred boats were in the harbor the first night. My grandfather's fishing boat was one of the first to leave and he took my father. My grandfather had made many trips from Cuba to Miami before that night—when it was illegal—always at night and always with the possibility of being caught and executed."

"If I recall my book learning from the Academy, Castro also used the opportunity to get a lot of the criminals out of Cuba."

"Which caused some friction with local residents in Miami. Anyway, when the influx was stopped, my grandfather continued to help Cubans get out and when my father turned sixteen or so, he made the trips with him. Castro denounced them saying they were like the water moccasins that slithered in and out of the harbors. His henchmen were always on the lookout and sometimes pretended to be Marielitos and jailed people who were trying to escape. The group my grandfather was in took Castro's words as a challenge and got tattoos of serpents so people trying to leave Cuba could identify them and know they weren't working for Castro. They continued as a small group and brought Cubans to Miami for several years."

Rosita paused as she fingered her salad. "A few years later, my grandfather mysteriously disappeared."

"Mysteriously disappeared?"

"They are Cuban code words for got caught and paid the price. After that, my father continued to help get refugees into Miami."

"And then?"

"Well, between his midnight runs, he married a nice Cuban girl in Miami and then I came along." Rosita gave a soft laugh and it seemed to put some perspective to her story. "He spent most of his time in Cuba so I only saw him once or twice a month, when he made his midnight runs bringing in refugees. I'd wake up in the morning and hear him snoring. I'd jump into bed with him and hold onto him so he couldn't get away and leave me. I called those days my *Daddy Days* because he belonged to me that day. A day I got to sit on his lap . . . show him my schoolwork and pictures I'd drawn for him."

Rosita stopped and lowered her head.

"And?"

"And everything ended when I was ten."

"What happened?"

There was a long pause before Rosita answered. "He mysteriously disappeared," she said.

"And your tattoo of the serpent?"

"I guess it's more a sign of respect for my father and what he did for our people. Even today people recognize it as a sign of hope and freedom."

"And then what happened?"

"Then I was raised by my mother. But things were different then. I mean . . . I grew up in Little Havana and it wasn't touristy like it is now. It was more like what I imagine Cuba was like. People congregating on doorsteps . . . neighbors helping neighbors . . . talking and laughing . . . singing and dancing . . . it was mystical, ya know? But residents—especially the men—were always being questioned and harassed by the police and accused of any crime within a fifty-mile radius. So I guess that's where you come in. Trouble kind of follows you around but you're usually only to blame for half of it." With that statement, they both laughed. Mario raised his glass. "To the unjustly accused," he said.

"Like your arrest for the killing of a cop. Even after that was cleared up, they still gave you eighteen months."

"Yeah, I guess the judge didn't take too kindly to me setting the boatyard on fire."

"At least my thesis got three months erased."

"And being a good boy got me another three."

"I'm still wondering how that happened. I just don't see you and good behavior ever going together. And now you're sitting on stolen diamonds?" She waited. "So, I'm guessing they were in the boat."

"They still are as far as I know. That's where my two friends in the car come in. They want the diamonds and I'm the only one who knows where they are."

"So . . . that's why I've been keeping an eye on it."

"Yeah. And all I have to do is get the stones and exchange them for the money. We can buy another boat here, or travel, or do whatever you want to do."

"But the boat's gone. How are you going to get the diamonds?"

"The best I can figure is one of two things happened. It was either a random act of thievery—which I doubt—or my old friend Hanson found it. Part of the deal over the damages at the boatyard was to give him clear title to *Miss Demeanor*. It's more likely he somehow stumbled onto it and hauled it back to his place. The thing is, he doesn't have a clue about the diamonds. They're still sitting on the boat if I can get to them."

"Won't he find them when he goes through the boat?"

"No. There's a secret compartment on board. It's passed every test imaginable. I just have to get on board for a few minutes."

"So what's your big plan?"

"Simple. We'll go to the boatyard. He's a sucker for pretty women so you go in the office and keep him busy. You can tell him you're interested in getting a slip for your boat or something. I'll go down to Miss Demeanor and get the stones."

"What about this guy Cohen you mentioned? Is he gonna keep up his end of the deal?"

"I talked with him from the car. He's here in Melbourne Beach and says he still wants the stones. At this point I'd be foolish to trust him, but it's doable if we work it right. He's a business man and he'll still make out okay after he settles up with me."

"I might have another idea for you to think about."

"What's that?"

"Well, when my mother died last year, she left me some money. It wasn't much in the scheme of things but after I took care of her funeral and other expenses, I still have about forty-five thousand dollars . . . which is sitting in my bank account. There are certainly things I can spend it on, but right now it's just sitting there."

"What are you saying?"

"I'm saying that it may not be a fortune, but it's probably enough for you to get your boat back from that asshole who owns it and get a new mast. You could just give the diamonds to this Cohen guy and forget about any risks. I mean, he had my tires slashed and sent two guys after you this morning. Just leave the diamonds somewhere and tell Cohen where to get them and get yourself out of this mess. You can have the money."

"It's a very generous offer, and I appreciate it, but I just spent twelve months of my life locked up because of those stones and I mean to get paid for my time. I'm sorry about this morning and if you want out right now I understand, but this is something I have to see through."

"Earlier today you said, 'we'll' go to the boatyard. If that's the case, you tell me what's going on with us. I've got a life too ya know."

Mario slipped into his best impersonation of Humphrey Bogart. "Well, I sure ain't plannin' on sailin' anywhere without ya, sweetheart."

49

W hen Andy stepped back on board from the *Bonnie-K*, Ollie's face displayed shades of green. Remembering what he must've looked like with specks of blood on his face and clothing, Andy held up a reassuring hand. "It's okay. Looks worse than it is."

"What the hell happened?"

"I got a lesson on the making of chum along with a reminder to not become part of the recipe," Andy said sarcastically. "How'd everything go here? Are we loaded and ready to weigh anchor?"

Ollie was pushing *Miss Demeanor* away from the trawler. Lombardi's men looked on, seeming to be interested in a sailboat with no mast heading to Miami powered by a nine horsepower outboard.

"I need you to fire up the motor and head out while I go below and clean up. Just follow the coastline. I'll chart the course and give you a compass setting once I get into a clean shirt."

The look of worry that Andy saw when he first boarded reappeared on Ollie's face. "Something else wrong?" Andy asked.

"You might wanna take a deep breath before you go below."

"Why? Don't tell me it's skunk grass like that stuff you had last year."

"It's not any smell I'm worried about. Fact is, the keys are bundled really tight. It's just . . ."

"Just what?"

"Well, ya know Eric never did give us a definite answer regarding the quantity we'd be picking up."

Andy moved quickly to the companionway and looked down into the cabin. From his vantage point, the only things visible were hundreds of tightly wrapped red and green bundles that left room for nothing else. "What the fuck? Are you tellin' me all those things are filled with grass? How much shit did they load on here?"

"By my count, it worked out to five-hundred keys."

"Five-hundred keys! We can't be sailing out here with five-hundred keys. You should've told them not to load it."

"Hey man, these aren't guys who you renege on, if you know what I mean. What was it you were saying about being made into chum or something?"

Andy returned his attention to the cabin and went below. Individual keys—some wrapped in red packaging and some in green, were piled on the floor, both berths, and most of the cabin's interior space. He climbed over them and worked his way to the V-berth only to find more of the same. He returned topside and glared at Ollie.

"Doesn't leave much room for sleeping does it, man?" Ollie said, trying to make light of a bad situation.

"Sleeping! Who's worried about sleeping? I'm worried about spending the rest of my life in prison. We may want to consider getting rid of this shit right now?"

"And how would you suggest we do that? Throw it overboard perhaps, or maybe go ashore and sell it on a street corner?"

"This is not good," Andy continued. "If we get caught with this load . . . I mean, we've got over a ton of this stuff on board. We can kiss our futures good-bye. I mean, you may be used to dealing with this kind of load, but count me out."

"Okay, let's just think this through. We've got maybe another seventy miles to Miami. I'm thinking with this motor we're gonna pull in there in the middle of the night. The Coast Guard focuses on boats coming in from sea, not mastless sailboats that are chuggin' along the coastline bein' propelled by an outboard. The odds of getting checked is a near impossibility. So, instead of worrying about getting busted, why don't you take out that calculator you've been playin' with since we left and figure out our profit margin. You were all excited about the money two days ago."

Andy was too concerned to do any calculations. He spelled Ollie on the tiller and stewed in silence for several hours. It wasn't until the two sat together in the cockpit, eating bowls of hot soup Ollie had prepared that the tension eased a bit. With the soup warming them and Ollie taking his turn on the wheel, they made small talk. After eating, Andy retrieved his calculator and entered some numbers.

"So how's it look?" Ollie asked him.

"Well, we never did get any firm numbers from Eric so I'm using the information you gave me which was, conservatively, three-hundred dollars an ounce. If that's true, the street value of five-hundred keys works out to . . ." He stopped as he pushed in the last few numbers and hit the equal sign. "Holy shit, if these figures are correct, it's over five-million dollars. Ten per cent of that is over half a million bucks!"

"So, you feel better now? And don't forget, you're getting a new boat to boot."

"I'll feel better when we get there and get it off-loaded. Speaking of which, how about getting below and stashing as much of it as you can. Anything else taking up space can be thrown overboard. All we need now is food and water."

Ollie made some headway in the cabin by squeezing the packages into every available cavity. It was his investigation into the smaller storage units that brought on the scream. Andy tied off the wheel and scrambled below. Ollie was backing out of the V-berth.

"Water moccasin!" he yelled.

Penelope had coiled herself in a small storage compartment beneath the V-berth. "Musta got in when the boat was on the river and been hangin' out since. Thing is, you don't want to let one of these suckers bite you . . . and we're out here in the middle of nowhere."

"Can you get it out of there?"

"Yeah, well, mocs don't really like to be bothered. They tend to take a dim view of having their space invaded. I guess we could just close the compartment and leave her to her dreams."

"Do you think that will work? Your screaming obviously didn't wake it. Are you sure it's alive?"

"Oh yeah, man, she's alive all right. I guess if we want to leave her in there though, we oughta lean something heavy against the door."

Ollie shut the compartment very gingerly. Andy went topside and returned with the plow anchor and Ollie set it against the door. Andy returned to the cockpit and Ollie continued with storing the keys wherever he found space.

Andy charted their course and they motored along with an eye on the compass. A tank of gas was lasting several hours and Andy's calculations regarding the two remaining cans indicated they had more than enough to get them to Miami. Their motoring continued for the remainder of the day and into the evening. Just after midnight, however, they ran into a fog bank. The makeshift lights they had duct taped to the bow were poor substitutes for the larger ones that were inoperable.

Andy located a horn in one of the seat compartments and instructed Ollie to blow on it every minute or so. They wore lightweight rain jackets and sipped fresh brewed coffee as *Miss Demeanor* purred through the mist. Ollie rolled a joint. He took a hit and passed it to Andy who took a long pull on it and filled his lungs. "Ever sailed in fog?" his voice was altered by his attempt to hold in the smoke.

"Not really," Ollie responded. "I've surfed in it though. Kind of interesting."

"Yeah, you find yourself in sort of a circle. I mean, you're obviously limited in the distance you can actually see in any direction."

"Never really thought about it."

"In nautical terms it's called the *Radius of Vision*."

"Hey, kinda like *void of course*," Ollie countered.

"Actually, it refers to the distance you can see in whatever direction you look, except that it keeps changing. You know, the circle moves with you. I mean, here we are in the middle of the ocean and all you've got is a distance of let's say, fifty feet in any direction. You try to see farther, but you just can't, no matter how hard you try. To make matters worse, there could be another boat near you in a circle of its own and you don't even know it's there . . . which is why you're supposed to be blowin' on that horn by the way."

Ollie gave a blast, and after Andy waved off the joint, took a final hit and flicked the roach overboard. Andy continued. "Kind of a metaphor for life really . . . everybody's out there ya know—in the real world I mean—walking aound in their own little radius of vision. Sometimes the circles intercept or collide into each other and sometimes they just sail on by. And no matter how hard any of us tries to see beyond our own circle, we're stuck . . . stuck in our own little radius of vision."

"Or maybe we don't want to go beyond our radius."

"Yeah, there's those people walkin' through life who're just out there in their own little circle."

"I think the whacky tobacky's got *you* goin' in circles, man."

Their thoughts were interrupted by a distant horn. "Sounds like we've got company. Sounds pretty big too," Andy said.

"How far do you figure?"

"Not sure, but you should give them a response."

Ollie blew a long blast and they waited. The second ship sounded again, closer this time.

"Blow another one," Andy instructed. "It sounds like its coming toward us. I can't believe they didn't veer off."

Ollie sounded another blast, but it was obvious the other ship was continuing to move toward them. The sound of several heavy engines chugged louder and powerful lights cut luminescent paths through the fog. The beams threw a wide berth of light across the water, broken by the choppiness of the waves. The intruders had entered their radius of vision. Ollie took a deep breath and gave another long blast on the horn. They waited.

Ollie looked at Andy. He began screaming to be heard over the roar of the approaching engines. Engines that pushed the oncoming ship through the mist and became deafening. "Remember what you said about sometimes people in life pass by each other and never know of the other's existence? I think tonight we've met some people who want to eliminate our existence. Did something happen on board the *Bonnie-K* you failed to tell me about?"

The lights that had given the earlier appearance of a giant sea monster became blinding. It was obvious to Andy they were about to be rammed. He spun the wheel, forcing the boat into an abrupt heel and Ollie lurched forward.

"What the hell are you doing?"

"It's going to ram us," Andy yelled. Even if we survive we're screwed. We're gonna have five-hundred keys of grass floatin' around us." Andy pictured their cargo floating on the water. Hundreds of neatly wrapped packages drifting to shore—washed up and opened by little children, wondering what the stuff inside the packages was, or stoners jumping for joy, or parents searching for the nearest cop. He heard the voice of Lombardi in his head saying "don't become chum." With those visions and thoughts, he hollered to Ollie over the now deafening sound of the ship that was about to ram them. "Life can't get much worse than this."

Ollie, who had regained his balance, focused on the oncoming ship and its menacing bow as it parted the waters. Within seconds of a collision, it made an abrupt turn and threw a spray of water into the cockpit, soaking both of them. Ollie focused on the bow, wanting to know the name of the boat about to sink them. Seeing the lettering caused his heart to momentarily stop. His blood turned an icy cold. "Did you say it couldn't get any worse?" he yelled to Andy.

"That's what I said."

"I think you might be wrong about that."

"Why, what is it?"

Before Ollie could answer, a voice blasted through a megaphone and pierced the night air. "You are being approached by the United States Coast Guard. Prepare to be boarded."

♦ ## don't shoot the messenger

Mario made an initial drive-by before he parked Rosita's car and walked across the highway to the boatyard. He saw no signs of Hanson's truck and became more optimistic with his attempt to board *Miss Demeanor*. He chuckled at the sight of the trailer that was replacing Hanson's coveted shanty and walked directly to the dock. A quick scan showed no signs of his boat. He became uneasy thinking perhaps it hadn't been Hanson who'd taken it but possibly someone who had noticed its inactivity and felt it was there for the taking. It was also possible it had been impounded by the authorities during their annual quest to round up abandoned boats that were eyesores reported by local home owners.

Not seeing the boat, and knowing Hanson wasn't around, he decided to take his chances with Connie, presuming she was still employed. He knocked on the door of the trailer and went inside, and in a strange way, he was relieved to see her. She was packing items in a carton and when she looked up, she hesitated before Mario's face registered. Once she recognized him, she became instantly friendly.

"Well, hello stranger," she greeted. "The last I heard you were coolin' your heels in the hoosegow. Although, according to Ernie, you should've gotten the electric chair for burnin' down his precious shanty. How do you like the new digs?" she waved her arms around the inside of the trailer.

"Nice," Mario told her, trying to be cordial. "I'm guessing with no truck outside, he's not around."

"He's not. Although I wouldn't think he's anybody you'd care to see. Unless you stopped by to give him a good uppercut if you know what I mean. If that's your plan, I'd like tickets to that show, but unfortunately, he's probably half way to Miami by now. Left outta here a couple of hours ago. As a matter of fact, he's goin' down there to get your boat . . . 'course it's his boat now."

"*Miss Demeanor*?"

"Yup."

"She's in Miami?"

"Well, she's on her way, at least according to the guy at West End Marina. He was gonna do some work on it—had it out of the water and everything—and then the two guys who towed it in said they was goin' to Miami. They put it back in the river and high-tailed it outta there."

"Do you know where in Miami?"

"Nope, and from what I gather, West End didn't know either."

"What about the two guys? Did he say anything about them?"

"Just that they seemed a little off, whatever that means." Connie studied Mario and recalled the good old days when he came into the office and she fantasized about him taking her to his boat and having his way with her. "I'm getting' married next week," she announced.

"Really? Good for you. Who's the lucky guy?"

"One of the marine supply guys who sells to Ernie. His company's movin' him up to the Carolinas so I'm through with this dump." She threw a few more things in the box she was packing. "Ya know, you coulda had me if you played your cards right," she teased. "I was always just sittin' around here waitin' for you to propose."

"Guess I missed my chance," he said, and they both laughed.

"And for the record, I always thought you got a bum deal on that whole prison thing and losin' your boat and everything to that asshole."

"Yeah, well I just dropped by in the hope of seeing her one last time."

"I guess you're a day late and a dollar short on that account."

Mario turned as if to end the discussion and leave the office when Connie was suddenly struck with an idea. "Hey, wait a minute. How'd you like to own her again?"

"What are you saying?"

"What I'm sayin' is I know more about this business than that moron ever gave me credit for. I've done a lot of paperwork for boat owners in the yard here who buy or sell a boat during their stay."

"Which means what?"

Connie picked up the packet containing the ownership papers. "These are the papers Ernie got from the arbitrator in your case. They prove his ownership of the boat. And I happen to know that when he heard your boat was at the bottom of the river, he never bothered to transfer the ownership and have the boat documented in his name. Until he does that, it's still legally yours."

"And those are the papers?"

"Yup. And it gets better. He left it up to me to get a courier to take these papers down to Miami so he can claim it all legal like. Seein' as how I'm in charge, then I guess if you were thinking of goin' down there, I could make you the courier." Connie extended the packet toward Mario. "I'm sure you would see these are put into the right hands."

"What about you? What about when he gets back here?"

"Like I said, I'm getting' married. I'm all through with this place."

Mario took the envelope and studied the court seal on the outside. "And this is it? You're sure . . . these make me the owner?"

"Actually, without those being filed, you still are the owner. Like I said, the transfer was never made."

"And he doesn't have any other proof?"

"Well, he did tell me to make copies before giving them to the courier, but I guess this bein' my last day and all, I've got more important things to do before I get outta here. With everything goin' on here, I guess I just forgot to make any copies."

The unlikely allies smiled at each other as Mario held up the packet. He put his hands on both her arms, leaned in, and gave her a big kiss on the cheek. "Thanks, and I hope you have better days ahead with your marriage."

"Nothing could be worse than this place," she sighed.

Mario turned and made his exit. It was the last time he'd see
Connie . . . and the last time Connie watched his ass as he
walked away.

MARIO CLIMBED INTO THE car and tossed the packet
to Rosita.

"What's this?"

"I believe it's our ticket outta here. Take a look through the
envelope. Supposedly there's proof in there that Hanson owns
the boat, but according to his secretary it's still mine. Not only
that, it's the only copy. The boat's headed for Miami. I'm going
to take you home and drive down there."

"Without me?"

"Afraid so. I don't know what I'm gonna find when I get
there. It's better you stay in Melbourne. I'll get the diamonds
off the boat, and when I get back, I'll get the money and then
we can decide what we're going to do."

"Really? ¿Comó es tu español?"

"What?"

"That's what I thought. I said, how's your Spanish? You're
heading to *my* neighborhood now. You may be a dark-skinned
Italian but nobody where you need to go is going to talk to you.
Even if they do, they'll be speaking mostly Spanish. How are
you going to find out anything? I grew up there remember? Not
to mention, it's my car you're taking. I'm going with you."

Her argument held no room for Mario to disagree. A
translator would be an asset and Rosita wasn't the kind of
woman who would shy away from risks. Since he'd told her
about the diamonds and his plan to cash in and cash out, she
had been all in—reluctant at first—but all in to see it through.

They returned to her house and while she put a few things
in a small travel bag, Mario roamed her apartment. It was small
but nicely decorated. Several fish tanks with bottoms covered
with rocks and straw were strategically placed to avoid giving it
the look of a pet store. The tanks sat empty, and when
questioned, Rosita told Mario that after putting Penelope on the
boat, she decided to give up her last two remaining snakes.
"Neither was poisonous," she told him. "So I took them to the
river and gave them their freedom."

It was almost seven o'clock when they were ready to leave. It had been a long day and both were tired. Rosita suggested they stay and spend the night and get an early start in the morning. "Besides," she persuaded, "you can practice your foreplay."

CONNIE HAD TWO MORE visitors that afternoon. Rovelli and Romance had been sitting in their car waiting for Hanson and watched Mario come and go. Posing as FBI officials, they told Connie the boatyard was under surveillance and they were seeking information on a sailboat named *Miss Demeanor*. "Do you know anything about it?"

Connie knew enough about police procedures to know they had no affiliation with the FBI. She also knew enough not to ask for identification. The men questioning her were not the type to mess with and she wanted them out of the office without any trouble. Her only goal was to close up early and get on with her life.

"Yeah, I know the boat you're asking about. It's over at the West End Marina. The owner wanted some work done and we didn't have the equipment he needed." She hoped her voice didn't reveal her nervousness and she rested her hands on the desk to prevent them from shaking.

Rovelli and Romance seemed to buy the explanation. Before leaving, they explained their investigation was on-going and she was to tell no one they'd been there. They climbed into their car and drove to West End. Connie breathed a sigh of relief, collected her things, locked the office, and left to get married.

THE OWNER OF THE West End Marina was no more fooled by the FBI act than Connie. This time they used the story that some merchandise had been on board and they were investigating a smuggling operation. It was doubtful that Cohen would've appreciated the amount of information they were doling out but their goal was to get the stones, get paid, and get back to New York.

"The stuff was in a small pouch," they told the owner.

"The only pouch I know about is some moldy thing the girl found. There was just some old beach glass in it . . . nothin' of value."

Romance turned to Rovelli in an attempt to remove any suspicions regarding the diamonds. "Probably samples of the crystal meth we've been lookin' for." He turned back to the owner. "Who's this girl you're talkin' about?"

"I don't know, just a girl that was helpin' clean up the boat. I think she was the girlfriend of one of the owners."

"Where can we find her?"

The owner was obviously nervous. His forehead became wet and his eyes darted around the room. "I don't know. She was just here helping out. I never saw her before yesterday."

Any pretense to the proprietor of being FBI agents disappeared. Rovelli grabbed the front of his shirt and twisted it as he pushed him against the wall. The back of his other hand came down and raked him across the face. The owner's want of self-preservation caused him to recall Ding-Lee's business card. "There," he said pointing to the office bulletin board covered with want ads. "She left her business card. It's somewhere on that board. She said she sells jewelry and stuff. That's all I know."

The grip on his shirt eased, and Romance ripped the card off the board. After studying it he looked at his partner and then to the owner. "Ding-Lee?" he questioned. "What the hell kind of a name is that?"

"I don't know. Like I said, I never saw her before yesterday."

"Any address on it?" asked Rovelli.

"No address, but it says here she's at Tomosca Park on Mondays, Wednesdays, and Fridays. Looks like today's our lucky day."

DING-LEE HAD SPREAD HER blanket in its usual location. Her jewelry made from sea shells, diamonds in the rough, and other trinkets were being arranged when Rovelli and Romance arrived. Tomosca Park was isolated from the city and not a place where vendors usually sold their wares. A few people sat reading beneath shade trees, an artist had set up an easel and was painting a section of the landscape, and a guy who had the appearance of being homeless sat with three leather bracelets on his lap with the impractical intent to sell them.

This time, Cohen's goons made no pretense of being FBI agents. It took only a minute to conclude that the girl selling jewelry was Ding-Lee. A few more questions and the mention that they were friends of the owner of West End Marina gave them the reason to casually mention how he'd told them about her finding a pouch on the boat and how fortunate she was to find the sea glass.

Ding-Lee's only concern seemed to be that they were there to claim the sea glass. Romance assured her that was not the case and then ascertained all the sea glass from the boat was present and accounted for on the blanket.

"Except for some real tiny pieces that I threw back into the ocean," she admitted.

Rovelli and Romance stared at one another. "And you haven't sold anything yet today?"

"No, I just got here."

Romance looked at the necklaces and earrings that ranged from five to fifteen dollars. Rovelli grabbed his partner from behind and pulled him aside for a strategy meeting. "This chick is a space head. She doesn't have any idea what she's got here. Just offer her some money and tell her you'll take all of it. Let Cohen sort out the real stuff from the junk. What do we care?"

Romance liked the idea and returned his attention to Ding-Lee. "What do you want for all of it?" he asked. "The whole shitload here."

"Wow. You want all of it? I guess I'd have to add it all up."

"Listen, we're kinda in a hurry." As he spoke, he peeled off five twenties from a wad of bills and tossed them toward her. The bills floated to the blanket. "Let's just say I give you these and take it all."

"Oh, but this is too much."

"I'll tell ya what, honey—you throw in the blanket to make up the difference and we'll call it even." Without waiting for a response, he put the four corners together, turning the blanket into a makeshift sack. He threw it over his shoulder like a sailor returning to his ship and he and Rovelli left for Cohen's condo.

51

Several lights from the Coast Guard cutter continued to sweep *Miss Demeanor*'s deck, moving from side to side like spotlights highlighting the center ring of the circus.

Through squinting eyes, Andy saw figures making the leap from the intruding ship onto his deck. Voices came from the Coast Guard vessel. Phrases such as "check the cabin" and "areas under the seats," and "give it the usual going over" cut through the fog. The megaphone blasted again with a question. "Do you have any weapons on board?"

"No," Andy shouted back. "We don't have *anything* on board."

Two men from the ship had made their way from the bow to the cockpit. One put a bright light directly in Andy's eyes and all but one of the sweeping beams from the cutter were extinguished. The officer in charge stared down at Andy from his higher perch. "Hold off," he yelled to the men who had boarded the sloop. He continued staring at Andy and then put his hand to his forehead to shield his eyes from the brighter lights. "Dugan? Is that Andy Dugan?"

Before Andy could respond, the officer jumped from the cutter into the cockpit and looked more closely. "Holy shit. It is Andy Dugan!"

Andy, still in a state of semi-shock, said nothing.

"Don't you remember me? From Maritime, man . . . the Academy. I was a year ahead of you. We played some ball together. It's me, man, Marshfield. Kevin Marshfield."

Ollie, who was standing in the companionway to block the attempt of anyone going below, made the first acknowledgement. "Wow, you two went to the Academy together?"

The comment gave Andy time to compose himself. Finding his old schoolmate in a position to bust him and send him to a life of making license plates was the last thing he expected.

"Yeah . . . yeah . . . Kevin. How've you been, man? And what the hell are you doing out here in the middle of nowhere?"

"After I graduated I joined up. All those years of study paid off, I guess. I've got my own cutter and crew. We're all out here just keepin' America safe, ya know? Been spending most of tonight helpin' tourists in their fancy yachts find their way outta this soup." He made a sweeping gesture indicating the surrounding fog.

The conversation regarding their acquaintance at the Academy quickly changed to talk of the rescue boat. The recollection by Andy that Kevin had always been sort of a braggart at school gave him a possible out by inquiring about his importance in the Coast Guard. It also explained the recklessness in the way the cutter had made the approach.

Kevin began the speech he usually reserved for picking up women during his onshore leave, explaining how he was in command of a rescue cutter. Because of their link to Maritime Academy, he slipped into some academia. "You remember when we studied a guy named Witter? He was the guy who designed the forty-four foot rescue boat. We studied his work in design class."

"Kinda rings a bell," Andy feigned.

"Well, this is the newest version of the rescue boat," he said, pointing to the cutter. "I'm in charge of this forty-seven foot baby that's practically unsinkable. What am I sayin', practically. It *is* unsinkable. I've got these recruits out here on a training mission."

"You want us to go below and check things out, sir?" The question came from one of Marshfield's trainees.

Andy said nothing. Ollie stiffened.

"Whaddaya think, Andy? Might be good training for these guys to let them have an inspection. See if we can find all that pot you two are smuggling." The comment was followed by a hearty laugh. "Speakin' of you two, I haven't met your mate yet."

Andy introduced Ollie, who extended a handshake but remained in a blocking position.

"If you're out here to save people tonight I'd guess your time would be better spent searching for the helpless than wasting it on us," Andy countered.

"Not to mention the water moccasin we picked up on the river," Ollie added. "We've got it corralled for the time being, but it's not a good night to be nursing a snake bite."

Kevin glanced at his two crewmembers awaiting orders. "He's right," he agreed. "These guys are okay. This guy here was one hell of a tailback when I quarterbacked our pickup games at the Academy." He then eyed the missing mast and shifted his look toward the outboard.

"You motoring this thing with that?"

"We are until we get to Miami. I've got a new mast and diesel engine waiting."

The statement from Andy triggered the normal response to a boat in trouble. Marshfield shot a quick look at the trainees. "Secure a bow line from this tub to our boat. Let's get this guy outta here." He then looked at Andy. "We're not going as far as Miami, but we can give you a tow for twenty miles or so. That's the end of our quadrant. You'll make better time and save some wear and tear on that ridiculous outboard."

"Hey . . . not necessary. I mean, I appreciate the offer but we can just mosey along here. You've got more important shit to do than hassle with us."

"It's no hassle, man. It's what we're out here for anyway. We can at least tow you until we get a call for real help. Besides, it'll give me a chance to show off my boat."

The United States Coast Guard towed Andy and Ollie and five-hundred keys of marijuana along the Atlantic coast of Florida until a distress call came from a boat similar in size to *Miss Demeanor.*

"Gotta go," Kevin hollered back to Andy. "Got a lost family with kids on board and they don't know where the hell they are." He ordered his crew to cast off the bow line and Andy and Ollie watched the cutter's stern lights disappear into the blackness. The fog lifted during the next hour and Andy and Ollie continued to Miami under a starlit sky. They agreed the towing event probably wasn't the kind of rescue the Coast Guard was normally involved in and would've probably been upset had their cargo been discovered. But Kevin had been right. They made better time and saved wear and tear on their ridiculous engine.

SOMEWHERE BETWEEN TWO AND three a.m. *Miss Demeanor* stole her way into North of the Keys Marina. Andy cut the outboard and let her drift toward the main dock in silence. He was met immediately by a dock worker. He looked to be in his seventies and held a coiled line in one hand. "*Miss Demeanor?*" he asked.

"That it is," Andy responded.

"I'm Henry," he told him. His voice was gritty, but friendly. Andy envisioned him to be an integral part of the yard. Someone who'd worked there all his life. Someone who knew things other people would never be told. "Any trouble comin' in?"

"None," Andy told him, figuring any acknowledgement of getting a tow from the Coast Guard wasn't necessary.

"Good. Take this line and secure it to your bow cleat. I'll set you up with a spring line."

The man went about his work in the manner of a dockworker who was securing a boat for a passing tourist. As he secured the stern, he continued. "We're gonna want you and your friend off the boat. Anything we need to know? Any of the cargo stashed in places we might miss?"

"Not really." And then Andy remembered the snake. "We did pick up a water moccasin along the way. Not sure where."

The worker didn't seem fazed by the information. "Where is it?"

"In the starboard compartment under the V-berth."

"Let's have a look, shall we? I may not be around for the unloading and the guys'll get all pissy if someone gets bit." He spoke as if snakes on board were a common occurrence.

Andy led Henry past Ollie, who was in the cockpit rolling a joint.

"Not here, friend," Henry told him. "Maybe you're forgetting where you are. Put that shit away." They continued to the V-berth and Andy pointed to the anchor they'd set against the compartment door. "Right in there," he said.

The worker removed the anchor and opened the door. The moccasin opened its eyes, seemingly annoyed at being disturbed. As if by magic, a gun appeared in Henry's hand, and without any fanfare, he discharged two rounds into the head of the cottonmouth.

He looked at Andy whose face showed surprise at the loud discharges from the gun in the early hours of the morning.

"A bit excessive wouldn't you say?" Andy asked. "You probably woke up everyone in the harbor."

"Ah hell, they all gotta get up to unload this tub anyway. Besides, most of 'em will either sleep through it or ignore it."

"What about my boat?"

"Ah, I doubt if this little pea-shooter went through to the bottom. If it did, Davy Jones'll have two more bullet holes in him. We're fixin' it all up fer ya anyway, aren't we?" Without waiting for an answer, Henry draped the snake around his neck and wore it topside where he threw it overboard. "If you've got some things you want to take ashore, now's the time to pack up. With work bein' done on your boat here I expect you'll be put up somewhere for a coupla days. I'm to tell ya to go to the harbor master's office. I guess he's got the details. The office is the little red shack at the end of the dock."

"Should I wait 'til morning?"

"No. He'll be up. If not, wake him up. He's gonna want to get you unloaded right away."

Andy and Ollie checked in with the harbor master. He was polite—professional. Andy began to see a pattern with the men he'd recently encountered. He recalled the words of Captain Lombardi describing the work force as men who trusted each other—men who had wives and children . . . mouths to feed . . . and how they relied on one another. It was a business. Their product was an illegal substance, but it was a business all the same. They took it—and all the risks that went with it—as part of their daily routine.

The harbor master didn't have the aged look of Henry, but he was in his early sixties. A Meerschaum pipe sat in an ashtray sending a small spiral of smoke upward. He seemed to be cross-checking figures in a ledger when Andy and Ollie entered. Classical music was coming from a small stereo and he turned in his chair and lowered the volume. "You must be the boys from Melbourne Beach. I saw you motor in just now." As he spoke, he pointed to one of several surveillance cameras that allowed different views of the dock and the yard.

Andy looked at the cameras for several seconds before responding. "Yeah, Andy Dugan." He then crossed the room and extended his hand. "My friend here is Ollie." Ollie nodded. The harbor master failed to return the courtesy of introducing himself.

"I guess we're supposed to let you know we need a meeting with . . . ." Andy was cut short by the harbor master's raised hand. "Yes, yes, I know. I'll set you up with a meeting with the Librarian, but it won't be at this hour of the morning." He turned his chair again and pushed a button on an intercom that threw his voice out to the yard. "Henry?"

After a short pause, Henry acknowledged the harbor master through the crackle of static and then waited for his orders.

"I need you to bring the car up and take our friends here to the Teal Cove." He released the button. "The Teal Cove's a nice hotel. You'll find it's quite comfortable. We've made arrangements for you. The Librarian will be in touch in the morning, so hang there until you hear from him. Order breakfast from room service."

Andy noticed that, like Henry, his tone was businesslike—neither friendly nor unfriendly.

"Henry will pick you up in a minute and drive you over. You can wait out front." He nodded toward the door as he made the statement, indicating their meeting was over. It was his way of saying good-bye. Once said, he returned to the ledger.

IT WAS A SHORT ride to the hotel. Henry had offered no information since leaving the yard.

"What happens once we're at the hotel?"

"You'll meet the Librarian and get paid, I expect."

"Librarian? Who the hell is this Librarian?" The question came from Ollie who sat in the back seat.

Henry glanced in the rearview mirror to respond. "He's the guy who'll pay you."

"Yeah, I heard that part. Why do you call him the Librarian?"

Henry's eyes shifted back and forth from the highway to the rearview mirror. "He keeps the books," Henry laughed. He then wheeled into a large horseshoe sweep at the entrance to the Teal Cove Hotel and Andy and Ollie got out.

Before Andy closed the door he received a final word of advice from Henry. "Captain Dugan," he said. "The Librarian is a highly respected man in our organization . . . he appreciates respect . . . it would be wise not to do anything to upset him."

Andy and Ollie were scrutinized as they passed the doorman. Inside, the lobby floor had been tiled in an off-white marble that matched large pillars. Palm trees towered into the cathedral ceiling and a sweeping staircase wound its way to the second floor balcony overlooking the foyer. Although it was nearing three o'clock in the morning, there was more activity than Andy expected.

Ollie surveyed the surroundings. "Not bad digs if we're to be prisoners."

"Nobody said we're prisoners."

"Didn't he say don't leave the room?"

Before Andy could respond, they had reached the desk and the night clerk gave him a cordial greeting. "Good to see you, Mr. Dugan." As he spoke he extended a hand holding two key cards.

"Have we met?"

"No, sir. It's just that I saw Henry dropping you off outside and we've been expecting you."

Andy and Ollie looked at each other, recognizing the probability that the hotel was owned by whoever it was they were working for. With that thought, a closer scrutiny of the lobby revealed an abundance of surveillance cameras.

The offer to have their bags taken to the room was declined and they took the elevator to the fourth floor. In the room, Ollie grabbed two beers from the courtesy bar. They collapsed on the beds and in a matter of minutes, fell into a much needed sleep. The unfinished bottle of Andy's beer sat on the nightstand. Ollie's had slipped out of his hand and drained itself onto the sheets. Both slept under the watchful eye of a camera.

♦   angel from heaven

Hanson's truck rumbled along the outskirts of Miami. He scanned the roadside for a motel—something within his budget that offered free HBO and WIFI. A neon sign on the Palm Beach Inn offered both and included a small restaurant advertising Miller High Life. Combined with the gas station and convenience store that sat on the opposite side of the highway, Ernie Hanson had found paradise—a place to hang his soiled captain's hat while he located his boat and waited for the repairs to be made.

It was past five o'clock when he got settled in. He called the office in an attempt to contact Connie. When she didn't pick up, he recalled her threat to quit. If she had been serious, he had no idea whether or not she had done anything to obtain the list he needed or attempted to find a messenger.

Rather than eat in the restaurant, he paid a visit to the convenience store and bought several bags of chips, a twelve-pack of Budweiser, and four cigarillos. As an afterthought he grabbed an egg salad sandwich from the store's cooler. In the room he made another call to Connie. This time to her cell. When she didn't answer, he ate his sandwich and chips, drank four beers, and watched the last half of *The Outlaw Josey Wales*.

On his third call, Connie picked up. Knowing his predicament, he attempted a civil tone. "Didn't want to bother you at home," he began. "I was just wondering how you made out with the list of marinas down here or if you had a chance to call anyone."

"It got real busy after you left Ernie. I'm afraid you'll have to make your own list. Try using the Yellow Pages." Hanson felt the ice in her voice reaching all the way to Miami.

"What about a messenger to get my papers down here?"

"Yes, I did find a good messenger."

Hanson breathed a quiet sigh of relief. "Can you call him tomorrow and let him know where I am?" He followed the question with the address of the motel and Connie pretended to write it down. "Give him my cell number too, in case I'm not in my room when he gets here."

"Sure Ernie, consider it done."

"Were you serious about quitting?"

"Yeah, and I'm not picking up any more of your calls, either. I only answered this time 'cause I don't want you buggin' me the whole time you're down there. I locked up the office. I'm through." There was no good-bye from Connie's end of the phone, and Hanson knew he was on his own. He hoped she had found a good messenger.

The next morning, he loaded the remaining beers into a small cooler and drove into Miami. His strategy to find *Miss Demeanor* was to perch himself on vantage points that overlooked boat-filled harbors. A good view would allow him to scan the multitude of moorings with the hope of spotting the singular boat that lacked a mast. From what he learned from West Coast Marina, there hadn't been time to step a new one. He surveyed several harbors before taking a break for lunch.

Hanson had never been a particularly lucky man, but the interruption of his plan to grab a burger at a roadside stand turned out to be the beginning of a fortunate chain of events. After leaving the congestion of the city, he came upon a stranded limousine headed back to Miami. The driver was out of the car waving frantically for him to stop. Hanson pulled over and the driver pointed to his flat tire and explained that he had to get his client to the airport.

Against his better instincts, Hanson agreed to turn around and take the guy's client to Miami International. During the ride, the man questioned Hanson about being in the city and Hanson explained he was looking for a boat and planned to be in town for a few days. In lieu of money as a means of compensation, the rider offered him something better.

"I'm the ambassador to the U.S. from Bosnafara," he told Hanson. "It's a small country in eastern Europe. I've been called back home unexpectedly—which is the reason for my haste, and I should like to offer you my suite at the Stonis Inn.

It is fully paid for through the end of the week, and if you haven't found a hotel yet for yourself, I would be honored to allow you to use it . . . as my guest."

Hanson's acceptance was purely from an economical standpoint. He had no idea the Stonis Inn was one of the premiere hotels in Miami. The ambassador promised to call the manager from the airport and let them know Hanson was going to be using the suite as his guest. He gave Hanson his VIP card which, as he explained, was a swipe card that would allow him to use the private elevator and access the suite.

"Be comfortable," the ambassador told him. "Use the minibar and room service. I will tell them to put everything on my bill."

The remainder of the day left no room for boat watching. He drove to the hotel, parked his pickup in the garage and went inside. He bypassed the lobby and followed the ambassador's directions to the private lift. He swiped the VIP card and went directly to the luxury suite.

Within minutes, he was stripped down to his underwear drinking a cold beer and watching a movie on HBO. Occasionally he walked to the window and looked down on the city. From the room's elevation, he overlooked one of the marinas he planned on checking. Believing it was possible to locate the boat from the window, he saw no reason to leave the room.

The ambassador caught his flight, but with phones being turned off during take-off, he lacked the opportunity to call the hotel on behalf of Hanson. Once in the air, he dozed from exhaustion. Not only was the call to the Stonis Inn never made, the ambassador also forgot to call the *Angel From Heaven* escort service and cancel his angel for that evening.

THE KNOCK ON HANSON'S door came around eight o'clock. Not being one for any sort of protocol, he answered it wearing his blue and white striped boxer shorts and the sweaty sleeveless T-shirt he'd worn since leaving Melbourne. The shorts and shirt, combined with his navy blue socks, gave him the appearance of an actor in a B-rated porn flick. It was in that attire he opened the door and stood staring at the most

beautiful woman he'd ever seen. She was in her early twenties
. . . blonde hair that cascaded to her shoulders . . . a full bust
that tapered into a tiny waist . . . and high heels supporting
perfectly shaped legs accentuated by the shortness of her skirt.
Hanson stared as he remained speechless. She held out a hand.
Her voice was friendly. "I'm your Angel from Heaven," she
announced.

"You certainly are." Hanson said, still staring.

"You called earlier . . . for an arrangement?"

Hanson didn't quite understand the significance of the
word *arrangement* and continued to stare in silence. She looked
over her shoulder and glanced down both hallways. "Are you
going to invite me in?"

Ernie stepped back, still a bit dazed. As she stepped past
him, he breathed in her perfume. She gave him a second look,
and as he closed the door, she glanced at the number to
confirm she was in the correct suite.

"How are you getting on?" she asked him. "Has your trip
been successful so far?"

"G . . . good," he stammered out.

"I can stay for an hour or stay the night," she told him.
"The agency left the timetable open so I guess it's up to you."
She unbuttoned the top button of her dress and smiled.

Hanson began putting the pieces together. The woman was
obviously a final thank-you gift from the ambassador. She was
his and he could have his way with her.

"I guess I'll go for the whole kettle of fish then. Let's just
do it up right."

As she studied him he realized he was standing in his boxer
shorts and he became embarrassed. A wave of paranoia swept
over him as he wondered if he smelled from his failure to
shower that day. He felt the stubble of whiskers on his chin,
realizing a woman of this beauty expected better. The fact that
she was a prostitute was irrelevant. She was obviously a high-
priced prostitute and certainly expected quality clients. His
sudden guilt caused him to make an attempt to straighten up
the room. He grabbed empty bottles and threw them into the
waste basket. Notes that he had scattered on the bed containing
information from the phone book were grabbed and thrown

into the drawer of the night table. All of it done while apologizing for the appearance of the room.

"The room should be the way it makes you comfortable," she told him, and then motioned to a chair. "May I sit down?" "Oh, sure . . . I'm sorry. Would you like a drink? I've got a fully stocked bar here." He studied her as he spoke, infatuated with her beauty. The mirror behind her reminded him of his appearance. "As long as we're going to make a night of it, why don't I hop in the shower real quick. I guess I could probably use a shave as well." As he talked, he walked backward toward the bathroom. His steps were awkward and he stumbled, nearly falling.

"I'll tell you what. You go ahead and shower and I'll fix myself that drink you offered."

Angel was on her second scotch and Hanson had yet to reappear. He hadn't seemed to be shy but it wasn't unusual in her business for guys to get cold feet when faced with a moment of paid intimacy. Not having provided services to this particular ambassador before, she had no idea what he might be thinking. She walked to the bathroom door. The shower stopped and she heard the glass door slide open. If he was anxious about the impending evening, she felt she might be able to soften things a bit and she knocked lightly.

Hanson still hadn't shaved and he became a bit irritated at the intrusion. If he had all night with this woman, he didn't want to be rushed. After all, she was his gift and he would call the shots. She knocked again, this time a bit louder.

"What is it?" his voice was tense but he tried to avoid sounding annoyed.

"Just checking to see if there is anything I can help you with."

"Yeah, I'll tell you what, there's a bottle of lotion in here. How 'bout I bring it out there and you put some on me and give me a nice body massage?" Angel remained silent. "Or, if you prefer, I could smear it all over you and give *you* a massage." This time, when he shouted through the door there was no attempt to hide his irritation at being rushed.

Unsure of what he was thinking, she again tried to sooth him. "If you think it might help, I could perform fellatio for you."

"Why the hell would I want you to come all the way up here to my suite and perform some play about a puppet whose nose gets longer every time he tells a lie?"

Hanson's response caused Angel to step back and think about the man on the other side of the door. She turned and surveyed the room. She saw no evidence of things that might be indicative of an ambassador. There was no briefcase or expensive luggage—no garment bag in the closet. She returned to the bathroom door. "Ambassador Howard?"

"Ambassador Howard?" Ernie hollered back. "You mean that geeky guy with the fancy jewelry? Hell no, he left this morning. Why, does he like that Shakespeare stuff?"

The second response caused Angel to procure her cell phone from her purse. "Billie? I think you better get up here. Something's not right with this guy."

Angel's driver arrived at the ambassador's suite as Hanson made his grand entrance from the bathroom. The driver looked as though he was the one who belonged there. He was dressed in an expensive suit, his hair was professionally cut, and his nails were manicured. The driver stood in the small entry way and was unseen by Hanson who stood wearing one of the hotel bathrobes. Freshly showered and shaved, he exhibited signs of renewed confidence. He spread his arms wide apart inviting a big hug and then Billie stepped forward. Angel grabbed her purse and took a few steps toward her driver.

"Who the hell are you?" Hanson asked.

"No, the question is, who the hell are *you* and what are you doing here?"

"I'm Ernie Hanson and I'm here lookin' for my boat if it's any of your business."

The conversation deteriorated further when Hanson was informed he owed Angel five-hundred dollars for her wasted time. When Hanson refused to pay, Billie landed a well-placed punch to the stomach. While he was doubled over, the driver followed the punch with an upward knee to the chin. Hanson dropped to the floor and Billie took the wallet from the vanity and pulled out all the bills. "Sixty-two dollars? That's what you've got in here, sixty-two dollars?"

Hanson looked up from his position on the floor. "The bitch wasn't even worth that."

Billie added a kick to Hanson's side and then removed the lone credit card before throwing the wallet to the floor. In the lobby, he took Angel into the hotel jewelry store where she picked out a three thousand dollar necklace. Billie presented Hanson's credit card for the purchase and there was no question of identity, although the clerk did offer to have the item charged to his room. Billie believed buying Angel a gift was the least Hanson could do. In the hotel lobby he tossed the credit card into a wastebasket and then escorted Angel to the car.

Hanson remained on the floor for several minutes after his Angel made her exit. Only then was he able to get to all fours and think about his situation. His only remaining cash was a twenty dollar bill he kept in the ashtray of his truck for emergencies. He had not seen the driver remove his credit card and figured his plastic and the twenty would get him through the next few days while he searched the harbors for *Miss Demeanor*.

He stumbled into the bathroom where he studied the dried blood on his lip. Pulling it upward revealed a small cut inside and pink stains between his teeth where blood had accumulated. While cleaning himself, there was a knock on the door. En route to answer it, he rummaged through his bag and took out his Glock. A glance through the peephole to the hallway revealed a mealy looking man who was rocking back and forth from soles to heels. Hanson was relieved to see it wasn't the driver coming back for round two. He set the gun down and tightened the sash on the hotel robe to make himself more presentable before opening the door.

The man in the hallway was the night clerk and was obviously distraught. Seeing spots of blood on the hotel robe did little to calm his nerves. Although Hanson was showered and clean-shaven, his hair was tousled and his lip was a bit puffy.

"I'm afraid I've had several complaints," the clerk told Hanson. "And I'm not quite sure how you got into one of our VIP suites in the first place."

"Maybe because I'm the best friend of the ambassador guy who stays here who said I could use the place for the rest of the week."

"Be that as it may, I'm afraid that despite any agreement you had with the ambassador, you'll have to check out."

"Just where in the hell do you expect me to go at this hour?"

"I can let you stay until morning, but it would be with the provision that there are no further disturbances. You should also be aware I cannot put any of your expenses on the ambassador's account without his official say so."

"He told me he was gonna call you about me stayin' here."

"As I said. There has obviously been a mix-up and you'll have to leave in the morning."

Hanson gave a surly response indicating he would settle up when he checked out and then closed the door on the clerk. In the morning, he made his exit in the same private elevator he used for his entrance. Once in the parking garage, he felt good about his successful escape.

Realizing his credit card was missing and having only enough cash for his return to Melbourne, he made two attempts to reach Connie. Both went to her voice mail. Without more money, his last ditch effort in finding *Miss Demeanor* was parking his truck in an area where boats leaving Miami heading north would most likely pass. It allowed him a final day of surveillance before returning to Melbourne empty handed. He planned to spend every hour of daylight waiting and watching every boat sailing north.

53

Mario and Rosita departed Melbourne at the crack of dawn on Saturday. When they arrived in Miami, Rosita gave him directions to her old neighborhood in Little Havana. "It's not far from the wharfs," she told him. "I know someone who might be able to get us some information on the boat."

The guy Rosita was referring to turned out to be a burly mechanic named Tobias, who owned a neighborhood garage. When they pulled in, he was working on the underbelly of a car and he rolled out from its shadow. Rosita told Mario to wait in the car and walked toward him. When Tobias recognized her, he grabbed a rag from a barrel and began wiping his hands in preparation for a hug. His arms were then outstretched and his embrace accompanied a genuine smile. From the driver's seat, Mario heard bits and pieces of the conversation, but being in Spanish, understood little. The smiles continued and the accompanying body language indicated old scenarios being relived and a reunion that was long overdue.

After a minute of catching up, Rosita then got right to the point. Her expression became serious, and being a woman who let her hands do much of her talking, Mario tried to follow what was being said through her gestures. Her arms flailed while she pantomimed the shape of a sailboat. She then made a sharp horizontal karate chop which Mario assumed was her reenactment of the mast being cut off. In the midst of her chatter and arm waving the mechanic stole glances at Mario between acknowledging Rosita with nods or shrugs.

The conversation ended and Rosita took the mechanic by the hand and led him to the car. Mario climbed out of the driver's seat for the introductions.

"This is Tobias," she told Mario. "He's an old friend of my father."

Tobias studied Mario as he extended a greasy hand. "Hola."

"Hola," Mario returned, using one of the few words in his Spanish vocabulary. "I'm Mario."

The stare from Tobias continued as he studied Rosita's friend. The smile he had given Rosita had disappeared. She put her hand on Tobias's arm. "It's okay," she reassured him. "He's good people."

The tension seemed to ease a bit and Rosita filled Mario in on their conversation. "I gave him the information on *Miss Demeanor.* He told me with sailboats going in and out of the boatyards every day there was no reason such a boat would raise any suspicions, but to give him some time. He said a lot of the guys who hang around the garage either work in the boatyards or know someone who does. I gave him my cell number in case anything comes up".

"I appreciate anything you can find out," Mario told him, not sure whether or not he understood. He and Rosita left the garage and checked out two boatyards but reaped no reward. Mario conceded the likelihood that *Miss Demeanor* hadn't even docked yet. "Whoever these guys are, they certainly aren't sailing her down here with no mast. And I'm not sure after sitting in the river for a year what condition her engine is in. I suggest we check into a motel and get settled in. We can visit a few more marinas and put the word out while we wait for a call from Tobias."

The remainder of Saturday was spent familiarizing themselves with possible harbors and marinas the Beneteau might use for repairs. Most of the focus was on the bigger places that had the equipment needed for stepping the new mast. Tobias called Sunday morning and informed Rosita that he might have a lead on the boat they were looking for, but she should come to the garage. It was closed on Sundays and they could talk more privately. When they arrived, Tobias opened the office door and motioned for them to come inside.

"I try English," he said to Mario. "But not so good," this time he smiled.

A slender man dressed in work clothes sat in one of two wooden chairs in the office. His clothing and boots carried a slight scent of fish from the docks and it had already begun to permeate the small room. He appeared nervous and snapped to his feet when Tobias entered with Mario and Rosita. When he saw Rosita, he removed his cap advertising Penzoil motor oil. Tobias spoke to Rosita in Spanish and she turned and explained to Mario that the man worked at a nearby boatyard. The conversation continued in Spanish as Tobias instructed the worker to tell Rosita what he'd told him earlier. Mario struggled to understand the language, getting some of what was being said through gestures and body language. It was obvious the man was nervous about giving out the information. His hat remained in his hands, and while he talked, it was twisted and squeezed as if he was wringing out a wet sponge. The wooden chair was old and when the man fidgeted, it squeaked beneath his weight. Between sentences, Rosita stopped him and translated for Mario.

"He said he thinks the boat we're looking for is at the North of the Keys Marina where he works. A boat came in last night and the boss had the men get started on it right away. He said it's not usual for them to be in such a hurry, especially on Sunday because it means overtime."

Tobias grabbed a bottle of water from a case next to his desk, unscrewed the top, and handed it to the worker. He raised a second bottle in the air and gestured to Mario who waved it off. The man continued but this time he directed his statement to Tobias. Rosita then turned to Mario. "He's scared," she said. "The men he's talking about use the yard as a front for running drugs. He saw some of the men unloading a shipment from a sailboat before he and the regular workers got started on the repairs. The boat didn't have any mast, like the one Tobias told them to look for."

Tobias said something to Rosita and Mario picked up on the word *morté* before she made the translation. "Tobias said the worker believes if they find out he's here he'll be killed."

The man then made a short plea to Rosita. She explained he wanted to leave and get home to his family. Rosita thanked him for the information with words even Mario understood.

"We should give him some money for helping us," she said to Mario. Mario withdrew his wallet which brought a reaction from the worker. He put his hand on Rosita's arm. This time he spoke in English. "No, no," he told her. "No money." He then looked at Mario and continued in English. "These are bad men." He looked at Tobias, who thanked him and opened the door for him to leave. "Remember, bad men," he said.

Rosita talked with Tobias to gain more information about the marina before she and Mario left the office. In the car, she explained Tobias' concern for their safety as he emphasized the dangerous nature of the men and the drug operation. Before backing out of the lot, Tobias emerged from the office and approached the car carrying an envelope and a soiled rag. At the car he leaned on Mario's door. He reached across Mario and gave Rosita the envelope. "You take this money," he said. "I'm doing good here . . . and your father . . . you know . . . I owe him. You take this and be careful."

Rosita started to object to taking the money but was stopped by his raised hand. "Please, I need you to have this." He then looked at Mario and held out the rag. He flipped over the top portion to reveal a small handgun. "And you take this. Nine bullets in the clip," he said to Mario. "It is small, but easy to hide and packs a punch." As he made the statement he punched the air.

Mario hesitated, but then thanked him and took the gun. "Hope I won't be needing it."

From the garage they drove straight to the North of the Keys Marina. Mario knew from experience that most wharf areas are readily accessible to the general public. Tourists and locals often walk the docks to view the yachts that come in and out of the harbor. The Miami Beach marinas have more restrictions than most to ensure privacy for celebrities who motor in on their luxury yachts. Many of the harbors post signs to dissuade visitors from disturbing boat owners. Anyone continuing past the posted areas usually received a polite warning and reminder of the rules.

Under the guise of innocent tourists, Mario and Rosita parked at North of the Keys Marina and walked toward the wharf. As they neared the gate, they found security was much tighter. In addition to the normal signs prohibiting access to boats, the area was protected by a full-time security guard prohibiting entrance to the yard. Employees wore ID badges and legitimate owners and their guests were screened at the gate. The security measures were no surprise in light of what Tobias and his friend had told them but none of the sloops visible from the gate proved to be *Miss Demeanor*.

The prohibited access resulted in Mario driving to a small hill overlooking the Marina, and with the use of binoculars, he scanned the harbor. Rosita stood at his side. "These guys don't waste any time," he told her. "*Miss Demeanor* is there all right and if what Tobias's friend told us is true, these guys got a new mast up and rigged in a hurry. There must be five or six guys scurrying around the deck scrubbing and polishing as well. I guess it would be to my benefit to let them finish before making a scene. If I can get the boat as well as the diamonds, I can deal with Cohen and you and I can still sail off into the sunset." He put the binoculars down and smiled at her. "Just like in the fairy tales."

"I don't think what Tobias told us has any kind of a fairy tale ending. Just how do you propose to get the boat?"

"I guess I'll do what any upstanding citizen would do. I'll present my papers of ownership and claim it. It *is* legally mine."

"I'm not so sure they're gonna see it the same way."

"Maybe not, but it's probably a better plan than blasting my way in with the pea shooter and nine rounds of ammo Tobias gave me."

As they drove back to the marina, Rosita thumbed through the money in the envelope. She looked at Mario and tears ran down her cheeks.

"What's wrong?"

She held up the envelope. "There's four hundred and thirty-six dollars in here. It's probably every cent he has to his name."

"I guess he's a better friend than you thought."

"A friend to my father. He believes my father saved his life when they were kids. My father pulled him onto my grandfather's boat in the Cuban harbor."

"Well, you know he's a man you can trust with your life."

"I know that. He's always been like an uncle to me."

"A bit more than an uncle, I'd say."

"What do you mean?"

"When he gave me the gun . . . I guess I got a slight taste of the reassurance your people felt like when they searched out a friend."

"Really? What do you mean?"

"I noticed the serpent tattoo on his arm."

◆ the arrival

A ndy and Ollie waited in their hotel room as instructed. Late Sunday afternoon a man came to the room to take them to the Librarian. They were subjected to the standard frisking they had become used to and then escorted to the elevator. When they got off at the penthouse, it was hard not to notice the black spheres embedded in the ceiling which hid surveillance cameras. The suite itself was three or four times larger than their own accommodations.

Their escort took a seat near the door. The man assumed to be the Librarian sat at a large desk, the top of which was much too organized. Two wooden trays were stacked on one corner and a stapler and scotch tape dispenser sat next to a chrome cylinder on the other. The chrome cylinder was filled with pens and pencils. An open ledger, similar to the harbor master's, sat on the desk in front of him. Beneath it was a large blotter. Close to his right hand was an old-fashioned adding machine with a lengthy strip of curled paper winding out of the top. The Librarian neither stood nor looked up to show any sign of recognition. He ran his left index finger down the ledger while his right hand punched keys on the adding machine with the proficiency of a court stenographer. After each group of figures was entered, he pulled down on the handle as if playing a slot machine. Andy and Ollie waited. Andy likened the scene to his days in school when he'd been called to the principal's office for a reprimand and was then made to wait to be yelled at.

Ollie broke the silence. "Nice view." His comment was made in reference to the panoramic view of Miami Beach from the wall of glass that looked out over the city.

The Librarian said nothing. He continued hitting number keys and cranking the handle. The sound of the figures being printed out was the only sound in the room. He then stopped, slammed the book shut and looked up for the first time. He was a frail man in his fifties and sported a pencil thin mustache. When he looked up he removed his glasses. His eyes were dark and tired. "You boys did okay for yourselves," he said. "Your boat's been unloaded and everything's present and accounted for."

"Good," Andy said. "So now what?"

"Normally, we'd pay you your money and send you on your way, but I understand part of this deal was to get your boat fixed up."

"Where does that leave us?"

"That leaves you with some time to kill. I don't know how long the repairs will take, but I'm sure the harbor master wants your boat out of the yard as soon as possible. We'll give your boat top priority. Ever been in Miami?"

A 'yes' and a 'no' came simultaneously from the duo. The 'no' was from Andy.

"It's got a lot to offer. Take a day and enjoy yourselves around town . . . or relax here around the hotel pool. Feel free to charge your meals and incidentals to the room." He then motioned to the man who'd accompanied them to the suite. "I'll have Smitty let you know when your boat's ready and we'll settle up and send you on your way."

"I think we'd just as soon settle up now if that works for you," Ollie said.

"You should tell your friend here he needs to have more trust." The Librarian's words were filled with a tone of indignation and they triggered the memory of Captain Lombardi's lecture on trust and his advice to "not become chum."

Andy tried to soften Ollie's comment. "I guess part of the problem is we're a little short on cash right now. If we're gonna see the sights of Miami, we could use the money we agreed on." In making the comment, he realized they had never really agreed on anything. Any figures they had used had come from Ollie.

The Librarian opened one of his desk drawers and removed a small cash box. He withdrew stacks of twenties before dividing them into two piles. "There's a coupla hundred for each of you," he said as he slid them to the front of his desk. "That should hold you until your boat's ready and we settle up for the cargo." Andy stared first at the money and then at the Librarian. "On the house," the Librarian added and the stare he returned was one of finality. Smitty stood and moved toward the door indicating the meeting was over.

♦   the payoff

O n Monday, Mario left Rosita at the motel and drove to the
    marina. He hoped to persuade the harbor master to allow
him on board alone. He only needed a few minutes to get the
diamonds, knowing proving his ownership and getting *Miss
Demeanor* returned might still be a problem. He had to
determine whether his boat was being refitted for the two guys
who stole her or was being modified for use in the marina's
drug fleet.

He parked and went into the office. "Name's Costello," he
told the harbor master, attempting to sound casual.

The handshake was accepted. "What can I do for you?"

"Well, I do believe you have my boat here in the harbor.
The sucker was stolen from me a week or so ago and I've traced
it this far."

"Traced it?"

Mario realized it was a poor choice of words. "Actually, I
guess I should've said found it. It was stolen up in Melbourne
and I got word the thieves were heading to Miami. I've been
searchin' the marinas around here for two days . . . finally
spotted her in your marina last night."

"What's the name of the boat?"

"*Miss Demeanor.* She's a thirty-five foot Beneteau. I've got
the papers here." Mario pulled the packet from his back pocket
and dropped them on the desk.

The harbor master looked a bit puzzled but picked them up
and studied them. "I'll have to check on this with the owners
who brought her in. Papers can be made anywhere."

"It might help if I could go on board. Maybe I'm mistaken
about it being my boat. I've only seen it from a distance."

"I'm afraid I can't let you go on board without the owner's
permission."

"Yeah, but I *am* the owner. Those are the papers that prove it. If I thought there was going to be a problem, I would've brought the authorities with me." Mario hoped the word *authorities* might move things along. If these guys were running drugs they weren't going to be receptive to cops nosing around.

"I'll tell you what . . . why don't you get yourself a cup of coffee somewhere while I check into this. Give me an hour or so and I'll see what I can find out."

Mario's departure triggered a phone call from the harbor master to the Librarian. The call resulted in Andy and Ollie summoned for another audience.

"I guess we knew you two stole the boat you brought in," the Librarian told them. "We just didn't figure on the real owner showing up. You either, for that matter. I thought you told our guy up north it was abandoned."

"It was abandoned," Andy responded. "The thing's been sitting up there on the river for over a year. What do you mean the real owner showed up?"

"That's what he said, and I'm told he's got the papers to prove it."

"But the boat's clean right? I mean, your cargo is off and safe."

"Oh yeah, the boat's clean all right. We just don't need anybody making a big scene at the marina and complicating matters."

"So now what?"

"So now I settle up with you. You can either make things right with the owner or take your money and get a bus outta town." He turned in his chair and fetched two small canvas bags from behind him and set them on the table. "Three hundred keys of marijuana at four hundred per key nets you a hundred and twenty thousand for the grass . . . ."

"I counted five hundred keys when we loaded," Ollie told him. "You might wanna use your fancy machine there to recalculate." The Librarian's man near the door stirred and the Librarian raised a hand indicating he had the situation under control.

"Yes. Five hundred keys . . . if you let me finish. Three hundred grass—two hundred cocaine."

Andy shot a look at Ollie and then back to the Librarian. "Cocaine?"

"Yes, that was the deal Eric laid out." He then continued with a tone of condescension. "You must have known that. I can't imagine two experienced dealers such as yourselves would get into a transaction without knowing the details. Any runner knows the green keys are grass and the red packets are coke. Your friend here certainly knew the deal." Andy's fists tightened, but he remained silent.

The Librarian picked up on the tension. "Or maybe your friend Ollie here forgot to mention a few things. Actually, it worked out pretty well for you. Coke is an extra hundred a key so it adds another hundred thousand. Two hundred and twenty thousand . . . not a bad paycheck for a couple of days work."

He pushed the bags toward the front of his desk. "Which one of you owns the boat?"

"I do," Andy said.

"Then this one's for you," he said and slid one closer to Andy. "I took the liberty of deducting our fourteen thousand for the repairs. Our expenses were a bit over that, but I kept it in round numbers."

"Eric told me fixing the boat was part of the deal."

"Eric says a lot of things. It's what I say that counts. If you question that, I suggest you take the fourteen grand up with him."

The Librarian looked down and opened his ledger, indicating the meeting was over. The calculations Andy had made were a far cry from what they were getting but Ollie was walking away with over a hundred grand and Andy had a bag containing ninety-six thousand to go with a like-new Beneteau. It was nothing to sneeze at. He was also anxious to see her refurbished, regardless of who showed up claiming to be her owner.

The Librarian nodded toward the bodyguard. "Smitty will drive you back to your boat . . . or the bus station. I'll let you decide where it is you want to go. I'm sure you understand that, under the circumstances, we can't help you with this guy claiming to be the owner. It brings unwanted attention to the marina. I would suggest you don't do anything that brings unwanted attention as well."

Once Andy and Ollie left the office, the Librarian called the harbor master. "If the guy claiming to be the owner of the Beneteau has the proof, let him have the boat. I just finished our transaction with the Melbourne guys and turned them loose. They can duke it out with him if they're so inclined. Just make sure if they show up there you tell them to take their feud out of the marina."

ANDY AND OLLIE FOLLOWED Smitty to the car. Andy's insistence on returning to the boat wasn't something Ollie could argue against. The fact that Ollie had not only known the quantity of what they were picking up, as well as knowing about the cocaine in the shipment, left no room for debate.

"If you want to bus yourself back to Melbourne, be my guest," Andy hollered. "As a matter of fact, I'd prefer it! As far as the boat goes, I believe it's mine. I've come this far and I'm going to see it through."

The ride to the boatyard was made in silence as the two sat in the back seat. Ollie attempted to make amends when they reached the marina. "Look, I'm sorry. I should've told ya. I just didn't think if I gave you all the details you'd follow through on the deal."

"You're right! I wouldn't have followed through. Do you realize how much time we'd be lookin' at if we got caught? We were damn lucky I knew that guy runnin' the Coast Guard patrol boat or we'd both be starin' at the world through bars."

"Actually, the twenty-five keys would've given us the same result. I figured if we were gonna get busted we should make it worth our while. Think about the money we just got . . . and I knew you wanted the boat."

"Oh no, don't push this back on me because I wanted a boat."

"Well, if it's any consolation, I'm seeing this thing through to make sure you get it. Whoever this guy is who claims to be the owner might find himself thrown overboard."

The sudden change in Ollie's personality made Andy laugh. "What about your 'void of course' concerns. What if the timing's not right for tossing somebody overboard?"

"I've been thinking you may have a valid point on the lunarium stuff." He fingered the necklace Ding-Lee had made that hung around his neck. "Of course, I've always got this chunk of sea glass for good karma," he laughed.

Andy gave him a friendly slap on the side of his arm. "Okay," he said. "Let's go get my boat."

56

Mario used the harbor master's suggestion to get a cup of coffee to return to the hotel. He felt not being threatened or tossed out of the office was encouraging. He updated Rosita on the progress, and when she heard the news, she suggested a new path.

"From what you're telling me, work on the boat is about done and it's probably ready to sail. I say we pack up our things and check out of this place. There's a branch of my bank here in Miami. We can stop on the way to the boat. If we're sailing off into the sunset in your fairytale ending, I'm not leaving the money sitting here. Besides, it'll give me an excuse to use that famous secret compartment you're always braggin' about. You know, the compartment hiding your precious diamonds."

"I'm not sure we should just rush into this."

Rosita put her arms around Mario's neck. "Hey, we're in this together or we're not."

"What about your car?"

"You mean my twelve year old VW that's got a knock in the engine, burns oil, and needs a new exhaust system?"

"Yeah, that's the one," Mario laughed.

"I'll leave it at the marina. Better yet, I'll call Tobias and tell him he can have it for parts. It might make up for the money he gave me."

At Rosita's insistence, Mario drove to the bank on the way to the boatyard and she emptied her account. With money in hand, and armed with proof of ownership, they continued to North of the Keys Marina. They now had little fear that any harm would come to them at the boatyard and Mario could also follow through on his threat of bringing in the Miami police if they ran into any trouble. If the work on the boat was finished, Rosita's idea was appealing. There wasn't anything for Mario back in Melbourne and another year or two selling doughnuts while Rosita finished her degree could certainly be put on hold. They both agreed if the boat wasn't ready they could drive her beat up car to another hotel and wait it out.

The harbor master offered no resistance when Mario and Rosita showed up. He explained that he hadn't talked with the two gentlemen who'd brought the boat in, but he did call the marina's attorney who advised him to make copies of Mario's papers and release the boat.

"I don't think you'll have any trouble finding her," he said. "Although you may not recognize her. She's pretty much a new boat now."

Mario did, in fact, give *Miss Demeanor* a double take. She sat bobbing gently on her slip and her pristine condition was more than he'd hoped for. He stood at the base of the new mast and checked the attached hardware and rigging. The deck had been refurbished and the hardware glistened. Rosita, who had only seen the sloop in the worst of times, was amazed. The two admired the deck briefly before going below. The interior teak had been brought back to life and varnished to perfection. The brass fixtures emitted a warm glow that Mario had never before seen. Rosita twirled around in the cabin with excitement.

"It's all very nice, but you're forgetting there's a small fortune on board," Mario reminded her. He pulled the cushion from the starboard seat and pushed the hidden button to open the compartment that housed the diamonds for more than a year. His face paled.

"What is it?"

"They're not here."

"Are you sure that's where you put them?"

"Yes, I'm sure. It's the safest place on the boat. There's no way anyone could've found them."

"Maybe when the men did the work on it someone stumbled onto the compartment. Maybe that's why the harbor master was so willing to give it back to you."

Mario went topside to decide on what their next move should be. Rosita seemed content to set sail for the Caribbean and offer charters like they had talked about. She tried to convince Mario that with his new boat and her insurance money, they could still start the life they wanted without the diamonds.

Appealing as that thought was to Mario, he had no desire to spend the rest of his life wondering if his old friends Rovelli and Romance might be around the corner. It was a thought he was reluctant to share with Rosita. He had no idea what Cohen would do when he discovered someone else had the diamonds from the deal he'd financed.

Rosita stowed what little gear they had brought on board and made a quick inventory of the compartments. The excitement over starting their new adventure was still in her voice. "I'm going to take a quick nap and then I'll go ashore for groceries. I'll catch up with Tobias and have him drive me back and he can have the car." She then collapsed on the V-berth where *Miss Demeanor* rocked her into a sound sleep. Mario went topside to ponder their fate.

Henry appeared with two beers and introduced himself. Mario recognized him as the stereotypical old salt, and when he extended one of the beers and asked for permission to come aboard, he welcomed him into the cockpit.

The old man admired the new beauty of *Miss Demeanor* and gave deserved praise to the men who had done the work. He then reminisced about his days in the Merchant Marines and after the two swapped sailing stories for over an hour, Henry realized the love and appreciation Mario had for fine sailboats.

"I've got a boat on one of the other docks you might like to see. Matter of fact, you could have it if you've got a quarter of a million in your pocket," he laughed. "Are you familiar with Fairlie yachts?"

At the mention of the word Fairlie, Mario's heart skipped a beat. Owning a Fairlie yacht was a fantasy he kept in his basket of dreams.

"You've got a Fairlie here in the harbor?"

"Sure do, my friend."

"It's not a Fairlie-55 by any chance?"

"That's exactly what she is," Henry confirmed. "And I'm in charge of sellin' her. C'mon . . . we might be poor as dirt but there's nothin' says we can't go on board and take a look."

As they walked to another area of the wharf, Mario spotted her immediately. "Is the seller really asking a quarter mil?"

"Yup."

"You do realize she's worth four times that."

"I do. The thing is ya see, the boat was owned by a woman who died and left it to her nephew. He lives somewhere in Indiana or some ungodly landlocked state like that. Anyway, he's payin' the marina a hundred bucks a day for the dock fee. He just wants the damn thing sold and off his plate. From what I gather, he doesn't give a buckle's barnacle about sailin'. His exact words were 'get rid of the damn thing and send me a check.' He didn't sound like a guy who really needed any more money, if ya know what I mean. You wait right here and I'll get the keys."

Henry returned from the office and Mario got the full tour. It not only dwarfed *Miss Demeanor* in size, but the craftsmanship, both inside and out, was meticulous. He had been on board a Fairlie-55 only once but it was a memory he hadn't forgotten. Every sailor has a dream boat, and this was Mario's. When the two returned topside, his eyes swept over the deck with a longing admiration. The boat creaked as it listed from side to side. "There just isn't any sound like a wooden boat talkin' to ya," Henry said. Mario smiled in wholehearted agreement.

"The woman who owned it said she was some distant relative of that actor fella, Steve McQueen. Whether that's true or not I don't know," Henry pointed to the stern. "Thus the name," he said. "named it after one of his movies." Mario took note of the name and smiled.

He returned to *Miss Demeanor* and went below. After being on board the Fairlie, she seemed a bit cramped. He was still arranging gear and going through cabinets when he felt *Miss Demeanor* rock from the weight of someone stepping into the cockpit.

"Ahoy on board."

Mario said nothing and seconds later the face of Andy Dugan appeared in the hatchway. "Afternoon," Andy greeted. "Okay if my friend and I come aboard?"

"Looks like you're already on board."

"Yeah, well we wanted to check on our boat."

"Check on *your* boat? Let me guess. You two are the ones who stole it up in Melbourne and brought it down here."

"I guess you could say we got her here, I'm not sure saying we stole her is the right choice of words." As Andy made the statement he climbed down into the cabin. Ollie followed.

"You took a boat that didn't belong to you. From where I come from, that's stealing."

"I rescued an abandoned boat," Andy corrected. "By rights of salvage and the rules of the sea she belongs to me. Not to mention I paid fourteen grand to get her back in sailing shape."

"And I certainly appreciate that, but you know what you can do with your line of bullshit. I've got the boat, the papers to prove it, and I'm sailin' her out of here tomorrow."

The voices awoke Rosita. She emerged from the V-berth and gave the visitors a questioning look. "These are the two boat rustlers," Mario told her.

"Like I said, we thought the boat was abandoned," Andy directed the correction to Rosita. "You realize it had been sitting there for over a year."

"Bein' my boat, I guess I can leave it where I want for as long as I want."

"Well, the thing is, as you know, the mast was gone. We brought it down here to get a new mast stepped. I also had a new engine installed and everything else that needed to be done . . . none of which came cheap."

"You cost me a lot of time and aggravation, so I hope you don't expect to get reimbursed." As Mario talked, Ollie moved forward to get a better view of Rosita. In doing so, the uncut diamond Ding-Lee had given him became visible. From what Carmine had told Mario about their proportioned value, he calculated it was worth enough to buy a dozen *Miss Demeanor*s if it was cut correctly. After twelve months of talking to Rosita in code, Mario fell into their old habit of playing with words. "That looks like the necklace you lost, doesn't it?" he asked her. And then he looked at Ollie. "It went with a pair of earrings she had." His voice then gained a tone of nonchalance. "Did you find that on the boat?"

Ollie fingered the stone. "No. It was my girl who found it. It's not your necklace though, it was mixed in with a whole pouch of sea glass. She makes jewelry to pick up a few bucks on the side."

"If the pouch was on the boat I guess you could say it's rightfully mine." Mario forced a laugh.

Rosita then took the lead. "She found my stash of sea glass?"

"Yeah, I guess she did," Ollie answered.

"And she's making jewelry with it?" Mario asked.

"Yeah, like I said, man, that's what she does. She makes jewelry out of shells and beach glass and shit."

"Is she down here with you?"

"No. She stayed behind up in Melbourne."

"So you're down here with a stolen boat and she's up there with the rest of the sea glass makin' jewelry." Mario didn't want to show more interest than necessary in the stones, but wanted to pinpoint their location.

"Yeah, I guess you could say that."

"How'd you like to part with that necklace so Rosita here can replace the one she lost and put it with her earrings. It's a close enough match, don't you think?" he addressed the question to Rosita who nodded.

"Matter of fact, you give me the necklace and your girlfriend can hang onto the rest of the beach glass." Mario gave another forced laugh in an attempt to neutralize any importance of the stones.

"No can do, man. The glass may have been yours but she spent a lot of time making pieces of jewelry she can sell. She gave me this one to bring me good karma."

"Yeah, and how's that workin' out for you so far?" Mario was reluctant to bring any more attention to Ollie's necklace, but believed the guy had no idea what he was wearing.

Andy's thoughts were still on getting *Miss Demeanor* and he was tired of the talk about Ding-Lee and her jewelry enterprise. He lifted the bag containing his money. "How about I buy her. I'll give you fifty K . . . in cash."

"Fifty? This boat's worth twice that, especially since you prettied her up for me."

"Well, like I said, you're getting the fifty thou for what the boat was worth in the condition I found her. I'm the one who paid to have her prettied up, as you say."

Mario didn't flinch. "And like I said. *Miss Demeanor*'s worth twice what you're offering."

Andy became impatient and dropped the canvas bag containing the money and kicked it to Mario's feet. "Okay . . . ninety-six thousand then," he said. "That's every penny in the bag."

Mario saw Andy's desperation to get the boat. He shifted his eyes to Ollie, who was holding an identical bag and wondered if his friend had an equal amount of cash.

"I don't think so," he told Andy.

The twelve month obsession with the boat seemed to take over Andy's brain. His mind raced for a solution. While *Miss Demeanor* seemed to be slipping through his fingers, his entire life of sailing went through his mind like a slow-motion movie. He relived his performance on the deck of his father's schooner . . . his childhood summers of maneuvering his sailboat around Boothbay Harbor . . . his teen years racing friends along the coast, and after high school, his time at Maine Maritime Academy and the superiority of the school's racing team. All of the thoughts were processed in a few short seconds, and during those seconds, his eyes remained fixed on Mario. He was certain the man he was staring at was no match for the amount of expertise he had with boats. The words that left his mouth seemed to escape from a dark cavern of his mind he was unaware of. "I'll race you for it," he blurted out. Ollie stood in silence trying to grasp what was happening.

Mario seemed surprised and took a moment to respond. "Race me for it? Why should I race you for a boat I already own?"

"Because I'll throw in the money, the ninety-six thousand. Winner take all."

Mario studied Andy but said nothing. It was an interesting challenge. Like Andy, he thought about his own life of sailing. *Sweet Vanilla* . . . the Commodore and the club . . . racing with Maggie and the men's racing team. He had been sailing on his own for as long as he could remember. He knew there was no possible way the guy challenging him to a race could best him in sailing. He looked at Ollie's bag a second time. "I'll tell you what, if your friend wants to throw in whatever's in his bag, you've got a deal."

"Hey man, I'm just a member of the crew," Ollie said quickly.

"That's exactly my point. You're a member of his crew and I've got my first mate as well," Mario said, nodding toward Rosita.

Andy turned and whispered to Ollie. "You owe me this much after this whole bullshit deal you forced me into to come down here."

Ollie hesitated, knowing after what he'd done he owed Andy a big one. He leaned in and whispered. "Can you really take this guy?"

"Yeah, I can really take this guy."

"Okay," Ollie told Mario. "I'm in."

"What about boats?" Andy asked.

"Obviously, I'm sailing *Miss Demeanor*. I own it, remember? I'm sure there's something in the harbor you could rent for the morning. After I win, I'll even pay the rental fee."

"Distance?" Andy questioned.

"Let's say we start at the first channel buoy. From there, we'll race to the third can out and back. Should be a good distance to allow me to teach you the fine art of racing."

"Agreed," Andy said and picked up his bag to leave.

"The money stays here," Mario told him.

"Why the hell should the money stay here?"

"Because your little trip down here with my boat cost me a small fortune. I'm willing to give you a racing chance to make things right but if you guys don't show tomorrow, I'm out a bundle. If the money stays here, you can show or not show. Either way I'll make back some of the money you cost me."

"If you win you mean."

"There's no question that I'll win," Mario said.

"And when I win, what's to prevent you from taking the money anyway?" Andy asked.

"I guess you'll have to trust me on not doing that. I'm giving you my word, sailor to sailor. So . . . as I said, the money stays here." As Mario made the statement, he opened a drawer and withdrew Tobias's gun.

Andy stared at it. "So what does that thing mean? If I don't leave the money you're gonna shoot me?" Andy's question held a tone of sarcasm.

"That's exactly what I'm gonna do. I'm gonna shoot you . . . and then I'm gonna shoot your friend there. After that I'm gonna set sail now instead of tomorrow and when we get far enough out to sea, I'm gonna weight you down and toss you overboard. Do you really think anyone is going to miss you two assholes?"

Mario's expression and his tone gave no appearance of a bluff. Andy recalled the loud sounds from the gun when Henry shot the cottonmouth. No one seemed to notice. No one seemed to care or hear anything. Shots seemed to be a normal occurrence, and those thoughts were punctuated by the memory of Captain Lombardi saying "no ser cebo de pescado."

"His bag too," Mario ordered, pointing to Ollie who clutched it a bit tighter and held his ground.

"Now," Mario said, moving the slide forward and back forcing a round into the chamber. Reluctantly Ollie set his bag down.

"See you in the morning," Mario told them.

With Andy and Ollie gone, Mario and Rosita each took a bag and counted the money. He stowed both bags and instructed Rosita to stay in the boat. "I have to check on something," he told her. "You know how to use one of these?" he held out the gun.

"My guess is you point it at something and pull the trigger?"

"Yeah . . . well, I meant what I said. If those two clowns come back, don't hesitate to use it."

"Easy for you to say."

Mario ignored her reluctance. "How much insurance money did you say you had?"

"A little less than forty-five thousand, why?"

"How'd you like to invest in *Costello's Charters?*"

◆ settling accounts
_____

Mario left Rosita to safeguard *Miss Demeanor* and walked to a secluded area of the marina to call Cohen. The twenty-four hour agreement for Cohen to call him had expired and Cohen's number was listed in Rovelli's phone. Mario assumed Ollie's girlfriend was under the impression she had a wealth of sea glass on her hands and his intent was to give up the diamonds for his freedom. If using the money he planned to win from Andy and Ollie was enough to satisfy Cohen for the stones he lost, he'd wire it leaving him and Rosita to sail off to sandy beaches. When Cohen answered, Mario wasted no time in giving his pitch.

"I don't have your diamonds," he told him. "but I know where they are and you shouldn't have any trouble getting them."

"You say you know where they are?" Cohen was somewhat amused at Mario's statement. Rovelli and Romance had already made their delivery and without giving anything away, he let Mario continue.

"Before I give them up I want your guarantee that no one gets hurt."

"And then what. I'm supposed to get the stones and give you your cut? Where the hell are you calling from anyway?"

Mario ignored the question. "My cut's over. You can have the stones free and clear. I just don't want anybody getting hurt. The person who has the diamonds doesn't know what they are. Everyone and their mother is fighting over what they think is a pouch full of sea glass."

Cohen remained silent and Mario was about to offer up the money as a ransom for his freedom when Cohen responded. "You mean like the little girl who lives down the lane?" he paused. "Who makes jewelry?"

Mario froze. He had never met Ollie's girlfriend, but he knew she had no knowledge of what she had in her possession. "You're a day late and a dollar short, Costello," Cohen said. "My guys have already had a little chat with her."

"There's no reason to do anything to her. Like I said, she doesn't even know what she's got."

"Yeah, you're right and you can relax. I've already got the merchandise, and as you said, she didn't know what she had and she's a hundred bucks richer for her ignorance. Your problem is the money I lost on the stones that went missing. Did you know that little girl actually threw some of them back into the ocean? And then, of course, there must be a couple of good sized ones missing because I'm a little light on the weight."

Mario pictured the stone Ollie was wearing around his neck. He was about to speak when Cohen started up again.

"I don't know what you think those missing stones are worth, but combined with the aggravation you've caused me and the twelve month wait to get this deal done, I figure the whole thing comes to the half million you were supposed to get." Mario remained silent.

"You're out of the game now, Costello. So if you plan on coming around looking for a piece of the pie you can forget it. Or, to put it in your language, that ship has sailed. If I see hide or hair of you nosing around, my two friends are just a phone call away and I know they would love to have another meeting with you, if you get my drift." Cohen hung up the phone and Mario stared out at the scores of boats on moorings. The wheels in his head turned quickly. Cohen was out of the picture . . . Mario had possession of *Miss Demeanor* and two bags full of cash. It was time to talk to his new friend Henry.

AFTER MEETING WITH HENRY, Mario took *Miss Demeanor* out for a test run of the course. While they sailed, Mario noticed the ease which Rosita handled the lines. "Where did you learn to tack like that?"

She tossed her head back and laughed and it reminded Mario of Maggie during their first racing encounter. "I grew up down here, remember? Do you think you're the only one who ever sailed a boat?"

He moved away from the wheel and motioned for her to take it. "It's good to know I've got a good first mate," he said.

"It's better if you know I'm your only mate," she hollered back.

He experimented with a few more maneuvers and she demonstrated skills of a veteran sailor. After he clocked the distance between the start point and the first buoy, he made a few marks on the chart and chuckled. "We're done here," he told Rosita. "Let's get out of these head winds and fill our sails with something more favorable."

"What about the rest of the course?"

"The first distance is all I needed. I talked to Henry about the channel and he said there's a constant head wind in here. If that's true, the right timing on the first tack tomorrow will put us in the lead to the first buoy. We agreed on a slalom style race so when I force him off to starboard at the first buoy, he'll have to come about to retake it. There's no way he'll be able to overtake us. The race is too short."

"You're sure about that?"

"Yeah, I'm sure. I've also got a racing jib on board that will increase our sail space. He didn't use any sails coming down here so he's probably not aware I have it."

ANDY MANAGED TO RENT a thirty-four foot Pearson for the race and spent most of the night studying charts and planning his strategy. Ollie watched TV and awaited his orders as first mate. The bed in their hotel room was converted to a makeshift boat. By substituting a towel for a jib and shoelaces for sheets, Andy instructed Ollie on the fine art of tacking. After a frustrating hour, his final words to his teammate were, "just do what I tell you and do it fast."

The remainder of the night was spent with Ollie insisting the Costello guy was going to sail off with their cash while Andy assured him he would race, and when he did, there was no chance of them losing.

The race time was set for "high noon" and Andy and Ollie arrived at the Pearson around nine o'clock. They were halfway down the dock when Henry came chasing after them. "Didn't know if I'd catch you or not."

"Why? What's up?"

"I've got your papers here. Captain Costello asked me to make sure you got them."

Andy and Ollie looked at one another.

"Your bill of sale," Henry continued. "and your documentation papers, although I left a blank where the name of the boat goes."

"What boat? What the hell are you talking about?" Andy asked.

"*Miss Demeanor.* He told me you settled things last night. Said you offered to buy the boat and he was accepting your offer. He told me you were takin' possession this morning."

"No, I didn't buy his boat. I mean, yes, I made an offer but we didn't agree on anything. Where is he now? We're actually supposed to race for the boat today."

Henry rubbed his chin and looked away. "I'm just not quite sure what his plans were after sellin' you his boat. I do know he sailed outta here just after sunrise on his new boat. I'm not sure if he was just testin' her out or had plans for a longer voyage."

"Tell me Henry, just how much exactly did we pay for the boat?"

"Don't recall the exact figure. Two hundred and some thousand I think it was. The figure's on the bill of sale there."

Andy stared at Ollie in disbelief before returning his attention to his ownership papers.

"Why did you say you left a blank line for the name of the boat?"

"Well, I don't know its history, but comin' in here with the cargo you were carryin' and well . . . you know . . . a lot of stuff goes on around here that I don't talk about. Sometimes guys come in here with one boat and leave with another if you know what I mean. It's just somethin' you might want to think about. If you're gonna be here all day, I can have the guys put any name you want on it this afternoon. All they gotta do is remove *Miss Demeanor* and throw on any name you want. You can fill in the new name on your papers there and your documents will be good and legal."

Andy and Ollie tried to grasp what had happened. Henry had other things to do and seemed to grow impatient. "Anyway, here's your paperwork. You can sail her outta here any time you want. She's paid up for today, but startin' tomorrow, you're gonna have to pay for the space. If ya want somethin' a bit cheaper, I could arrange for a mooring."

"No, that's okay," Andy told him. "I'll spend the day checking her over, but it's supposed to be a clear night and I haven't sailed under the stars in quite a while. I think we'll head out at sunset."

The two remained stunned for several minutes before going on board *Miss Demeanor* to look her over. Andy had admired the new look the day before, but hadn't had the opportunity to check her over with the proper amount of scrutiny. Ollie was upset about losing the money, but Andy thought about how he'd pined over the boat for a year and how he'd come into the cash, and rationalized it was a good deal.

Ollie picked up the canvas bags to find them empty. He threw one the length of the cabin. "I told you that fucker was going to take off with our money."

"Actually, you said he would take off with our money and the boat. I mean, he did leave us the boat and it is worth every penny."

"He didn't leave us the boat, he *sold* us the boat and it was worth the money you offered. The rest of the money he took was my share."

"Look on the bright side, you're now the half-owner of a fancy yacht."

"That's very generous but if we're talkin' shares here, I believe I put in a bit more on this tub than you did."

"But my difference was to pay for the refurbishment. I say we're equal partners."

After the bickering, Andy and Ollie agreed that Henry's suggestion to rename *Miss Demeanor* was a good idea. Leaving for Melbourne meant they would need supplies. Andy went for groceries and other necessities, and in his absence, mistakenly gave Ollie the task of arranging *Miss Demeanor's* name change. His only advice was to "pick out a good one."

WHEN MARIO AND ROSITA returned from their test run of the course Mario tracked Henry down to follow up on their earlier meeting. He then returned to *Miss Demeanor* and took Rosita off the boat telling her he had something he wanted to show her. Minutes later, they stood on the deck of the Fairlie. She stared in awe of its beauty.

"Whaddaya think," he asked her.

"What do I think? I think it's beautiful."

"I have the keys. Henry said we could come aboard and check her out if we wanted to. It was up for sale until this morning."

"What about the new owners?"

"That's my surprise, *we're* the new owners."

"What are you talking about?"

"It's ours. I mean, you did invest in Costello Charters right? I had Henry call the owner while we were checking out the race course to see if he would take a little less than the asking price. He got the price down and the owner took my offer."

"But my money wasn't enough for this. How do you expect to pay off the rest of it?"

"From the sale of *Miss Demeanor*. I sold her this morning."

"Sold her for how much?"

"The two hundred and six thousand the guys had."

"They paid that much?"

"Yeah, well sort of. They just don't know it yet. I put their money together with a little of yours and she's ours free and clear. We've even got a nice nest egg left over."

"And so those guys now own *Miss Demeanor*?"

"Yes, I had Henry do up a bill of sale to make it all legal. Besides, don't forget about Hanson. If that guy ever gets wind of anything that went on down here in Miami, he'll be all over those guys—not that he has a leg to stand on—but he can fight it out with them. You and me? We're transferring our bags to our new home and sailin' out of here. I gave Henry a list of supplies earlier and she's loaded and ready to go. And you, being a partner in *Costello Charters*, are now part owner of this custom built yacht."

The continued tour of the boat left Rosita with the feeling she was in the luxury suite of a five-star hotel. Mario smiled as he pointed out the features and she giggled as one surprise after another unfolded. Midway through the tour, she stopped him.

"But what about the race?"

"There is no race. We're leaving with the morning tide."

"But the money. Do you think it's fair just taking it?" Rosita's tone was not only questioning, but carried a note of concern.

Mario thought for a minute and then found a piece of paper and a pen. He talked as he wrote. "I'll tell you what. How about if I leave them a thank-you note?" As he asked the question he handed her the paper. "Will that clear your conscience?"

She read the note and smiled. "Okay," she said. "Yes. I feel much better now. Why don't you get the boat ready and I'll walk over and say good-bye to *Miss Demeanor* and leave the note." She started topside but then turned. "I didn't think to ask, what's the name of our new boat?"

"Well, it's certainly a good omen for us. Henry told me the woman who owned it was a relative of Steve McQueen. It's named after one of his movies."

"I always liked Steve McQueen. Don't tell me she named it *Bullit?*"

"No. It's more appropriate than that . . . for us anyway."

"Why, what was the movie?"

"*The Great Escape*," he laughed.

58

A ndy and Ollie set sail for Melbourne just before sunset. With a boat complete with mast and sails, they left the security of the coastline, and like pirates, they ventured out to sea. Andy manned the helm and smiled most of the time. Ollie rolled joints and smoked on the bow. The two friends were bonded by a boat. Andy had forgiven Ollie for his misrepresentation of his dealings with Eric realizing the money gained from his misdeed had been invested in the Beneteau.

As habit dictated, there was a new bone of contention between the two of them. Andy's complaints regarding Ollie's choice for *Miss Demeanor*'s name change lasted for the entire sail home while Ollie, as half owner, felt his decision was well-founded. Andy vowed to change it again, regardless of Ollie's logic.

Shortly after casting off, they found the thank-you note Rosita had taped in one of the cabinets. Ollie read it, smiled, and then scurried topside with the news. "If this means what I think it means, we may have reason to celebrate," he told Andy.

"Why, what is it?"

"It's a note from Costello. I knew it. I suspected something when that guy kept tryin' to get my necklace."

"Knew what? What's it say?"

"It's actually to you. It says:

My apologies for taking all the money, but if you get stuck for cash, tell your first mate to take his necklace to a reputable jeweler."

As they sailed on with the good news, they neared the area where Hanson sat in his truck. *Miss Demeanor* had not appeared as he had hoped and as it was past sundown, desperation was setting in. He started the truck for the return trip to Melbourne. As he was about to pull out of the parking area, he spotted a sailboat that might possibly be the one he'd been waiting for. His years in the boatyard told him it was a thirty-four or thirty-five footer and his heart jumped a beat. Feeling he may have found *Miss Demeanor*, he raised his binoculars for final confirmation. His hope dissipated when she came into focus. It was a Beneteau all right, but certainly not *Miss Demeanor*. The name on the stern was *Void of Course*.

MARIO AND ROSITA SAILED *The Great Escape* on a course for the Bahamas. Each nautical mile brought warmer winds that filled the genoa and gave the Fairlie a picture perfect heel as she glided through the water. Mario planned to stop and anchor at Andros Island where, a year earlier, he had picked up the diamonds for Carmine. The anchorage was secluded and well protected. It now seemed a lifetime ago since he'd met with Lopez for a pouch of diamonds in the rough. He and Rosita could spend a day or two on the island before continuing.

Since leaving North of the Keys Marina, it had been a lazy day of sailing and Mario sat at the wheel while Rosita sunbathed on the bow. He eyed her and realized how lucky a hand fate had dealt him. She stood and stretched. Her body glistened. She caught him looking and they both smiled, happy with each other and to be where they wanted to be.

It was nearing the cocktail hour and on the way to the galley, Rosita retrieved her bikini top from a mast cleat and slipped it on. After going below for several minutes, she magically reappeared balancing two glasses. A bourbon for Mario in one hand, and her salt-rimmed margarita glass in the other. He sipped the bourbon slowly and it filled him with warmth . . . a peace he had not known in many years.

Rosita sat next to him and sipped her margarita. The two gazed out over the horizon and the fading sunlight danced on the water.

"How do you feel after all the time and fuss over the diamonds and then not getting them?" she asked.

He put his hand on her thigh and smiled. "I've got the only jewel that counts." His comment was followed by a peaceful silence before Rosita spoke. "Do you want me to spell you on the wheel?"

"No," Mario responded. "I'm fine." He studied her again as she looked out at the horizon. The same wind that filled the sails drifted through her hair and she tossed her head, letting the breeze flow through it. Mario heard the occasional, yet unmistakable click from the winch as the line tightened a bit as if asking the Fairlie's permission to surge a bit faster. She glided through the water with the grace and elegance that matched her lines. Rosita slid closer to Mario and snuggled into him. He leaned back and put his arm around her.

"I can tell you're still thinking about diamonds in the rough aren't you?" she asked.

"Kind of."

"Kind of?"

"Yeah . . . I was thinkin' about us."

Author's notes

Following the completion of this book:

Eileen Beckett took a long-awaited vacation to Melbourne Beach to visit her sister. She was the wife of an Idaho potato farmer and when she returned from her vacation, she filled a glass jar with shells and sea glass she had collected during her morning walks on the beach. When she finished filling the jar, she placed it on the windowsill where, in Idaho, nothing looked so out of place. But out of place or not, it was her reminder of her wonderful vacation and that was where it stayed. Over the years, the jar was moved from room to room until, one day, it was passed on to one of her children who later sold it at a yard sale for twenty-five cents. The uncut diamonds she had mistaken for sea glass were never discovered. It is unknown if other visitors to the beach returned home with similar treasures.

Ding-Lee terminated her jewelry business and enrolled in a six-month course in hairdressing. She gained employment in a small salon in Melbourne, and after two years became involved in politics and won a seat on the city council. During her first term in office she announced her goal was to become the mayor of Melbourne Beach. Her campaign is currently underway.

Carmine, who was serving three to five for illegal trafficking of automatic weapons, used his time on the inside to run numbers, make book on prison fights, and oversee the drug operations. He also served as a loan shark and offered avenues of legal assistance to inmates who claimed to be innocent. During the third year of his sentence he was sent to the infirmary after suffering stomach wounds inflicted during a fight in the exercise yard. The infirmary physician found him the next morning with his carotid artery severed. Other patients were reportedly sleeping when it occurred, and despite the fact that no weapon was found, his death was listed as a suicide.

Cohen continued to operate his jewelry store in New York City. After being badly beaten and thrown into an alley, it was alleged that the punishment came from the Russian mob as a reminder of how and where his stones were to be purchased in the future. A monetary fine was also imposed by the Russians for eliminating them as middlemen. The fine far exceeded the profit on the uncut diamonds. No further runs were made to Cuba.

Jennine Barbosa no longer works for Cohen. She is currently on the short list for the next vacancy on the Supreme Court.

Silo was made a trustee at Bower Correctional. In addition to the honorary duties that went with the title, he taught transcendental meditation and offered classes in the teachings and beliefs of Eastern religions . . . most of which he cannot pronounce. No parole is seen in his immediate future.

Rovelli and Romance continued to hang out at a local bar and do odd jobs for Cohen until Rovelli got married. Three months after the wedding, police were summoned to the Rovelli household to investigate a charge of domestic violence. A severe beating preceded a fatal gunshot wound to the head. The District Attorney listed the death as a justifiable homicide stating Rovelli had it coming and no charges were filed against his wife. Romance is in search of a new partner.

Hanson returned to Melbourne Beach. Without Connie, the boatyard became more disorganized and he took to drinking. His battle with the credit card company to replace his lost card ended when he refused to pay for a three-thousand dollar necklace he claimed not to have purchased. His card was terminated and his credit rating suffered severely. Eventually, he sold the boatyard and invested in a coin-operated Laundromat. He was later sued for a hazing incident involving two college students who were injured when their fraternity brothers stuffed them into one of the industrial dryers and gave them a tumble. Hanson, not wanting to pay an attorney, represented himself in court. The outcome is still pending.

Connie married Harold Frye, the salesman from Marine Supply Unlimited. She and Harold live in North Carolina. She keeps the books for Harold and both are happy enough with each other that no "Small Fryes" are expected. Each year Connie makes a New Year's resolution to lose weight, and during Lent she gives up bubblegum. Her sex life with Harold is very satisfying, but occasionally, she closes her eyes and pretends she is with Mario.

Ollie cashed in on his necklace and signed his share of the boat over to Andy. He returns to Melbourne Beach each spring to assist the baby turtles in getting from their nests to the water. The remainder of the year he gets high and surfs . . . anywhere he wants.

Andy sailed the Beneteau to Maine. He accepted a position with a top firm in the yachting industry. He is currently working on a new keel design which he believes will revolutionize the sailing world. Because of his fond memories of his adventures with Ollie, the boat's name was never changed. To Andy *Miss Demeanor* will always be *Void of Course.*

THE VAUDEVILLE
REVIEW

**Harry Berry
and the
Sunkist Vanities**
*(One hour and twenty minutes of fast,
clean entertainment)*

A final thank you to Cheryl Gerding and Keith Hall, the great niece and great nephew of Vaudeville performer Harry Berry. I thank them for sharing their family's Vaudevillian poster depicting *Harry Berry and The Sunkist Vanities* (and Harry's faithful dog Fanny.)

The Story Behind The Story

In 2012, my wife and I were visiting Melbourne Beach and spotted an anchored sailboat (pictured on the book's cover and below) on the Indian River. There was a disarray of equipment and miscellaneous items on deck along with an outboard motor dangling off the stern rail.

I thought nothing of it at the time, but the following year when we returned, the boat was still anchored in the same spot, and apparently, hadn't moved.

This continued for two more years, although in 2015, the boat broke from her anchor rode and was almost touchable from shore. The following day I noticed the outboard motor was gone.

I will be returning to Indialantic next month and will be curious to see if the sloop is still there. Not knowing the "why" or "how" of the boat, I wrote my own story. For me, this is how novels are brought to life.

Diamonds In The Rough is Leggett's second novel. His first, *The Five-Cent Gang*, published in 2014 is a coming of age story that takes the reader back to the 1950s as the normally mischievous deeds of five twelve-year-olds escalate to unexpected consequences. Armed with ropes, a hatchet, and walkie-talkies, their carefully made plan evolves into a crime of terrible errors. With no solution in sight, they are forced to remain guardians of the secret or face horrible consequences.

www.ingramcontent.com/pod-product-compliance
Lightning Source LLC
Chambersburg PA
CBHW060154260626
47160CB00001B/255